THE CANDYMAKERS

AND THE GREAT CHOCOLATE CHASE

wendy mass

Little, Brown and Company

New York Boston

Copyright © 2016 by Wendy Mass
Illustrations by Steve Scott

Little, Brown and Company

Hachette Book Group
1290 Avenue of the Americas, New York, NY 10104
Visit us at lb-kids.com

Little, Brown and Company is a division of Hachette Book Group, Inc.
The Little, Brown name and logo are trademarks of Hachette Book Group, Inc.

The publisher is not responsible for websites (or their content) that are not owned by the publisher.

First Edition: August 2016

"Time is the coin..." quote on page 1 by Carl Sandburg.

ISBN 978-0-316-08919-7

10 9 8 7 6 5 4 3 2 1

RRD-C

Printed in the United States of America

For all the readers of *The Candymakers* who
told me what they wanted to see in this book,
I hope you're pleased.
May your lives always be sweet. (See what I did there? ☺)

P.S. Read with candy!

"You will travel in a land of marvels."

—Jules Verne, *Twenty Thousand Leagues Under the Sea*

FROM THE DESK OF MR. J.

You! With the dirty knees and the leaf in your hair. You with the sticky fingers and the smudge of chocolate on your chin. And you with the flashlight under your covers after Mom said lights out. And, yes, YOU with this book in your hand, trying to decide whether you're going to read it. You don't know me very well—not yet, anyway. But a lot of people went out of their way for me, so I figured I'd pay it forward and look out for you. I'm not gonna lie—this is a long book, and there are things you should know if you're going to spend your precious time turning the pages. After all, what is more valuable than your time? As a man much wiser than I once said, "Time is the coin of your life. Don't let anyone else spend it for you."

If you do read this book, here's what's
in store for you: Hidden treasures.
Secret worlds. A decades—old mystery.
The open road. A River of Light. A
Map of Awe. A sky of many colors.
Gadgets and gizmos. New friends and old
relatives. Love. Fear. Bravery. Hope.
One very small cat who thinks she's
a dog.

And candy. Lots and lots of
mouthwatering candy. Soft and chewy,
hard and crunchy, sour and sweet. Some
of it plays music. There's also the
small matter of a comet hurtling toward
Earth at a hundred thousand miles an
hour, but try not to worry about that.
It happens a lot.

If any of this stuff doesn't interest
you, feel free to close the book now.
No hard feelings. I won't take it
personally. I should mention, though,

that if you don't stick around, you'll
miss seeing how one of the world's best
magicians utterly blurs the edges of
reality, and that's not something you
soon forget. Trust me, I've seen it.

I'd better go now. I need to sleep. Got
a big day tomorrow. So do Logan, Miles,
Philip, and Daisy. Only to them it's
just an ordinary Tuesday. Life is like
that, ya know? It's never the things
you worry about that get you.

PART ONE

LOGAN

CHAPTER ONE

Monday

After spending exactly twelve years and five months living inside a candy factory, Logan Sweet knew all the best places to hide. That's not to say he hid often. In fact, all the folks responsible for creating, packaging, selling, and shipping the dozen different types of candy produced at the **Life Is Sweet?** candy factory considered Logan to be a visible, helpful (some would add *indispensable*), and always cheerful presence on the factory floor. But from time to time, he found the need to be alone. Usually these times coincided with the final due date of a homework assignment. Since all his teachers worked at the factory (and in the case of his parents, lived in the same apartment), he had to be creative if he wanted to ditch them.

Logan found his first hiding spot at age seven and a half, while trying to avoid finishing an assignment on the Amazon rain forest. In between Max's duties as head candy scientist, he was teaching Logan about the effects of water saturation and drought on various types of cocoa beans.

Logan didn't mind having to make a diorama. All he had to do was visit the factory's Tropical Room, which was as close to a real rain forest as one could get without visiting the equator. He took an old shoe box, shoveled some dirt into it from around his favorite sapodilla tree, taped some fallen leaves to two Pepsicle sticks, strung a green shoelace from stick to stick to make a vine, dangled a brown plastic monkey from the vine, and called it a day.

But he really, *really* didn't want to do the second half of the assignment—going to the factory's library to find books and write down facts. Particularly in his younger years, Logan was more of a hands-on, in-the-moment type of person, the kind of boy who looked closely at things and tried to figure them out on his own. When he couldn't, he enjoyed the not-knowing just as much as finding a solution. He would rather wonder how an ecosystem such as the rain forest gave life to so many different types of flora and fauna than find out an answer that might not be as exciting as he'd hoped.

So he decided he simply wasn't going to do it. Having no interest in actually telling Max that news, he figured his only option was to hide. But he couldn't just wander into the factory and pick some random storage room. Preparations had to be made. He carefully gathered his supplies and then parked himself in one of the oversized chairs in the library and pretended to do his reading. He waited as patiently as possible (which is to say, not patiently at all) while, one by one, the workers shut down the factory's candy machines for the night. This process was a lot more complicated than merely turning off some switches. The oil that made the machines run smoothly had to be drained and disposed of properly. All the pipes, tubes, trays, bins, compressors, oscillators, tumblers, conveyor belts, ovens, stovetops, kettles, vats, pots, pans, funnels, and barrels had to be scrubbed and stored until the machines would start back up again twelve hours later. Logan nearly fell asleep in the chair!

When the coast was finally clear, he grabbed his stash from behind the chair and slung the duffel bags over both shoulders. He hurried down the quiet hall toward the room with the perfect Logan-sized hiding spot. With one last glance to make sure he hadn't been followed, he ducked inside the Icy Mint Blob Room and wedged a pile of pillows behind the stack of old peppermint-oil barrels. He stocked his new space with comic books, drawing pads, and snacks of both the candy and the healthy variety. He made it back up to the apartment just in time for his mom's famous Veggie Loaf Surprise dinner. (It should be noted that his mom's substitution of chocolate chips for peas hadn't been a surprise for many years.)

Even though he ultimately had to finish the report, Logan wound up spending many lazy midday hours tucked away in that hiding spot, lulled into an almost dreamlike state by the thumping of the nearby panning machine. The panner—which looked to him like a space-age washing machine—spun the Icy Mint Blobs and coated them with blueberry syrup until they sparkled with a sugary glaze. It also muffled the sound of Logan crunching/slurping/chomping the latest candies that had been deemed NQP (not quite perfect) by Randall, the head of the quality-control team. As much as Logan loved all the candy **Life Is Sweet** produced, he particularly loved the pieces that came out too oddly shaped to fit in the packaging, or that were stuck together, or that came off the conveyor belt too sticky or too hard or the wrong shade of brown/red/orange/yellow/neon green. He possessed an uncanny ability to show up exactly when a new NQP batch appeared on the counter of the employee lounge.

By the time Logan was nine, his legs had grown so long that his feet stuck out from behind the peppermint barrels. Rather than risk being discovered, he found a new hiding spot in the barn's hayloft. This one worked out even better because the open windows let in a lot of fresh air (which also helped offset the smell of the cows below) and allowed him to play Name That Cloud without lying outside in the open. In one direction, he could gaze at the wheat fields and cornfields, the fruit trees and sugarcane grove, and the great lawn with the pond and boats and painted picnic tables. A glance in the other direction revealed the gleaming windows, the tall chimneys, and the deep red brick of the back of the factory.

When not drawing dinosaurs in his sketchpad (many of which looked a lot like his favorite gummy dinosaur, Gummzilla), he would play one of his grandfather's old hand-carved wooden puzzle games. He wasn't very good at solving them, but he enjoyed the challenge. He could hum as he worked, and the noises of the busy barn drowned out the sound. The farmers below him milked the cows for fresh milk and collected eggs from the chickens, and if they knew he was there, they never let on.

As he got older, Logan enjoyed learning more and more and started hiding less and less. Eventually, he forgot about hiding at all. But tomorrow was the big Kickoff. Candy history would be made when the very first Harmonicandy glided down the conveyor belt. A new product was always a big deal, but the introduction of the winning candy in the Confectionary Association's annual New Candy Contest was a *massive* deal. All eyes were on Logan.

So, obviously, he needed to hide. And he needed to hide *fast*.

Unfortunately, the options were slim. A frenzied energy buzzed through the air. Visitors from all parts of the candy community filled the factory halls, the candymaking rooms, the library, the cafeteria, the Tropical Room, the Bee Room, the great lawn, and even his family's apartment upstairs. This made it very hard to hide in shadowy corners or to slip into back rooms unnoticed. The factory hadn't had this many people in it in seven years, and Logan was finding it hard to adjust. He rested his hand on the pocket where he'd stuck his poem of the day. Ever since the contest, his mom had let him select his own. Today he'd chosen this one:

I am the boy
That can enjoy
Invisibility

It was written by an author named James Joyce. He'd found it by looking up *hiding* in the index of one of the poetry books his mother had given him. So far it hadn't helped him hide, nor turn invisible, but it gave him a slight sense of hopefulness, and he was glad he had it.

He wished his friends from the candymaking contest were there. They were the only people who knew him well enough to understand how he felt. Miles O'Leary, Daisy Carpenter, and Philip Ransford the Third were so different—not only from each other but also from anyone else he'd ever met. Each of them made his small world bigger, and every night when he recited what he was grateful for, they were at the top of his list. Even Philip. Not that Logan would ever tell him that.

At least Miles would be there after lunch. Even though it was summer vacation, he had a new hobby that kept him away each morning. Miles wasn't the best at hiding anyway. He'd most likely sneeze or forget they were supposed to be hiding and then start to tell a story and blow their cover. Poor hiding skills aside, Miles was the best friend Logan had ever had. It helped that neither of them had had a best friend before. They were learning together how to be one.

If anyone could figure out a way to help him now, it would be Daisy. Hiding was basically her full-time job! But she was away on a spy mission, and even though she had given him one of her secret communication devices that would allow him to reach her wherever she was, she'd made it clear that the gadget was for emergencies only. He hadn't even turned it on. No one knew when her mission would be over, but she'd promised to be back for the factory's annual picnic, at the end of the summer. As momentous as the next day's event was expected to be, the factory's first picnic in seven years would be an even bigger deal, but one that he was looking forward to. He wasn't exactly dreading tomorrow, but the tight feeling in his stomach felt something close to it, and the instinct to hide was strong.

Since Miles and Daisy were out, that left only Philip, who really wasn't the world's best listener. Not by a long shot. Still, he was much better than he used to be. After winning the contest, Philip had started hanging around the factory at least a few times a week. The Ransfords' personal assistant, Reggie, would drop him off after school in a fancy limo and pick him up before dinner.

For a kid who hadn't eaten candy for seven years, Philip was making up for it big-time by sampling everything he could get his hands on. He'd follow all the workers around, learning how they did their jobs and always volunteering to help. It was obvious he was trying to compensate for having been so obnoxious during the contest. Logan would say he was successful at achieving that goal about 70 percent of the time; Miles put it at 50. Logan had called Philip yesterday to invite him to come that morning, but Philip had a dentist appointment scheduled. That boy should probably cut down on all the candy eating, just to be on the safe side.

Logan pressed himself against the wall outside the Oozing Crunchorama Room to plot his next move. Maybe he could claim that his skin felt clammy and hide out in the nurse's office. It was always empty, so he'd have lots of privacy. The worst thing the nurse usually saw during the course of the day was a bee sting. The Candymaker made safety his number one priority, which made it even worse that the only serious workplace accident had been when his own five-year-old son tried to reach into a vat of boiling-hot fudge and sustained third-degree burns on his arms and face and neck.

Logan quickly dismissed the idea of the nurse's office. He'd spent more than enough time as a patient, with doctors treating his burns after the accident. Plus he would feel terrible lying to anyone.

He glanced behind him. Last month the Oozing Crunchorama had fallen to third on the candy best-sellers list, after being at the top for nearly a decade. Max and the other candy scientists responded to this disappointing turn of events by tweaking the recipe a little. All they did was chop the hazelnuts into smaller pieces and add a touch more cream to up the "ooze factor," and the candy community went wild. A week later the Crunchorama was back on top. Now the room bustled with activity as they tried to keep up with the demand. Logan sized up the corner behind the hazelnut-warming table. It would provide good cover from the workers pouring the hazelnut-praline mixture into the huge vats of dark chocolate. First he'd have to figure out a way to distract them, though.

"I don't think I've ever seen you stand so still," a familiar voice said with a chuckle.

Logan jumped. Then he turned to face Henry, the man who had single-handedly run the Marshmallow Room since the factory opened fifty years earlier. Henry had always been like a grandfather to him, even when Logan's own grandfather—the original Candymaker and founder of **Life Is Sweet**—was still alive. Since the candymaking contest a few months back, Logan had been so busy that his usual morning visits with Henry had become less frequent. But with his mess of white hair and easy smile, Henry was the only grown-up Logan didn't mind seeing right now.

"Can we go back to the Marshmallow Room?" Logan asked, tugging on Henry's sleeve. He knew they'd have privacy there. Henry guarded the marshmallows the way a mama bird guarded her eggs, and he was extremely choosy about who he let get too close. Plus the walls of the Marshmallow Room were made of a special tinted glass that allowed Henry to see out but kept people from seeing in. Henry insisted the walls were tinted to keep the room cool, but Logan suspected that was just an excuse.

Without waiting for an answer, Logan took off at a run. He darted through crowds of smiling guests, their arms laden with bags of free treats. He did his best not to meet anyone's eyes and pretended he didn't hear their whispered comments. Not being friendly was uncharacteristic of him, but he couldn't handle even one more person gripping him on the shoulder and offering words that were supposed to make him feel better but had the opposite effect. Comments like "You're always a winner to us!" or "This must be tough, but hang in there. Your time will come!" Or, if it was a particularly nosy or thoughtless journalist, "Your grandfather won. Then your dad won. What's it like watching your father's company produce the contest-winning candy when you're the first member of your family in three generations to lose?"

He told them the truth, but no one seemed to believe it.

By the time Henry showed up in the Marshmallow Room, Logan already had the large Bunsen burner up and running and two marshmallows speared onto the tips of their favorite toasting sticks.

"Let's hear it," Henry said, sitting down on the wooden stool next to Logan's. The stool groaned under Henry's considerable weight.

"No one believes me when I say I'm okay," Logan complained as their marshmallows toasted over the low flame. He didn't like the way his voice sounded, but until recent events, he'd never had reason to complain about anything. Now he couldn't help it.

"They pat me on the arm," he explained to Henry, "and tilt their heads at me with their eyes as gooey as a fresh batch of chocolate." It wasn't until the contest that he'd begun to realize that people had always looked at him with sympathy—or at least ever since he'd gotten the scars. Other than the need to massage aloe into them, and the occasional itch or throbbing, and the fact that the ones on his hands sometimes made it hard for him to grip small objects, he never gave his scars much thought. It hadn't occurred to him that others would think about them. He was embarrassed that he hadn't been smart enough, or aware enough, to realize that of course others noticed. And now with all the strangers at the factory, he was aware of the second glances thrown his way.

"You can't really blame folks for thinking you might be disappointed," Henry replied. "You have to watch the Harmonicandy get all the glory. Under your own roof, no less! And after you'd worked so hard on your Bubbletastic ChocoRocket."

"I might not have worked *that* hard," Logan admitted.

"Perhaps it wasn't your best effort," Henry agreed. "But most people don't know that. All they know is that the kid who was rude to everyone won the contest, and you didn't get what you wanted."

"But losing the contest actually *is* what I wanted," Logan insisted. "I mean, not before it started, but once I got to know the others, everything changed. The Harmonicandy was really a team effort, even though Philip has to get the credit officially. You know he's only half as obnoxious as he pretended to be while he was here, right? And then when we were able to save the factory, I really *did* win!" Logan shoved his marshmallow into his mouth to keep himself from rambling even more.

"*I* know all of that," Henry said gently. "And I understand your frustration. But you have to see it from the other side."

Logan let his shoulders slump and crossed his arms.

Henry chewed his marshmallow and laid his stick next to Logan's on the counter. He turned off the burner. "Perhaps you're being oversensitive and a bit overdramatic."

Logan would have argued that perhaps he wasn't being dramatic *enough*, but then Randall rapped on the glass door, and Logan immediately straightened up. He didn't want Randall to see him sulking.

Randall balanced a large brown box under one arm while he chomped on a green apple held in his free hand. He grimaced with every bite. He'd once confided to Logan that he didn't like apples but had to eat them when he was taste-testing different candies. Sour apples neutralized chocolate. Bread neutralized hot, spicy foods, and fortunately, Randall liked bread.

Randall could also always be counted on to have packets of crackers stuffed in his coat pockets because they neutralized almost any taste—spicy, sour, bitter, or sweet—just not as well as the apples. While Logan loved learning anything about the candy-testing process, he didn't need to use any of those tricks. His taste buds were always on high alert.

Logan jumped up to open the door.

Randall tossed the apple core into the trash can. "I'm sorry to interrupt, gentlemen," he said, laying the box on the counter beside the marshmallow sticks. "This package arrived a few minutes ago, so I offered to deliver it on my way to the Harmonicandy Room. Only a few more tests to go before the first one comes down the conveyor belt. Exciting, don't you think?" He glanced at Logan, and his grin wobbled a bit.

Logan looked pointedly at Henry. This was exactly the kind of thing he'd been talking about.

Henry leaned over to look at the shipping label. He squinted and mumbled that the return address was blurry. "Is this the new vanilla-bean grinder I ordered?" he asked Randall. Halfway out the door already, Randall called back, "Nope. It's for Logan."

Logan and Henry looked at each other in surprise. "Me?" Logan asked.

He pulled the box closer. The return label was printed in neat, even letters. Maybe Henry needed better glasses (even though his lenses must have been a half-inch thick already). The handwriting didn't look familiar to Logan, and the address—a post office box a few states away—didn't mean anything, either.

"Maybe it's from Daisy," he suggested to Henry. "It doesn't look like her handwriting, but maybe that's on purpose to cover her tracks." Henry was the only adult at the factory who knew Daisy's true identity. He'd promised to keep her secret, and Henry always kept his promises.

Logan pulled at the thick tape on the side of the box but couldn't get a good grip. He would need scissors or a knife to cut through it. Logan and sharp instruments didn't mix well. "Will you open it for me?" he asked.

Henry nodded. "Certainly."

As Henry crossed the room to his metal supply cabinet, Logan thought how much he appreciated that Henry hadn't jumped up to help before Logan even asked. He'd become very aware of people doing that for him.

Henry returned and got to work cutting through the thick tape. He was very careful. When the flaps were loose enough, he stepped back to let Logan pull the box open.

Logan thought maybe it might contain a game or a puzzle or something funny that Daisy had come across on her travels. She knew he didn't leave the factory very often, so she liked surprising him with random things from the outside world. The week before, she'd sent him a (not very good) painting she had found at a rest stop on the highway. It showed a cat waving a magic wand while wearing polka-dot pajamas. The painting had a title (*Abra-Cat-abra*) and the signature of the artist (a woman named Ava Simon) in the lower right corner. It now hung proudly over his bed.

"So what's in there?" Henry asked.

Logan carefully lifted out a thick stack of yellowed newspapers and dusty spiral notebooks tied together with brown twine. A folded-up map, the back yellowed with age, remained at the bottom of the box. "I don't think it's from Daisy," he said, moving the contents from his arms to the counter. His new friends were well aware that he didn't have much patience when it came to reading. He'd once told Miles that he usually read the last page of a book first, and

Miles was so horrified he didn't speak to him for the rest of the day. Talk about being overdramatic.

"I bet this will tell us," Henry said, pulling a long, thin envelope out from underneath the twine. He handed it to Logan, who turned it over in his hands. The envelope was new, while the rest of the stack looked as if it had been rescued from someone's attic or basement. Logan tore open the envelope and unfolded a typewritten letter. He held it up so that he and Henry could read it together.

Logan had only gotten as far as the first sentence when Henry asked if he minded reading the letter out loud, so Logan began again.

Dear Logan,

We have never met, but your grandfather—the one and only Samuel Sweet—and I spent our boyhoods together. We lived two houses away from each other, and I believe I spent more time at his home than at my own. I would be lured over by the most wonderful smells of whatever Sam was cooking up! (Unlike your great-grandmother's cabbage, which did not smell good AT ALL!)

I recently found a bunch of Sam's old journals and candymaking research in my basement. I know he would want you to have them. Even though my life took a different path, I do keep up with candy news because it reminds me of my dear friend and the world he treasured. I heard that you were defeated at the candymaking contest and that your family's factory was given the honor of producing the winning Harmonicandy. I hope you will be comforted by seeing all the notebooks your grandfather filled with ideas for candies that failed. Don't give up! I am old and coming to the end of my days faster than I want to accept, but there is greatness ahead for you. I can smell it from here.

Very sincerely yours,
Franklin O. Griffin

Logan stared down at the letter. "Even strangers feel sorry for me. Still think I'm being oversensitive?"

When he got no answer, Logan looked up. Tears were streaming down Henry's cheeks in two even rows until they dripped off his chin. When Logan thought about that moment a month later, after so much had happened and so much had changed, it felt like a turning point, with a clear *before* and *after*. But at the time it was happening, all he could think about was how unprepared he was to deal with Henry's reaction. The random thought occurred to him that if they were eating slices of chocolate pizza, Henry wouldn't be crying. *No one* could cry and eat chocolate pizza at the same time.

CHAPTER THREE

L ogan shifted from foot to foot. Crying at the **Life Is Sweet** candy factory was usually reserved for the confectionary scientists after taste-testing a new batch of red-hot chili peppers. Randall went through two whole loaves of bread in one day before giving the final approval to begin production on the new Fireball Supernovas. (To make the candy, which would be labeled *For Adults Only*, the farmers had cross-bred two kinds of hot peppers to create something so fiery they had to handle it with gloves—and if they wiped their eyes by mistake, well, they'd have to go home for the rest of the day and soothe them with wet cotton balls.) Spontaneous eye-watering was common enough, but out-of-the-blue, real-life crying? It had never, ever happened in Logan's memory. He put his hand on Henry's arm. "Are you okay, Henry? Is there anything I can do for you?"

Henry only shook his head and continued his silent weeping.

Sure, Henry was an emotional guy. Everyone knew that. Every time Randall posted the list of new candies that had passed Max's rigorous testing and been accepted for production, Henry's eyes would water, and he'd turn away to blow his nose. And last year when the *Spring Haven Herald* selected **Life Is Sweet** as the "Best Place to Work" for the fifth year in a row, Henry got so choked up he had to close down the Marshmallow Room for three hours while he sat outside and fed the swans and wouldn't talk to anyone.

But now Henry's tears were getting the collar of his shirt wet and threatening to land on the stack of papers. Logan looked around the room, hoping to find something to distract his friend. He reached across the counter and grabbed two warm marshmallows from the cooling tray. They were still gooey in the center, exactly how Henry liked them. Logan offered them up, but the man's tears kept coming.

When Logan was little, Henry used to make the marshmallows talk. The two of them would have whole conversations that way. Logan held up the one in his right hand. He ignored the fact that the marshmallow was leaking and to anyone *without* scars on their palms would have been really hot.

"Wut up, marshmallow?"

He lowered his voice and pretended the one in his left hand was speaking now. "Yo, other marshmallow dude. Wuz up wit you?"

Logan thought for a second he spotted Henry's mouth quivering at the corners, but if so the tiny movement had disappeared as quickly as it came.

Then a flash of bright yellow out in the hall caught Logan's eye. The candy groupies had arrived! Even though the launch of a new candy was by invitation only, the Candymaker always welcomed a small number of confectionary enthusiasts to attend. These were the people who knew which candy factory in the world made which candy. They wrote fan letters singing the praises of their favorite treats, and if a recipe was tweaked and they didn't like the new version, they were not shy about letting the factory owners know about that, too. They'd have found a way to get their hands on a still-warm Harmonicandy even if they didn't have an invitation, so the Candymaker knew enough to open his doors.

Logan had found his distraction. He popped the marshmallows into his mouth and pointed out to the hall. "Quick, Henry, look at their shirts!" Henry followed his gaze, but only halfheartedly. A large group of parents and kids was heading toward them, all wearing matching T-shirts the exact same shade of yellow as the Neon Yellow Lightning Chew. The words LIFE IS SWEETER AT LIFE IS SWEET ran across their chests.

"Aren't those T-shirts great?" Logan asked. "They must have made them themselves."

Henry gave a polite nod of his chin but didn't stop crying. Logan watched in horror as the group turned almost as one and pressed their faces up to the window. He couldn't blame them, really. Marshmallows were a vital ingredient in so many of their chocolate candies (most famously Some More S'mores), so who wouldn't want to watch them being made and catch a glimpse of the man who had become something of a legend in the candymaking world?

Logan knew the groupies weren't able to see through the one-way tinted glass, and thankfully no one tried the door. They eventually moved off toward the factory library, where Mrs. Gepheart had set up a "Life Is Sweet Through the Ages" display. She was working on a much bigger one for the return of the annual picnic.

When the threat of interruption had passed, Logan said, "Um, Henry? Are you planning on stopping anytime soon?"

Henry sniffled and shook his head.

Logan knew he had to do something to break Henry out of his mood. Something he would never normally do inside one of the candy rooms (and not very often outside of them, either).

Logan began to dance.

His arms flailed as he twirled around the marshmallow cooling table, narrowly avoiding the glass jars of raw honey lined up at the base. He hummed and kicked out his legs and glanced every few seconds at Henry, who was finally wiping his eyes with his sleeves. Logan kept dancing, right up until he bumped into a basket of fresh eggs that he hadn't noticed by the sink. The basket teetered on the edge, and both he and Henry reached for it at the same time.

"That was close," Logan said, skidding to a halt.

Henry steadied the basket and then grabbed a tissue and blew his nose. He sat back down on the stool and took a few deep breaths to pull himself together. "I don't think you have a career in musical theater," he finally said. "But thanks."

"You're welcome," Logan said, pleased that his distraction had worked. He had to admit that he felt better, too. Maybe he should dance more often. "Can you tell me why you were crying?"

Henry looked down at Logan like he was sizing him up, deciding how to reply. Logan waited, trying to make his face look like the kind of face people would want to confide in. He feared he probably only looked like he needed to go to the bathroom.

"It's . . . complicated," Henry finally said. "I should get back to work." He stood up and straightened his lab coat.

"Do you want me to leave?" Logan asked.

"Yes," Henry said.

"You do?" Logan took a step backward. Henry was generally a matter-of-fact kind of guy, but Logan hadn't expected such an abrupt answer.

"Yes," Henry repeated. He lifted the stack of papers and notebooks and dropped them into the box. "I'd like you to go back to your apartment and sit down with these. Learn a little more about your grandfather." He thrust the box at Logan, who saw no choice but to take it.

"But I already know tons about Grandpa," Logan reminded him. "He only died a few years ago."

"You knew him as a grown-up and your grandfather," Henry

said, ushering him across the room. "Now get to know him as a boy and a young man. People will always surprise you if you let them."

"What do you mean by that?" Logan asked as Henry practically shoved him out the door. He tried to wedge his foot back in.

Henry only shook his head, closed the door the rest of the way, and turned the lock.

CHAPTER FOUR

Logan hurried down the crowded halls as fast as one could hurry while being weighed down by a fairly heavy box and the possibility of a surprise.

This time he didn't mind the nods and greetings that flew at him. No one tried to stop him to engage in conversation about the Harmonicandy or anything else. Clearly a man with a box was a man with a mission. If he'd known this before, he would have loaded up his arms sooner! He made a mental note to remember this the next time he wanted to be left alone.

He stopped as he neared the chocolate fountain by the front entrance. He had a hunch Miles had just arrived. Admittedly, the hunch was based on the fact that he had just heard Mrs. O'Leary's tires squealing as she peeled out of the driveway. She had driven him and Miles to Verona Park last week, and he'd dug his fingers into the backseat the whole ride.

He stood by the fountain and waited for Miles to come in. After a few seconds (which seemed longer thanks to the awkwardness of balancing the box while nodding at people walking by), he rested the box at his feet, ran across the large front entry hall, and grabbed a piece of grape taffy from one of the huge barrels kept there. With the bright noontime sun streaming in through the glass roof, the taffy practically glowed.

A surge of laughter rose up behind him. The Neon Yellow Lightning Chew group had gathered in front of the long window that looked into the Cocoa Room. Steve and Lenny were each juggling three football-shaped cocoa pods. Then they tossed one across to the other and kept juggling! They'd been working with cocoa pods since they were old enough to hold them without dropping them on their toes. They loved showing off their skills for guests. Usually Logan would stay and watch, too, but that whole man-with-a-mission thing was calling out to him.

He hurried back to his grandfather's box, feeling a pang of guilt for having left it while strangers were milling about. If *he* had seen a mysterious box on the floor next to a chocolate fountain, he'd certainly have wanted to peek inside. Until told otherwise, Logan usually figured people felt the way he did.

Miles still hadn't come in, but Logan didn't really find this too strange. He himself often took longer to get someplace than one might expect. Who knew how many interesting things might have distracted Miles along the way? The exhaust pipe from the factory cafeteria let out right above the front door. Maybe the smell of the chocolate pizza had temporarily frozen him in his tracks. Maybe he'd spotted a rare flower or bug or leaf and had stopped to admire or draw it.

"There you are," a voice said from behind him. "You must have your walkie-talkie turned off. That's a first." Logan hadn't heard Max approach over the sounds of the group oohing and aahing as Steve and Lenny poured the cocoa butter into the chocolate mixture in perfect swirls. That was one of Logan's favorite parts of the chocolate-making process, too.

"I'm sorry," Logan said, pulling the walkie-talkie off his belt loop. With a little pang of guilt, he flipped the switch to On. When one had been planning to hide, one couldn't very well be reachable, or what would be the point of hiding?

"You must come see this!" Max boomed. "The caramel for the first Harmonicandy batch is the most beautiful shade of amber I've ever seen. It's almost a shame to cover it up with chocolate! Randall approved it already, but he can't stop eating it."

Max always got excited when a new product rolled off the assembly line, but the Kickoff of the Harmonicandy had ramped up his excitement level at least five notches higher than usual. His bald head glistened even though the indoor temperature held steady at seventy degrees.

Logan hesitated. Up till then, the Harmonicandy Room had been considered a construction zone and was off-limits. It would no doubt be crowded with people who would ask the same questions he'd been avoiding all day. But could he turn down the chance to see (and, most likely, *sample*) one of the most important ingredients in the whole Harmonicandy? The caramel was the glue that held it all together.

Then he thought about the contents of the box. As much as he wanted to learn about his grandfather's early ideas, did he really want to spend a sunny summer afternoon sorting through them? Pulling apart delicate objects like newspapers was a task he usually avoided at all costs. Max tapped his foot and Logan decided. The contents of the box had sat for more than fifty years. They could wait a little longer.

"I'll be right there," Logan promised Max. "Miles just arrived. I'm sure he'll want to see the caramel, too."

"The more the merrier," Max said, walking over to the group of visitors, who were now arguing about whether you could eat raw cocoa beans straight from the pod. (You could, but they tasted like dirt until fermented and roasted.)

Logan began to use his foot to push the box behind the fountain, then hesitated. He undid the flaps, pulled out the letter addressed to him, and resealed the box. He shoved the letter deep into his pocket, pushed the box the rest of the way out of sight, and then ran to the front door. More cars were parked in the visitors' lot than he'd seen in years. And this was the day *before* the big day!

Miles sat on the front stoop on top of the old-fashioned tin milk jug that had been there forever. Logan had been right; Miles had indeed found something to distract him—a book. The jug, with its flat top, made a perfect seat for a boy.

Miles held his book (*How to Make Your Own Alphabet*) right up to his face and hadn't noticed Logan yet. Even though Logan was eager to see the caramel, he had learned that Miles entered another world when he was reading. So Logan sat down on the stoop beside Miles, pulled his knees to his chest, and waited for his friend to finish.

This close to the jug, he could tell that some work had been done to it. After decades in the sun, the large white *M-I-L-K* across the middle had faded, and the letters hadn't been legible for years. But now they were brighter and more distinct. The paint must have been touched up, along with the picture of a cow below the word. He leaned closer. Yes, it definitely looked fresher and newer.

Logan wasn't really surprised. The whole factory had been swept, scrubbed, waxed, and polished. Even the red brick walls had been power washed and regrouted. The brass and steel and glass had already sparkled; now they all *gleamed*. His mom had become a bit obsessed with how everything would appear to the guests, pretty much from the second they'd learned their factory would be the one producing the Harmonicandy. The rules didn't specifically state that the honor (and a large percentage of the profits!) of producing the candy would go to the factory that had hosted the winner, but that's what had happened every year so far.

Miles gave a little gasp and burst out laughing.

Logan grinned. "That must be a really funny book!"

"Gnipael sdrazil!" Miles shouted. He jumped straight up, tripped over the milk jug, toppled backward off the stoop, and landed faceup in the rosebushes.

CHAPTER FIVE

I t was the faceup part that saved him.

"Ouch!" Miles yelped as the factory nurse pulled the last thorn out of his thigh with her tweezers. Logan winced along with him. He had paged the nurse on his walkie-talkie as soon as Miles landed in the bushes. She'd run outside immediately, proving Logan's point that she never had much to do.

A few dabs of ointment later, Miles was deemed good to go. "Stay out of the bushes," the nurse warned, rolling up her first-aid kit.

"Yes, ma'am," Miles said, pushing up his glasses. His cheeks were red, and Logan didn't think the flush had come from the sun.

"Sorry for startling you," Logan said once they were alone. "I know how wrapped up you get in your books. I'm like that sometimes when I'm watching at the Cocoa Room window. An hour could go by and I'd swear it was a minute."

"It wasn't your fault," Miles said, rubbing the back of his leg. "I shouldn't have been sitting there in the first place. I mean, I could have broken that old milk can thingy."

"I've sat on it for years," Logan assured him, "and it hasn't broken yet. Dad says they made things sturdier back in the day."

A dark blue spot was starting to spread from the pocket in

Miles's tan shorts. "Um, Miles?" Logan said, pointing to the spot. "I think your pen broke when you fell."

Miles looked down at his shorts. "Rats," he said. "That was supposed to be a surprise." He reached into his pocket and pulled out a small plastic bottle. Not a pen after all. Logan recognized it right away, even though he hadn't seen one in years. "That's disappearing ink!"

Miles looked up in surprise. "You know about this?"

Logan nodded. "My grandfather used to love those kinds of tricks. Explodable cigar, a pen that shocks you, itching powder." He hadn't thought about that in a long time. He smiled at the memory of his grandfather sprinkling itching powder down the collar of Avery's shirt on his first day at work in the Tropical Room. Avery tried so hard not to squirm. Finally he leaned up against a cinnamon tree and rubbed his back up and down while trying to act natural. Logan would never forget the tiny strips of cinnamon bark wafting all around him in curly brown rings. Avery hadn't forgotten it, either; he brought it up each year on Samuel Sweet's birthday when all the workers gathered on the great lawn to share their favorite memories of Logan's grandfather.

The ink had gotten all over Miles's hands now. "Looks like it's cracked down the side," Logan pointed out.

Miles went over to his backpack, which had been propped against the porch step, and pushed the small bottle into a side pocket. He wiped his hands off on his shorts and grinned. "Good thing it disappears!" The original spot on his shorts was already almost gone. "Hey, you don't see my book anywhere, do you?"

Logan had a gift for spotting anything out of place, or missing, or extra. This talent came in very handy when helping out in the candy rooms and sometimes outside the candy world, too. It took him only a few seconds to spot the corner of Miles's book between two raspberry bushes on the other side of the porch. He reached for it. "Too bad you didn't fall off on this side. Instead of getting thorns in your legs, you could have had a snack."

"I'll get it!" Miles said, darting in front of Logan. He quickly stuffed the book into his backpack. Logan stepped aside, a little hurt. Had Miles just assumed he'd drop it? He didn't drop *everything.*

"Want to hear something interesting?" Miles asked, heading inside the factory as though nothing weird had happened.

Logan took a few seconds longer than usual to answer. They were standing in front of the statue of Samuel Sweet before he nodded.

Miles whispered so the guests still milling around the front hallway wouldn't hear him. "Turtles can breathe through their butts."

Logan looked at him. "Is that really true?"

Miles nodded and grinned. Logan grinned back. The weird feeling about the book slipped away. "Hey, I have something to show you!" he said, remembering his grandfather's box.

"Okay, but then I have to get to the Advertising Room," Miles said. "Sabrina and the others are going to pick the final slogan today."

"This won't take long," Logan promised. "You're gonna love it."

Thankfully, the box seemed undisturbed. Miles leaned over Logan's shoulder as he opened it. "This is my grandfather's old research and stuff from when he was young," Logan explained. "An old friend of his I'd never heard of before sent it to me."

Miles was already eagerly digging through the contents.

"Wow!" he said in an awed whisper. "Notebooks and journals and newspapers and maps. *Maps*, Logan, *maps!*"

"Glad you like it," Logan said, pushing the box toward Miles.

Miles's eyes glowed as he looked up from the box. "Really?"

"You can pull out the highlights for me. If you don't mind, I mean."

Miles closed the box back up and clutched it to his chest. "Mine, all mine."

They both laughed. "That's settled, then," Logan said. He was about to tell Miles about the caramel when his walkie-talkie buzzed and Max's voice came through.

"How's it going, boys? We're not getting any younger down here! Unless Miles wants to keep playing in Mrs. Sweet's prized rosebushes?"

Word traveled fast in the factory! Miles shook his head, reddening. "I've had plenty of thorns for today, thanks."

Logan pressed the Talk button and said, "Sorry, Max! I'll be right there."

Dwarfed by the pack on his back and the box in his arms, Miles hurried down the hall. Now *he* was the man with the mission.

"I'll save you some caramel!" Logan called after him just as three chimes sounded over the factory loudspeaker. An announcement was coming on. Logan's mom's voice soon rang through the air.

"We hope all our guests are having a very sweet time at **Life Is Sweet** today! Visiting hours are now over for the day, so please make your way toward the front or back doors. We have a lot of preparation to do for the Kickoff tomorrow, when the first Harmonicandy enters the world! We hope to see you all outside on the great lawn at noon!"

Logan grinned as soon as he realized what his mom had just said. The public wouldn't actually be there—in the room—when the Harmonicandy rolled down the belt! It would be a private moment after all, with no one whispering how it should have been the Bubbletastic ChocoRocket instead. The crowd would be waiting outside for the official presentation and sampling. Feeling as though a huge weight had been lifted off him, he ran all the way to the Harmonicandy Room, high-fiving anyone who reached out for him (and one person who, he was pretty sure, was waving to someone behind him).

"I'm here!" he shouted as he pushed open the door. His dad, Max, and Randall stood behind the long conveyor belt that stretched from wall to wall. They stopped sorting through the stacks of cooking supplies laid out on the belt and broke into wide grins. Logan's jaw dropped. He began turning around the room. The bright lights danced down upon the new brass and copper candy machines, some that reached nearly to the ceiling. Ingredients bubbled in large vats and small pots on burners at three different cooking stations. A jazzy tune played on what could only be a harmonica, the music filtered through small speakers built into the walls. This was most definitely the only room with harmonica music!

But even with all there was to see (and hear), the thing that hit him the strongest was the incredible smell. Philip once joked that Logan had a nose like a dog, a species well known for being able to distinguish different odors easily. It was true that smelling and tasting went hand in hand, so it stood to reason that if Logan was good at one, he'd be good at the other. But someone didn't need to have Logan's heightened abilities to notice *this* scent.

The room smelled like a combination of all the other candy rooms, and yet like something totally different at the same time. The shortbread cookie that formed the basis for the Harmonicandy gave the room a savory smell, more like food than candy. He picked up the earthiness of the dark chocolate, the salty, buttery sweetness of the caramel, the hint of vanilla. It was an irresistible combination. A lump formed in his throat. He had been a part of bringing this into being!

The door opened behind him, and Henry walked in. His eyes widened. He inhaled deeply, and his chin began to quiver. Uh-oh. A second later came the waterworks. After all that work to get him to stop crying and now it was starting again! At least this time Logan knew the cause. And truly, he couldn't really blame the man.

Seeing Henry cry made Max start crying. Then the Candymaker joined in. That did it; Logan was done for. They all huddled together and sobbed and beamed at each other and laughed and sobbed some more.

That was how Logan's mom found them when she walked in. "Oh dear," she said as she took in the scene. The men (and boy) quickly pulled apart and wiped away any remaining tears with their sleeves.

Then they all started talking at once. Max and the Candymaker eagerly showed Logan and Henry where the Harmonicandy molds would go, how the chocolate would be piped in from the Cocoa Room and funneled directly to the enrober, how the wrappers would be affixed. Logan's attention kept flying from place to place as he turned around in circles again, making himself dizzy with the wonder of it all.

Finally Max brought out the copper pot with the caramel in it, and everyone gathered around in a circle. Logan could see why they had been so excited about this particular batch. The deep amber-brown color, the brittle candied edges, the swirl of the cream, the tiny dots of salt—it looked perfect. The Candymaker handed everyone a spoon. They all clinked them together in the air, then reached in for a taste.

It may have been the best batch of fresh caramel Logan had ever tasted. And he'd tasted a *lot* of caramel. He knew what this meant— and so did the others. If the rest of the ingredients came out this well, the Harmonicandy was going to be *huge*.

With a glint of rebellion in their eyes, they all dug their spoons back in, fully ignoring the factory's rule against double-dipping. Laughter bubbled up inside them, and soon spoons were flying in and out of the pot as gooey strands of caramel dripped onto chins and splattered onto walls. At one point Logan's spoon slipped from his fingers and into the bowl. He didn't mind—more to lick off!

Then the door swung open and everyone froze, like kids caught by Mom with their hands in the cookie jar.

"I was told you wanted to see me?" Philip asked. Then he took one look around the room, dropped his briefcase with a thud, and burst into tears.

CHAPTER SIX

Logan remembered Daisy saying that musicians were, by their very nature, dramatic. They "felt their feelings" more strongly than regular folk. They had to, in order to translate emotion into musical notes and the notes back into emotion. He could now say with certainty that her theory was correct. He had seen Philip pitch fits before. He'd seen him shout, he'd seen him shut down, he'd even seen him cry. But this current outburst topped all of those.

Philip's eyes were so wide Logan couldn't imagine how they were staying inside his head. He kept opening and closing his mouth, clearly at a loss for words, which was unlike him. Finally he wiped his eyes and shouted, "All this! Everything! Me! It's real!" He gestured wildly around the room, pointing in turn at the conveyor belt, the Harmonicandy molds (where each stainless-steel tray had slots for forty candy bars), and the enrober, which would coat each harmonica with a stream of chocolate. He spent a full five minutes craning his neck back and pointing at the tubes that, as of tomorrow, would be filled with the Harmonicandy's special blend of milk and dark chocolate.

It took four spoonfuls of caramel and a really tight hug from Logan's mother before Philip calmed down. Then he instantly began peppering the grown-ups with all kinds of questions. Had the machinery been properly tested? Were the molds to the exact specifications from the blueprints? Would the cleaning supplies be all-natural? How many Harmonicandies would be produced in a day? Was that too many for Quality Control to handle, or did they plan to hire more staff? And about a dozen more questions Logan would never have thought of, including one to the Candymaker about the price per unit versus per carton, and the profit margin after advertising and distribution costs. Logan had never thought about that last part in his entire life.

Exhausted, Philip finally slumped on a stool in a corner of the room, taking deep breaths as if he'd just run the length of the factory. (Although the only time Logan had seen Philip run was when Max had sent them out to the chicken coop to collect some eggs, and a rooster had taken a liking to Philip and chased him clear across the field.)

"Satisfied?" Henry asked Philip kindly.

Logan had noticed over the last few months that Henry and Philip had built a special friendship. It didn't make Logan jealous—that was an emotion he had no real experience with. He just found it interesting and wondered what it was about each of them that drew them together so easily, since they were such completely different people.

"For now," Philip replied. "I'm sure I'll have more concerns within the hour."

"I'll look forward to hearing them," Max said with a grimace.

The Candymaker stood off to one side and spoke into his walkie-talkie for a moment before clipping it back on his belt. "Miles will be joining us in a few minutes," he announced. "Once he arrives, we have some very exciting news that will affect all our young candymakers."

Logan snapped his attention away from Philip. "Really?"

Another surprise! And one for all of them together! This day had definitely taken a turn for the better.

His dad patted Logan on the shoulder. "We wanted to tell Daisy in person, too, of course, but when we called her house this morning, her grandmother said she was out of the state for a while. I hope she's somewhere fun. A lovely girl. So spirited."

"She's at sleepaway camp," Philip volunteered.

Logan tried not to laugh. If he ever needed lessons on being able to lie on a moment's notice, he would go to Philip. The idea of Daisy doing something as normal as going to camp, making art projects, and singing campfire songs with a hundred other girls was hilarious. Whatever secret mission she was on would be a lot more exciting than that. Before his dad could ask any more questions about Daisy that they wouldn't be able to answer, Logan decided to change the subject. "What's the surprise?" he asked. "Tell me, tell me, tell me." For good measure, he added, "*Pleeeeeease?*"

The Candymaker only shook his head. "Patience, my dear boy, patience." Patience, like jealousy, was a character trait Logan spent little time entertaining. And who knew how long it might take Miles to get there. The boy was easily distracted. Logan turned to his mother. She could usually be relied on to cave in.

But she simply looked away and busied herself scrubbing the sticky caramel off the wall with vinegar and a rag.

He tried Max next. When their eyes met, Max gave a little hop and then scurried off to the sink to run boiling water into the caramel pot. "Sorry, Logan," he said. "You know how it is. Once caramel hardens in the pot, it's a bear to scrape off the bottom."

"Uh-huh," Logan muttered, even though he did know that to be true. When they were all making the Harmonicandy in the early-morning hours of competition day, Daisy had to use her cut-through-anything laser pen so they could chisel the burned caramel out of the pot. A good candymaker never left a mess behind.

Logan turned away from Max and quickly ducked under the enrobing machine. "Randall, are you going to tell me?" But Randall continued to fiddle with a knob that clearly did not need to be fiddled with. "So this is how it's going to be," Logan declared, turning away. Only one person was left. "Henry!" he said. "What about you? Are you going to keep me in the dark, old friend, old pal?"

Henry shook his head. "Sorry, Logan. I don't know any more than you do. Honest."

Logan assessed Henry's answer. Eye contact, not scurrying away to do something else. He decided Henry was telling the truth. Whatever the news was, Henry didn't know, either.

Logan finally faced Philip, who was now using the bottom of his shirt to dry the water drops that had landed beside the sink. "Help me out here, Philip. Aren't you curious?"

"I'm sure Miles will be here any minute," Philip replied, tucking his shirt back in. "Since when did you get so impatient?"

Logan stared at his friend. "Me? You're the most impatient person I've ever known!"

"Maybe," Philip admitted. "Guess that means you're becoming more like me."

The adults in the room got quiet. Logan felt his cheeks begin to heat up. Was that true? Sure, Philip had some good qualities. He worked hard, he never gave up, he actually finished things he started. But Philip had such a hard edge to him, while Logan was so easygoing and happy. Wasn't he? He used to lie on the great lawn and stare at a blade of grass for hours and still not tire of looking at it. Could he still do that? Would he even want to?

Thankfully, the door opened before his self-examination went any deeper and brought down his mood. "Hey, everyone!" Miles said, bounding into the room. He waved a folded piece of paper in the air. "We did it! We came up with the top four slogans!" He turned to the Candymaker. "Once you pick the final one, Sabrina wants to announce it tomorrow at the Kickoff!"

"Wonderful," the Candymaker boomed. "I'll look forward to seeing that list."

Everyone else remained quiet, watching Miles expectantly. Logan figured they, like himself, were waiting for Miles's response to seeing the Harmonicandy Room for the first time.

"What's everyone staring at?" Miles asked, looking from person to person. He rubbed his nose and ran his tongue over his teeth. "Do I have something on my face?"

Mrs. Sweet smiled and ruffled Miles's hair. "No, dear. We're just waiting for your reaction to seeing the room. It was an emotional experience for some of us."

Everyone's gaze slid over to Philip, who put his hands on his hips and snapped, "Do I need to remind everyone how I found you when I arrived?"

That got a laugh. Miles raised one eyebrow, then dutifully glanced around the room. "It looks awesome!" He said it enthusiastically, but without tears or the need to be soothed with caramel. "I heard there's a big announcement?"

The Candymaker smiled. "Everyone, pack your bags. We're going on a road trip!"

••••••••••••••••

CHAPTER SEVEN

••••••••••••••••

A road trip? Logan dared not breathe, afraid he'd heard wrong. What if his dad had said *nose dip*? Or *toad lip*? Or...Logan searched his brain to think of other options but had to admit they all sounded unlikely. And there was that part about packing a bag, so maybe he'd heard his father correctly after all! But other than the annual Confectionary Association's convention, Logan's parents had not taken him farther than the other side of town in *years*.

Philip and Miles came to stand beside him as they awaited more information. Logan was grateful for their company.

With the usual twinkle in his eyes turned up a few notches, the Candymaker announced, "I've already gotten Miles's mother's blessing and left messages for Philip's father and Daisy's grandmother. Mrs. Sweet and I would like to take the four of you on a week-long publicity tour to introduce the Harmonicandy before it launches! We are expected at three of the country's biggest and most famous candy stores to give them samples. It will give me and Mrs. Sweet a good chance to visit with the store owners to discuss product placement, shelf life, and other grown-up business while you guys have fun showing off the candy bar to what will no doubt be a lot of interested folks. Max and Randall and Henry will hold down the fort here. What do you think so far?"

Logan and Miles hesitated for about a second before jumping up and down. They grabbed each other by the wrists, then jumped up and down some more.

"I'll take your enthusiastic response as a yes," Logan's father said.

"Yes!" Logan shouted. "Definitely yes! How will we get there?"

"We'll take one of the factory's vans," his dad replied. "I wouldn't call it roomy, but everyone will be comfortable. A few members of the publicity department and the sales team will be going as well, in their own vehicle."

"Will we eat at truck stops with real truckers?" asked Miles. "Will we stay in hotels? Can we go geocaching on the way?"

The Candymaker ticked the answers off on his fingers. "Probably, yes, and I don't know what that is." Then he turned to Philip, who had been very quiet. "How about you, Philip? You in? You're the main attraction."

"Isn't the candy bar the main attraction?" Philip snapped, his old personality coming back. "That's what people want to see, not me."

"Yes, of course," the Candymaker said patiently. "But people want to meet the boy behind it."

Logan's mother chimed in. "And the boys and girl behind him."

"That's us and Daisy!" Miles said. He and Logan high-fived.

In the time since the candymaking contest, Logan's parents, Max, and Randall had pieced together much of what had happened leading up to Philip's win. They didn't know Daisy and AJ's role, or Philip's father's plans to take over the factory, or that Henry knew more of what really happened than the other grown-ups did. But they did know that the four contestants had worked as a team. Inviting them all on this trip proved it.

"Don't you want to go, Philip?" Logan asked. "Five minutes ago you were running around here making sure everything was perfect for the Harmonicandy's big entrance into the candy world. This would be your chance to make sure all the store owners display it exactly right."

"Of course I want to go," Philip snapped. "And proper placement on store shelves is very important." He looked down at his feet. "But there's no way my father would allow it."

Logan hadn't expected that response and couldn't think of what to say.

Miles had no trouble jumping right in, though. "Why not? Isn't he the one who always wants to win all the time? Why wouldn't he want your candy to be successful?"

Philip glanced around the room. He pressed his lips together and shook his head. Miles grabbed him by the arm and dragged him toward the door. Philip, being much larger, could have stopped him, but he let Miles lead him away. When Miles sensed an injustice, his size didn't hold him back. Logan quickly hurried after them.

"Boys, wait," the Candymaker called after them. "Let's see how it plays out when we hear back from Mr. Ransford."

Henry put his hand on Logan's dad's arm. "Let them go," he said calmly.

"We'll be right back, Dad," Logan promised, closing the door behind him. Whatever was going on, Philip clearly wouldn't say it in front of the grown-ups, and Logan didn't want to miss it.

"What's the problem?" Miles asked Philip when the three of them were alone in the hall. "We can't do this without you, and I *really* want to go."

Logan nodded in agreement. "If *my* parents are letting me go out into the world, your dad has to let you. He just *has* to!"

Philip shook his head again. "You don't understand. My dad

45

hates this place and anything to do with it. He doesn't care what happens to the Harmonicandy."

Logan felt his face grow hot. His first thought was to worry about the factory's candy becoming unstable in the heat; then he realized the temperature had only risen in *him*.

"Philip!" Miles said, stomping his foot.

"Sorry," Philip said to Logan. "Nothing personal."

A squeaky sound escaped Logan's lips. He swallowed and tried again. "Why?" he managed to get out. "Why would he . . . hate us?"

"Honestly, I don't know." Philip checked the door behind him before continuing. "I think it's because he lost this one. He had to promise not to take over the factory if I won the contest. You may have figured out that my father doesn't like to lose. And he especially doesn't like to lose to his youngest son."

Neither Logan nor Miles could argue with that. "Maybe he's over it," Miles suggested. "He lets you come here all the time."

Philip shook his head. "My father doesn't know I come here. Reggie brings me on his own."

Logan searched for something to say, and again nothing came. He could tell his own father anything. Not that he always wanted to, but he could. Finally he said, "So what are we going to do? We're not going without you."

"We're not?" Miles said.

Logan shot him a look.

"Fine, we're not," Miles agreed.

The door to the Harmonicandy Room opened, and the Candymaker stuck his head out. "Big news, Philip!" he boomed so loudly Logan bet they could hear him in the Taffy Room, clear across the factory. "Your father said yes!"

Philip couldn't have looked more surprised if he'd just learned a spaceship had landed on the great lawn. His eyebrows rose so high they almost disappeared under his hair. "He *did*?"

The Candymaker nodded. "He just returned our call. He was funny, actually."

"My father was . . . funny?" Philip repeated. His brows rose even higher, if that was possible.

"Yup. He said to make sure to bring some yarn with you for the long drive. Said you'd have time to knit a whole blanket!" The Candymaker chuckled. "You don't strike me as the knitting type. Still, you never can tell with people's hobbies, I suppose."

Philip's mouth opened, then closed, then opened again, exactly the way it had earlier, when he'd first seen the Harmonicandy Room. Logan considered himself better than average at reading people's faces. It was his way of making up for all the years when he'd paid more attention to what people were saying than how they were saying it. Philip's face was going through a range of emotions now, almost faster than Logan could register them. First had been the shock, and then he'd looked puzzled, then angry, then amused. Finally his features settled back into something that looked like acceptance, with a hint of defiance and gratitude. A bizarre combination, but somehow on Philip it worked.

"You okay?" Logan asked. "This is good news, right?"

Philip let out a long breath, straightened his shoulders, and nodded. "Looks like I'm in!"

"What are you boys standing around for, then?" the Candymaker asked. "You've got packing to do! I know this is short notice, but the timing of the trip will work out well. It will take two weeks for Max and his team to gather the necessary supplies to get the Harmonicandy production under way, so it will be ready to go when we return. Plus, as you recall, at the contest Big Billy announced his retirement and the end of the **Mmm Mmm Good** candy factory. He will arrive in two weeks to announce which of their candy recipes he's going to give us."

Personally, Logan hoped they'd be inheriting the EnchantMints.

That was his favorite **Mmm Mmm Good** product. Soft peppermints with sparkles on the surface that made tiny pops on your tongue when you sucked on them. Refreshing *and* entertaining!

"But, Mr. Sweet," Miles said, "you haven't told us when we're leaving."

"I didn't? Oops. Sorry about that. We leave tomorrow as soon as the Kickoff is over."

Miles and Logan began jumping up and down again. *Tomorrow!*

"Wait," Miles said, landing on one foot. "What about Daisy? We can't go without her."

"We may have to," the Candymaker said. "She might not want to leave sleepaway camp."

Miles's eyes widened. "Daisy's at *sleepaway camp*?"

Logan leaned over and whispered, "No! Philip made it up before. We couldn't tell my parents Daisy's on a mission."

"Right!" Miles said loudly. "Camp! Probably braiding some girl's hair right now and telling ghost stories around the fire."

Logan cringed. "I don't think Daisy's the hair-braiding type."

"Too much?" Miles whispered.

Logan nodded.

"*Anyway*," the Candymaker said, "I mean it about packing. Tomorrow's going to be a busy day for all of us. Let's have our bags ready to be loaded onto the van before the Kickoff."

The three of them nodded. The Candymaker went back into the Harmonicandy Room, leaving them alone in the hall again. Miles turned to Logan. "I'm going to bring my road maps and my swag bag—that's a geocaching thing I'll teach you all about—and some books and my travel chess set and..."

Miles paused to take a breath and Logan jumped in. "And I'll bring my sketchpads and pencils and puzzles and we can share my comics and I can bring the painting Daisy sent me and we can hang it up at each hotel room and—"

"Hold on there, boys," Logan's mother said. Logan looked up, surprised to see that his mom had appeared and Philip had slipped away. When did that happen? She handed them each a sheet of paper. "Before you start packing all your earthly belongings, I thought you might have trouble figuring out what to bring. This is all you'll need."

Logan glanced at the very, very short typewritten list. "That's it?"

"Yup. Think one van, six people, eight days. You do the math."

Logan looked the list over again. "So no seashell collection from when I was three and we went to the beach with Grandpa and he had the idea for Sour Fingers when I spilled my orange juice on the sand?"

His mom shook her head.

"And I can't bring the giant stuffed whale my dad won for me at a carnival two years ago that may or may not sleep on my bed at night?" Miles asked.

Mrs. Sweet smiled. "Not unless you want it to take someone else's seat."

Miles looked thoughtful. "Hmm, Philip or Whaley... Can you give me a minute to decide?"

"Where is Philip, anyway?" Logan asked, looking behind him.

"I thought he was out here with you," his mother said, "but clearly he's not anymore. Hopefully he went home to pack. Miles, I think Mr. Sweet is ready to take a look at the list you gave him. Logan, let's head up to the apartment to get our stuff together before we run out of time."

Without another word, Miles shot past them and into the Harmonicandy Room.

"And then there were two," Mrs. Sweet said, putting her arm around Logan.

"Thanks, Mom," Logan said as they moved together down the hall. "For letting me go. I know you think people will stare at—"

"Ugh, what's this?" Logan's mom broke away. She bent down to pick up a blue Sour Finger wrapper. A few grains of blue sugar spilled out. "Great," she muttered, sweeping it into her hand. "I've got to get this place cleaned again before tomorrow."

"Mom, the factory looks great," Logan insisted. "It's one wrapper—don't worry." As soon as the words were out, he spotted two Leapin' Lolly sticks on the floor behind the heel of his mom's shoe. If she saw them, she'd freak out over more trash, and who knew where it would lead. He had to act fast.

Hoping the sticks didn't harbor any spit from whoever had eaten the lollypops off them, he pretended to tie his shoe, then grabbed the sticks and slipped them into his back pocket. Usually something that skinny would be hard for him to pick up, but his fingers had a little caramel stuck to them, which allowed him to grasp the sticks with no problem. He'd have to remember that in the future!

"Like I was saying," Logan continued as though nothing had happened, "I know you and Dad have always tried to—"

His mom stood back up, spun around, and gave him a tight hug. "I know what you're trying to say, honey. We've been protecting you all this time, and you've proven you're ready to face the world. We'll be right there with you, and if you feel uncomfortable at any point, you'll let one of us know. But right now I've got to call a meeting of the cleaning crew." She planted a kiss on his cheek and hurried off. Just before turning the corner, she called out, "Now go pack!"

Now go pack, he repeated to himself. He couldn't remember ever hearing those words before today. He really liked the way they sounded.

Once he was sure he was alone, he pulled out Daisy's vid com. He pressed all the right buttons, but a light just flashed NOT AVAILABLE over and over. When it offered the chance to leave a video message, he told her honestly how much he wanted her to go on the trip. With a sigh, he pressed the Off button. Daisy was probably out saving the world or something else really exciting. He couldn't expect her to drop everything.

Sure would be nice, though.

CHAPTER EIGHT

Logan stared down at the sunshine-yellow suitcase his mother had left on his bed. He hadn't seen it in years—not since his last hospital stay, seven years ago. His mother had picked out the color because she thought it was cheery. Just seeing it made him think of the big-as-his-head sunflowers in the field out back that would reach their full height just in time for the picnic next month.

He fully expected to find the suitcase empty, but when he unzipped it and flipped the top open, the smell of chocolate was almost overwhelming. From the strength of it, he'd have thought the suitcase would be filled with the stuff! Instead, all he found was the corner of something white peeking out from an inside pocket. Logan gripped the corner firmly and pulled it all the way out. He smiled when he recognized his grandfather's handwriting on the homemade card.

The front of the card had a picture of a stick-figure boy drawn in crayon. An arrow pointing to the boy said *Logan*. Next to the boy his grandfather had drawn a tree with rainbow-colored, football-shaped fruit growing right out of the trunk. The pods were much bigger than they should be in comparison to the tree—more like watermelons than cocoa pods—and real cocoa pods weren't rainbow colored, but Logan knew it was supposed to be a cocoa tree. Plus it read *Chocolate...yum!* underneath. Logan had only the faintest memory of seeing the card before. He traced his hand over the tree and tried to picture his grandfather holding on to the little crayons with his big hands.

He figured he'd see a *Get well soon* message, or maybe even one of Grandpa's practical jokes, like sneezing powder or some kind of flat rubber snake that sprang out when you opened the card. But the only words inside were the days of the week, written in a circle. Every day except Sunday had a small rip in the paper beneath it, like something had been stuck there and then peeled off.

Logan turned the card over, but the back was blank. He laid it on his dresser. His mom would get a kick out of seeing it.

It took only fifteen more minutes to find everything on his mother's short list. He didn't know how she expected him to get by on four changes of clothes. She must be planning on doing laundry along the way, because he could go through four outfits in a single day!

The suitcase was barely half full. Hmm...it would take up the same amount of room in the van whether it was full or only half full. May as well add a few more things.

First in was his latest batch of comic books, a sketchpad, and a pack of pencils. They hardly took up any space at all. He lifted his stuffed dinosaur off the shelf, tossed it into the suitcase, then snatched it back out. Somehow bringing a stuffed animal to sleep with didn't exactly scream, "I'm mature enough to go on a road trip." Still, it would be nice to have something that reminded him of home.

He knew what to do. He yanked his pillowcase right off his pillow and ran toward the front door. First stop, the employee lounge, only to find the NQP shelf totally bare. "The groupies cleaned us out," Randall explained, getting up from one of the round tables. He tossed out his apple core and joined Logan. "Can't blame 'em. What do candy lovers love even better than their favorite candy?" Without waiting for an answer, he said, "Their favorite candy all messed up!"

Logan laughed. That's exactly why he was such a fan of the NQPs, too. He held out his pillowcase. "I'm loading up for the trip."

Randall nodded in approval. "Smart. Although I'm pretty certain your dad wouldn't hit the road without plenty of candy within arm's reach."

"True," Logan agreed. "But you may have noticed my father's not the best at sharing his personal candy with others."

Randall laughed. "Also true! Here, you can bribe him with this, if necessary." He reached into his pocket and pulled out a Fireball Supernova, freshly packaged and ready to ship.

Logan opened his pillowcase and Randall tossed it in. "Thanks!" He felt more grown up already, having a "for adults only" candy!

"Hey," Randall said as they headed out of the room together, "what was in that box I delivered this morning? If you don't mind my asking."

Logan realized he hadn't thought about the box at all after giving it to Miles. "It was a whole bunch of Grandpa's old papers and journals. Miles is going through it for me. He even found a map or two, so he's happy. He loves maps."

They were right outside the Cotton Candy Room now. As much as Logan loved his cotton candy (which was *a lot*), he knew it wouldn't travel well. He inhaled deeply, then began to walk on, expecting Randall to stay in step. When he didn't, Logan looked over his shoulder, ready to say his goodbyes. He had a lot of candy to collect, and the closing bell would ring in a few minutes. But Randall's expression made him come to a full stop.

"What is it?" he asked. "Do you smell something weird? Is it the grapefruit-flavored cotton candy? Takes some getting used to but tastes delicious, as you must know."

Randall shook his head. His face looked pale, or maybe it was just the lighting in the hall. "Who did you say sent the box?"

"I didn't say," Logan replied, trying to picture the signature at the bottom of the letter. "But it was Franky, or Franco, then something with a G, I think." He could swear Randall's eye twitched.

"Franklin Griffin?" Randall asked.

"Yes, that was it," Logan said, eager to be on his way. His dad took closing time very seriously. And if he waited until tomorrow to collect the candy, the visitors would likely have left only crumbs behind. "Gotta go," he told Randall. "See ya in the morning."

"Okay," Randall said, but still he didn't move. Logan wondered why Randall cared who'd sent the box, but he wasn't curious enough to ask—not when it could mean the difference between eating candy on the road and not eating candy on the road.

By the time he got down to the Tropical Room twenty minutes later, Logan had collected samples of every candy currently in production except the Pepsicle and Some More S'mores. Those he put in a category with cotton candy in terms of their low odds for survival on the road. He temporarily stashed the bag in the large refrigerator in Avery's office for safekeeping. It wouldn't take long for everything to melt into one big blob of chocolate and sugar in the tropical heat.

He headed to his destination—the aloe plants. He broke off a few of the spiky green stalks and stuck them gently into his back pocket before reaching for some more. He'd never had to plan ahead before, and he didn't want to run out on the road and not have enough to put on his scars. He may have limited knowledge of life outside the factory, but he did know aloe plants didn't grow on street corners.

"G'day, road tripper!" Avery called out across the room.

Logan scanned the treetops until he spotted Avery waving his blue bandana from the top of a cinnamon tree. Logan stuck the rest of the stalks in his other pocket and headed over. "You heard already?"

"You know how fast news travel here," Avery replied with a grin. "Especially good news. I knew before you did." He stuck his knife into the holster on his belt and tossed down a burlap satchel, which landed beside the tree with a *plop*. Logan knew that at this time of day it would be filled with long ribbons of bark. The lower part of the tree was already bare. He watched Avery slide down the trunk, wishing as always that one day his parents would let him try climbing one of the trees.

"You excited?" Avery asked as his feet touched the ground.

Logan nodded enthusiastically. "So excited!"

"It's a big deal," Avery said, gripping Logan's shoulder. "Leaving home for the first time, facing the great unknown on the road. You could return a whole different boy. You could return a *man*!"

Logan stopped nodding. "I didn't think of it that way. I wasn't nervous before, but maybe I should be?"

"Nah," Avery said. "You'll do great. You'll have all your best mates with you. What could go wrong?" He slung his satchel over his shoulder and sauntered off with a wave. "Send me a postcard from someplace supercool."

Logan waved back, but only halfheartedly. Unless a miracle happened and Daisy left her mission, he'd only have two out of three of those mates. But he knew Daisy never left a mission unfinished.

A few minutes later, Logan stepped through the factory's back door and inhaled the scent of chocolate from the vents that opened out onto the lawn. The scent blended with the smells of ripe summer fruit. He loved that each season smelled different here and wondered whether it was like that everywhere. He wished he could bottle the great lawn's special smell, but since that wasn't possible, he'd have to find something else outside to remind him.

Logan's dad was walking toward him, his arms full of ears of corn. "I thought you were upstairs packing," he said when they met halfway to the strawberry patch.

"I am," Logan said. "I mean, I was. Just had a few pit stops to make." Logan reached around the sack of candy slung over his shoulder and pulled an aloe stalk from his back pocket. He held it up.

His dad nodded. "Smart."

"I've just got to grab one more thing from out here."

"Judging by the bulk of that pillowcase, I'd say you've collected quite a lot as it is. Remember, small space, lots of people. And some of us take up more room than others." He jiggled his belly.

"No one wants a skinny Candymaker, right?" Logan asked as he stepped around his dad and started down the path. "Isn't that what Grandpa used to say?"

His dad laughed and called after him. "I'm pretty sure that was just to get out of exercising like the doctor told him to."

The great lawn was usually quiet at this time of day, but not the day before the Kickoff. Logan was in such a good mood that it didn't even bother him when people called out to him or when the occasional son or daughter of one of the lingering visitors stared at him a little too long. He stopped to pick a strawberry and ate it while measuring himself against a giant sunflower. A huge field of sunflowers sprouted up every year at that time. The farmers who grew the crops for the different products had contests to see who could grow the tallest one. The current winner came up to his shoulder. Just a week earlier it had only reached his chest. Maybe by the time they got home from the tour it would be over his head!

It took Logan longer than he thought it would to find the right white clover bush. He'd spent so many weeks kneeling in front of it, drawing the caterpillar's metamorphosis into a butterfly. He figured his feet would know where to go, but in summer the bushes got so full with leaves that they blended into each other. He couldn't see any caterpillars or a chrysalis. He *especially* didn't see a butterfly. He still found himself wondering whatever happened to the chrysalis he'd watched so intently, the one with the black, yellow, and red-winged butterfly inside. It still made him sad that he never got to see it emerge.

All he wanted now, though, was one leaf from the bush to remind him of home. He reached to pull one off, but his hand slowed as it neared the bush. Ripping a leaf off the living, healthy bush suddenly felt wrong. Breaking off the aloe stalks felt different—maybe because they were grown for medicinal purposes. He decided he would take something that was already on the ground, like an acorn, maybe.

He spent a few minutes combing the ground for acorns before remembering that they didn't drop until fall. He was about to scoop up a nice-looking pinkish-gray rock when he spotted an unusual stick down by the path to the picnic tables. It was smooth with three lumps on one side. He picked it up and slid it into his pocket, next to the aloe. He was about to turn back toward the factory when he heard Miles's voice. He stepped out from behind the row of trees that lined the path to see Miles kneeling on the ground, the box from Franklin Griffin open on one of the tables.

"Hey!" Logan said. "Find anything cool?"

Miles jumped up in surprise, but at least this time he didn't throw anything in the air. He did scramble for his vid com, which he'd balanced on a rock. He quickly closed the cover and stashed it in the box before turning to face Logan.

"Were you just talking to Daisy?" Logan asked.

When Miles hesitated, Logan added, "I called her, too. To get her to come on the trip with us. I had to leave a message, though."

"Yes!" Miles said loudly. "Me too!" He began stuffing notebooks, newspapers, and maps back into the box. "I'm sorry. I just need to run to the factory library before it closes. Can't go on a road trip with nothing to read, right? Then home to pack. See you tomorrow!" He ran off, clutching the box.

"You didn't tell me if you found anything cool!" Logan called after him. But Miles must not have heard him, because he didn't slow down. Oh well, plenty of time on the long drive tomorrow to hear all about it.

CHAPTER NINE

Logan tossed and turned but couldn't sleep. Usually at this time of night he could count on finding his dad in the living room, checking supply lists for the next day or going over the accounting ledgers. No matter how busy he was, he would always stop working to play a game or to tell Logan a story. But tonight both of his parents were still downstairs in the factory, trying to get everything ready to run in their absence. Maybe that's why he couldn't sleep. He wasn't used to being alone.

He ran through his gratitude list twice more, then stared at the ceiling for a while, thinking how strange it was that he didn't know where he'd be sleeping the next night. That thought certainly didn't help him fall asleep any faster, so he flipped on the light and went through his suitcase for the third time since he'd packed it. At least now it made sense that it smelled like chocolate when he opened it.

Even with all the candy, clothes, comics, pads, and pencils, it still felt like something was missing. He looked around the room and saw an empty space on his bookshelf where his favorite wooden puzzle from his grandfather usually sat. That's what was missing! He'd left it up in the loft over the barn. He had to get it. How could he have thought of leaving without it? His grandfather had carved it by hand, sanding down each of the small interlocking pieces until they slid together like butter. The puzzle would remind him of his grandfather.

He threw his sweatshirt on over his pajamas, slipped into his sneakers, and scribbled a note for his parents in case they returned while he was gone. As he ran down the walkway from the apartment into the factory, his resolve faded. It was dark outside, and he'd forgotten his flashlight. And really, when he thought about it, he hadn't actually played with that puzzle in weeks. Maybe months.

Plus a piece was missing, so you couldn't solve it.

His feet slowed. Maybe he could find something else to remind him of his grandfather. He stood at the back door, looking out the small window, trying to decide. The moon hung directly over the barn. It had a slightly bluish tint, and it reminded Logan of an Icy Mint Blob with a big bite taken out of it. How could he be scared with a giant piece of one of his favorite candies hanging in the sky?

He pushed open the door and stepped out into the warm night. He couldn't remember the last time—if ever—he had been outdoors this late alone. Sometimes his dad would host an outdoor movie night for all the factory employees and their families, but that was like the opposite of being alone. He looked up at the moon for courage and hurried across the lawn to the barn.

Unfortunately, he hadn't considered how the chickens and cows would react to his unexpected presence. As soon as he started to slide open the barn door, he was greeted with *kuh-kuh-kuh-kuh-KACK*, followed by a loud, sharp trilling sound from a recent batch of baby chicks and angry growls from their protective mothers. He didn't even know a chicken *could* growl! The cows just gave lazy moos. Logan scurried backward and bumped right into something soft. He yelped and turned around to face an amused-looking Henry.

"Sleepwalking?" Henry asked. "Or just out to visit the animals?"

"I left something in the couldn't sleep."

Henry tilted his head. "Huh?"

Logan realized he hadn't made much sense. "I mean, I left something in the barn, and also I couldn't sleep."

"Too excited about tomorrow?"

Logan nodded. Over Henry's shoulder he caught a streak of light arcing across the sky. A second later another whizzed by. "Did you see that?" Logan asked, pointing.

Henry turned around. "See what?" he asked.

"That!" Logan said as another streak of light soared overhead. "I think it's a meteor shower! I've never seen one before. I had to do a report on them for Mrs. Gepheart a few years ago." Logan couldn't tear his eyes away from the sky. So this is what he'd been missing all these years by staying inside when it was dark out! Another whizzed by. "Aren't they awesome?"

Henry shook his head. "These old eyes can't see that far."

"Are you sure?" Logan asked. "Maybe you're not looking in the right place. They're really bright."

Henry put his hand on Logan's shoulder and turned him back toward the factory door. "It's late and you should be sleeping. Who knows how well you'll sleep on the road."

The road! It had such a grown-up ring to it. He was going out on the road! He followed Henry to the door and realized that his friend had a long walking stick in one hand, the kind he'd use if he were going hiking in the woods or up a hill.

"I didn't get to ask what *you* were doing out here in the dark," Logan said. "Going for a midnight hike?"

Henry smiled. "You know me, always up for adventure."

They both laughed. Logan knew that the only person who traveled outside the factory grounds less often than he did was Henry! "I'll be inside in a minute," he promised.

Henry nodded. "Sleep well, Logan. You're gonna need it."

Logan knew his old friend was right. He just wanted to watch a few more stars streak across the black sky. In his head, he was drawing them in his sketchpad—the way they all seemed to come from one part of the sky but went in different directions. The way they lit up the stars they passed closest to and left a brief impression on the sky, like skywriting, before fading away. It seemed like he could hear some of them, even though they were really far away and probably didn't make a sound anyway. When Logan got back upstairs, he quickly drew a picture of the shooting stars to show to Miles, who liked that kind of stuff.

As he turned off the light, he felt a little silly for letting the chickens (and Henry!) scare him off. But as he drifted to sleep with the smells of the new candy he'd collected mixing with the old chocolate odor from his suitcase, Logan knew he wouldn't need the puzzle to remind him of his grandfather anyway. Almost everything he knew about candy he'd learned from Samuel Sweet. That knowledge lived inside him. He would take it everywhere he went, and it wouldn't even need to fit in a suitcase.

CHAPTER TEN

Tuesday

L ogan could hardly contain himself. He shifted his weight from side to side and had to concentrate on keeping his feet on the floor and not jumping up and down. He and his parents stood by Miles and *his* parents, who stood next to Philip, who had worn a tie for the occasion. Only a handful of others would be the first to see the Harmonicandy come down the belt. The head candymakers from each room were there, including Fran, from the Taffy Room; Avery, from the Tropical Room; Paulo, from the Bee Room; and of course Steve and Lenny. Sabrina, the head of advertising, and three other "suits" from the sales and marketing teams ran in just as Max pressed the button to start the machine. He'd offered to let Philip do the job, but Philip had declined. The gears began to move, and a cheer went up from the small crowd.

Outside, hundreds of employees and guests were waiting on the great lawn for the Kickoff to officially begin. The crowd included the judges from the candymaking contest, who always got to celebrate the newest winner. They would also be presenting Philip with his winning plaque, just like the ones in the front lobby of the factory. The Candymaker had bought everyone plastic harmonicas to practice with, so the crowd was no doubt keeping busy while they waited.

"Here they come!" Miles shouted. He pointed as the first tray of naked Harmonicandies slid under the enrober and chocolate cascaded down upon them. He really didn't need to point, as all eyes had been glued on that first tray. A dozen more trays followed right behind it. They'd all be wheeled outside so everyone could try them together.

Amid his joy, Logan felt a pang of sadness that Daisy couldn't be there. She loved the enrober even more than he did, and he loved it a *lot*. They'd all tried to reach her, and no one had heard back. He couldn't imagine wanting to be anywhere other than where he stood right then. But if he were the world's best teenage spy, maybe he wouldn't want to leave his supersecret assignment to watch a candy bar being made. Daisy was probably on the other side of the world, rescuing a kidnapped princess or recovering a priceless work of art.

The trays moved past them toward the cooling tunnel, where it would take five minutes for the Harmonicandies to solidify. When the real ones were ready to be packaged for sale in a few weeks, the tray would have a longer journey. After cooling, it would flip over, gently releasing the Harmonicandies onto the belt and funneling them, one at a time, into the wrapping machines. At the end of the line, they would drop into a specially made box that would cushion each one so the inner workings of the harmonica wouldn't get crushed.

Each person cheered as the first tray passed in front of them. Philip just wiped away a tear. He didn't even try to hide it. Logan was at the end of the line. When the tray reached him, he cheered like the rest of them. How would they wait until all these had cooled before they tasted one?

The Candymaker's walkie-talkie buzzed, and he stepped away

from the group to answer it. The rest of the group watched the clock, counting down the seconds. But when the Candymaker returned, his eyebrows were scrunched together. Everyone stopped talking and gathered around him.

"What is it?" Logan's mother asked. "Is everything okay?"

The Candymaker paused. "I hope so. Big Billy from **Mmm Mmm Good** is here."

"So?" Mrs. Sweet said. "You invited lots of other candymakers, right?"

He nodded. "Yes, but he just told the crowd he had an announcement to make after the unveiling of the Harmonicandy."

"You don't think he changed his mind about letting us produce some of his candy, do you?"

Mr. Sweet shook his head. "I hope not. It's his choice, of course. Maybe he thinks we'll be too busy with the Harmonicandy to give his the time they deserve."

"Come now, Richard," Henry said, stepping forward. "Nothing's wrong till something's wrong, right? This is a day of celebration. We'll worry about Big Billy if he gives us something to worry about."

"You are wise beyond your years," the Candymaker said, putting his hand on Henry's shoulder.

"There ain't much left beyond my years!" Henry joked.

Logan relaxed. His dad and Henry had been having that exchange for as long as Henry had been handing out advice. Which was as long as Logan could remember.

"The first batch is done!" Max announced, transferring the now-cooled tray to the bottom shelf of the cart. "You can all go join the party, and I'll wheel these out as soon as the rest are cooled off."

Logan, Miles, and Philip lagged behind as the others filed out. "I'd like to stay," Philip said.

"I bet your family's anxious to see you," Max said.

"They're not here." Philip said it like he didn't care, but Logan wondered whether he really did. It seemed as though Philip was very used to his dad's not coming to things.

"*I'm* here," a man's voice said from behind them.

They turned around to find Reggie heading into the room. Logan had begun to suspect that Reggie meant more to Philip than just someone who worked for his father.

"What are you doing here?" Philip asked, two red patches appearing on his cheeks. "I said you didn't need to come."

Logan cringed to hear Philip talk to Reggie that way.

Reggie held up Philip's violin case. "You left this in the car."

Philip looked surprised. He mumbled thanks, took a quick peek inside like he was making sure his violin was still in there, and stuck the case in a cabinet.

Max's assistants had been busy pulling the finished trays off the belt, and the carts were now full. "We're ready to introduce the Harmonicandy to the world," Max said. "Boys, a little help?" Logan and Miles each grabbed a cart and lined up behind Max. Philip got behind the last one, giving Reggie one more wary glance.

The bright sunshine was a stark contrast to the last time Logan had stood in that spot outside the back door, only ten hours before. The shooting stars seemed almost like a dream. Now balloons and banners hung from trees, boxes of chocolate pizza sat piled high on picnic tables, and colorful beach balls flew through the air, chased by laughing kids. It was a beautiful sight, and Logan's heart swelled.

The crowd welcomed him and Miles and Philip with cheers and chants of "Harmonicandy! Harmonicandy!" They had the honor of handing out a Harmonicandy to each person lined up in front of their cart. If some of the people Logan handed them to looked a few seconds too long at his hand or arm or face (which some definitely did), he refused to let it bother him. He thought again that it wasn't fair that Daisy had to miss this, even if she was out saving the world somewhere. Philip caught his eye and smiled at him. A real, genuine smile, which was rare for him. Logan smiled back extra wide.

When everyone had a Harmonicandy clutched (but not too hard!) in his or her hand, the Candymaker stood at the podium to make a speech. He gestured for Philip to join him, then spoke about having dreams, about the joy of teamwork and of believing in oneself. Logan knew people were still giving him sideways glances and whispering that he was probably wishing he were standing up there instead of Philip. But he wasn't. He was too excited about taking the first bite of the Harmonicandy before it melted.

It had been four months since he'd last tasted one, and that was four months too long. He knew back then that they'd created something special, and it wasn't only that the candy bar played music. Somehow the ingredients had combined to taste so much better than the sum of their parts. He'd always regretted that they hadn't made any extra candy, but they were lucky they'd even had enough for the contest judges.

The Candymaker handed Philip the microphone. Philip, who was normally anything but shy, seemed at a loss for words as he stared out at the crowd. Finally he raised the microphone and said, "Thank you, everyone, for your support. It's a great honor that wouldn't have been possible without my friends Logan Sweet, Miles O'Leary, and Daisy Carpenter and all the other wonderful candymakers at **Life Is Sweet⁹**."

Logan and Miles gave a wave to the crowd as everyone clapped. Then Philip added, "Now let's see what this thing can do!" He quickly moved the Harmonicandy up to his lips. Everyone else did the same. He blew into it and moved his fingers over the tiny holes. The notes flew through the air. The crowd immediately joined in! It wasn't as easy for them, without having practiced, but soon the great lawn was filled with music. A really bad, not-harmonious-in-any-way type of music, but it was *music*. Out of a *candy bar*.

Logan couldn't wait even one more second. He took a bite, chewed, swallowed, and took another. His heart began to pound. Sweat broke out on his forehead. His hands shook as he took the final bite.

Around him people of all ages cheered and called for more. Logan scanned the crowd for Randall, locating him leaning against a tree, munching away happily. His parents, Max, Philip, Miles, the three judges from the contest—everyone he saw was smiling and laughing as they ate the bars.

And then his eyes landed on Henry. There must have been fifty people standing between them, but Henry's unusually pale face wore an expression Logan had never seen before. His thick glasses magnified the sadness and worry in his eyes, along with something else Logan couldn't quite identify. It was almost like Henry was looking at something the rest of them couldn't see. This only confirmed what Logan was thinking. There was no denying it—the candy bar was delicious. The dark chocolate took the edge off the milk chocolate base, the caramel was sweet yet salty, the cookie had just the right crispiness, and the vanilla complemented the marshmallow perfectly. No doubt they had a winner on their hands.

But Logan knew, and clearly Henry knew, that this was not the Harmonicandy. This was not the candy bar that had won the Confectionary Association's annual New Candy Contest and had indirectly saved **Life Is Sweet** from being taken over by Philip's father.

Something was very wrong.

Logan tried to make his way through the crowd toward his father and Max without passing out from panic. He only half registered that Big Billy had taken the stage and had just announced he was giving **Life Is Sweet** four of **Mmm Mmm Good**'s most popular candies—more than he was giving any other factory—and that a bunch of his employees were now tossing samples of those candies into the cheering crowd.

What *did* hold Logan's attention was when Billy said that his trucks would be arriving the next day. The next day! Not in two weeks, as planned. He was taking his whole staff on a surprise vacation to thank them for their years of service and loyalty, and that bumped up the delivery date.

Logan reached his dad at the podium just as the Candymaker leaned over to shake Big Billy's hand. "Your faith in **Life Is Sweet** has not been misplaced. We will do you proud."

"I know you will, Richard," the old man said, leaning on his cane. "And you've got another winner on your hands."

The Candymaker smiled. "The Harmonicandy is certainly delicious."

"It is," Big Billy agreed. "But I meant him." He nudged the

Candymaker and pointed to Logan. Then he went to join the throng of well-wishers.

"Dad!" Logan cried out, too focused on getting his dad's attention to be flattered or embarrassed by Big Billy's kind words. "I have to tell you something!"

But before he could start, his father said, "Logan, I'm so sorry. I don't see how we can go on the publicity tour now. There's just no way, with those trucks coming tomorrow. Your mother and I need to be here to figure out how we're going to get the new candies into production while fulfilling all the initial Harmonicandy orders."

Logan was stunned. They were supposed to leave in two hours! Their bags were sitting in the front hall by the door. Three crates of Harmonicandies had just been picked up for overnight delivery to the stores!

"I hope you understand," his father continued. "I'd still send you boys without us, but you'd need a chaperone, obviously, and we can't spare anyone now. We'll reschedule the trip when things settle down, okay?"

At least he wasn't saying the tour would never happen. But how could it happen without a Harmonicandy to sell? Logan had to tell his dad.

"The Harmonicandy isn't right," Logan blurted out, nearly shouting over the music and laughter.

"What?" his father said. "The Harmonicandy isn't ripe?"

Logan shook his head. "Right. Isn't *right*."

"It's too noisy here," his dad said. "We'll catch each other back inside. I'm sorry again about the trip. I know you're disappointed." He gave Logan a squeeze, then let himself get drawn into the crowd, all eager to speak with the famous Candymaker.

Frustrated, Logan blew out a stream of air. He turned to look for Max and Randall. Randall stood taller than almost everyone in the crowd, and Max's bald head was easy to spot. But they were also surrounded by visitors and happily answering questions. And when it came down to it, even though Randall had the best sense of taste in the factory, he hadn't tried the original Harmonicandy, so he wouldn't notice the difference. Max *had* tasted it while Philip was working on the recipe, but Max's skills were different from Randall's and Logan's. Max was an expert on measurements and temperature and the actual science behind combining ingredients. Logan would have been surprised if he had noticed any difference between the taste of the Harmonicandy now and the way it had tasted four months ago, when he'd only had a small sample.

Logan gave up and went in search of Henry. Before he got far, Philip and Miles pulled away from the group and ran up to him. They'd been laughing and grinning until they saw his face. Their smiles faded fast. "What's wrong?" Miles asked. "You look all panicky."

Logan gave one more glance around for Henry, who had apparently disappeared into thin air, and then led his friends around the side of the barn, where they'd have privacy. He took a deep breath and in a rush of words said, "Remember how the rules of the contest clearly state that the ingredients of the winning candy have to be identical to what was submitted? And that's why the I Scream was eliminated?"

Miles and Philip nodded.

"Well, the rules also say that the ingredients have to be ones that any of the chocolate factories can easily find in large supply— nothing too rare or expensive. I mean, the point of the contest is to make a candy that can be sold, after all. Normally this isn't a problem—many candies use the same ingredients. It's all about the preparation, the combination, how much you use of each one, that sort of thing. No one even focuses on that part of the rules because it's so obvious."

"Okay," Philip said, "so what's the problem?"

"The Harmonicandy is the problem," Logan said, his heart sinking as he said it. "It's not the same as the one that won the contest."

Miles and Philip stared at him. "What do you mean it's not the same?" Philip demanded. "Max had the same list of ingredients. It looks the same, it sounds the same, and as far as I can tell, it tastes the same. Right, Miles?"

Miles nodded. "No one else seems to notice anything wrong. Even the judges loved it. They're over there now, congratulating Max. But..." He glanced at Philip apologetically. "If Logan says something's wrong, then something's wrong."

Philip crossed his arms. "Well, even if he's right, it's too late to do anything about it."

"You're missing the point," Logan insisted. "If Max and his staff followed the directions we gave them—and I know they did—but it still tastes different, that means we left something off our ingredient list when we submitted it."

Philip shook his head. "Not possible. We knew exactly what we put in there. Bottom line—production starts in two weeks. The Harmonicandy tastes great, and people are excited for it, and the stores have preordered hundreds of cartons. End of story."

Miles, who had gone a bit pale, turned to Philip. "Of course *you'd* still want to make it, even though Logan's telling you something's wrong. You'd lose all that money otherwise. I heard you talking with Reggie about the profits you'll make on each bar."

Philip glared at Miles. "That's not fair. What I do with my portion of the profits is none of your business. It has nothing to do with that."

Logan took each of them by the arm. "C'mon, we can't fight. We have to figure this out together. I don't want to stop production any more than you do—trust me."

Miles looked down. "Sorry," he grumbled in Philip's general direction.

"Whatever," Philip muttered back.

"And it's not true that no one else noticed a difference," Logan said. "Henry did. I could tell from his face that he knew it."

"Let's go find him, then," Miles said. "I'm sure he has an explanation."

They ran all over the great lawn checking out any men with wild white hair (which were more plentiful than one might expect). When they couldn't find him anywhere, they went down to Henry's favorite bench by the pond. A family of four was sitting on the bench and taking pictures. A few scattered playing cards littered the ground, no doubt remnants of a game abandoned when the excitement started. Henry wasn't on any of the other benches. Logan couldn't shake the feeling that he was hiding. But why would he do that?

Once the family recognized Philip, they wanted to take pictures with him. Philip posed stiffly, but at least he wasn't frowning. More and more people wanted pictures, and as the minutes passed, Logan grew more and more anxious. He told Philip that he and Miles would go look inside for Henry and would meet him back there.

The Marshmallow Room was empty. With everyone outside still celebrating, it was a little spooky having the factory so quiet during the middle of a workday. Miles ran into Henry's small office. After a minute or two Logan called out to him. "We should keep looking."

When Miles rejoined him, he had a strange expression on his face. Before Logan could ask if everything was okay, Miles said, "We must have missed him outside." Back out they went.

They grabbed Philip away from his adoring fans and started searching the grounds in a big loop. They finally spotted Henry near the marshy side of the pond, where the mallow roots grew. He was walking in the tall grass, clearly deep in thought. The boys were almost upon him before he noticed them. And when he did, he immediately turned the other way and bumped right into a tree.

"Seriously?" Philip said, marching toward him. "You're trying to ditch us?"

Henry turned to face them, rubbing his nose and fixing his glasses. "Saw that, eh?"

Philip said something else to Henry in a low voice, but Logan didn't hear. He doubted it was very nice.

"Are you okay?" Logan asked. He noticed that the bottoms of Henry's pants were wet. He'd gotten too close to the marsh and wasn't wearing his tall wading boots. "Where have you been? What's going on?"

Henry sighed. "I wish I knew."

"But you agree something's wrong with the Harmonicandy?"

Henry stuck his hands in his pockets and nodded. Logan had held out a shred of hope that maybe only *his* Harmonicandy had been off, or that he'd misinterpreted Henry's reaction while he was eating. That last shred was now gone.

Philip threw up his arms. "This is crazy. There's nothing wrong with it. It was delicious!"

"I agree with you," Henry said. "It tasted wonderful. But it was not the same as the one you submitted to the contest. I . . . I should have told you then. I should have stopped you. . . ."

"Stopped us from what?" Miles asked.

"From using the wrong chocolate."

"The wrong *chocolate*?" the boys repeated in unison.

Henry nodded. "I sampled some of the chocolate Philip was using while I was helping him work on the recipe. I knew right away that I'd tasted it before—only once, and it was a long time ago. But you don't forget a thing like that. Never expected to taste it again."

A worried feeling had started to settle in Logan's stomach. Henry wasn't making any sense. Why would the chocolate they used have been from some old batch? "What are you talking about, Henry?"

Henry gave a sad little shrug. "I don't know how else to explain it. Wherever Philip got that batch from, he wasn't supposed to use it. I didn't tell him because I wanted to give the Harmonicandy the best chance to win. I wanted to save the factory. Not for myself. I'm old, and I've been here perhaps too long. It didn't occur to me that of course Philip wouldn't be able to use the same chocolate again if he won. I didn't know about the clause in the contest rules that says the exact recipe has to be followed. Not until that other contestant got disqualified, anyway. And by then it was too late, of course. All I could do was hope that when the time came—when *today* came— no one would notice the difference."

"And no one did," Philip said firmly. "I mean, no one but the two of you. So let's keep it that way."

Ignoring Philip's remark, Logan asked instead, "Do you remember where you got the chocolate from?"

Philip threw up his hands again. "Of course I don't. Some shelf in the back of Max's lab, probably, with all the other ingredients."

Logan turned to Henry. "Can't we just find more of this chocolate? Steve and Lenny should know where all the different batches are, right?"

Henry shook his head. "There is no more. I am certain of it."

"We'll just need to look again," Philip said, already turning back toward the factory.

"There is NO more," Henry repeated firmly. Philip hesitated, then nodded.

No one spoke for a minute. "So what do we do?" Logan asked. "Production of the Harmonicandy is scheduled to start in two weeks." He looked at Miles, who had been very quiet since they'd left Henry's office. "What do you think, Miles?"

"I don't think we should say anything to anyone," Miles said softly.

"Exactly!" Philip said.

"We'll wait until we get back from the trip," Miles continued. "And then if it's still a problem, we'll tell them what's going on."

"I agree," Henry said. "While normally I would never suggest hiding anything from your father, he has enough going on right now with the rush to get the **Mmm Mmm Good** product line up and running. I'll work on it here, you work on it on the road, and hopefully we can sort it out before production starts."

Logan couldn't imagine how they could change anything from the backseat of a van, but it hardly mattered. He had to break the bad news. "We're not going on the trip."

"What?" Philip shouted. "That's crazy. We'll figure this out. We are going on that trip!"

"It's not because of this," Logan insisted. "Like Henry said, it's going to be crazy around here for the next few weeks. My parents have to be here to deal with all the new equipment and supplies coming in. But listen, it's a good thing to put off going to the stores. This will give us time to figure out what's going on, and—"

"No," Miles said in a loud voice. He cleared his throat and repeated it. "No. Philip's right, and you know I don't say that easily. We need to go on the road trip. Not later, now."

Logan had rarely heard Miles sound so forceful. "Why?" he asked.

Miles hesitated, then looked Logan right in the eye. "Tsurt em. Esaelp. I tnac llet uoy ereh."

Logan stared at him. He knew how to decipher Miles's backward talk by now. What could Miles have to tell him that he couldn't say in front of the others? He glanced at Philip and Henry. Henry looked at Miles blankly. Philip was scowling. He'd once said that learning Miles's backward talk would encourage him to use it more, and they should break him of the habit. Logan was pretty sure it annoyed Philip so much because he couldn't understand it.

"Even if we could still go," Logan said, "I told you, my parents can't take us. Neither can the suits who were going to drive the other van."

"Henry can drive us," Miles said, looking at him pleadingly. "Will you do it, Henry?"

"Of course he can't do it," Philip snapped. "You heard Big Billy. He's giving the Marsh-Wiggle to the factory. That thing's, like, half marshmallow. Henry needs to be here to get it up and running. Obviously."

Logan and Miles stared at Philip. "How do *you* know what's in the Marsh-Wiggle?" Miles asked angrily. Miles almost never got angry at anything. Whatever he knew that Logan didn't was clearly getting him worked up.

Philip shrugged. "I make it my business to know the top sellers at each factory. Plus the name kind of gives it away."

"He's right. I can't go," Henry said. "I'm sorry. But don't worry. I found—"

"What I still don't understand," Philip said, interrupting him, "is what you meant when you said you tasted the same chocolate a long time ago. When?"

"I don't recall," Henry said, rubbing his head as if it hurt. "I just know that it was a very special batch of chocolate, and you used up the rest of it."

Out of the side of his mouth, Miles said to Logan, "Eh si gniyl."

Logan's eyes widened. He sure hoped Henry hadn't figured out *that* one! Logan leaned close to Miles. "Lying about what?" Logan whispered.

"I'm not sure," Miles whispered back. "But about some of it."

"You know that's rude, right?" Philip said loudly.

"Sorry," Miles muttered. Then he said, "Hey, maybe Reggie could take us?"

Philip shook his head. "My dad's coming home in a few days. No way would he part with Reggie. Being driven all over town is a status thing for him."

"Figured that was a long shot," Miles admitted. "And I know my parents can't leave their jobs."

Henry shook his head at them. "As I was saying before, I'm sorry I cannot drive you. But I know someone who can."

"Who?" Philip demanded.

"Let's go find out," Henry replied. "He's waiting out front right now."

PART TWO

MILES

CHAPTER ONE

Monday

Miles tied up his bike and ran over to the wooden bench at the entrance to the park. In the four months since he'd helped create the Harmonicandy, Miles rarely did anything slowly. He had so much living to catch up on!

He tossed his backpack onto the bench, then ran his hand along the underside, being extra careful not to get a splinter in the process. He soon felt the paper scroll and carefully pried it loose from the tape.

Miles smiled to himself. Being friends with a real-life spy had taught him a thing or two. One of those things was that a *real* secret mission would be scary, but a make-believe one was fun!

He looked around to make sure he was alone—a totally unnecessary step in this case, since he wasn't actually *on* a spy mission, but Miles liked following directions. He was decidedly *not* alone, as it was a breezy summer day and school was out and this was the best park in town, with its hiking trails and lake and merry-go-round and vendors selling hot dogs and ice cream and pretzels.

He unrolled the scroll anyway.

The first thing he noticed was his name written in Norse runes. Last time it had been in Sanskrit. The time before that it was Egyptian hieroglyphs. A chill of delight ran up his spine. He loved ancient languages almost as much as he loved candy and maps. And he loved candy and maps a *lot*.

WHO:

WHEN: SECOND MONDAY IN JULY, 10 A.M.

WHERE: VERONA PARK

WHY: TO LOCATE THE LAST REMAINING GEOCACHE IN THE PARK

HOW: WITH THE COORDINATES SENT TO YOUR GPS AND YOUR OWN GEO-SENSES

NECESSARY SUPPLIES: GPS, RUBBER GLOVES, PEN, SNACKS, SWAG TO LEAVE IN THE CACHE, WATER BOTTLE

Being well trained and a fast learner, Miles had brought all the correct supplies. He tucked the scroll into his sock, slipped his backpack over his shoulders, and picked up the GPS attached to the strap around his neck. As promised, Arthur Wu, Spring Haven's new reference librarian and second-to-none geocaching tour guide, had loaded the coordinates into the device. Arthur was the reason Miles was at the park today instead of at the candy factory. During Arthur's first week on the job, he'd convinced the library to purchase five GPS devices that patrons could check out for free, just like a book. He then posted a sign-up list for a geocaching expedition where he would teach the game of geocaching.

Geocaching. Miles loved that word. *Geo*, meaning of the earth and ground. And *cache*, with its soft *sh* sound, meant a hidden collection of items that might one day prove useful. Pirates hid them to return to when safe from pursuit; soldiers hid them in preparation to hunker down in one spot; and now regular people hid them for sport, and other regular people found them. People like Arthur, and now people like *him*! Hurrah!

Miles's mom did not hide that she was anxious for him to do something other than go to the candy factory after school every day. She'd made it clear that running through the factory with Logan for hours on end wasn't exactly an educational pursuit. The minute Arthur had posted the sign-up list, she wrote Miles's name in bold letters on the first line.

Miles could admit it was possible he had become a bit obsessed with the candy factory and the upcoming release of the Harmonicandy, and he might talk about it a little too much, but the last four months had been the most amazing of his life. At least his father was always happy to take him to the factory. Every time Miles went to spend time with Logan or use the library or learn more about making candy from Max, he brought home enough free samples and NQPs to satisfy his dad's sweet tooth for a few days. If his mom had a sweet tooth, she probably wouldn't complain so much.

As someone who loved words and their histories and meanings, Miles knew that Arthur's last name meant he was Chinese, and that fact likely had something to do with why his mom wanted them to spend time together. Before Arthur moved to Spring Haven, Miles and his family were the only Chinese people in town besides Mrs. Chen, the librarian for the children's room who'd encouraged him to enter the candymaking contest last year. His own last name—O'Leary—definitely wasn't a typical name for a Chinese family. His mom's last name had been Yang, which Miles knew from his research was the seventh most common Chinese last name.

He knew that O'Leary was an Irish name (he had made a really excellent family tree in fourth grade, with real leaves attached to it, that went all the way back to Simon O'Leary, born in Dublin, Ireland, in 1842!), but he didn't know much about that side of his family besides their names.

His father's parents had passed away when Miles was only a few years old, and he didn't really remember them. When he was first designing his afterlife for the-girl-who-drowned, Miles had added a house for his grandparents, complete with a huge garden because his dad said they'd loved growing their own vegetables. Old pictures of them showed a smiling, blond-haired, blue-eyed couple. When he was younger, he'd asked why his grandparents looked so different from the rest of them, but his dad had always changed the subject. Eventually Miles gave up asking.

When the day of the first geocaching hike arrived, Miles turned out to be the only one on the list! He didn't mind at all. He could ask more questions, which he loved to do. Providing answers brought reference librarians great joy, and Arthur was no exception. They hit it off right away.

Miles's dad had tagged along that first time as Arthur explained that geocaching involved using GPS coordinates to find small treasures that other players hid in public outdoor areas around the world. At first Arthur seemed a bit shy around them, but he quickly warmed up. As they hiked the park's long trail system, Mr. O'Leary started lagging farther and farther behind while Miles and Arthur chatted enthusiastically about longitude and latitude, the various types of caches (large, regular, micro, and the tiny nano), common and tricky hiding places, and the proper way of recording your discovery in the cache's logbook. The conversation turned from treasure hunting to ancient maps and languages. Eventually Mr. O'Leary stuck in his earbuds and switched on his music, no longer even bothering to pretend that he was engaged in their conversation.

Over the last few weeks, Miles had become Arthur's best patron at the reference desk. Most people asked for basic information, like how to find a newspaper article published in the *Spring Haven Herald* five years back. Either that or they asked for directions to the bathroom. But not Miles. With all the tools of the library at his fingertips, Arthur was able to find nearly anything Miles asked for, and he was always up for a challenge. Miles was just the guy to give it to him. A map showing the topography of ancient ruins in Rome? *Certainly, I have that right here.* An aerial view of the Mississippi River basin in 1850? *No problem! I'll bring that up from storage.* The latest Ultra Deep Field image from the Hubble Space Telescope? *Let me print that out for you in high-definition color.* And when Miles told him he'd read that real "X marks the spot" treasure maps had never actually existed, Arthur found him a true-to-size replica of the two-thousand-year-old Copper Scroll from Israel that supposedly gave instructions on where to find more than sixty buried caches of real silver and gold.

Neither Miles nor Arthur expected to find real treasure in a plastic box in the middle of Verona Park, but anything was possible. That's what made it fun.

"Fifty more feet!" Miles shouted as his handheld GPS counted down the distance to where the last geocache on their list was hidden. He practically skipped along the hiking trail as he followed the arrow of the built-in compass. After a few more feet, the arrow swung to the west and Miles found himself veering off the dirt path and into a clearing. Even though he hadn't seen Arthur since he'd arrived at the park, he knew the librarian wasn't far behind. For this last one, they'd agreed that Miles would try to get to the location on his own. Next time he wanted to program the coordinates in himself, too. "Nineteen feet!" he called out. "Six!"

When the GPS told him he had one foot to go to reach the correct coordinates, he stopped, proud of himself for having found the spot on his own. He looked up to see that his feet were at the edge of a brook he'd never noticed before, even though his family had been coming to this park his whole life. Good thing he'd stopped when he did, or he would have wound up in the water!

"Almost there," Arthur called out from the end of the dirt path. "Just trying to get Fluffernutter to stop sniffing at every single pebble!"

When Arthur found out that Miles had named the Harmonicandy, he'd asked him to name something else—his family's brand-new puppy! Miles had literally bounded upstairs to his desk to work on it. Miles *loved* naming things. Dad said his afterlife map was as beautiful and detailed as any in the front of the fantasy novels they both loved to read.

Miles had never named a dog before, though, and he must have considered a hundred names before he landed on the perfect one. Not only was Fluffernutter a cool word (all those double letters!), but also it was one of his favorite sandwiches to eat at the **Life Is Sweet** cafeteria. It's always more fun to eat something you've had a hand in making, and Henry sometimes let him and Philip help pull out the mallow roots. Or, more accurately, Miles and Henry did the pulling (it required wading into the middle of the swamp, and Philip said once was enough for him) and then tossed the thick, slippery roots to Philip on the shore, where he blotted them dry with thick towels. Henry worked his magic and turned the roots into marshmallow cream. Ah...mazing!

According to Arthur, Fluffernutter was an "amazing" dog, so the name fit perfectly. Miles had yet to see proof of the dog's amazingness (Miles was a cat person), but Arthur claimed that not only could Fluffernutter roll over on command already, but she'd sniffed out six geocaches on her own!

Of the ones he and Arthur had found together, Arthur had spotted the first one (a small metal box hanging from a low tree branch), and yesterday Miles had found the second, inside a fallen log, after nearly an hour of searching the wooded area. That one—a large plastic bin—had rewarded his efforts with a small bottle of Hocus Pocus Disappearing Ink.

Usually the trinkets hidden in the boxes were common objects—pencil toppers, plastic rings, rubber toys, dominoes, dice, key chains, stickers, crayons, that sort of thing. So to find something as exotic and unexpected as disappearing ink, even though the bottle was half-empty, well, it made Miles giddy with excitement. He couldn't wait to show Logan and then try it out on Philip. Philip hadn't shown much of a sense of humor and probably hated practical jokes. That would make it even sweeter when a stream of blue ink shot out onto his tie, only to disappear a minute later!

Arthur finally showed up, out of breath from trying to keep Fluffernutter from pulling away on her leash. He had his three-year-old daughter, Jade, with him, too. She ran up to Miles as soon as she saw him and wrapped her arms around his waist.

"Um...hello to you, too?" was all he could think to say. Now, Miles was a hugger himself. But he couldn't recall a time when a young child had hugged *him*. It was...interesting. But not altogether bad. They'd met only once before, and that had been at the library when Arthur's wife, Tina, had brought Jade to visit. Miles had been poring over a collection of old candy bar wrappers Arthur had found while cataloging a storage room. **Life Is Sweet?** had donated them to the library twenty years earlier, but they had sat on a shelf since then. Arthur was planning to put together a display, and he let Miles and Jade organize the wrappers by color and shape. Mostly Miles organized and Jade threw them up in the air and laughed, even though you're supposed to be quiet in a library and she should know that since her dad worked in one and some of the wrappers were *really rare* and should be handled with respect.

Miles patted her awkwardly on the head a few times, and she finally let go.

Arthur grinned. "What can I say? She likes you!"

They eventually turned to the job at hand and began looking for anything out of the ordinary, like a random stack of branches, or a rock pile too orderly for nature to have built it. Those are easy places to hide a cache. But nothing like that jumped out at them.

Miles returned to the water's edge. He bent down to more closely inspect the rocks that formed a natural wall on one side of the stream. He slid his hand along the rocks, feeling for some sort of crevice or gap. If a cache was hidden there, it would have to be a small one. He moved his hand over to the next row, and instead of feeling the dry rock, he got a handful of wet nose!

CHAPTER TWO

Arthur laughed. "She beat you to it!"

Okay, so Fluffernutter really *did* have a nose for geocaching! If this actually was the cache, the dog had found it only seconds before Miles. After a minute, she yanked her snout out of the hole and ran around happily in circles. Miles peeked in. It was too dark to see much, but he could spot something silver reflecting the sunlight. Yup, Fluffernutter had found the last cache in Verona Park, all right. He tried not to be resentful but couldn't help thinking that this never would have happened if Fluffernutter had been a cat. Well, unless someone had hidden tuna in the cache!

"I think Fluffernutter deserves a treat for that display of geocaching skill," Arthur said, reaching into his pocket.

"There's a Pepsicle in my backpack," Miles offered, proving he could accept defeat with grace. To date, the Pepsicle was the only candy approved for both people and animals. "My friend Daisy's horse, Magpie, loves them, so maybe Fluffernutter will, too. I brought a few extra if Jade's old enough for one."

"Thanks! Much better than a dog biscuit." Arthur reached into the small cooler inside Miles's backpack and pulled out a mostly frozen Pepsicle. Fluffernutter and Jade both immediately sat up at attention when they saw (or, in the dog's case, smelled) the treat. Arthur grinned. "I think that's a yes for both."

Miles showed Arthur how to pull out the stick before giving it to the dog. Fluffernutter gobbled it down in a few licks and a bite. Jade sniffed at hers, then gave a tentative lick. Miles could tell when the peppermint taste kicked in, because Jade's eyes opened wide. She beamed and then plopped down on the grass to enjoy it at her leisure.

While Fluffernutter happily slurped up the juice left behind on the ground and Arthur snapped pictures of Jade with blue ice dripping down her chin, Miles put a glove on and used the discarded Pepsicle stick to root around in the small hole. Daisy would probably have something to say about the fact that he didn't just reach his hand in, but one never knew what might be lurking in a hole between damp rocks. Worm, spider, bee, snake, pointy nail. Better not to take chances. Certainly Daisy would agree with that. Or maybe not. She didn't seem the type to look for long before leaping.

A little more maneuvering with the stick, and the geocache slid out into his hand. It was cylindrical, made of black plastic with a silver lid, and only about two inches high. He rolled it on the ground to loosen the dirt that clung to the sides.

Arthur chuckled. "That's an old film canister, from back in the day when you had to get film developed. Imagine having to take pictures with your camera, being careful not to waste a single shot because film wasn't cheap, waiting till you filled up a whole roll of film, which could take months, sticking it into one of those canisters, and delivering it to a store. Then waiting for the photos to be printed before you could see how they looked and by then you'd forgotten what you took pictures of in the first place." He shook his head. "In the last two minutes I've taken thirty-six shots, deleted nine, cropped three, taken out a shadow in one, and sent them to six relatives with the caption *Jade's First Geocaching Pepsicle*. Man, modern technology!"

Miles had never owned a camera or a photo-taking phone, but all that waiting did sound awful. He flipped the rubber cap off the container and tipped it over in his hand. Two marbles and one rectangular wooden magnet with the words I LOVE GEOCACHING engraved on it fell out. He held up the magnet and admired the craftsmanship involved. Someone had clearly carved it by hand.

"Cool," Arthur said, admiring the magnet, too.

"Do you want it?" Miles asked, offering it up to his friend. "I got the disappearing ink, so it's your turn."

Arthur shook his head. "I'll take a marble. The magnet will be a good keepsake of your first solo find." Fluffernutter rolled onto her back and barked as if to say, "Hey, I helped, too!"

They all laughed, even Jade. "Well, mostly solo," Arthur corrected. He scratched Fluffernutter's belly, and the dog's legs kicked out like she was riding a bike.

Miles traced his finger along the letters, then happily slipped the magnet into his pocket. "Thanks. Here's the log." He pulled out the rolled-up piece of notebook paper from the canister and handed it over. For these first three finds, they'd agreed that Arthur would write his own handle, StormingTheCastle, in the log, along with the date. Miles hadn't yet chosen his own geocaching handle—the nickname he'd go by as long as he played the game. Even though he found it easy to name everything else, he was stumped trying to pick out a handle for himself. Nothing felt quite right. Apparently Arthur's handle was based on a line from a famous movie that involved sword fighting, true love, a giant, and a man named Miracle Max. When he first heard that, Miles wondered if Max Pinkus, the head candy scientist at the factory, knew about this other Max, who could make miracles. But then again, Max made miracles himself every day with only a handful of ingredients!

Miles pulled his swag bag out of his backpack and began rummaging through it. Each person to find the cache should *take something and leave something.* That was the geocaching motto. "What do you think the next person to locate this cache would hope to find inside it?"

"Impossible to say. Could be anyone, of any age." Arthur looked at the few items Miles had spread out and said, "We should restock the swag bag for next time. I'm sure I have some trinkets that Jade doesn't need or want anymore."

"I'll add some, too," Miles said. His mother had packed away all his little-kid toys and stashed the box in the attic. Miles suspected she'd kept it because she thought Miles would have a little brother or sister one day, but that had never happened. He was sure she wouldn't miss the stuff now.

He spread out the few small items they had collected so far. First he stashed the disappearing ink in his pocket; that one was definitely a keeper. He looked over the remaining choices. They could leave the yellow plastic compass. When they'd found it in the first cache, they both doubted it would work. But Arthur had showed Miles the correct way to hold it (flat in his palm, chest height) and then how to use the position of the sun to orient himself. As Miles slowly turned, the arrow swung directly north. This led to a lively discussion about true north (the direction along Earth's surface pointing toward the North Pole) versus magnetic north (the direction the north end of a compass needle points due to Earth's magnetic field) and how you have to adjust for the difference if you use a compass to guide you somewhere. Miles placed the compass back down on the grass. It would be a tight squeeze, but it would fit in the container.

For the second item, they could leave the sticker of a kitten in a basket. Other than the compass, it had been slim pickings in that first cache. His choices had been either the kitten sticker or a three of hearts playing card. He couldn't think of anything he could do with one playing card, so he kept the sticker by default. He was torn. He kind of wanted to keep the compass, and what if the next person didn't like kittens?

"Go ahead and leave the coupons," Arthur said. "You know you want to."

Miles grinned sheepishly. "Thanks." He put the swag back in the bag and pulled out the same thing he'd left in the other caches—coupons for a free Oozing Crunchorama at any candy store across the country. Mr. Sweet had given him a whole stack a few weeks ago to thank him for working so hard on the new slogan. Miles had tried to hand them back, insisting that he was just happy his interest in playing with words had actually been helpful to somebody other than himself. But the Candymaker had pressed them into his hand, and he didn't want to be rude. And, hey, they were free Oozing Crunchoramas! No one could say no to those twice.

As he rolled up the coupons and slid them into the container, he felt himself shiver in anticipation.

"Are you all right?" Arthur asked. "You did some weird shaky thing. Are you drinking enough? Have some water." He handed Miles a water bottle. Jade, who still had half of her Pepsicle left, let it topple right out of her hand and came running to Miles's side.

Miles laughed. "I'm fine, I promise! I was just thinking that maybe one day a geocacher would find a coupon for a Harmonicandy. Something I named is going to be out in the world! It will exist as a *real* object."

As he said it out loud, though, he realized that all the places on his afterlife map felt real, too. But he couldn't explain that to Arthur. Unless one of Miles's parents had said something, Arthur didn't know about any of the stuff that had happened with the girl who he thought had drowned (but was now one of his best friends), and he wanted to keep it that way. For one thing, it sounded crazy. And for another, Miles knew if he talked about it, he might slip back into that place halfway between fantasy and reality. It hadn't always been such a bad place. Sometimes he even missed it.

"Drink some water anyway" was all Arthur said, apparently unconvinced that Miles wasn't actually suffering from dehydration.

Miles obliged and drank, then pushed the film canister back into the hole. He stuffed it in deep enough that the next geocacher couldn't see it sticking out, but not so deep that he or she wouldn't be able to reach it easily.

Arthur gathered up the Pepsicle wrappers. "There are sixteen more caches hidden around Spring Haven. Once you find all those, maybe you'll want to hide your own."

Miles lit up. "I can do that?"

"Definitely," Arthur said. "Maybe you and your dad could start scoping out some spots." He took Jade by the hand and passed Miles the end of the dog's leash. "It's a great family activity. Jade already helps me, right, honey?"

But Jade had caught sight of a butterfly on a nearby bush and wasn't listening. Miles watched it flutter from leaf to leaf for a moment, too, its yellow-and-black wings opening and closing lazily. Every time he saw a butterfly now, he checked to see if it had any red on its wings. But the butterflies never did.

They started back down the path that led to the parking lot. "I'm not sure my dad's that into it," Miles said. "I think he was kind of bored last time."

"I sensed that when he started pulling the petals off a dandelion during our conversation about how the library prepares a book to go into circulation."

They both laughed. "Sorry about that," Miles said. "He's not as interested as I am in the art of bookbinding and bar codes."

"Not many are," Arthur joked. "Your dad works at the college, right?"

Miles nodded. "He's the director of financial aid. He helps kids with their tuition if they can't afford it."

"Cool," Arthur said.

"Cool beans!" Jade said, skipping ahead. "Cool beans, cool beans, cool beans!"

Fluffernutter started barking and pulling on her leash. Miles had to strengthen his grip to keep it from being yanked out of his hand.

"She doesn't like Jade getting too far away," Arthur explained.

"Or maybe it's because Metal Detector Boy is back!" Miles pointed through the trees toward the site of the recent 4-H carnival. The area was still marked off by temporary fences, and they could see that the grass was smooshed down from the rides and food booths. The guy they'd nicknamed Metal Detector Boy looked a lot like Daisy's cousin Bo. Even though Miles had learned that Bo wasn't really Daisy's cousin, and that his real name was AJ, he would always think of him as Daisy's tractor-pulling cousin Bo.

They'd met Metal Detector Boy yesterday when hunting down cache number two. The Bo/AJ look-alike told them he was searching for coins dropped from the pockets of unsuspecting carnival-goers. Apparently right after a carnival left town was the best time to swoop in. Today he was crisscrossing the area, sweeping his metal detector back and forth in front of him as he walked.

When he saw the three of them (four, including Fluff), he slipped off the headphones that were attached to the top of the metal detector by a thin cord. "Find any geocaches today?" he called out to them.

"Just the one," Miles replied. "Find any quarters today?"

He held up three fingers. "Seventy-five cents. Enough to pay for another year of college."

They all laughed and waved goodbye as Fluff started barking again. This time she really was pulling Miles toward Jade, who was rooting around in the grass a few yards behind Metal Detector Boy. As they caught up with her, she picked up something shiny and held it high over her head. "Look what I found!" she squealed. "Can I keep it?"

"Finders keepers," Metal Detector Boy told her. He turned to Miles and said, "Your little sister's a much better treasure hunter than I am. She found a silver dollar. That's more than I made all day! Not *too* embarrassing."

"Oh, she's not my sister," Miles said quickly.

Metal Detector Boy looked surprised, then glanced over at Jade and Arthur. "Oh, sorry. Just assumed that was your family. Well, see ya. I'd better make sure this thing's working!" He knocked on the side of his metal detector.

Jade pushed the silver dollar into the pocket of her shorts before the guy could change his mind. They left him to get back to his work.

"That was kind of a weird thing to say," Miles said when they reached the spot where he'd tied up his bike. "About Jade being my sister."

Arthur chuckled. "She *is* fond of you."

Jade stuck out her tongue at Miles.

"Hmm, I'm not so sure about that," Miles said.

"But seriously," Arthur said, "don't let it bother you. There aren't a lot of people around here who look like us. As you know, of course, having lived here much longer than we have."

"I guess," Miles admitted. "But still. My dad is *much* taller than you are."

Arthur laughed again. "True. He got all the height in the family." He winked as he and Jade climbed into their car.

"You have the same sense of humor, though!" Miles called out as he climbed on his bike.

Arthur lowered his window and asked, "See you at the library tomorrow? I'm going to start putting up the candy wrapper display."

"I'd love to," Miles replied honestly. "But tomorrow's the big Kickoff at the candy factory. The first Harmonicandy will be made."

"Sounds great!"

Miles smiled. "Tastes even better!"

Arthur laughed. "Good one! I'll look forward to finding out."

Miles made a mental note to add *Sounds great, tastes even better!* to his slogan list.

Jade waved out of the backseat window, her newly found dollar clutched in her hand. Miles waited for the car to pull away before starting home himself. If he had to have a little sister, he supposed Jade wouldn't be such a bad one. For the first time in his whole life, he wondered if his parents were disappointed that he was an only child. He'd never spoken to them about it, just as he'd never asked why Dad's parents were Irish. Maybe it was time for a serious discussion.

But first he wanted to try out the disappearing ink.

● ● ● ● ● ● ● ● ● ● ● ● ● ● ● ● ● ●

CHAPTER THREE

● ● ● ● ● ● ● ● ● ● ● ● ● ● ● ● ●

Miles found his parents having lunch outside on the back porch. A place was set for him with a bowl of noodle soup and a grilled cheese sandwich under one of those tent things that keep flies off your food. His mother jumped up to hug him.

"Um, Mom? I was gone for less than two hours."

"I know," his mother said, smoothing down his hair. "I'm still not used to you being out on your own. It's a mother's job to worry."

"I'm fine," Miles insisted, pulling away a little. It wasn't that he minded the hug, but he was afraid if she hugged him any harder, the bottle of disappearing ink would get squished. It would be fun to try it out on his parents, but his mom had zero sense of humor when it came to messes.

"Did you have fun at the park?" his father asked, gently prying them apart.

Miles scarfed down his sandwich (geocaching made him hungry!) while he filled them in on his adventure. When he got to the part about Fluffernutter beating him to the cache by a nose, his father shook his head and said, "Wouldn't have happened if she was a cat."

"I know, totally!" Miles said. "Something else kind of weird happened."

"What?" His mother stopped eating her soup midslurp. He almost didn't want to mention it now, but he knew she'd keep asking.

"You know that guy with the metal detector I told you about?"

They nodded.

"We saw him again today. He thought Arthur's daughter, Jade, was my sister."

His mother laid down her spoon. "Well, I suppose we can understand why he would think that."

"I told Arthur he wasn't tall enough to be my dad."

Mr. O'Leary puffed out his chest. "I *am* blessed in the height department."

"Your dad was a lot taller than you, though, right?" Miles asked. "I mean, it looks like that in the picture from your high school graduation."

Dad looked momentarily unsure how to answer. He took a few sips of lemonade, then said, "Yes, your grandfather was similarly blessed. Over six feet two inches in his prime. He played college basketball."

"Wow," Miles said, sliding the noodles onto his spoon. "What else did he do?"

Once Miles's dad started talking, he couldn't seem to stop. Over the rest of lunch Miles heard more stories about his grandparents than over all the lunches that had come before, combined. His grandparents didn't only grow vegetables and fruit for themselves; they donated most of it to the town's food bank so people in need would have fresh food along with the canned goods. His grandfather was the town pediatrician, and his grandmother was his nurse. Miles hung on every word while his mom looked on with misty eyes.

"I wish I'd gotten to meet them," Miles said.

"They would have been really proud of you," his mother said.

His father tried to say something, but then his lip quivered and he reached for his lemonade instead. Miles looked back and forth between his parents. He'd gotten really good at reading their signals. For all the times they'd told him he needed to get out of the house last year, there were ten more times when they'd wanted to tell him to move on, to stop blaming himself. They wanted him to accept that he'd never know what really happened (turned out they were wrong about that part!), but most times they just busied themselves with some minor task rather than risk upsetting him. When his mother started quickly piling up the lunch plates, he knew for sure that's what was happening. The conversation had ended.

And then it was just the two of them. Miles smiled at his dad, trying to send out telepathic vibes that he wanted to know more. Clearly his mind-to-mind powers weren't very strong, because the only thing his dad said was "Don't forget you have a meeting at the factory soon."

On his way upstairs to get his notebook, Miles swung by the kitchen and grabbed two Blast-o-Bits from the treats drawer by the fridge. "Really, Miles?" his mom said. "You're on your way to the factory and you still have to eat more candy?"

Miles looked down at the grape candies with their bright purple wrappers. "But, Mom, the factory only makes these every three days, and today is an off-day. Mondays are High-Jumping Jelly Beans, Tuesdays are Leapin' Lollies, and then they convert the machines back to Blast-o-Bits on Wednesdays. Do you expect me to wait until then?"

She sighed. "Why am I not surprised that you know the candy production schedule?"

Miles grinned. "If you'd prefer, I can go back to talking about the afterlife."

She leaned down and kissed him on the cheek. "No thank you. Now go on. I'd like to see what you came up with for the slogan."

"Be right back." Miles took off before she changed her mind. He stopped at his bedroom door and cringed before entering. He'd always kept his room relatively neat (at least compared to Logan's room, where he sometimes couldn't see the floor), but now sheets of paper covered not only his floor but the desk and even his bed. He'd been so focused on coming up with a creative slogan that researching it had taken over both his brain *and* his room.

Miles had let go of most of the habits he'd picked up after the girl-who-drowned incident (although he still sat out on the roof to think, and when he got superexcited, he still spoke backward, so maybe not most of the habits). But some had proven harder to break. He still tended to get very focused on one single thing to the point where he tuned out everything else. His father told him that wasn't always a bad quality and that every new invention or discovery came from someone who was willing to put the time and effort into focusing on the solution. Most recently that one thing was the Harmonicandy slogan.

He wished he had a slogan he really loved, but none had made him jump up and shout, "This is it! This is The One!" He grabbed his notebook and added the new one he'd thought of (with Arthur's help) when he left the park.

He found his parents still in the kitchen. They stopped talking as soon as he appeared, a fairly common occurrence in the O'Leary household. Usually he'd assume they were talking about boring, grown-up stuff like mortgages (whatever they were) or taxes or retirement plans or who to vote for in the school board elections. But now he was beginning to suspect otherwise.

"So what have you got for us?" Dad asked.

Miles flipped open his notebook. He took a deep breath and belted out, "In no special order: *Tap your feet to the beat of this delicious treat!*"

"Hey, that's pretty good!" his dad said. "I like the rhyme. Are there more?"

Miles scanned the list in front of him. He flipped over the page and scanned again. He looked up and announced, "Thirty-one."

"You have *thirty-one* different slogans?" his mother said, glancing at his father with that oh-so-familiar look of concern. "Didn't they want you to bring two or three?"

Miles looked sheepish. "I couldn't decide."

His dad checked his watch. "We'd better get going. I need to drop you on the way to a meeting at the university."

"Don't you want to hear more?" Miles asked, trying to keep the disappointment out of his voice.

"You can tell me on the way," his dad said, reaching for his briefcase.

Miles hadn't expected to leave so soon. He still had one more thing he needed to do in his room. "Can I have ten more minutes?"

"Five," his dad replied.

Miles turned toward the stairs.

"Can I read them over while you're up there?" his mom asked.

Her offer made him feel a little better. "Sure, let me know your top three." He handed her the notebook and bounded up the stairs, two at a time. He couldn't believe he'd almost forgotten to check his books!

He had to scramble on the floor to find them under all the papers, but eventually he had five library books opened up to random pages. He closed his eyes and let his finger drop. Then he scribbled down a sentence from each on the last page of his school notebook.

Turtles can inhale and exhale through their rear ends. It costs the U.S. Mint almost twice as much to mint each penny and nickel as the coins are actually worth. Nothing exists except atoms and empty space. Be where you are. Honey can prevent seasonal allergies, heal a cut, soothe a burn, and get rid of your pimples.

Miles felt the tip of his chin. He'd noticed a little bump growing there the last few days. He might be getting his first pimple! The universe had already spoken to him! He tore the page out of his notebook and shoved it into his pocket with the disappearing ink. His parents were sitting together on the bottom stair. They looked over their shoulders when they heard him coming down. His mother had eye makeup streaked on her cheeks. It was clear she'd been crying.

"Mom!" he called out, hurrying toward them. "What's wrong?"

She pulled him into another hug. "I'm just so proud of you. You came up with all these clever ideas on your own? They're brilliant. Every one."

Miles doubted *every one* was brilliant, but he didn't mind hearing it.

She pulled back and held his arms and looked him in the face. "Forget anything I ever said about your time at the candy factory not being well spent. Look what's come out of it." She dabbed the corner of one eye with her sleeve, then waved the list in the air.

His dad spoke up. "Well, three new friends and one award-winning candy bar, too."

She handed Miles the notebook. "Go show 'em what you've got, sweetie. They'll love them."

"Thanks, Mom," Miles said, tossing the notebook into his backpack. "I'll let you know. By the way, do we have any honey?"

CHAPTER FOUR

Wow," Miles said as their car wound through downtown Spring Haven. "I've never seen the streets so crowded before. Who *are* all these people?"

"I don't know," his dad replied. "Maybe a convention's in town. Maybe they're office supplies salespeople. Or exotic-flower dealers."

"Or tightrope walkers in the circus!" Miles suggested.

"Yes, definitely carny folk," his dad agreed with a wink.

"So did you have a favorite slogan?" Miles asked.

"I particularly liked *Candy for your taste buds AND your earbuds!* Also, *Harmonicandy: A symphony of sweetness.*"

Miles beamed. "Those were good, weren't they?"

"Like your mom said, you're a very talented writer. You could have a career in it one day if you wanted to."

For a brief second Miles pictured himself grown up, scribbling away in a notebook, telling stories or writing about the world. But he also could envision maps spread out all around him and tacked up on the walls. How could he tell his dad he missed the time he'd spent creating his own version of the afterlife? He couldn't. It would sound crazy.

"You miss it, don't you?" his dad asked.

Miles's pulse quickened. "Miss what?" he asked cautiously.

"The afterlife," his dad replied, looking straight ahead. "You spent a year designing a place, visiting it in your mind, and now you're supposed to put it aside like it never happened."

Miles's eyes grew big. "It's like you read my mind!"

His dad smiled. "I just know you."

Miles took a deep breath. "Part of why it's hard to let it go is that my grandparents—your parents, I mean—are there. The girl and I used to play in their garden. They built a swing set for the two of us in their yard even though there are swing sets all over the afterlife."

His dad was quiet for a minute. "I know," he finally said. "I mean, I saw that on the map. I especially liked how you made their house on a hill, overlooking a river. Very different from the flat little town I grew up in. Your grandmother would have loved a view of water."

Just ask him, Miles thought. *Ask him now.* But he couldn't. He could see his dad's lower lip begin to quiver again.

The car pulled through the factory gates, and Miles was surprised by the full parking lot. All the people they'd seen milling about in town must have come for the Kickoff tomorrow! Judging by all the cars here, many had come today, too. His dad pulled up to the front door, and Miles agreed to call his mom when he needed to be picked up.

He closed the door and waved, but his dad didn't pull away. Miles walked slowly to the porch, glancing over his shoulder. His dad simply stared straight ahead, his hands still on the steering wheel. Finally, after another minute, the car began to move slowly down the circular driveway. Or did it just seem slow in comparison to how his mom exited driveways? No, it was definitely slow. Like, turtle slow.

A bit unnerved, he decided to wait before going inside until he felt able to shake off the uneasy feeling and bring his focus back to the Harmonicandy slogan. The meeting wouldn't start for a little while anyway.

Now that Arthur had planted the idea in Miles's head of one day hiding his own geocache for others to find, he couldn't help approaching the factory with that in mind. The grounds weren't public property, though, so he wouldn't be able to actually hide one there unless he got the Candymaker's permission.

His eyes landed on the large rosebushes to the right of the porch. They were dense enough that he could tie a bit of string to the end of a small container and hang it from a back branch so it wouldn't be visible to people visiting the factory. Although on closer inspection, he wouldn't want to stick his arm in between the branches and risk getting scratched by a thorn or two... or twelve.

The large old-fashioned milk can on the porch looked inviting. He could glue a magnet onto a cache and stick the whole thing on the back of the can. Although once again, as he got close enough to the can, he realized it wouldn't work. He rapped his knuckles on the flat top and could tell by the resulting sound that the milk can was made of tin, with maybe a little copper mixed in. It would need to have iron in it for a magnet to stick. Finding a good hiding spot was harder than it seemed!

He felt better, but he still wasn't ready to go inside. He couldn't stop thinking about the things his dad had said—and *hadn't* said—about his grandparents. Miles took a deep breath. He knew what he needed to do. He took off his backpack and held it in front of him, then sat down gently on top of the milk can. It was solid and had no trouble holding his weight. He reached into his backpack, grabbed his hardcover copy of *How to Make Your Own Alphabet* (he had it in paperback, too), and opened it up to the middle.

Only instead of seeing instructions on how to use vowels when creating your alphabet, he found himself looking at the blank screen of the vid com Daisy had given each of them. It was the next generation of her old video communicator and apparently could do all these superneat spy tricks that she had forbidden any of them to try out. Last week he had very carefully sliced out the pages of the book and attached the device to the inside covers with straps and staples. It wasn't pretty, but it looked convincing. Ever since Daisy had revealed that she hid hers inside that romance book she was always pretending to read, Miles had wished he had something like that. And now he did!

He turned on the vid com and began punching in the series of numbers and letters Daisy had given him. This would allow Miles to reach her wherever she was. Unlike a mobile phone or tablet, Daisy's device didn't use radio waves to connect, or need cell towers to bounce a signal from place to place, or rely on the Internet, with its satellite links and tangle of copper and fiber optic cables. Hers also never ran out of power. He had been the only one to ask her for the details when she handed them out before her first post-contest mission. She refused to give specifics on how it did work, though, claiming that was on a need-to-know basis only. Miles respected that. A spy had to keep her secrets.

Since the contest four months ago, he had seen Daisy only a few times, when she'd been between jobs. She'd sent him postcards from around the world (which he was pretty sure she had some-one else mail), but they hadn't spoken for three weeks. He needed someone to talk to right now, and as great a friend as Logan was, this required someone with more life experience.

As soon as he hit the last number, the screen flashed on. "What is the nature of your emergency?" Daisy chirped. He could hear her clearly, but the screen remained dark. He quickly held the fake book up to his face so it would look to any passersby like he was reading. He'd learned that trick from Daisy, too.

"Um, Daisy? Are you there? I can't see you."

"Oh, hi, Miles," Daisy's voice said, brightening up even more. "I thought you were Philip."

"Sorry to disappoint you," he said, tilting the screen in different directions in the hope of getting Daisy's face to appear.

"Trust me, you're not," she said. "In fact, I have something cool to tell you about a code we found that—"

Her words were drowned out by the loud screech of tires in the background. At first he thought it was on Daisy's end, but the smell of exhaust made him peek over the top of the fake book. He could just see the rear of a black car zoom out of the factory's long, circular driveway. Guess the driver was in a big hurry. He turned his attention back to his book. As curious as he was about what she was saying, he knew he had to talk fast. "I know you said only to call if I really needed something, and I really need your advice. I can't see you, though."

"Sorry about that," she said, lowering her voice to a whisper. "My location isn't secure right now. These devices are equipped with the ability to read lips. We'll need to put them on silent mode so that when I mouth the words, they will show up on your screen, and vice versa. Little red button, lower left corner."

Miles nodded and pushed the button. "I won't take long," he mouthed, hoping the words were appearing on her screen, since he couldn't see them on his.

A few seconds later, text from Daisy began to appear across the top of his screen: *You won't bake frogs? I would hope not! You have to mouth the words a little slower than normal talking, and it will pick it up better. I mean, unless you actually meant to discuss frogs.*

Miles giggled at the mistake. "Sorry! Will try harder. Here's the thing, you know how me and my parents are Chinese?"

Yup.

"Well, my dad's parents aren't. They were Irish. From Ireland."

After a short pause, she replied, *Okay.*

"So, we haven't done genetics in school yet. Is that even possible?"

After another, longer pause, she answered, *No. Was your dad adopted?*

Miles leaned back, nearly slipping off the milk can. He sat up again. His dad was adopted! Of course that was it! He must have known deep down. But his dad had never mentioned anything like that. Miles mouthed, "I guess he must be! But why wouldn't he talk about it?"

You sometimes don't talk about things. Maybe you get that from him.

Her words surprised him. "Me? I'm an open book. Just ask Philip—he wanted to punch me every time I talked about the afterlife."

Yeah, but that was more about losing his mother than really being annoyed at you.

Miles realized she was right. Insights like that were the reason he was calling her and not someone else.

Daisy's words started coming again. *You talked about the afterlife, but you never really talked about what you saw at the lake, or about hiding in your room and always being scared something was going to happen to someone you cared about and all that stuff that you told us later, when you were ready. Maybe it's like that with your dad. It's too hard for him to talk about. Is he close with his parents?*

"They are in the afterlife now. You and I used to go visit them. You liked the red swing the best."

That's sweet.

"I never knew them, but yes, he was very close with them and loved them a lot."

I think you have your answer. He doesn't want to hurt them by implying they weren't his real parents. Even though they aren't alive anymore.

Miles thought about that lip quiver every time the conversation could have turned toward the adoption. Obviously the topic upset him. And upsetting his dad was the last thing he'd want to do. Daisy was totally right.

"Thank you!" he mouthed.

You're welcome. Really gotta go now. Got a bit of a thing happening here.

"Anything I can help with?" Miles mouthed.

You wouldn't happen to know how to get honey out of hair, would you? Max never taught us that in our candymaking classes!

"I actually do know a thing or two." He recited the sentence about honey he'd copied earlier, feeling the sticky spot on his chin. Nope, the honey hadn't cured him yet. The pimple was still there.

More text appeared on his screen. *Helps burns? Wonder if it would help Logan with his scars.*

As soon as he read Daisy's comment, Miles immediately knew why he'd picked that line out of the book on natural remedies. He was supposed to help heal Logan's scars! His mind began to race. Maybe part of why he missed thinking about the-girl-who-drowned wasn't only because he missed the creativity of making his map. Maybe he missed helping someone. Each day he had thought of a way to make the girl's afterlife better. He could channel that into helping a real person now. And if that person just happened to be his best friend, then all the better!

Miles, I really gotta go. I need to figure out a believable story for AJ to get me out of something.

Miles snapped his attention back to the screen. "How about Bo Dinkleman, the cowboy who pulls tractors with his teeth, could pretend you're needed back on the ranch for corn-shucking season."

That's actually a great idea! Just for that I'm going to give you a treat. Hang on. I'm taking a picture for you.

A few seconds later a photo of Daisy filled Miles's screen. What was on her face? He pulled the book closer to him and then burst out laughing. Her cheeks had bright orange dots sprinkled all over them, like the worst fake freckles he'd ever seen. But the funniest part had to be the pieces of hair clumped together with honey. Oh, and the honey had small white feathers stuck to it. He couldn't imagine how she'd wound up in that situation.

"That must be a really funny book!" Logan's voice said from very close by.

"Gnipael sdrazil!" Miles cried out, launching the book in one direction and his body in another. This turned out to be a very bad idea.

CHAPTER FIVE

Miles was about to tell Daisy that he had honey on his face as well (what were the odds?), but Logan surprised him, and everything happened fast after that. He felt bad about snatching his book before Logan could retrieve it for him, but he didn't want Logan to know he had talked to Daisy. He was just glad that they'd been mouthing the conversation, so Logan hadn't heard them talk about the scars. That would have been awful.

It meant more to him than he knew how to express that Logan gave him the box with Samuel Sweet's old papers. He'd never had a friend who understood how much he'd love something like that. He'd wanted to jump up and hug him, but there were a lot of strangers around and he didn't want to embarrass Logan.

As Miles carried the box toward the library, he could barely believe his good fortune. Sure, his mom was bound to ask later why he was covered in Band-Aids (and he was pretty sure he still had a few thorns in an area he wasn't about to ask the nurse to check!). And yes, his disappearing-ink bottle had exploded, soaking not only his shorts but the list of random thoughts from his books. As irksome as those events were, it was impossible to be bothered by anything when presented by his best friend with *a box full of old journals and maps!!!*

Barely able to see over the top of the box, Miles pushed the library door open and stumbled in. Mrs. Gepheart, the factory's long-time librarian, popped up from behind the desk.

"Watch out for the—" she started to shout.

"Oopf!" Miles ran straight into the table that had definitely not been there the last time he visited the library. He realized too late that she was trying to warn him about the display she'd been working on for all the visitors. He and the table collided. His glasses flew off his face, and the box dropped to the floor, taking Miles and half the items on the table with it.

Well! That was certainly embarrassing. "So sorry!" Miles said, sticking his (fortunately unbroken) glasses back on his face. He scrambled to pick up the fallen items—a framed dollar bill signed by Samuel Sweet; an old Pepsicle carton from the days when a whole box cost only a dime; a handful of black-and-white photographs, including some that showed a row of people Miles didn't recognize standing on the factory's front steps; and a certificate awarding **Life Is Sweet?** the official trademark for the name of the company. The sign, now knocked sideways on the table, read A VERY SHORT AND SWEET HISTORY OF **Life Is Sweet?**.

"That was some entrance!" Mrs. Gepheart said, doing her best to rearrange the samples of each candy, now lumped together in random piles. They had been carefully lined up in the order of when they were released, a project that had taken longer to put together than one might think. Max and Henry had argued for nearly two hours over whether the Leapin' Lollies should go before the Snorting Wingbats. Apparently they had hit the stores on the exact same day, fifteen years ago. Max had thought the order should be determined by which had been invented first (Leapin' Lollies). Henry thought it should be the candy that came off the conveyor belt first (Snorting Wingbats). They finally agreed to let the sales record speak for itself. In a close tiebreaker, the first candy store to log in sales for that day—**The Candy Basket**—reported that a pack of Snorting Wingbats had sold one minute and twenty-three seconds before the first Leapin' Lolly. The winner had been crowned and the correct order set.

Miles stood back to get a good look. "That one goes here," he said, replacing the High-Jumping Jelly Beans with the Sour Fingers. "And the Magic Bar should be here," he announced, gently picking up the rarest item on the table and moving it between the Pepsicle and the Some More S'mores. The bar, wrapped tightly in blue foil, felt both solid and airy beneath his fingers, but of course by this time it would be stale beyond recognition. This was the first time he'd seen one up close. The box of wrappers from the library hadn't contained the rare Magic Bar wrapper.

Many candies had been discontinued over the years as tastes and trends changed. Some never really took off to begin with, like Flo's Forever-Flavor Gum. The flavorful treat—named in honor of Logan's grandmother Florence—had to be pulled when reports of jaw injuries began trickling in. It turned out that if gum never lost its flavor, kids didn't know when to stop chewing it.

But the history of the Magic Bar—the very first chocolate bar the factory had produced—was shrouded in mystery. One brief, shining week of glory, and then it disappeared from shelves across the nation, never to be seen again. Only whispers of its greatness remained. This had happened decades before Miles was born, but it had not escaped his notice.

Mrs. Gepheart looked the display over and nodded. "You're right, that's more accurate. Not that I'm surprised. Between you and Philip, it's hard to decide who knows more about our candy and its illustrious history."

"That's easy," Miles said. "I knew it even before the candymaking contest. So the answer is clearly me."

Mrs. Gepheart smiled. "Probably."

"How did you get a Magic Bar?" he asked, tempted to touch it again. "I asked Logan about them once, and he said he's never even seen one."

She leaned over to straighten the DO NOT TOUCH sign. "That's actually a chunk of foam with a Magic Bar wrapper around it. As far as I know, there's only one Magic Bar left in existence, and it's locked in the vault for safekeeping."

"Wow," Miles said. "I didn't even know the candy factory *had* a vault."

"It's more like a safe in the wall," she explained. "It contains all the original recipes, prototypes of most of the candies, and I'm sure other things that I wouldn't know about." She glanced down at the box at their feet. "Now, what have you got there that caused all this commotion? We don't have much room to expand right now, but I'm still collecting memorabilia for a big display at the annual picnic."

In all the excitement, Miles had momentarily forgotten about the box! He bet one of the old notebooks or journals in the box would make a perfect addition to the display. He was about to share that idea with Mrs. Gepheart but stopped himself. Samuel Sweet could have brought these to the factory anytime over the half century he'd spent as Candymaker. The library shelves were full of booklets he had written, on topics like how to succeed in the candy business, how to build a safe and happy workplace, and how to set up a working farm and cultivate crops. There was even a booklet on the proper way to eat a chocolate pizza (hint: any way you like). Many of his original sketches and designs for the factory's machines hung on the hallway walls for every passerby to see, along with framed letters from candy-loving kids and dozens of awards and newspaper articles highlighting the various charity groups the Candymaker supported. Bottom line—if Logan's grandfather had left the material in this box behind, he'd done so for a reason.

"It's just some stuff of Logan's that he asked me to keep here for a few hours," Miles finally said. This was, essentially, the truth, if not the whole truth. "But I actually do know where some more stuff is. My friend Arthur at the Spring Haven public library found a whole collection of old candy bar wrappers. I'm sure he'd lend them to you for the picnic."

"That would be wonderful," she said. "Now that visiting hours are over, I'll be heading out. The door will be unlocked for you and Logan to collect your box of . . . whatever it is." She pushed the box under the table and out of harm's way.

"Thanks, Mrs. G," Miles said. He ducked out of the library and ran two doors down to the Advertising Room. Before he met Logan, Miles hadn't been much of a runner. Now he could barely sit still. His mother was not convinced this was a good thing, but Miles liked being so excited about a place that he had to run to it.

The door to the Advertising Room opened just as he arrived. Miles felt instantly more at ease when he saw the smiling face of Sabrina Katz, the head of advertising at the factory. At only twenty-eight, Sabrina was the youngest department head. She wore purple-framed glasses and a different hat every day. Whenever she spoke, she kept her hands busy solving a Rubik's Cube, or using a calculator to calculate pi to the four thousandth decimal place, or sketching animals that were combinations of other animals. (Miles's favorite was the caticorn, a half cat, half unicorn that used its magic horn to grant wishes to children.) Sabrina often stayed late into the night to work on one brilliant idea or another, or occasionally to play floor hockey with the cleaning crew, using brooms and bars of soap. Miles had never met anyone like her before, and he thought she was supercool.

Sabrina grinned widely. Today she wore a soft black baseball cap over her long blond hair. "Young Miles has arrived!" she announced, ushering him into the room. "Ready to wow us with your ideas?"

"Um, I hope so?" Miles said, suddenly feeling shy. At least twenty men and women from not only Advertising but also Sales and Marketing and Publicity stood around the large conference table in the center of the room. He wasn't even sure of the differences between marketing and publicity and advertising, but he knew that they all had to do with trying to think of new ways to introduce the public to **Life Is Sweet**'s products, and that the people in these departments wore regular clothes instead of the factory's uniform. He suddenly wished he'd dressed better that day.

All the chairs and desks (and the beanbag chair they'd gotten for him to use during their previous meetings) had been pushed to the back, and large mock-ups of the Harmonicandy wrapper lay across the conference table. Sabrina guided Miles to a spot at the head of the table. Talking stopped, and everyone smiled up at him. Only one or two of them showed any uncertainty in their eyes.

Sabrina said, "A few of you may not have met Miles O'Leary before, but he's the brilliant mind that came up with the name of the Harmonicandy, and now he'll get a chance to help create the advertising slogan for our initial ad campaigns. The floor is yours, Miles!"

The group clapped. One or two of the guys he'd gotten to know even cheered. Miles smiled gratefully at them and cleared his throat. "I thought about this for a while, and I have a bunch to run by you." He took a deep breath and flipped open his notebook. "Okay, so these slogans would all go after the word *Harmonicandy* on the wrapper, or, like, underneath it." He took another breath and told himself to pretend he was reading to his parents again. With all the drama he could muster, he began to read the list.

Candy for your taste buds AND your earbuds!
Music to your ears AND your taste buds!
Sounds delicious!

Now kids can finally play with their food!
The only instrument you can eat!
Now you just need the rest of the band!
Chew to the tune!
Hits the spot and the right note!
It really plays!
The musical treat!
Music for your mouth!
Chew in harmony!
Candy never sounded so delicious!
Tap your feet to the beat of this delicious treat!
A new tune in every bite!
Taste the tune!
Play it and eat it!
Music you can eat!
It's a melody in your mouth!
Taste the music!
A tune you love to chew to!
The candy that strikes a chord!
Such sweet music!
A symphony of sweetness!
It makes your taste buds sing!
Play with your food!
Sounds as good as it tastes!
Tastes as good as it sounds!
Bring harmony to the whole family!
Play your troubles away, then eat them!
Sounds great, tastes even better!

When he finished, he tore the page out and handed it to Sabrina. At first the room was silent. He swore he could hear his own heart thudding. Then almost at once, the room erupted. They all talked over each other, shouting out which one they liked best. Sabrina thumped him on the back.

"Wonderful job, Miles!" she said. "Now you've left us with the hardest part—picking one!"

"Thank you for giving me the chance," he said. "Where are all the other suggestions?" The group usually brainstormed their ideas on the dry-erase boards stuck on each wall, but the boards were blank.

"There *are* no other ones," Sabrina replied. "We didn't want to freak you out by letting you know it was all up to you." She winked and joined the group crowding around the list.

Shaking with excitement, Miles snuck off to the back of the room. He pulled his beanbag chair out from under a desk, plopped down, and instantly jumped back up. He'd found that last thorn. Since he couldn't very well pull it out there, he settled for leaning casually against the wall.

Listening to the grown-ups argue whether "Sounds as good as it tastes" was better than "Tastes as good as it sounds" counted as one of the highlights of his life.

At one point the Candymaker checked in with Sabrina on the walkie-talkie. Miles heard his name but didn't want to be caught eavesdropping. After saying "Over and out," Sabrina called for a vote. She handed out pieces of paper and instructed them all to write down their favorite slogan. Miles got one, too!

When all the votes had been collected, Sabrina opened the papers while a guy from Sales tallied the results on one of the boards. In the end, four slogans tied for first place:

HARMONICANDY: SOUNDS GREAT, TASTES EVEN BETTER!
HARMONICANDY: TASTES AS GOOD AS IT SOUNDS!
HARMONICANDY: SUCH SWEET MUSIC!
HARMONICANDY: PLAY WITH YOUR FOOD!

Everyone clapped, and the room became a flurry of activity again. Desks and chairs were moved back into place, and the advertising folks hurried to their computers to start designing the four slogans so they'd be ready to go with whichever one the Candymaker chose.

As the workers from other departments streamed out the door, they stopped to give Miles their congratulations and many slaps on the back. (He learned to plant his feet firmly, shoulder-distance apart, in order to stay upright.)

Sabrina scribbled the final choices on a slip of paper and handed it to Miles. "You get the honor of sharing these with Mr. Sweet. He also has a special announcement, but he's waiting for your arrival before sharing it."

So he *had* heard his name before. Miles gave her a grateful hug and headed out to the Harmonicandy Room. He hadn't planned on a pit stop, but the Marshmallow Room was only a few doors down, and Miles couldn't wait to share his excitement with someone.

"Henry?" he called as he pushed open the door. But the room was empty. Well, empty of people, but certainly not empty of marshmallows. There were stacks of those cooling on the counters. He popped a still-warm one into his mouth on the way to check the small office in the back. Maybe Henry was having a late lunch at his desk. Miles ducked his head in. No Henry, just one very overcrowded desk with a bulky old computer off to the side. Even though four pairs of eyeglasses with really thick lenses were getting second lives as paperweights, stacks of papers and folders threatened to slide to the floor at the slightest breeze. Miles thought it must be hard to have to do boring things like paperwork when all you really wanted to do was make marshmallows.

He scribbled a note to Henry letting him know he'd stopped by, and then Miles set forth again. The Harmonicandy Room was all the way at the other end of the building, so he had to face many temptations along the way. The candy scientists in the lab had their door propped open, which wouldn't help him get to his destination any faster. He would almost definitely get sucked in by the smell of whatever they were testing; it happened every time. Maybe today they'd be developing cabbage candy or asparagus icing or candied beets, and he could easily hurry past. Ah, no such luck. As soon as he passed the Cotton Candy Room, where the smell of grapefruit-flavored spun sugar (smells and tastes better than it sounds!) filled his nose, the unmistakable smell of peanut butter from the lab hit him full force. One whiff and he was powerless against its pull.

He stood by the open door, breathing deeply with his eyes closed. A few of the candies at Life Is Sweet? included nuts (hazelnuts in the Oozing Crunchorama, peanuts in the Snorting Wingbats, peanut-flavored taffy, and you always had the option of sprinkling sugared pecans on the chocolate pizza), but none of the recipes used straight-up peanut butter. Miles's curiosity kicked in, and he would have gone into the lab if his attention hadn't been pulled away by the sound of someone whistling. Miles turned around to see one of the assistant candymakers heading toward him, a huge bag of Leapin' Lolly sticks slung over his broad shoulder. One of the bags had a hole in the bottom, leaving a trail of sticks that went as far back down the hall as Miles could see. The scene reminded him of Hansel and Gretel dropping breadcrumbs through the forest so they could find their way home.

The man nodded at Miles as he passed, whistling away, clearly unaware of the leak. "Hey, your sticks are leaking," Miles called out, pointing to the trail. The assistant candymaker stopped.

"So they are! Thanks." He lifted the bag off his shoulder to inspect the hole. Miles bent down to grab the nearest sticks and felt something flutter onto his shoulder. He turned his head to see what it was. The guy laughed and said, "I've heard the expression money doesn't grow on trees, but I've never heard it said about growing on boys!"

"What do you mean?" Miles asked, then craned his neck a little farther. Resting on his shoulder was a *fifty-dollar bill*! He snatched it up and held it out. "Is this yours?"

The guy shook his head. "Nope. Finders keepers. And that bill clearly found *you*!" He picked up the bag again, careful to pinch the hole closed with his fingers, and whistled on his way.

Miles stood still, staring at the bill in his hand. He'd never held fifty dollars before! Where had it come from? His mind spun with all the possibilities of what to do with it.

No doubt about it, this was shaping up to be one of the *best days ever*!

CHAPTER SIX

S uch was his overwhelming happiness that Miles had to keep himself from skipping out of the Harmonicandy Room to the library and then skipping out to the great lawn. Even though the box he carried weighed him down a little, he felt as if he were floating. In the last hour he'd had one of his slogans selected to go on every Harmonicandy wrapper, found fifty dollars, seen the Harmonicandy Room, and been told he was going on a road trip with his friends to visit famous candy stores (a road trip! A dream come true!), and now he was about to sit at a picnic table and open a box of old journals and maps that hadn't been seen in decades. It made all the earlier drama with his dad seem very far away.

As usual, the lawn was bustling with activity. Even though the factory had closed to visitors in order to prepare for the Kickoff the next day, many of the guests had lingered to enjoy the outdoors. Balls flew between parents and kids, music played, and factory workers carried bales of hay to the barn and boxes of strawberries from the field. Thankfully, the smell from the peppermint leaves helped cover the odor of the manure spread around the flower beds. And Miles had never seen the pond so full. The only boat not on the water was the Candymaker's private canoe, painted bright yellow in honor of his award-winning Neon Yellow Lightning Chew.

He walked past the spot where Max had set up their picnic lunch the very first day of the contest. Miles had to shake his head at the memory of telling the others he was allergic to rowboats and the color pink. What they must have thought of him! He was so glad he could tell them anything now. Or almost anything, anyway.

After making his way around a spirited game of lawn chess played with giant pieces that took both hands to lift, Miles rested the box on the only picnic table that didn't have families crowded around it.

The breeze was picking up, so he gathered some stones and sticks to use as paperweights before getting down to the task of sorting the contents of the box into piles. He loved the feel of the old notebook paper beneath his hands. He expected it to be rough and crackly, but instead the pages were soft, almost buttery. Even the musty smell of the newspapers reminded him more of the storeroom of the library than an attic. He breathed the smell in deep, wishing he could absorb all the information just by doing that. Sure would save time.

A small crowd began to gather around him. Perhaps they thought he was setting up more freebies. Most drifted away when they discovered he was pulling out notebooks and papers, not candy, but two boys—around ages eight and ten—stayed. Miles had thought doing this outside would be more private than spreading the material out on the factory library floor, but he was beginning to doubt his judgment. The younger boy actually reached into the box and began pulling things out! The other started tossing around the rocks and sticks Miles had piled up.

"Um, can you guys not do that?" Miles asked, pulling the box away. "This stuff is really valuable."

"C'mon, Cole," the older boy said, tossing a few of the sticks from the table into the box. "I told you there's no candy here."

Cole dropped the spiral brown notebook he'd been holding,

then peered into the box one last time before following the other boy. Miles was tempted to catch up to them and give them a lesson on manners, but as an only child, he had no experience scolding other children. He straightened the piles and then pulled the sticks out from the box and tossed them to the ground. It wasn't that windy anyway. He was looking forward to the factory's return to normal after tomorrow, when people would once again respect other people's property.

Finally the visitors slowly began heading around the side of the factory toward the parking lot. Miles rubbed his hands together in anticipation and dove into the pile. He started with the newspaper clippings because they were the most fragile and looked like they'd be the easiest to read. Miles could see from his quick glance at one of the notebooks that Samuel didn't have the neatest handwriting. They would take longer to get through.

First, Miles sorted the papers chronologically. The dates only spanned a ten-year range, from fifty-five to sixty-five years ago. Most were from Sam's hometown paper, the *Brookdale Gazette*. The earliest article told the story of how ten-year-old Samuel Sweet started a lemonade stand during a heat wave and raised four dollars and fifteen cents, which he donated to buy fans for the community center.

Most of the newspaper clippings weren't about Sam. Some reported on the accomplishments of local businessmen; many were recipes for homemade cakes and cookies; a few told of advances in technology or machinery, which Miles only skimmed. Many, in fact, were about new inventions or discoveries, including one article titled "Local Student Invents Sneezing Powder!" Miles set that one aside to show Logan. Maybe that's where Sam's interest in practical jokes came from.

By far the longest article was the one announcing Sam's win at the first New Candy Contest, sponsored by the newly formed

Confectionary Association of America. It included a very grainy photo and an interview with Sam, along with comments from his parents, his teachers, and the contest judges. Miles set that aside, too. He bet Logan would love to hear that it took his grandfather two solid years before he figured out how to combine the ingredients so that the Pepsicle would taste just right, and then another six months learning how to keep it frozen without it losing flavor. Clearly the man's ambition and determination had been there since his youngest years. It gave Miles a chill of excitement. From a tiny lemonade stand to the enormous **Life Is Sweet?** factory. What a journey!

Eager to learn more, he turned to the journals next. Most of the notebooks were plain, with thick brown covers and metal spirals on the top. He liked the weight of them in his hand. In comparison, his own notebook, with its flimsy cover and plastic spirals, seemed very unimpressive. Sam's notebooks were the kind one would fill with truly deep thoughts, thoughts that would one day change the world. Miles had no doubt that's what he'd find when he opened the first one.

So imagine his surprise when he found nothing of the sort.

Instead, drawings and sketches of trees, houses, treasure chests, and all kinds of animals filled the unlined pages. Miles flipped through the other notebooks. He found more of the same, along with recipes crossed out and rewritten, mazes that went on for pages, lists of rules for made-up games, diagrams of three-dimensional puzzles, and short, direct, to-the-point reviews of everything from the newest superhero comic at the comic-book shop ("splendid art and gripping story line") to the new socks his aunt had given him for his birthday ("scratchy and unpleasant to look at").

Miles had to laugh. He didn't have an aunt, but if he did, he bet she'd give him ugly socks, too. The last few pages of one of the notebooks were filled with drawings of the Pepsicle from all angles.

The final notebook contained more of what he'd expected. The handwriting looked more grown up, with fewer flourishes at the ends of the letters, and the words tended to go straight across the page instead of slanting down to the right. Here Samuel finally spoke about how the prize money helped his family buy a modern refrigerator with a separate freezer on top and enabled his mother to buy herself some new dresses for a change, instead of getting hand-me-downs from the ladies in town. He wrote a list of goals for himself—college, then maybe a candy store of his own, a family. Sam had reached his early goals and gotten a lot more than he'd dreamt of.

Miles closed the last notebook. It seemed odd to him that Samuel would have stopped writing when still young, before he even began his career. Although he'd written about a lot of that business stuff in the pamphlets now available inside in the library, those were more formal, and meant for others. And the library pamphlets didn't have doodles of gum balls and lollypops down the edges. Maybe whoever gathered this material and sent it to Logan just didn't have the batch in between.

He stood up to stretch. It had to be close to dinnertime, and he'd need to pack. He knew he should call home for a ride, but he couldn't do it before turning to the last, most highly anticipated items on the table—the maps.

He reached for the rolled-up map first and was a bit disappointed to see that it was a map of Samuel's hometown of Brookdale. He didn't know what he'd been expecting, but the town—with its downtown, bus station, movie house, and school—just wasn't very exciting. Nicely drawn, though.

He turned to the next map. This one had been folded instead of rolled, and he opened it very carefully, figuring the creases might rip otherwise. But the thick paper had held up well. The paint had faded, but the colors were still vibrant and beautiful. With a thin brush, the mapmaker had written three words across the face of the map:

MAP OF AWE

Miles gasped. Now, *that* was more like it! What could be cooler than a map of awe? He read the words over again, out loud. He'd always liked the word *awe*. It made the bottom of his throat vibrate in an interesting way when he said it out loud.

The map showed a hazy landscape with rolling hills; a deep, sandy valley with a stream running through it; a few clumps of trees; and a cloud with the words *FOG to the North* running through it. The words *River of Light* drifted along with the stream. The art style and the lettering didn't match anything he'd seen of Sam's so far. Maybe he'd gotten the map as a gift and it had become mixed in with his old papers. Miles looked in the lower right corner for the signature of the mapmaker but found only a drawing of a large gray boulder with some smaller rocks scattered around it.

He knew that sometimes mapmakers wrote their names or initials inside features of the map or in the borders. This map didn't have borders, though. He peered more closely at the leaves in the trees, then checked for any patterns in the sparse grass, but spotted nothing. He turned his attention to the boulder.

Faint lines crisscrossed the face of it, like cracks in the stone... but not all of them were perfectly straight. He tilted the map up to the sun and pulled his glasses a few inches away from his face to magnify the image. The numbers 43127 appeared, ever so faintly. From what he'd learned recently about GPS coordinates, there weren't enough digits to represent longitude or latitude. Maybe it was the mapmaker's birthday, or his lucky numbers.

Miles carefully, and reluctantly, refolded the map and set it aside. He leaned over the box to double-check that he'd gotten everything out and spotted one thin brown pocket-sized notepad that blended in with the bottom of the box. A gray rubber band that must once have been pink held it together. When he went to pull it off, the rubber band crumbled in his hand.

At first glance he thought the lined pages were blank. Closer inspection revealed that the faintest of pencil writing actually filled not only the lines, but the blank space around the edges of every single page. Time had faded the words so much that they were impossible to read. Holding it up to the sun didn't help. Whatever notes Sam had written in there were lost to history.

When he got to the end, he discovered a folded sheet of yellowed paper stuck between the last page and the back cover. The outer edges of the paper were almost completely burned off, as if it had been held over a fire and yanked back.

Holding his breath, Miles put down the notebook and ever so carefully unfolded the note. Unlike all of Sam's other writings, this one had been typed on a typewriter; he'd only used ink to sign his name below the single paragraph of text. Beneath Sam's name Miles could see tiny bits of ink, but they were covered in black soot. He was afraid to even breathe on the paper in case the whole bottom half crumbled right off.

His eyes drifted up to the text. The words *swear never to reveal the location of the special beans* jumped out at him from the first line. He stared at them.

Special... *beans*?

Heart pumping hard, he began reading from the beginning.

We, the four signers of this contract, do hereby solemnly swear never to reveal the location of the special beans, nor how Samuel Sweet came to be in possession of them. If questioned, we agree to say we don't remember any details about our time spent

there. We promise to uphold our vow to help keep
the valley hidden, whatever that might take in the
future. This contract binds us together for life,
both in friendship and in secrecy. We have been
given a great gift, and we hereby agree to repay
that debt whenever possible, anonymously, asking
nothing in return. Once this binding contract is
signed and sealed, it shall be destroyed.

Miles's eyes darted back down to the bottom of the contract.
Only Sam's signature had survived the flames. And he'd only
signed his first name. *Sam.* Somewhat of an expert on the man's
handwriting by now, Miles could tell he was perhaps eighteen or
nineteen years old at the time he signed it. So who were the other
three mentioned above?

Miles read the document twice. What did it even mean?
Did Samuel Sweet steal something? Did he steal *beans*? Like,
chocolate-making beans? Miles was pretty sure they weren't the
Jack-and-the-Beanstalk kind of beans, although he found himself glancing up at the sky to see if a giant beanstalk had suddenly
sprouted from the ground.

Why had Sam kept the paper instead of fully destroying it, like
the contract said? Had the factory been built on a lie? Miles knew
he needed to ask someone better at solving mysteries than he was.
Good thing he knew someone like that.

He looked around to make sure he was still alone, then pulled
out his vid com and propped it up on a rock. He knelt down and
called Daisy. He expected her to answer right away, like she had
that morning, but he had to leave a message this time. He had just
held the letter up to the screen when he heard Logan's voice behind
him ask, "Hey, find anything cool?"

W hen Logan showed up looking like Santa, with his dancing-gumdrops pillowcase filled with candy slung over one shoulder, Miles's first thought was that he needed to protect Logan from any speculation about Samuel Sweet's wrongdoings. He couldn't show him the contract, not before he found out what it meant.

So he threw things back into the box, mumbled an excuse to Logan, and ran off, cringing as he pretended not to hear Logan calling after him. He needed to find out if the original Candymaker got his job by stealing something that belonged to someone else. There had to be some information in the library that would help.

He figured he'd be alone in there, but as he approached the library, he could see Sabrina though the glass wall. She was standing at the candy bar display table, peering closely at the items.

Miles pushed the door open slowly so he wouldn't startle her.

Sabrina looked up, then broke into a grin. "Sounds great!" she said.

Miles smiled back and set down the box. "Tastes even better!"

They both laughed. "Guess you've heard, too!" she said.

"Yup! Mr. Sweet just told me in the Harmonicandy Room."

"All us suits love the slogan!" Sabrina said.

Miles laughed again. "I didn't know you knew people called you that. Even though I've never seen you in a suit. Or, like, a dress."

"We think it's funny," Sabrina said. "And it's true that being on the business end is very different from the work of all the people who actually make things." She pointed down at the table. "I was just in here researching a good font to use. The art director wants to find one that hasn't been on any other wrappers before but still feels like it belongs." She lifted the fake Magic Bar and the real Oozing Crunchorama. "I was thinking something between the two of these."

"The Magic Bar wrapper is a little old-fashioned looking," Miles said. "It's sparkly, but the rest of the design is kind of like a sign you'd see in an antiques store."

"That's part of its charm," Sabrina said, admiring it and setting it back down. "But I see what you mean. Well, gotta run. We have to print up a bunch of banners to hang for the Kickoff tomorrow." She tipped her cap at Miles in a salute and dashed out.

Miles straightened the Magic Bar and turned his attention toward the row of pamphlets Mrs. Gepheart had added to the display. Maybe there was something about the history of the factory that he'd missed before. He grabbed the whole stack of them and stuck them on top of the stuff in the box. He left a note in his neatest handwriting telling Mrs. Gepheart he'd return them first thing in the morning.

As he set the note on the table, he noticed a framed black-and-white photo very close to the edge. He moved it a few inches so it wouldn't slide off. He'd seen this Opening Day photo before. A larger version hung on the wall in Logan's apartment, and in one or two other places in the factory, too. It showed a very young Sam— he didn't look older than twenty—standing on the front steps of the factory with two other men in suits and hats and two women in dresses, all holding a **Life Is Sweet** banner. He knew the woman to Sam's right was Logan's grandmother Florence, who had passed away before Logan was born. But when once he'd asked who the others were, Logan just shook his head and said it was a mystery, that even his dad didn't know.

Miles lifted the picture and squinted at it, as though a clue to their identities might jump out at him. The factory was much, much smaller than it was today, and their clothes were really old-fashioned. That same old milk jug sat on the porch steps! It didn't look so old then, though.

But no names were scribbled on the picture... at least not on the front. He turned the picture over and was about to slide it out of the frame to check the back, when he heard the library door shut behind him. Without thinking, he tossed the photo into his box and folded up the flaps.

He turned around to see Philip watching him. "You know that stealing is a crime, right?" Philip asked, pointing at the box. He tried to look stern as he said it, but Miles could tell he wasn't too serious about teasing him. After all, Philip's strict, unreasonable, candy-hating father had just given him permission to go on the road trip. Even Philip couldn't pretend he wasn't in a good mood, and Philip was a good actor.

"Why are you still here?" Miles asked, changing the subject. He didn't want to have to show anyone what was in the box until he had more answers than questions. He pushed past Philip into the hall.

"I'm not still here," Philip said as he followed. "I mean, I'm leaving." He pointed toward the front hall. "See?"

Reggie was heading toward them, swinging a key chain on his finger. "Gotta get moving, Philip. Hello, Miles."

"Hi, Reggie." Miles gave a nod of his head, since his arms were full.

"Need a lift home?" Reggie asked.

Miles's eyes widened. "Did you bring the limo?"

"Actually, I did," Reggie said. "I just dropped Mr. Ransford at the airport."

"I thought he wasn't leaving until tomorrow night," Philip said.

"His meeting was moved up a day."

Philip looked like he wanted to say more, but he pressed his lips tight instead.

"I'll even let you play with the divider," Reggie said. "Philip and his brother used to love putting it up and down when they were little."

Philip grunted and trudged after them. Miles knew Philip wouldn't want him along for the ride—he didn't like to mix his home life and his factory life—but no way was Miles turning this opportunity down! Who knew when he'd ever get to ride in something as cool as a limousine again! He gave Reggie his address and pushed to the back of his head any concerns over whether Samuel Sweet had founded the factory based on a lie. He'd worry about that later.

The inside of the car looked even bigger than the outside! Miles put the box at his feet and bounced up and down on the soft seat. Philip climbed in after him, and Reggie shut the door. Miles beamed as he took in the wood-paneled walls, the long windows, the plush carpet. He wanted to slip his sneakers off and run his toes through it, but he knew Philip would hate that (which made it even more tempting!). "This is the life!" he said.

"Don't get too used to it," Philip grumbled.

Miles used the phone built into the car to tell his mom he'd saved her the drive.

As the limo pulled away, Miles pressed the button to put up the window between the front of the car and the back. The top of Reggie's head kept appearing and disappearing. Reggie was right—that *was* fun! "How long has your family had this car?"

Miles asked. "How many people can fit in here? Does this thing have a TV?"

Philip didn't answer.

Miles's thoughts turned to the trip. "I've never stayed overnight anywhere," he admitted. "Except at my grandparents' once and at the factory a few times. I bet you've traveled a lot."

Philip shrugged. "I guess. With my family or on school trips. Not with my fr..." He trailed off and turned toward the window.

"It's okay," Miles said with a nudge. "You can admit we're your friends."

Philip just grunted again.

A few minutes later the car pulled up in front of Miles's house. He noticed Philip staring out the window at it. He was probably thinking how small it was in comparison to the huge house he lived in. Miles had never been invited over, though, so he could only imagine what kind of house the town's most successful businessman owned.

"Do you, um, want to come in?" Miles asked. Logan had been over many times, and Daisy a few times, too. Philip had never accepted his invitation, though.

Philip shook his head. "Gotta pack," he mumbled.

Miles gave Philip a long look. Maybe he wasn't pretending to be annoyed at Miles after all. Maybe he really *was* annoyed. "I'm sorry if I shouldn't have accepted the ride," he said. "I know you're a really private person and all."

"Don't worry about it," Philip said, still watching out the window. "I just have a lot on my mind."

He seemed sincere enough. Miles nodded. "Anything you want to talk about?"

Philip quickly shook his head again.

"Okay, then. See you tomorrow for the Kickoff." Miles saw his dad come out of the house, and it felt weird waiting for Reggie to open the door, so he let himself out.

His dad whistled as they watched the car pull away from the curb. "You sure are coming up in the world, son."

"Yup. Soon I'll be flying off in my private plane."

"I thought it was just a road trip," his dad joked, taking the box from him.

"So I'm really going?" Miles asked.

"Oh, you're going, mister. Your mom and I are already planning some nice child-free activities after work each day."

"I'll try not to take that personally."

"What's in here, anyway?" his dad asked, placing the box on their front-hall table. "Candy?" he asked, his voice full of hope.

"Sorry, just some research on the factory." He was used to telling his parents most of the truth without telling them all of it.

Miles's mom came in from the kitchen, holding a piece of paper. "Mrs. Sweet read me off the packing list so I could get started," she said. "All you need to do is add your toothbrush in the morning and a book or two for pleasure reading on the long car rides."

"Wow, you really *are* anxious for me to leave!" Miles said, only half joking. His mother came over and put her arms around him. "I will miss you every second you're gone." He believed her.

That night in bed Miles stared at the ceiling, thinking about what he'd read. Only one of Sam's pamphlets included anything to do with the founding of the company. It focused more on the steady growth of the company but still gave a brief history of the small-town boy turned candymaker.

After he won the big contest, Sam chose not to have any of the other candy companies manufacture the Pepsicle for him. He used some of the money he'd won to take classes at the local business school and to purchase supplies to test more candy recipes. His goal was to make, in addition to the Pepsicle, a chewy candy, a hard candy, and a chocolate bar. When he had all four ready to go, he put the rest of the money into opening the factory. Many of the members of the Confectionary Association chipped in to help him, and Sam repaid their generosity in the years that followed by always being willing to help other candymakers in any way he could.

While the pamphlet was very inspiring and educational, it didn't include any mention of secret beans, half-burned contracts, or a mysterious place that had to be protected at all costs.

Miles flopped around some more. Even tracing paths through the maps he'd taped up on his walls didn't help him relax like it usually did. His latest addition had been a gift from Henry for his birthday last month. It was a pencil drawing of a small village—not much more than a sketch, really—but it gave Miles a warm feeling, as though the mapmaker who drew it truly loved that place.

Then he sat bolt upright as a new thought struck him. Maybe the contract had just been a joke, like a gag or something! Why hadn't he thought of that before? Logan had said that Sam enjoyed a good prank every now and again. Maybe that's all this was! Sam and his friends being goofy—like he and *his* friends could be sometimes!

Miles grinned. Now he could put the worry behind him and focus on the trip. He glanced around his dark room. Goodbye, desk. Goodbye, bed. Goodbye, house. He giggled to himself and thought of the picture book his mom had read to him when he was a child, the one where you're supposed to say good night to the moon. The next time he saw the moon, it would be out a different window!

He kicked off his covers and got his glasses from his night table. The window over his bed was already open a few inches to let in the breeze, so he pushed it the rest of the way and stuck his head out.

"Goodbye, moon," he whispered. As soon as the words were out of his mouth, a flash of light sped across the sky in front of him. Then another! A person less skilled in astronomy might have thought Spring Haven was putting on a fireworks display.

But Miles knew better. He couldn't believe he'd forgotten about the meteor shower expected to start that night in the wake of that big comet he kept hearing about on the news! He propped his elbows up on the windowsill and watched. Usually he would go get his parents to watch with him, but now his first thought was to wonder what Logan and Daisy and Philip were doing at that moment and whether they were seeing this light show.

He reached over the side of the bed and pulled the vid com out of his suitcase. It was definitely too late to contact any of them, but he could at least record it for them so they wouldn't miss it. Logan had taught him about watching the clouds turn into bunnies and castles and ducks; the least he could do was teach Logan about watching the stars turn into fireworks.

CHAPTER EIGHT

Tuesday

The doorbell rang at the O'Learys' house early the next morning. "I'll get it!" Miles shouted, bounding down the stairs. He looked out the window like he'd been taught. He certainly wasn't going to open it for someone he didn't know, especially not while he still wore his pajamas! But he *did* know the person standing on the front porch. He flung the door open. "Hi, Arthur and Fluffernutter! Were we supposed to go geocaching today?"

The puppy wagged her tail, slapping it against the door with a *thwak*. She dropped a soggy stuffed lamb that must have once been white on the porch and prodded it with her nose. Arthur shook his head. "I just came to give you this." He held out his hand and presented Miles with a small yellow gift bag.

Miles took it, surprised. "You know it's not my birthday, right?"

"I do indeed!" Arthur said. "Your mom was in the library yesterday afternoon when she got the call about your trip. This is a care package from me and Tina. Jade pitched in, too. It's a little random, I admit, but short notice and all."

Miles eagerly dug into the bag. There was a red envelope with his name on the front in another ancient language, a packet of tissues, two bags of potato chips, a pair of soft blue-and-yellow-striped socks, a deck of playing cards, and a paperback copy of *Let's Go Geocaching!* with some pages bent back at the corners.

Miles held up the card. "Old Hebrew?"

"Close. It's Aramaic."

"Nice," Miles said, nodding approvingly. He stuck it carefully into the book.

"I marked off some of my favorite parts for you," Arthur said. "I figured if you're out on the road, you might have a chance to find some caches. You'll have to set up your own account, though, so you can start keeping track of them."

"I will!" Miles promised. "I'll teach my friends, too."

"Hello, Arthur," Miles's dad said, joining them at the door. The men shook hands. "Would you like to come in?"

"Sure," Arthur said. "I won't impose too long. I know it's early."

"Not at all. I'll make you some tea. Susan will be home soon." They headed toward the kitchen together, Fluffernutter following obediently behind.

Miles was glad his dad hadn't mentioned that the reason Mom had run out so early was because she was buying him underwear for the trip. Apparently his old pairs weren't "road trip–worthy," whatever that meant!

He listened by the stairs for a minute, and when the conversation turned to sports, he ran upstairs to get dressed. As soon as his mother got home, they would all head off to the factory. He thought it was really cool that Mrs. Sweet had invited his parents to be in the room for the first tasting.

He added the care package from the Wus, and after the addition of his new undies, his suitcase would be ready to go. He'd already packed the pile of books from his night table because who was his mom kidding if she thought one or two would be enough? He'd also added a few of Sam's journals and the Map of Awe.

His globe would have to stay on his desk. It would be strange not to be here each night to give it a spin and then learn about where his finger landed. He'd just have to spin it seven times in a row when he returned. He thought about bringing some of his homemade maps, but he knew he wouldn't have much privacy—if any at all—to work on them, and he wasn't ready to share them yet.

He picked up the small brown notebook with the faded words. He had wrapped a fresh rubber band around it to hold it closed. It occurred to him now that this was the only notebook Sam had taken any trouble to securely close. Maybe because he'd stuck the fake contract in it and didn't want it to fall out, or maybe he had some other reason.

Stepping in front of the window, Miles undid the rubber band and opened the notebook again. He thought for a minute. He knew from his reading on creating alphabets and codes that if you found a piece of paper that had been sitting underneath a piece that had been written on, you could rub the side of a pencil over the blank page to pick up the indentations that had been pressed into the paper. Maybe that would work with the notebook.

He pulled a sharp pencil out of his desk drawer and gently rubbed the edge over the first few seemingly blank lines. The occasional tiny part of a letter showed up, but that was all. He ran his finger over the page. There really wasn't much indentation left behind. The years must have flattened out the pages. That, or Sam had written very lightly. Or both.

He tossed the notebook into his suitcase and zippered it shut before he found more stuff to shove in.

He stuck the pamphlets into his backpack and realized he'd forgotten to check the back of the old photo for names. The clips holding the frame together were rusty, but Miles twisted them carefully, and the front and back practically fell into two pieces. He lifted out the photo and held it up to the light. *Spring Haven Photographs & Fur* was embossed on the bottom in fancy lettering. *Photographs and fur?* That was a random combination! He put the frame back together. The identity of the unknown people posing with Logan's grandparents would have to remain a mystery until he returned.

Miles heard Fluffernutter bark, and then his dad's and Arthur's voices got louder as they moved from the kitchen toward the front door. They were laughing about both of them having the same favorite baseball player and remember when he did that backflip out in right field after he caught a pop fly? Miles was glad they'd finally found something in common to talk about, even if it wasn't as exciting as geocaching.

He hurried from his room so he could say goodbye. Halfway down the stairs he stopped short. Maybe the mystery of the photo *wouldn't* have to wait! There was someone in this very house at this very instant who would probably *love* the challenge of tracking them down. He ran back up to get the photo for his favorite reference librarian.

"Of course!" Arthur said when Miles explained it to him. "You know I love a good challenge!"

"I hoped you'd say that!" Miles said. He ran into his dad's office to make copies, and they each kept one. Arthur promised to let him know as soon as he discovered anything. Miles's dad was so used to his quest for knowledge about unusual topics that he didn't even ask what Miles was up to.

An hour later the pamphlets and photo were back on the display table in the library. Miles's note was still there, apparently unseen. He tossed it in the trash and ran to the Harmonicandy Room to join his parents and the others who'd been invited to the special event.

Seeing that first tray move along the conveyor belt was a moment he'd never forget. He kept watching tray after tray move toward the cooling station, even once everyone else had broken off and started chatting. He couldn't help overhearing a heated discussion between Philip and Reggie about the percentage of money Philip would get on the sale of each one and what Mr. Ransford would say about it. Sometimes Miles forgot that the candymaking business was actually a *business*. He knew he shouldn't be surprised that Philip was talking about money before the first Harmonicandy had even cooled down.

Wheeling the trays out to the crowd was awesome! He could tell Logan was thrilled, too, and Philip caught his eye and smiled really big in the middle of all the craziness. The smile felt real and sincere and special. Miles gladly returned it. He had to admit he'd been a little scared that the Harmonicandy wouldn't actually play any notes, but it totally did! And it tasted great!

And then everything fell apart.

Miles knew Logan would never have tried to ruin the Kickoff on purpose, but the event went from awesome to awful in just a few minutes when he said there was something wrong with the Harmonicandy. When they went into the Marshmallow Room to look for Henry, Miles ducked into Henry's office. The Marshmallow Room never smelled like chocolate. But back here he definitely smelled a faint odor. Maybe Henry was planning on branching out from marshmallows.

The tiny office looked much as it had the day before, although the stacks of bills and paperwork were lower and organized into neat piles. A small rectangular bin marked OLD RECEIPTS sat on the desk chair. Miles turned to go when something in the center of the desk caught his eye. He stepped closer. It was the picture he had just returned to the library! Not the same exact one, but a copy. Judging by the small size and the water stains, this might even be an original photo. His eyes darted across the desktop to see if he spotted anything else unusual.

That's when he saw it—and smelled it at the same time. Underneath the photo was a faded yellow envelope that it must have been stored in. The middle bulged out slightly. Miles picked up the envelope and turned it over. A bright blue ball fell out onto his palm. For a second he thought it must have been a gum ball, but since the chocolate smell multiplied by about a thousand when it hit the air, he revised his opinion. This could only be a cocoa bean. He'd seen a lot of cocoa beans over his months at the factory, but never one this round and certainly never this blue color.

Logan called out that they should keep looking. Miles left the picture and the envelope on the desk and stuck the bean deep in his pocket.

When they finally found Henry by the marsh, Miles stood quietly, hoping no one would notice the smell from the hidden bean. Maybe Philip had been right to call him out for stealing back in the library. His heart pounded. Why had he taken it? Was he just a common thief now?

As Henry tried to explain about the chocolate, Miles's heart sank. That contract wasn't just a joke; he knew that now for sure. Somehow the bean, the Harmonicandy, that old photograph, and Sam's secret were linked. Miles needed to find out as much as he could about these mysteries, and he needed time. They *had* to go on that road trip! He couldn't explain everything to them, though, not there and then. Not in front of Henry, who definitely knew more than he was admitting to. He had to let Logan know the importance of the trip, so he blurted it out the only way he felt sure Henry wouldn't understand it—backward.

Logan got it right away, even though it obviously annoyed Philip and left Henry confused. But then Logan pointed out that there wasn't anyone to drive them. "Henry can drive us," Miles suggested, fixing his eyes on him. "Will you do it, Henry?" Henry was their best chance of solving this mystery. Who better to accompany them? But Henry broke eye contact even before Philip annoyingly jumped in with his reasons why Henry couldn't do it. Miles snapped at Philip and then felt ashamed at his tone and almost missed it when Henry said someone else could drive them.

Miles felt uneasy as they followed Henry around to the front of the factory. What if the driver was someone he or his parents wouldn't feel comfortable with? Philip walked close to Henry, and Miles felt another flash of annoyance. Why did Philip have to remind Henry about the Marsh-Wiggle?

The sounds of the Kickoff gradually fell away behind them. Parked outside the front door was a blue minivan, with pretty much the last person Miles expected to see leaning against it.

"Who's up for a road trip?" their new driver asked.

As Miles stared in surprise, slowly but surely he felt the tension in his chest fall away.

PART THREE

DAISY

CHAPTER ONE

Sunday night

aisy watched as her camp counselor tugged on the piece of rope that hung from the rafters. The lone lightbulb clicked off, plunging the cabin into darkness. Only the faint moonlight outside allowed the girls to see the outline of the bunk beds and cubbies that filled the cabin. Daisy could see perfectly well in the dark. That's what a lifetime of training will do for a girl.

"Sleep tight...," the counselor sang.

All twelve campers replied with a chorus of "Don't let the ladybugs bite."

And then all the girls giggled. Honestly, Daisy didn't see what was so funny about living in a cabin infested with ladybugs. Plus everyone knew ladybugs didn't really bite. But she giggled along with the rest of them and even joined in when the girl on the bunk bed below her started a game of Toss the Stuffed Animal.

After a full day of swimming, arts and crafts, kickball, campfire songs, and scratching mosquito bites, everyone except Daisy quickly drifted off to sleep. She'd been there two weeks already, pretending to be Ava Simon, the shy, bookish girl from up north who didn't gossip and kept her cubby neat and organized. She didn't usually play this type, but at Camp Tumbleweed for Girls, it was best if she didn't stand out very much. That way she wouldn't be missed when she slipped away from the group.

And she slipped away *a lot*. Who could blame her? She was stuck at *sleepaway camp*! Her! The best and brightest thirteen-year-old spy in the country, deep undercover in the middle of nowhere, surrounded by nothing but trees and lakes and grass and more trees!

She had to constantly remind herself that she'd asked for this job. After the mission at the candy factory, she had insisted on taking a break from her crazy, busy life and the responsibilities that came with it. She didn't know if she could continue being a spy. At least, not without getting to make more of her own choices.

She had spent most of her first day off riding Magpie through the fields around the mansion, listening to pop music on her headphones and enjoying the breeze through her hair.

On day two, she'd walked the gentle curves of the labyrinth in her grandmother's Zen garden, trying to force herself into a state of calm and clarity, but all she got was dizzy from the twists and turns.

On day three, Grammy had presented her with a backpack, a bag lunch, and fake school documents created by her most skilled forger. Off Daisy went to the local public middle school. And not on an undercover assignment, either—as a real student! The situation turned out to be completely unbearable. Daisy lost her mind having to sit quietly at a tiny desk all day long and pretend she didn't know more about the world than the teachers did.

Plus she didn't have anyone to sit with at lunch.

After that brief glimpse of life as an ordinary school kid, she'd been ready to jump back into the spy game with both feet. It took many hours of begging and groveling (of which she wasn't proud) before her grandmother finally agreed. Daisy still wouldn't be allowed to choose her own cases, but she had figured out how she could do her job without worrying about whether she'd been hired by the good guys or the bad guys. It was a brilliant solution, really. Basically, she simply wouldn't dwell on the situation, which was exactly how she'd handled it before she'd started thinking about it! She would lock the question of right and wrong so far back in her mind that she'd forget where the key was. It would languish there along with other unanswered questions, like her real last name and did she really have a brother, questions her parents had skillfully dodged during their brief visit to the mansion the previous month.

The only downside to being back in the spy business was that her grandmother had made her promise to keep her distance from the candy factory and the friends she'd made during her short assignment there. Once you leave a job behind, you shed the person you'd been pretending to be. The fees for the gig got paid, the documents shredded, the files encrypted. The End.

But at the factory gig—for the second half of the job, at least— she hadn't been pretending to be anyone other than herself. She and Logan and Miles and even Philip had grown so close and been through so much that she couldn't simply turn her back on them. For now, though, she'd have to limit herself to short visits and letters from the road. Her grandmother wasn't trying to be cruel, but she had the whole organization to protect. Daisy knew it was the right thing to do, but that didn't make it hurt any less.

Her grandmother had insisted on starting Daisy off easy, with a straight-up surveillance gig at a museum where a young man was suspected of plotting to steal an extremely valuable statue. There had been a string of art thefts in the area in recent months, so the museums were on high alert for any suspicious behavior. They couldn't even trust their security guards.

Her assignment had been to watch from across the room as the man, dressed as a ponytailed artist, drew sketch after sketch of a marble statue of a bald eagle in flight. Sometimes he would sit there for eight straight hours, moving his stool in tiny increments around the roped-off statue. Close observation of his behavior led Daisy to believe he really was the art student he appeared to be, but the museum needed her to stay in place until he was gone, just in case. She knew this boring job was partly a punishment for what had gone down at the candy factory, but she was determined to take it seriously.

As the days wore on, she'd gained an appreciation for art and an admiration for those who loved it enough to stare at the same piece all day long. She missed seeing her new friends, though, and she missed riding Magpie. The only time she got outside was when the man took a short break to eat his salami sandwich on the museum steps and she followed at a safe distance.

After two weeks, he closed his sketchpad with a finality that indicated he had done whatever he came to do. He tucked his pencil behind his ear, stood up, and stretched. Then his eyes darted around the room. Usually he seemed oblivious to the world around him, so this last bit had Daisy on full alert.

His eyes passed over her, not even slowing down. Her disguise as a Girl Scout with a badge-covered vest made her seem particularly nonthreatening and also not very memorable. It's an old spy trick that if you wear a uniform, people will notice your clothes and not your face. They will assume you're part of a group and won't suspect you're there for them. The trick had clearly worked this time.

Brown and green wasn't *the most* flattering combination, but Daisy did enjoy wearing the vest. Even though she hadn't earned the badges the traditional way, she had earned every single one during her years of training and service. Now she finally had the chance to show them off with pride.

Apparently confident that no one was watching him, the young man stepped closer to the ropes. Daisy used the remote in her pocket to snap pictures with the tiny microcamera hidden behind her archery badge. Could she have been wrong? Was the man planning to try to steal the statue after all? She glanced quickly over at the security guard stationed at the entrance of the room. He was busy giving an older couple directions to the restrooms.

The art student (thief?) now stood against the rope, only inches from the giant bird. Was he going to grab it right there, in the middle of the day, surrounded by a dozen museumgoers? He couldn't hope to get very far, even if he could lift the weight of the statue, which she doubted. He didn't look as if he spent much time exercising. Only a few feet behind him, Daisy balanced on the balls of her feet, ready to spring into action.

The man leaned the top part of his body over the rope. With one last glance left and right, his head darted forward and he kissed the marble eagle right on its pointy beak. Then he backed away, tucked his stool under one arm and his sketchbook under the other, and hurried out the door.

In Daisy's official report to her grandmother, she'd concluded that loving art shouldn't mean *loving* art, and that grown men shouldn't wear ponytails.

Two more assignments followed before her current position at the camp. She'd enjoyed being a golf caddy at a fancy country club, where she recorded the private conversations of the wealthy businesspeople whose clubs she carried. Their discussions were boring, but the green rolling hills were beautiful, and she liked the triple-decker sandwiches in the clubhouse.

After that assignment ended, she and Courtney—who was still her closest spy friend in the mansion, even though she was nearly AJ's age—were hired by the local soccer association to join two rival all-girls soccer teams. They needed to find out whether the coaches were conspiring with each other to throw the games (they were). She always enjoyed the rare occasions when she and Courtney got to work together, and soccer was one of Daisy's best sports. She'd even scored a game-winning goal (made only slightly less gratifying because she knew that the opposing goalie had been ordered to let the ball through).

She'd taken those assignments in stride; she'd had dozens like them before. But deep-cover jobs like the one at Camp Tumbleweed were definitely the toughest. Being a sleeper agent meant that she had to fully immerse herself in being a camper, without getting to do any spy work until AJ activated her. She was Ava Simon *all the time*. She couldn't show even a little of her true self.

In the past this wouldn't have bothered her. But she couldn't deny that her experiences at **Life Is Sweet** had changed something inside her. The friends she'd made there had liked her for who she was, even when she wasn't pretending to be sweet and happy all the time. But now when the girl on the bunk below her got homesick, she had to pretend she knew what it felt like to miss a home with parents and a pet and a white picket fence around it all. (Her mansion *did* have a white picket fence around it, but it was electrified and had sensors that read the fingerprints of each resident before allowing the person to go inside. So, not really the same.) And the missing-her-parents part—well, she was so used to not seeing them for long stretches that being away from them felt more normal than being *with* them.

Maybe the most difficult thing was having to pretend she was only half as skilled at the camp activities as she actually was. She could climb/swim/run circles around the other campers without even breaking a sweat, but that would make her stand out. People would ask questions. If her cover got blown, like at the candy factory, it would mean she'd have to go back to middle school, and she'd already crossed the middle school experience off her list of things to try.

Daisy reached over to the top of her cubby to grab her journal so she could complain in print, then remembered that her pen had run out of invisible ink the night before. Apparently, *invisible* doesn't mean *endless*. She couldn't write her innermost thoughts with a real pen and risk someone's seeing it. And even if she wanted to write an online diary instead and encrypt it in secret code, the camp was an electronics-free zone, so she didn't have her computer. Tomorrow she would "borrow" a lemon and an onion from the camp's kitchen and make her own (smelly) invisible ink.

Daisy flopped back onto the bed and thought for the hundredth time how lucky AJ was right now. He got to hang out in his totally awesome tricked-out RV a mile down the road from the camp, watching TV till all hours of the night, while she was stuck in this drafty cabin, where a trickle of brown water passed for a shower and the smell of artificially scented coconut sunscreen always hung heavily in the air. When she got older, she'd get the cushy jobs.

Ah, who was she kidding. She'd be bored and a little creeped out living alone in the woods for weeks. But at least AJ had real running water in his RV, and both eggs and milk that weren't from powder. And he didn't have to pretend he loved to make birdhouses out of Popsicle sticks.

Daisy checked her watch. It was still too early to sneak out and meet him. She had to wait until even the counselors were asleep, and she'd discovered they did their own share of sneaking out of the cabins after lights out. She didn't blame them; having to pretend to be cheery and full of camp spirit all day couldn't be easy. Although as someone who pretended for a living, she knew most of them really were cheery and full of camp spirit, which, frankly, she found annoying.

While she waited for a safe time to go, Daisy allowed herself to drift into a sort of half sleep. She had trained herself to literally sleep with one eye open (it involved light meditation and wearing an eye patch), and whenever she was on a mission, that was how she slept.

After a few hours her pillow buzzed. She ripped off the eye patch. Finally some action! The spot they were watching was technically on camp property, but maybe AJ had seen something through his night-vision goggles/binoculars. (He couldn't see in the dark as well as she could, a fact that Daisy couldn't help pointing out whenever she saw him wearing those bulky things.)

She reached under the pillow and pulled out the fake book with her vid com hidden inside. She never claimed to have left *all* her gadgets at home. She needed to be able to reach the outside world, and the ear transceiver she usually wore wasn't meant for long jobs like this one. Most devices wouldn't get a signal in a place as remote as Camp Tumbleweed, but her vid com supposedly could work at the top of Mount Everest or at the bottom of the ocean. One day she planned to test that claim.

But now she threw the blanket over her head and made sure it was fully draped around her. A noise canceler was hidden between the thick layers of cotton. Soft *and* practical.

She switched on the screen, expecting to see AJ either in his RV or out in the woods. Hopefully he had news on the drop they'd been waiting for. Neither of them had any idea of what the item was for or what it looked like, but their job was to wait for its arrival, follow the instructions inside, and pass it on to the next dead drop, where another spy would retrieve it. *Please be good news*, she chanted silently.

But instead of seeing AJ's familiar face, she found herself peering into a small, well-lit room that she didn't recognize. Plastic bins and cardboard boxes lined the walls. Clothes and books and general household items were strewn all over the white marble floor. A familiar face popped up in the midst of the mess, and it wasn't AJ's.

CHAPTER TWO

Daisy groaned. "Philip Ransford the Third!" she said, using her best scolding voice. "I distinctly remember telling you not to contact me unless (A) you were on fire or (B) you were kidnapped and being held for ransom. I can clearly see you're not being held against your will, although I bet any kidnappers would quickly get tired of you and dump you back home. So that only leaves option A."

In response Philip held up a tangled ball of purple yarn with two knitting needles stuck at crooked angles. "What am I supposed to do with this?" he asked.

Ignoring his question, Daisy asked, "Well? Are you?"

"Am I what?" He tried to yank out one of the needles. There were still stitches attached to the bundle of yarn, so he didn't get very far.

Daisy asked matter-of-factly, "Are. You. On. Fire?"

"Not currently," Philip admitted. He dropped the yarn onto the floor beside him, then thought better of it and placed it on top of one of the few unopened boxes. "Would it help if I lit something *else* on fire?" He reached for a box at his feet and tilted it so she could see the contents. Candles of all colors and shapes toppled forward. He began rummaging through it. "I bet there's an old pack of matches in here somewhere."

"Please don't," Daisy said. "I don't want to be responsible for you burning your house down. Your fingers aren't that nimble. Remember the powdered-sugar incident?"

"Ruined a perfectly good tie that day," Philip grumbled, pushing the box away from him and standing up.

"I wouldn't feel too bad about that. It wasn't very nice."

He grinned. "You remember my tie?"

She felt her cheeks warm and hastily replied, "I'm a spy! It's my job to remember details. And I happen to remember you wore a particularly ugly tie that first day. The second day, too, if we're being honest here."

"Is this one any better?" He tilted the lens on his video communicator (she was now doubting her decision to give him his own device) and held up a blue tie with tiny yellow dots.

"It's the middle of the night!" Daisy reminded him in a loud whisper. "Why are you wearing a tie? That's a little weird, even for you."

"My dad dragged me to a fancy dinner thing tonight," he replied, letting the tie fall back into place. "It was supposed to be for charity, but from what I could see, it was really a chance for him to make some business deals. He did buy me a new suit, so it wasn't all bad." He moved the screen farther away and panned down to show off a black suit with silver buttons on the jacket.

"Okay, enough of the fashion show," Daisy said, growing impatient. Soundproof blanket or not, she didn't want to risk getting caught for something unrelated to the mission. "Why are you calling me?"

Instead of answering, he asked, "Where are you? It's so dark. Can I guess?"

"No."

"Are you hiding out from pirates, deep in an underground cave?"

"No." She considered slipping on her eye patch but didn't want to encourage him.

He reached into one of his boxes and lifted out an old-fashioned pink telephone with a twisty rubber cord hanging down. "I've got it! You're in a tunnel, tapping into telephone wires so you can over-hear the conversation of someone suspected of selling government secrets. Right?"

"Yes!" she replied. "That's exactly it."

"Really?" he said, perking up.

"Of course not," she snapped. But she couldn't help smiling back. Even though he'd changed so much and she no longer wanted to strangle him (usually), it still caught her off guard when he smiled. "Plus you'd be the last person I'd tell. You've already blown my cover twice!"

Philip placed the old phone down next to the bundle of yarn. "That's not really fair to say. You blew your own cover at the factory. With the old spelling-bee thing. I was just playing my violin in the music room, which was supposed to be private, and I walk out to find some random girl who didn't even go to my school stealing the spelling-bee words I'd studied for a year. Plus I was only nine years old. Can you blame me?"

"Yes," she replied. "But I forgive you. It's not your fault you play the violin so well that I thought someone had left on a recording of a famous violinist. I would have been more stealth if I thought you were real."

"I'm just that good." Philip said it jokingly, but he really *was* that good. He just didn't know it, or couldn't admit it to himself. But Daisy was not planning on feeding his otherwise very healthy ego in the middle of the night. She checked the time on the top of the screen.

"Philip, I've got to go. Why did you really call me?"

He reached for the ball of yarn and held it up again. "For this. I told you—I need you to tell me what to do with it."

Daisy exhaled loudly. "How should I know? Make a sweater or something!"

He looked at the ball thoughtfully. "Really?"

"Sure, why not. Knitting is very relaxing. You don't see too many stressed-out old ladies, do you?"

"I guess not," he agreed.

"Okay, well, good seeing you," she said. "Gotta go put the last pieces of wire together so I can start gathering all those government secrets."

"Wait," Philip said, moving nearer to his screen. This close up, Daisy could see the red mark under his chin that he got from holding a violin against his neck. He usually tried to hide it, but she could spot it peeking out from his shirt collar. She didn't know how Philip's own father hadn't noticed it all these years when Philip played. From what little she knew of Mr. Ransford, he didn't seem to pay much attention to anyone unless he made money out of it. She was too busy watching the red mark bobble as Philip spoke to actually hear what he was saying. "Sorry, what?" she asked.

"I said, are you going to the factory Tuesday for the Kickoff?" Philip repeated. "Everyone's making a really big fuss about the first Harmonicandy coming off the conveyor belt, like it's the first time they've seen a chocolate bar. Every time I go over there, I can barely get past the chocolate fountain without people slapping me on the back and whooping."

"No offense," Daisy said, "but isn't that what you like? Having people fuss over you when you win something? I mean, you're the guy who used to wipe down his trophies every day until he could see his reflection in them."

"I shouldn't have told you that," he said, frowning.

"Probably not," she agreed. "But to be fair, you weren't thinking very clearly. You'd just eaten an entire Gummzilla and a Gummysaurus Rex to help settle Miles and Logan's bet about which type of giant gummy candy tastes better. You were totally hopped up on the sugar."

Philip chuckled. "It was a tie, as I recall." The red mark bobbled faster when he laughed, but she did her best to ignore it. "Hey," she said, "wouldn't you rather they praise you than grumble about you behind your back—you know, like they did when no one liked you?"

Philip didn't reply right away. Daisy knew it had been hard for him in the weeks following the contest. Every time they were at the factory, people were pleasant, but no one went out of their way to congratulate him, except Henry and Max, and Logan's parents, of course. Most of the workers felt too sad about Logan losing to be happy for Philip. Especially when Philip had been so obnoxious during the days leading up to the contest. Everyone would have been nicer to him sooner if they knew what Philip did to save the factory and all their jobs. But no one could ever know that.

"I'm not so sure," Philip replied honestly. "I almost preferred it when they gave me the cold shoulder. That's really what I deserve. Logan was the one who figured out how to hold the whole thing together, and Miles thought of the name, and you made the molds out of that supercool secret spy wax. Even Henry gave me most of the ingredients. It's not fair that I get all the credit."

"Philip Ransford the Third," Daisy said, nodding appreciatively, "I believe you have officially changed. I hope you don't go all soft on me, though. I still need someone to argue with. Logan and Miles are *way* too nice for that."

"Don't worry," he promised. "There's still plenty of obnoxious left in me."

Daisy grinned. "Glad to hear it. But really, none of us mind that you're the face of the Harmonicandy. You came up with the idea in the first place. I'm sure Logan would be embarrassed if he got any more attention. And Miles definitely got credit for the name, and now he's helping with the advertising slogan. I bet Mr. Sweet even offers him a job one day. As for me, a spy's job is to attract as little attention as possible. It's much better if I'm left out of it."

Philip didn't look entirely convinced, but his face was now slightly less scrunched up, so she considered her speech a success. "Now go knit a sock or something. I've got to go. You may want to consider taking a shower before bed. You look all shiny. And not in a good way."

Philip sniffed under his arm. "Meh. Could be worse."

Daisy cringed. Boys could be so gross.

"Over and out," Philip said. The screen went dark, and she pulled the blanket back off. She barely had enough time to take a gulp of fresh air before the screen buzzed again and AJ's face popped up. Judging by his rumpled hair and puffy eyes, he must have fallen asleep. Her spirits sank a bit. She always looked forward to being the one to scare him awake with stories about Yeti or Bigfoot being spotted in the woods. But someone, or something, must have beaten her to it. She became instantly alert. She threw the sound-proof blanket back over her head and asked, "What is it? Did you discover that Bigfoot is real and he's at your front door?"

"Meet me at the Tree of Life, Oopsa," he said, zipping up his sweatshirt and throwing on a baseball cap. "It's go time." He ducked out of view and then back in. "And as cool as that would be, it's not Bigfoot."

CHAPTER THREE

Daisy leapt off her bunk bed and landed soundlessly on the floor. She reached into her cubby for the basket each camper received to store her shampoo, deodorant, brush, and other assorted grooming supplies. She was pretty certain no one else's toothbrush holder contained a laser that could cut through steel. Or a shampoo bottle filled with a chemical powerful enough to wipe someone's fingerprints off their fingers. (She had to be careful not to use that one by mistake!)

She stuffed her supplies and her vid com into a small Camp Tumbleweed–issued backpack, grabbed her sneakers, and tiptoed toward the front door.

"No, Mommy! I want to do my homework, not play a game!"

Daisy froze, then relaxed. It was only Amy Lynn, talking in her sleep again. Last night she'd had a whole conversation with an imaginary teacher about the proper use of *lay* and *lie* in a sentence. Amy Lynn had never woken up, even though the debate got pretty heated. Daisy (who hadn't had much formal teaching in grammar) had actually learned something.

She held her breath until she was sure no one else had awoken, and then she reached into her sweatshirt for her ball of spy wax. In one swift move she rubbed it against the door hinges to stop any squeaks and slipped out into the crisp night mountain air.

Once clear of the bunk, she slid into her sneakers, flipped up the hood of her sweatshirt, and sprinted toward the thick woods behind the cabins. She knew the dead drop was located a hundred yards due east, but AJ had kept the exact location to himself. She hadn't minded. Standard protocol dictated that when working as a pair, each spy knew only part of the information. That way, if they were caught, the details of the mission would still be safe. Also, neither could turn double agent and sell the information to the enemy. Not that the two of them distrusted each other. The candy factory gig had proven that even though AJ drove Daisy crazy, he always had her back.

The sounds of chirping crickets and hooting owls accompanied Daisy as she raced along the camp's nature trail. She loved this time of night. The skies over Camp Tumbleweed were the darkest she'd ever seen, with only a crescent moon illuminating the landscape. They were so far from any city that no other lights competed with the stars. She made a mental note to ask Miles to teach her something about the constellations when she got home.

In a few minutes Daisy reached the giant rock that marked the end of the dirt trail, the farthest point that had been cleared into the forest. Campers—some likely long gone and grown up—had covered the rock with friendly graffiti (*Camp Tumbleweed 4 Ever*, *CT Rocks!*, *Girl Power!*, that sort of thing). She climbed up on it to get a better look at the rest of the woods.

The ground sloped down gradually from where she stood until it leveled out about a hundred yards away. She needed to wait for a signal from AJ before heading down into the woods. Even though she had excellent night vision, they *were* in the mountains after all, and that meant snakes, sleepy bears that didn't want to be disturbed, and poison oak (or its cousin, poison ivy). Nothing could ruin a summer faster than poison oak. Except a snake bite. Or a bear attack.

While she waited, Daisy switched her vid com to the night vision/binoculars setting and looked through the camera hole. It only took a minute to find AJ. He stood about halfway into the valley. He spotted her, too, and waved his arms in a big arc. With his huge night-vision goggles, he looked like a giant bug. She waved back. A few seconds later her vid com beeped. She jumped off the rock, switched the setting to infrared, and pointed it at the ground. After a little sweeping of the area, the device soon picked up the heat trail AJ had left for her to follow.

She stepped carefully off the path, being sure to keep to the invisible trail he'd laid out. The heat dots would dissolve within a few days, but she should only need to take this trip once. Her vid com would buzz if she strayed too far from the path, so she had to keep the device very steady in front of her. After a while she got into the groove of it and began to feel like a fairy-tale kid following bread crumbs. But these were high-tech spy bread crumbs, and if you ate them, your insides would burst into flame.

AJ had clearly scouted out this route during the day in preparation for calling her into action. Stepping on a stick could bring a predator running, but she saw maybe one stick every thirty yards. The pushed-down leaves and cleared undergrowth were also signs that he'd worked to make the trek as easy and safe for her as possible. He could have just left her to bushwhack her way in. She doubted she'd have thought to do the same for him.

Fifteen minutes and only two branches across the face later, she approached her destination. The tree itself was wide, with exposed roots that ran far out into the surrounding woods on all sides. It looked old and taller than the rest of the trees around it. AJ leaned against it as though hanging out in the deep woods in the middle of the night was no biggie. He looked less bug-like now that his goggles were dangling around his neck.

"Come here often?" she joked, tucking her device away. Even

though the RV was fitted with a camera and microphone that rose out of the top like a periscope on a submarine, AJ couldn't use it for this mission. Spies spying on other spies when both were on the same side was expressly forbidden and also seriously uncool. She knew he'd had to watch for the drop-off the old-fashioned way. Like, with his eyes. (Plus the superstrong night-vision goggles.)

"Every day for the last two weeks, in fact," AJ replied. "But sometime today they finally came." He pointed his flashlight at a tree about twenty feet away. Someone had drawn a red slash mark on the trunk at about eye level. Once they'd retrieved the item, Daisy or AJ would draw a slash in the other direction. Leaving a signpost at a dead drop was a basic rule of spying and just plain considerate. Still, many spies either got lazy or forgot this step. The fact that these guys had left one showed they were professional.

"So you've been hanging out with the wild animals in the middle of the woods in the dark every night?" she asked.

"All in a day's work," he said. "So do you see it?"

Daisy began circling the tree, running her fingers lightly over the rough bark, looking for the hollow area. That was the unspoken hiding place at a dead drop. Surprisingly, she couldn't find one.

He grinned and pointed up.

She craned her neck back to see past all the tall trees. "Are you trying to show me a constellation?" she asked. "I couldn't tell you the difference between Orion's Belt and Andromeda even if I wanted to."

"Well, one of those is a *galaxy*," he said, an edge of impatience in his voice. "And the other is a constellation not visible in this part of the world in the summer. Don't you remember when we were kids and we went along on that mission with your parents to the Native American reservation?"

Daisy looked back at him, shaking her head.

"You're sure? Remember the chief taught us how to find our location on the planet if we were ever lost?"

"Turn on the GPS?" she suggested.

He shook his head. "Find the North Star."

Try as she might, no memory of stargazing with a Native American chief came back to her. "How old was I when this supposedly went down?"

He hesitated for a few seconds (a few seconds too long, which always made her suspicious). "You were only two or three. So of course you were too young to remember. Sorry."

A little chill went through her, and she pulled her sweatshirt tighter around her. "Are we here to talk about the stars or to pick up a package?"

"Package," he said firmly. "Which is what I was trying to show you." He pointed again at the tree. This time she lowered her gaze from the stars to the treetop until she spotted it, sitting about forty feet above their heads.

"A birdhouse?" she asked, taking a step back to see better. It looked like a more professional version of the ones she'd had to make in arts and crafts.

"Watch out," AJ called, grabbing her. "You almost stepped in that."

Daisy looked down. A pile of bear poop lay inches away from her foot. "Yuck, thanks."

"Yes, it's a birdhouse," AJ said. "But take my word for it—yesterday that branch was empty."

"So you're telling me the package we've been waiting two weeks for, the supersecret information that we're getting paid big bucks to deliver to the next dead drop, is stuck up in what might be the tallest tree I've ever seen?"

He nodded. "Sure looks that way."

"Fab." Daisy tossed her backpack to AJ. "Hold this while I climb." She kicked off her sneakers and approached the tree. The branches didn't begin until at least twenty feet above the ground, so she'd have to shinny up to that point. Unfortunately, the trunk was so wide she'd never be able to wrap her legs around it. She ran her fingers over the bark, trying to decide if it was worth using up her spy wax to try to make rungs that she could climb like a ladder. Or maybe her laser could melt away chunks of the bark to create tiny finger- and toeholds. That would take hours, though, and it would be bright. She was about to ask AJ if he had anything in his sack that would help, when she encountered something smooth under her palm. She stepped back and peered at the area more closely. Something was wound around the tree! At first she felt a pang of fear— *poison ivy winds around tree trunks!* But that kind of poison ivy rope was fuzzy, and this was smooth. Well, if it was poison ivy, the damage was already done, so she gave a little tug. The tree-colored rope easily pulled away from the trunk.

"AJ! There's a rope! I think it connects to the box like a pulley!" She looked over at AJ excitedly. He had his back to her, and his shoulders were heaving.

He was laughing!

She put her hands on her hips. "Let me guess, Aaron Jacob Whatever-Your-Real-Last-Name-Is, you knew there was a rope."

AJ turned around, wiping a tear from his eye. "I just wanted to see how committed you are to your job. You were really going to climb this gigantic tree in the pitch-dark? Without a harness?"

Daisy puffed out her cheeks. "I was still working on a plan, if you must know. But c'mon, let's get to it. I want to go home."

AJ tipped his baseball cap at her. "My hat is off to your bravery, Oopsa Daisy Dinkleman."

"Don't call me Oopsa! Or Dinkleman." But truth be told, she was starting not to mind his big-brother-like teasing as much as she used to.

They gently pulled on the rope until the birdhouse began to tip forward off the branch. Then they slid the rope through their

hands. The birdhouse started to descend, bumping occasionally into the trunk, until it landed safely in AJ's hands. He quickly
untied it and set about inspecting it while Daisy pulled the empty
rope the rest of the way down. She wound it up in a ball and stuffed
it into her backpack.

"The spies who left this for us have a strange sense of humor," he
commented, turning it over and over in his hands. "There's no way
to open this thing."

Daisy looked closely. Solid wood. No Popsicle sticks and glue here.
No opening for a bird to sit in, either. She shook it gently, hearing a
faint clink as something bounced off its walls. She knew they couldn't
force it open or slice it with their lasers. Not without risking damage
to whatever had been placed inside. "They must have left us a clue."

AJ turned the birdhouse upside down, but nothing was written
on the bottom. When he flipped it back over, Daisy noticed that the
chimney wobbled a bit. She reached one pinky inside and slid out a
tightly rolled piece of paper covered in jumbled-up letters. She and
AJ huddled on the ground and spread it out, careful to stay clear of
the gift from the bear.

"A straw wrapper?" Daisy said, for surely that's what lay before
them. But from what Daisy could tell, none of the letters formed
any recognizable words. No punctuation, either. "How is this supposed to help us?" she asked.

"It's a scytale," AJ replied.

"An Italy?"

"A *scytale*," AJ repeated. "It might *rhyme* with Italy, but it was
the Greeks who used scytales to pass secret information back and
forth. It's basically a note written in code. We need to find a stick
exactly the right size. Then we roll the paper around the stick, and
the letters will line up and form words."

She rocked back on her heels. "Really? That's a thing? How
come I've never heard of it?"

He shrugged. "I do have a few more years of experience than you do, you know."

"I don't think they had straw wrappers back in ancient times," Daisy pointed out.

"I guess our fellow spies didn't have vellum or papyrus to write on. The point is, if you don't have the right-size stick, you can't read it."

"Then how are we going to read it?"

AJ put his night-vision goggles back on. "We're going to find the right-size stick."

CHAPTER FOUR

Three quarters of an inch," AJ declared, tossing the stick over his shoulder, where it lodged in a bush. "Too thick."

"You don't even want to test it? Let me put the paper around it, at least."

"Be my guest," AJ replied, reaching for the next stick they'd gathered from the woods. "But we need to beat the sunrise, or your camp is going to go on full alert when they find the lovely Ava Simon missing from her bed."

"Fine, I trust you," Daisy said. "Even though you never mentioned your ability to judge the circumference of a stick simply by rolling it through your fingers."

AJ grinned and tossed the latest stick over his shoulder. "Never had much use for it till now." He held out his hand, and she placed the next stick in it. "Actually, I have your father to thank for teaching me."

"My father?" Daisy repeated. She knew that her parents and AJ had spent a lot of time together without her—some of it before she was even born—and she always enjoyed hearing him talk about it. It didn't make her jealous. Well, maybe a tiny bit.

"Twelve millimeters," AJ said, handing the stick back. "Too small. We need closer to fourteen millimeters."

"I think you're enjoying this a little too much," Daisy accused, holding out the fourth stick, so thin it was more of a twig, really. It didn't look any different from the last one. "So you were saying? About my dad?"

"Right," AJ said, taking the stick from her. "A few years ago your dad and I were on a mission together. He was undercover as a carpenter, and I was his apprentice. We both found we loved building things with our hands. That's why I gave you the last name Carpenter for the candy factory assignment, by the way. So we—"

"Wait, *you* make up my names?"

"Sometimes," he said. "Why, don't you like them?"

"They're fine," she said. "It's just that I wondered why Grammy let me keep Daisy as my first name on that gig. But that was your decision?"

He nodded, his fingers still judging the twig. "I thought you deserved it."

She wasn't sure what he meant by that. It almost sounded like he felt sorry for her, which would drive her crazy.

"Anyway," he continued before she could dig deeper, "we had to pretend to be master craftsmen at making these dowels that would go up staircases in these fancy houses. So your dad thought it would be more convincing if we could show off this skill. It made us so popular that they practically *handed* us the documents we'd come for." AJ held up the twig. "Fourteen millimeters exactly. Perfect." He picked up the paper and wound it around the twig, careful to line up each edge without overlapping.

Daisy could see the words appear before her, just as he'd promised.

"Oh! I get it now! Whoever wrote this wound the paper around a stick this same size, then wrote the note straight across. Then when you unwind it, it's impossible to read! I love it!"

"Yeah, it's pretty cool," AJ admitted. "Now let's see what they went to all this trouble to tell us." He turned his flashlight on at the lowest setting, and they hid the faint light with their bodies. He slowly rotated the stick until the only capital letter appeared in the first spot.

They both excelled at making and breaking codes and ciphers, so Daisy knew that, between the two of them, they would decipher this clue without too much trouble. When the kids in the mansion were growing up, Daisy's grandmother encouraged them to communicate with each other in code. (Except for the twins, Clarissa and Marissa, who were excused from the exercise, since they already had their own system of communicating.)

The others got pretty creative, though. Courtney could write upside-down as quickly as she could write the normal way. Daisy enjoyed leaving clues where the true meaning could only be discovered by pulling out the third letter of every word and stringing them together to form new words. AJ used to make up his own languages, complete with rules of grammar and punctuation. Daisy had always found the hand-drawn symbols he used in the place of letters to be pretty cool, but she doubted she ever told him that, since until recently every single thing he did seemed intended to bug her.

They all stopped writing in code when they got older, saving it for the occasional job when the ability came in handy. Daisy hadn't realized how much she missed it until she met Miles, who still spoke backward sometimes and made alphabets, too. Now, even though she and AJ were in a race against the sunrise, a part of her was excited to see how this one would challenge them.

She had expected a nearly unbreakable code, or a cipher so

sneaky it would take them days to figure it out. Instead, they got a nursery rhyme!

> *Greetings to my fellow spies*
> *it will come as no surprise*
> *we hid the key to this fine house*
> *in a space sized for a mouse*
> *but no mouse made this brown house*
> *if you don't know what to do*
> *our clue may be stuck to your shoe.*

When they finished reading the rhyme, Daisy and AJ looked at each other with matching expressions of disbelief. The note left little doubt as to the hiding place of the key. "They wouldn't," Daisy whispered. She was definitely reevaluating her first opinion of their professionalism. "Would they?"

AJ grimaced. "I think they might."

"Who *are* these people?" Daisy asked. "They really do have a very warped sense of humor."

He shrugged. "Maybe they got bored during their own stakeout and wanted to mix things up a bit."

She knew they were both stalling now, neither of them wanting to be the one to retrieve the key. "How many other spies do you think have passed along this same package?"

He shook his head. "No idea. We'll know more when we get the key."

"You mean when *you* get the key. Feels more like a man's job, don't you think?"

"Sure, the one time you act like you can't do something as well as me," AJ joked, but he grabbed one of the discarded sticks. He stood as far away from the pile of bear poop as possible and poked it with the stick. Daisy held her breath, assuming the stick would go right through. But to their surprise, the whole pile moved.

"It's fake!" she shouted, reaching for it.

"Or maybe it's just dried out and hardened," AJ warned just as she grabbed for it.

Daisy heard his words a second too late. Her fingers had already closed around it. She immediately dropped it, stepping back so it didn't land on her foot. It fell upside down, revealing a plastic bottom and the words *Open Me*.

"Phew!" Daisy decided then and there that she had to meet these spies. But right now she could see a glimmer of sunrise over the hilltops to the east. AJ would have to finish up here. "I'd better get to my bunk before anyone wakes up," she told him, slipping on her backpack. "Don't open the birdhouse without me." She quickly kicked up some leaves to make sure the spot didn't look disturbed. A good spy always cleaned up his or her tracks. "When everyone goes to breakfast, I'll pack up my bag and meet you at the RV." She flipped the setting on her vid com back to infrared and prepared to follow the heat dots back to the nature trail. She'd have to run from there to her bunk to make it on time.

"Nope," AJ said, grabbing the bottom of her sweatshirt. "You can't just ditch camp. They take the security of their campers very seriously. They'll have every police official in the state out looking for you."

"What do I do, then? No way you're going to tell me I'm stuck here till the end of summer, right?"

"No, of course not. We just need to figure out a way to spring you that's on the up and up."

The story of AJ and her father was fresh in Daisy's mind. It gave her an idea. "I can say I'm homesick. That I miss my dad and want to see him. If I cry, they have to send me home, right? It's sleepaway camp, not jail."

AJ stuffed the birdhouse and the fake poop into his sack and hoisted it over his shoulder. "Give it a try," he said. "The camp has listed me as your legal guardian, so I'll be there to pick you up."

With that, he walked off into the sunrise. She turned in the opposite direction and ran all the way back to her bunk. She slid into bed exactly thirty-two seconds before the loudspeaker clicked on and the camp director (always sounding way too cheery for the early hour) shouted, *"Rise and shine, everyone! It's going to be a beautiful day!"*

CHAPTER FIVE

Monday

Turns out they don't send you home from camp for being homesick, even if you cry actual tears and move your shoulders up and down at the same time. What they do is send you to "Aunt" Jess, the warm and fuzzy camp director with the single braid down her back, who gives you a nice cup of lemonade and a long hug and tells you that keeping busy and not thinking about home is the best cure.

Daisy was not the least bit happy with this turn of events. She emptied her last sip of lemonade onto the grass outside the camp director's cabin and stormed back to her own in a huff. How had that not worked? She wasn't used to being brushed off and dismissed so quickly. Were her acting skills not good enough? Not possible. She'd once convinced a Boy Scout troop that she was an Eagle Scout named Bill so she could get access to a storeroom of stolen goods. If Aunt Jess wanted a challenge, a challenge she was going to get.

Twenty minutes later, while her bunkmates were busy painting banners for the upcoming Color War, Daisy dipped a thin paintbrush into the red paint and dotted it on her arms and a little on her cheeks. She waved her arms and fanned her face until the spots of paint crusted a bit. Then she told her counselor she needed to go to the nurse.

As she passed the dining hall, she decided to make a quick detour for one more item. Three minutes later, she stood before Nurse Becky, a grandmotherly woman who was always chasing after the campers with bottles of sunscreen. If there was a weak link in Camp Tumbleweed's defenses, it would be Becky.

"I have chicken pox," Daisy announced as the screen door banged shut behind her. Nurse Becky looked up from restocking a bin of bandages. Daisy began to scratch at top speed. She figured if her arms moved fast enough, the nurse couldn't get a good look at the dots of red paint. "I need to go home before I give it to everyone at camp."

"Odd," the nurse said. "I haven't seen chicken pox in a number of years." She squinted at Daisy's cheeks without quite the level of concern Daisy had hoped for. Detecting a note of doubt in the woman's voice, Daisy ramped up the scratching, careful to avoid scraping off the dried paint. "Well, I'd better let you get back to the nursing," she said, waving her hand vaguely around the totally empty cabin as she scratched. "If you could let Aunt Jess know while I go pack my bags, that'd be great. Thanks." She turned to go.

"One moment," Nurse Becky said, blocking her way. She held up a white tube. "Let me put something on you to soothe the itch."

"No, really, it's okay," Daisy said, but Becky reached out and squeezed a few drops onto her arm anyway. The situation went downhill from there as the paint smeared under the slippery lotion.

"Weird!" Daisy said, rubbing her hand over her arm. "Didn't know that could happen. Guess it wasn't chicken pox after all."

"Guess not," the nurse agreed.

Neither moved. Then Daisy began to scratch again, only this time it was her scalp. "I forgot to mention," she said, pointing to her hair, "I also have lice. Better not get too close. People say they can't jump, but I'm not so sure."

"I'll take my chances," the nurse said, grabbing a comb and a magnifying glass.

Daisy began to fling her hair back and forth so the nurse couldn't get a good look. The woman took a step back, and Daisy's hopes rose. Maybe Nurse Becky would actually let her go. But then the nurse's face squished up and she sneezed. And sneezed. And sneezed again as the black pepper Daisy had shaken onto her scalp floated down around them.

Daisy felt her own nose begin to tingle. *Don't sneeze, don't sneeze*, she told herself. Years of having to remain absolutely quiet on various secret missions had trained her well. She knew the steps. With her back still turned to the sneezing nurse, she pinched her nostrils, tugged on her nose, and pressed her tongue against her top teeth. With her free hand, she wiggled her earlobe.

In between sneezes, the no-longer-even-pretending-to-be-nice nurse told Daisy that Aunt Jess would find her later to "discuss the situation."

Daisy had no choice but to rejoin her group, now having swim lessons down at the lake. She sat on the wooden dock, hugging her knees in frustration. In ten minutes flat she could swim under the entire lake, surface on the other side, have AJ meet her there, and never look back. It was extremely tempting, but she knew AJ was right. It was time to move on to plan B—getting kicked out. She had to tell AJ she needed a little more time.

Even though her vid com was securely hidden inside the binding of a book (not the romance book she'd used at the factory; she'd gotten enough grief for that one from the boys), she still never risked carrying it around with her during the day. AJ had come up with a much safer way for them to communicate. She ran up to the hill behind the tennis courts and flashed her laser pointer onto the satellite dish. In Morse code she spelled out *Need more time. Have plan.* The tilt of the dish reflected the signal all the way to the driver's-side mirror of AJ's RV.

A few seconds later, AJ replied. *Hurry.*

Thanks to a particularly nasty stomach bug that went around the mansion when she was ten, leaving the kids with no choice but to sit around watching old movies, Daisy knew the perfect prank that would be guaranteed to get her kicked out of camp. It had backfired on the characters in the movie, but they didn't have her training.

It only took ten minutes to gather the supplies she needed. She still had the rope from the dead drop. The art room provided the little feathers (normally used to decorate art projects), and she had seen where the kitchen staff stored the honey when she was there earlier for the pepper.

The plan would have worked, too, if her vid com hadn't gone off just as she was about to string up the bucket of honey. It beeped so loudly that, even though the device was buried in her duffel bag, the sound was nearly ear piercing. She must have switched the volume all the way up by mistake while packing it away. She was so startled that she let go of the pulley that held the bucket of honey over the rafters. The bucket flew down toward her, spilling the honey as it went, splattering all over the floor of the cabin and leaving her soaked.

She'd already packed her duffel and slipped it under the bed so she could grab it at a moment's notice. Now she lunged for it, landing right on the bag of feathers behind her. The bag burst open with a loud *poof.* Just enough feathers rose up in the air to stick to her cheeks and hair. She wanted to cry. *But spies don't cry. They think on their feet and they move forward, always forward.*

She knew the noise would attract visitors any second, so she slid the duffel out and fumbled for the zipper. When she grabbed the vid com and flipped open the cover, she knew before looking who was on the other end. Even without being in the room, the boy managed to mess up her plans. *Again.*

With sticky fingers, she turned on the audio feed but made sure the camera was off. She would never live it down if he saw her like this. "You have thirty seconds," she snapped. She was *definitely* taking his vid com away when she saw him again. "This'd better be good."

Philip blurted out his problem of the day while Daisy knelt and scrubbed at the floor. He sounded so worked up that she finally agreed to help him. It may not have been the best advice, but she was not in a particularly helpful mood. Her bunkmates would return soon and find this mess. She spent one more minute on the vid com following up on what she promised Philip she'd do for him, then switched the camera back on and called AJ. "I know I'm not supposed to risk using this during the day," she blurted out before he could comment. "But plan B was a bust."

"I guessed that from your appearance," he said.

She figured she deserved that, so she didn't argue. "I'm initiating plan C. You'll have to show up and tell them I'm needed at home."

"Cousin Bo to the rescue. Over and out."

She sighed and tucked the book back in the duffel. That Cousin Bo thing wasn't showing any signs of going away. At least he didn't give her a hard time. A few months ago he would have.

After a glance around at the mess she'd made of the bunk, she closed her eyes. She could have skipped plans A and B and gone straight to C from the beginning. Why had she thought she needed to prove something? To her grandmother? To herself?

She needed to calm down. She crossed her legs and took four deep breaths in through her nose and out through her mouth, the way her grandmother had taught her. Soon enough they'd be sitting together in the Zen garden, and she hoped they'd be laughing about all this.

Feeling a little bit better, she carefully tipped out some of the dissolving solution from her fake shampoo bottle, and the sticky honey sizzled and disappeared, taking a bit of the wooden flooring with it. Too bad it would also peel off a layer of skin if she tried it on herself. Maybe, in hindsight, it hadn't been such a good idea to store it in the shampoo bottle, even though it had been reinforced with fireproof plastic. She debated taking a shower, but AJ always got places faster than she thought possible. He was probably already in the camp director's office.

She pulled the hood of her camp sweatshirt over her head to cover as much of her face as possible. It was an odd look in the heat of the day, but better than having to explain why Ava Simon was covered in honey and feathers.

She slung her duffel bag over her shoulder and shoved the bucket and the feathers as far under the bunk bed as they would go. Hopefully they wouldn't be discovered until the cleaning crew came at the end of the summer. Otherwise her fellow bunkmates would have fun trying to guess their purpose. She could wait in the bunk until AJ arrived or until she was called into Aunt Jess's office, but she didn't have it in her to be Ava Simon for even one more minute.

Daisy took one last look at the place she'd called home for two weeks and opened the door to peek outside. One of the groups must have been toasting marshmallows, because a slightly sweet, slightly burned smell hung in the air. Camp Tumbleweed clearly didn't get the message that campfires should be a nighttime thing. She inhaled deeply. It reminded her of the factory, and of Henry in particular. After the contest he had pulled her aside and thanked her for everything she'd done for the boys and for the factory. No one had ever thanked her after a job before, but of course no one had ever known she was a spy before. Still, it had meant a lot to her.

Her throat tightened, and she felt a little pang in her chest. No need to have pretended earlier—she really *was* homesick!

Campers were now approaching from all sides, streaming toward the dining hall. She scooted out and ducked behind various trees until she had a clear shot down the nature trail to the mound with the satellite dish. Besides being a great place to bounce signals off, it was the only place in camp where she could hide while still being able to see what was going on.

Using her duffel as a pillow, she lay down in the shadow of the dish, waiting for AJ's signal to flash. She hoped it would come soon or she just might fall asleep. When she didn't have to sleep with one eye open, Daisy believed in getting a good, solid nine hours. The ride home would take a day or two, and then bed. Her own bed. Ah, how nice it would be to slip into her supersoft Egyptian cotton sheets, sink into the mattress that molded to her body, and hug the pillow that cradled her head so gently it felt like floating on a cloud.

Her vid com screamed again, and her peaceful daydream burst. Hadn't she turned the volume down? She *really* had to focus. She grabbed for it, being sure to keep the camera turned off on her end. She knew she should be annoyed that Philip was calling *again*, but she was in too good a mood. Even the fact that flies had begun circling her head couldn't bother her. As long as they didn't actually stick to the honey. That would take things to a whole new level.

"What is the nature of your emergency?" she joked.

But it turned out to be Miles's face smiling back at her, not Philip's. She sat up. She started to tell him about the scytale and the stick, but a loud noise on his end cut her off. It was just as well, because two counselors had just parked themselves on the nature trail not twenty feet behind her and were now arguing over who'd flirted with whom during the morning meeting. From what Daisy gathered, the guy had flirted with the drama counselor, who was also the girl's best friend. Not cool, dude. But what did she know about the world of romance? Blissfully, nothing. (Except the occasional stories the older girls in the mansion whispered to each other late at night. They always stopped when she appeared, though, probably worried she'd go and tell her grandmother, who had a strict no-dating rule. Daisy wouldn't tell, of course, but being the boss's granddaughter was a burden she was well used to.)

She told Miles how to switch his vid com to silent mode, and she pressed the button on her own. It was a good thing she could read lips, since every time Miles tried to say something, it came out garbled on her screen. When she pointed it out, he giggled and said, *Sorry! Will tie farther. Here's the bing, so you know how bee and my parents are cheese?*

Daisy would have laughed at how his words were translated, but she quickly realized the serious nature of his call when he started talking about his dad. She screened out the lovers' squabble taking place between the counselors and focused on how to help Miles. She felt a little weird giving advice on family matters seeing as her own family situation was so unusual, but it seemed to be helping. She'd just thanked him for his great suggestion on how to break her out and sent the photo when AJ appeared at her side, causing her to yelp. How did he *do* that?

He tipped his cowboy hat at her (yes, he was wearing a cowboy hat) and said, "Howdy, ma'am. Bo Dinkleman here to rescue you."

"One minute," she whispered, pointing to her screen.

AJ shooed the flies away while she finished up with Miles. After they hung up—or rather, after he tossed his book in the air and it shut off automatically—AJ grinned at her. "You have a soft spot for Miles. You knew we already had a plan to get you out of here, and yet you let him think he came up with it."

She tucked the book away and stood. "That kid built a whole world for me in the afterlife. Building up his confidence is the least I can do. So you sprang me?"

"Yup. Wasn't as hard as I'd expected."

She grinned. "I may have worn them down."

AJ opened his mouth to reply but sneezed twice instead. "I must be allergic to something."

"Could be the black pepper I sprinkled in my hair," Daisy suggested.

"Fake lice?" he asked, peering at her head.

"Yup. I even added some salt. You know, for the eggs."

He nodded. "Very thorough."

"Didn't work, though." They made their way down the mound, back toward the nature trail. Daisy looked around. "What happened to Romeo and Juliet? Last I heard, the guy was declaring his undying love."

AJ shrugged. "The girl must have spotted me and dumped the poor guy. Being this handsome ain't easy." Daisy tried to kick him, but he was too fast for her.

He grabbed her duffel from her shoulder and hoisted it onto his own. She almost complained—after all, she could carry ten of those and not break a sweat. But he was being nice, and that was rare enough.

"C'mon, Oopsa," he said. "Let's go see what's waiting for us inside that birdhouse."

CHAPTER SIX

Daisy sat on the edge of the surprisingly soft RV bed and ran a comb through her wet hair. She was not completely convinced that all the gooey honey and itchy salt and pepper had been rinsed out. She could have stayed in that shower for hours, but AJ had warned her the RV stored only enough hot water for ten minutes. Still, she felt much cleaner than at any time since her life as a camper had begun.

Plus the honey made her hair feel really soft.

AJ had left out a pair of his own sweatpants and a T-shirt for her so she wouldn't have to put on any of her grimy camp clothes again. His clothes were too big, but they were soft and cozy and smelled like the fabric softener Mrs. Peterson used on their laundry back at the mansion.

She allowed herself to flop backward, intending to rest for only a minute or two. But the plush mattress and the feather pillow proved impossible to resist, and her almost total lack of sleep the night before couldn't be ignored. Her eyelids closed, and she didn't fight it.

It felt like only five minutes had passed when AJ's voice over the intercom woke her, but a quick glance at the position of the sun outside her window told her she'd been asleep a few hours. It must be nearly dinnertime, and from what she could tell by the changing countryside, they had covered a lot of ground already.

AJ's voice came through the speaker again. "Wake up, Sleeping Beauty. Come out after you dry the drool off your chin."

Her eyes darted to the walls, then the ceiling. Was there a *camera* in the bedroom? Then she wiped at her chin. No drool. "Very funny," she grumbled. But she got up and grabbed her backpack from where she'd stashed it in the closet. It took her a moment to find it among the shelves full of hats, glasses, wigs, fake beards, foam, shoes, dresses, suits, and everything in between. If they ever needed a snap cover (or what a non-spy would call a last-minute disguise), they would have plenty to choose from.

The closet didn't look large enough to hold as much as it did. But the whole RV was like that. It was much bigger on the inside than it appeared from the outside. When the vehicle was parked, a simple press of a button pushed out both side walls a good five feet, expanding the floor to twice its current width. AJ didn't need anything so fancy for their straightforward dead-drop mission, but he'd convinced the guys in Research and Development that someone should take it for a test run before it was called into duty for a really big job. AJ could be very persuasive. She wasn't surprised that they'd given it to him.

She reached into the closet for an old stovepipe hat, the kind Abraham Lincoln was always pictured wearing. She plopped it on her head and headed out.

To anyone driving by, the RV looked like an ordinary motorhome a family would take camping. But there was nothing ordinary about it. The ride was so smooth that even when zooming down the highway, they barely felt like they were moving at all. It had been fully outfitted with everything a spy could possibly need, as well as many things Daisy hoped they'd never need—like the tubes that could pump oil or smoke out behind them in case they were being chased, and the cabinet lined with five inches of steel in case they needed to defuse a suspicious package. She hesitated a moment, wondering if they should have put the birdhouse in the cabinet for safekeeping. Maybe the whole dead drop had been a trick to foil their plans by blowing them up! Well, too late now.

The bedroom was all the way in the rear, so she needed to walk the length of the vehicle to reach AJ. She passed through the kitchen, with its gleaming, full-sized appliances and six-person booth for eating, followed by a small washer and dryer (which now held her honey-soaked clothes, and which she doubted AJ had used once in the whole two weeks), and then the bookshelves, where half of the books were real and the other half hid secret compartments of various sizes.

The entertainment area, with a huge TV screen and gaming consoles and a long, comfy couch, came next, then a climbing wall, which seemed like a strange thing to have, since the ceiling was only a few feet above their heads. Drawers and cabinets filled the rest of the empty space on the walls, probably filled with boring things like maps and spare parts and repair manuals. In the front, a wide, comfortable-looking seat sat next to the driver's seat, with another row of two seats behind them.

Other than the bedroom, she didn't see anywhere to sleep, which didn't seem very practical for long stakeouts with more than one person. Daisy swung her backpack onto the chair behind AJ and plopped down in the passenger seat. "Dibs on the bedroom tonight," she said. "You can have the couch."

Without glancing away from the highway, AJ said, "There's a rest stop coming up in a mile. I'll pull in there, and we can open the box. We need to figure out the next part of the mission."

She rubbed her eyes and yawned. "Aren't we going home first?"

He nodded. "Only for a day or two. I need to return this beast to R and D, and I'm sure your grandmother will want to see you. But then it's back on the road." He patted the steering wheel lovingly. "I'll miss you, my cool little tricked-out RV."

"Hardly little," she murmured as the RV made a wide turn into the rest stop. AJ pulled up alongside a big rig and turned off the engine.

He stood up and stretched. "Okay, hand it over," he said, holding out his hand.

"Hand what over?" she replied.

"The birdhouse. I know you took it and hid it before your shower."

"What makes you say that?"

"Because I've known you for thirteen years. It's in your pack, isn't it?"

Daisy glanced over at her backpack, which indeed hid the birdhouse—and not very well, since the square edges clearly bulged out. She'd known AJ wouldn't wait much longer to open it, and after all the trouble they'd gone to in order to get it, she hadn't wanted to miss out on the best part.

"Oh, so that's what that is," Daisy said, feigning innocence as she pretended to struggle with the weight of her backpack as she lifted it onto her lap. "I wondered why my pack had gotten so heavy."

"I'm sure," he said, and fished the fake poop out of his jacket pocket. In the light of day Daisy could see how fake it truly looked, with its rough edges and an inch-long slit cut out of the top. She leaned closer. It looked like a piggy bank! Sure enough, AJ turned the container over to reveal a round rubber lid where money would normally drop out. Below where the spies had written *Open Me*, she could now see small printed letters that spelled out *Poop happens, so save those pennies!* Miles and Logan would no doubt think it was hysterical. She had to admit it was pretty funny.

AJ rolled his eyes. "Let's just get the key." He pried open the lid and shook the hole over his hand. Daisy expected to hear the clanking of a key but didn't hear anything. "Is it empty?" she asked, preparing to be *really* annoyed.

AJ shook his head. "I can feel something hitting the sides." He reached his finger in and, after fishing around for a few seconds, pulled out a rolled-up slip of paper.

Daisy groaned. "Not another scytale! We don't have any sticks!"

AJ unrolled the unlined paper and held it up. This piece didn't have a stream of random letters printed along it like the other. In fact, it was completely blank. He handed it to Daisy, who turned it over to inspect both sides. The unmistakable odor of onion mixed with sour milk wafted up.

She wrinkled her nose. "Invisible ink."

"Really?" AJ said, taking the paper back. "How could you tell?"

"Don't you smell it?" she asked.

He shook his head. "Lost my sense of smell last month after that gig I had at the power plant." He held the paper right up to his nose and sniffed deeply before shaking his head again. "Not a thing."

Daisy looked at him with surprise. "So when you took me to the factory before camp to say goodbye to Logan, you couldn't smell the chocolate air?"

"Nope."

"That stinks," she said.

"Sadly, I wouldn't know."

She took the paper from him. "Maybe in exchange for taking your sense of smell, the power plant gave you special powers, like a superhero." She narrowed her eyes at him suspiciously. "You do move awfully fast. Maybe you have superspeed. Can you turn invisible?"

"I cannot."

"Can you melt your bones and slip under locked doors and then re-inflate on the other side?"

AJ didn't even respond to that one. He only said, "Don't tell your grandmother. Spies are supposed to have heightened senses—all of their senses."

"I won't," Daisy promised. He was right. They'd gone through extensive training to strengthen their eyes and ears, and their fingertips were so sensitive that reading Braille would be easy. They could even identify poisons that to everyone else were odorless and tasteless. But now AJ couldn't do that. She felt a shiver of fear for him. "Is it permanent?" she asked.

"I hope not, but none of the special nose doctors I went to would promise anything. I couldn't go to our regular doctor without it going on my chart."

"They have special nose doctors?"

"Sure."

AJ was definitely in a tough spot. "I'll just have to do the smelling for both of us, then," she declared.

She turned her attention back to the paper, running her fingertips lightly over the invisible message to figure out which side was faceup. Then she placed it on the nearly flat dashboard. The late-afternoon sun was still strong, and its heat would reveal the message soon enough. She didn't want to hold a flame to it and risk setting it on fire. The RV probably contained some high-tech way of doing it, but sometimes low tech was just as good, or even better. "Can we make it home tonight?" she asked AJ as he settled back into the driver's seat.

He shook his head. "We'll drive as far as we can before stopping for the night. Why don't you go get a jump on writing up the mission report."

It was more of an order than a suggestion, but Daisy didn't mind. She actually enjoyed writing up reports at the end of each gig. It made her feel grown up. Not that she often felt like a kid.

Her stomach rumbled when she sat down at the table. The

bowl of oatmeal she'd wolfed down at breakfast felt like ages ago. She popped back up to check out the contents of the fridge. The freezer compartment held only one item—a giant bag of ice. As for the fridge, besides a carton of milk and a hunk of cheese, all it contained were ham sandwiches wrapped in clear plastic. AJ may have stocked it with fruits and vegetables before he left, but either he'd eaten everything or he hadn't bothered to fill it in the first place. She'd have to talk to him about eating healthier on the road. It was very important for a spy to eat balanced meals. However, since her options were currently limited, she grabbed a donut and a bag of chips from the pantry. Then she poured herself a glass of milk to balance it out.

A small window above the sink gave her a view out the right side of the RV. Of course, the glass was tinted so no one could see inside. She leaned on her elbows and chomped her snacks, watching the farmhouses and rolling hills and cows go by. She thought of Logan and how she'd seen him sit so still sometimes, just gazing up at clouds or sketching a flower or a bug. His whole face would move and shift when he ate something. He drew the full flavor out of every bite. She wished she could be more like that, fully grabbing the life out of every moment. But after another minute at the window she was bored and settled in to write her report.

When she turned on the vid com, she immediately saw she'd missed four video calls while she was sleeping. And three of the four were marked URGENT.

CHAPTER SEVEN

Judging by the time listed next to each call, Philip had called first, followed by Logan, then Miles, then Grammy, all within a half hour of each other. Daisy glanced up at AJ, who had stuck on his cowboy hat and was singing along to the radio. He wouldn't notice if she snuck back to her bedroom to listen to the messages in private.

She debated playing her grandmother's message first out of respect, but hers was the only one without a red flashing URGENT sign next to it. Plus if she'd really needed to reach Daisy immediately, she would have called AJ, and AJ hadn't mentioned anything. So Daisy lay on her belly, propped the device on the pillow, and hit Play.

The pile of rubber ducks on the floor and the yellowish cast to the wall immediately gave Philip's location away. He was in that storage room in the factory, the one near the lab, where they'd prepared for the contest. She had to admit his hideout had its charms. He wore an expression she hadn't seen before—a little cautious, a little excited, a little rebellious.

"Daisy!" he barked. "Why aren't you picking up? Strangest thing. We're going on a road trip! I know you're at that camp, but you'd better get home and come with us. We leave tomorrow after the Kickoff. I really need some advice, too. I have to pretend that—"

Then a knock on the door made him turn away. He shouted, "I'll be right out." He returned to the screen and whispered, "I have to go. Call me back."

Daisy stared at the blank screen. Philip knew where she was? How could he possibly know that? And what kind of road trip was he going on? Hopefully Logan's message would tell her more.

She smiled as soon as his face came on-screen. He stood in the Tropical Room, grinning from ear to ear. He wore his long hair slightly differently than the last time she'd seen him. It fell over the corner of his left eye and hid some of the scars that ran alongside it. She wondered if that was on purpose.

Logan had one hand on the cinnamon tree and must have been holding the vid com with the other. "Your tree is waiting for you," he said, patting it gently. "It misses you, like the rest of us do. I know you told me to only call in case of emergency, and I don't know if your grandma told you yet or not, but my parents want to take all of us to visit three different candy stores. A road trip, Daisy!" Here his smile wobbled, but he recovered it. After a deep breath, he gushed, "I know you said you probably wouldn't be around until the annual picnic, but I really, really, really hope you can come, because I've never been on the road like you have, I mean, I've never been practically anywhere, but you know that, of course, so I really need you to come." He finally took a breath. "Okay. Got that out. No pressure, though. But it will be totally great." He smiled again. "Gotta finish packing." He leaned closer to the tree and made a big sniffing gesture. "Mmmm . . . smells so good." Then he winked and the screen went dark.

Daisy smiled. Guess she hadn't been as good at hiding her affection for that tree as she'd thought. She shook her head and started Miles's message. In contrast to Philip's sunless background, Miles had made his call from the great lawn. Two swans floated behind him. He had the vid com propped up on something and was crouching down in front of it. It didn't look like a comfortable position.

"Daisy!" he said, not as impatiently as Philip, but with more anxiety than she'd heard from him since the day of the contest. "When will you be back? I found something that used to belong to Logan's grandfather that I really need to show you." He glanced from side to side, then held a burned piece of paper up in front of the camera before yanking it away a second later. "This could change everything. Everything!" His face scrunched up into a worried ball.

Miles could be a bit overdramatic, and he got excited easily, but if he was so worried, something must be seriously wrong. She rewound the video and froze it on the paper. Even zooming in and sharpening the image couldn't bring it into clear enough focus to let her make out more than a few words of type. The paper looked old, though, and dark around the edges. She hit Play again. Now Miles had moved the vid com so close to his face that all she could see was his mouth and nose.

"I need you to help me figure out what this is," he whispered. "I can't show Logan until I know more." He sat still for nearly a full minute, clearly trying to collect himself. His face finally unscrunched, and he leaned in again. "But hey, guess what? Mr. Sweet is taking us all on a publicity tour for the Harmonicandy! You have to come, Daisy. It wouldn't be the same without you." Miles's expression turned serious again. "Call me when you can. Logan's grandfather might have done something—"

But he was cut off by a voice behind him asking, "Find anything cool?"

Daisy could only see legs, but she knew they belonged to Logan. She'd recognize those tanned knobby knees anywhere. The screen instantly went blank. Daisy sighed. Clearly the factory didn't offer anyone much privacy. What could Miles have meant? Logan's *grandfather* did something? Hadn't he been gone for years now? That didn't make any sense.

Her finger hovered over the space next to her grandmother's message. Maybe the call meant she'd be allowed to go on the trip after all! If she went, she'd have to stay in the background. She couldn't be photographed or interviewed or do any of the things required on a publicity tour. But she was an expert at staying in the background when necessary. And the Sweets had been so kind to her. They'd started to feel like family. Speaking of family . . . she had another reason to call Grammy.

Instead of playing the message, she pressed the link on the vid com that would track Grammy down wherever she was. It took a little longer than usual before she answered.

"Darling!" Grammy sang out as her face popped up on the screen. She wore an orange sundress with a necklace made of seashells. The sound of rushing water echoed around her, but all Daisy could see behind her grandmother was what looked like a wall made of large stones, glistening with moss and water. She had hoped to find her grandmother at home. But there was definitely no rock wall or rushing water in her grandmother's office. "Where *are* you?" she asked.

"I'm tucked away in a cavern behind a waterfall," her grandmother replied, switching to the back camera of her vid com. "It's lovely! See?"

Through the cascading sheets of water, Daisy took in a breathtaking view. A turquoise sea lay spread out before her, ringed on all sides by lush green grasses and palm trees. Daisy had been on missions in plenty of beautiful places, but nothing like that. Her grandmother always took the best assignments for herself. Not that Daisy was bitter about it. Grammy had certainly earned it. With all the other responsibilities they had, most directors of spy organizations didn't still go out on assignments. But her grandmother never gave to another spy what she could do best herself. Especially if it happened to take her to an interesting part of the world.

"When will your mission be over?" Daisy asked. "I was hoping to see you when we get home tomorrow."

"I won't be gone much longer," she said, switching the view back to herself. "The dead drop was successful?"

Daisy nodded. "Part of the instructions are written in invisible ink. We'll be able to read it soon."

Grammy's eyebrow rose. "Invisible ink? Strange that they would have bothered."

Daisy nodded. "Wait till you see where they stashed the note." Out of nowhere a pelican landed on Grammy's left, flapped its wings to dry off, and gazed over at her grandmother adoringly. Daisy giggled. "I think you have a friend."

Grammy scooted a few inches away from the large white bird. "Spies don't have friends, darling. You know that."

Unable to help it, Daisy cringed. Grammy must have realized her comment sounded harsh, because she added, "I mean, other than her fellow trusted spies, of course. Those kinds of friendships are priceless. You girls at the mansion are all very lucky to have each other."

Daisy didn't want to argue about how Courtney and the twins and most of the others were friendly enough but were all older than her. There was a difference between *friendly* and *friend*. But she knew her grandmother wouldn't want to hear it.

"Did you get my message?" Grammy asked.

"I didn't play it yet," Daisy replied. "I figured I'd call you instead."

The pelican peeked around Grammy's shoulder to get a better look at the vid com. Its face filled the screen and tried to poke it with its beak! Daisy burst out laughing. Her grandmother gently shooed the bird away, her hand all silver rings and red-painted nails. "It can wait until you get home," Grammy said. "I've got a long-term assignment to discuss with you that would start in a few months. I would only offer it to my best young spy."

"Me?" she asked, trying to ignore the pelican pacing back and forth now, hanging its head a bit.

Grammy nodded. "Last I checked, you were still my best young spy."

Daisy blushed.

"Everyone is allowed one slipup," her grandmother continued. "And let's face it, letting our client's son ruin our plans was a whopper of a slipup."

Daisy pressed her lips tight. They'd have to agree to disagree on that point. A slipup implied a mistake, and helping Philip stop his father's plan to destroy the candy factory had been no mistake. Her grandmother didn't know the full story, or else she'd call it a lot worse than a slipup. AJ had agreed they wouldn't tell her about the real part the two of them had played in helping Philip win the contest, nor that she had blown her own cover. Her parents didn't know, either. The fewer people who knew a spy's business, the safer everyone was.

"Was that all you wanted to tell me?" Daisy asked, hoping she wouldn't have to bring up the Candymaker's offer herself.

Grammy pushed a lock of surprisingly dry hair away from her forehead. "I think so."

"Oh," Daisy said, disappointed. "No phone calls about me?"

Her grandmother looked thoughtful. "Now that you mention it, Mrs. Peterson did patch an odd call through to me. Richard Sweet, the man who owns the candy factory, called with the strangest request. He offered to take you along on a publicity tour for the winning candy. He said he was inviting all the children who had prepared for the contest at his factory."

Daisy's heart was pounding fast. "What did you tell him?"

"I thanked him, of course, but told him you were otherwise occupied. Which is true. You must do the next dead drop."

Daisy had expected that response. Still, she had to try. "What if I could do both? I'm sure I can get the job done on the road without anyone noticing. I can leave at night, or—"

Grammy held up her hand to stop Daisy. "Sweetheart, even if you *could* do both without your traveling companions noticing, the problem isn't with you. It's them I don't trust."

"Wait, what do you mean? Logan, Miles, and Philip are really great." Hearing herself, she added, "Well, Philip's maybe not totally great, but he's soooo much better than he was. You'd hardly recognize him." Then she muttered, "Not that you've ever *met* them . . ."

Grammy's eyes softened. "I only meant that while you know your boundaries, they don't. They can't, of course; they're only children. They will get attached to you, and you to them. They will distract you on missions. And what happens when they ask why you never have them over to your home? Sooner or later they will interfere with your job, you will get tired of lying about your real life, and you will have to let them go. Let them go now. It's easier on everyone. Trust me," she added. "I've been in your position."

Daisy sighed. Even though her grandmother underestimated the boys, her points were valid. Bringing them into her life could put everyone at risk, not just her. Grammy didn't know that the boys already knew about her real life as a spy. If Grammy knew that, she'd *never* let Daisy see them again. "I get it, Grammy, I do."

"I knew you'd understand. Maybe go take in a movie with Courtney or one of the other girls when you get home." Grammy glanced at her watch, one Daisy had never seen her wear before. "I've got to hurry into a meeting, darling."

"One more thing," Daisy said, surprising herself. She'd wanted to bring up this topic many times over the last four months but always stopped herself. She understood that her safety as a spy hinged on others' not knowing her true identity, but she'd started to question whether she really needed to keep her true identity hidden from herself. Knowing her last name wasn't all that important to her. After all, she took names on and off like a new set of clothes every time she went on a gig. She could keep that question buried until the time was right. But her mother's offhand comment never quite stayed locked away well enough. It rattled the door and demanded an audience. After a deep breath she blurted out, "Mom said something once about going to see my . . . brother?"

Grammy's expression didn't change, not even a flicker in her eye, and Daisy was watching closely. Of course, her grandmother had decades of training in not betraying anything she didn't want to, but still, Daisy was sure she'd catch something . . . if there was something to catch.

She continued. "When I asked her about it later, she said she was only teasing me. And maybe that's all it was, but it sounded real."

Grammy tilted her head. "Honey, don't you think you'd know if you had a brother?"

"Maybe not," Daisy insisted. "Mom and Dad are away so much they could have five other families for all I know!"

Her grandmother paused to consider that. "Okay, good point. But trust me, you are an only child. Your mother just has a strange sense of humor sometimes."

Hmm, her mother was pretty laid-back and was good at making people smile, but Daisy had never found her to be laugh-out-loud funny.

Grammy blew a kiss at the screen. "See you soon, honey." Feeling a bit defeated on both the brother thing and the road trip, Daisy moved to switch off the vid com. This time it was her grandmother who called out that she should wait. Daisy pulled her hand away from the button. "Yes, Grammy?"

"How did the holojection do?" her grandmother asked with a wide grin.

"The what?" Daisy asked, assuming she'd misheard.

"The hologram projection. We call it a holojection. Watch, I'll turn it off." Her grandmother touched a button on the side of her new watch, and right before Daisy's eyes, the rock wall and the damp cavern disappeared. The pounding of the waterfall stopped abruptly.

Daisy blinked and brought the vid com close to her face. "Whaaa? Huh?"

Her grandmother was sitting at her desk at home, the giant world map behind her as usual. "So? Did it look real?"

Daisy could only gape at the screen as she nodded, stunned. Finally she said, "Where'd the pelican go?"

Grammy laughed. "No pelican. Just part of the computer simulation."

Daisy shook her head. Wow. R & D had really outdone themselves! "It looked amazing."

Grammy nodded. "Good! I'd been waiting for a chance to give it a test run."

"You may want to consider wetting your hair a little next time, though," Daisy added. "I did kind of wonder how you stayed perfectly dry behind a waterfall."

"Excellent idea," Grammy said, scribbling on a notepad beside her. "Bye, honey."

"Bye, Grammy," Daisy said, still shaking her head in wonder. Then she stopped. If Grammy could easily spin lies about where she was—even including that bit with the pelican!—she could easily be lying about the mystery brother.

Daisy debated calling back, but her stomach growled. She hadn't eaten a real meal in a long time. Camp Tumbleweed wasn't known for its food. Spaghetti would be awesome. Or, no...tacos!

Mmmm, tacos! But she'd pretty much settle for anything right now. Even one of AJ's sandwiches, if it came to that.

She made her way back to the front of the RV and sat down beside AJ again. The sun hung low in the sky, turning it all sorts of colors. The wide windshield made Daisy feel like she was watching a movie of a sunset rather than the real one. Her stomach growled again and reminded her of why she'd come up there. "So whatcha got that passes for real food around here?" she asked. "Other than sandwiches and donuts, I mean. You're the one who usually thinks about food all the time, and you haven't even once mentioned eating. It's unnatural."

"I know," AJ replied. "But when you can't smell, you can't taste very well, either. Food doesn't have the same appeal."

Daisy didn't say anything. AJ loved his sandwiches. She was starting to get a greater sense of what he'd lost.

"Don't you want to see the note?" he continued, changing the subject. "The words showed up."

She reached over to the dashboard and picked up the paper. She'd actually forgotten all about it. Grammy was right. Even thinking about her personal life with friends and a mystery brother had led to her forgetting about her job.

She'd expected the note to give them instructions on how to get into the birdhouse, but instead it said this:

leigynehnicng.nhsot,cdehaaqsdpbrNcooppbqzomnxhBeegyrpmesd
592034.023153076089844322,-1111126078.1541313450670436

"At first I thought you were right, that it was another scytale," AJ admitted. "But when I fed the paper into the RV's onboard computer system, it generated that coding." He nodded his head toward a paper sticking out of the dashboard, right below the navigation screen.

"Neat," Daisy said, pulling it out of the nearly invisible slot. She read over the computer code.

```
looking.text = input("Message?")
length = len(text)
for i in range (0, length, 3):
decoded = text[i]
print(decoded, end=" ")
```

It looked correct to her, but she didn't need it. She could tell at one glance that the spies had written an nth letter code—in this case, every third letter or number. She'd been cracking those since she was four. She picked up the spies' note again and carefully picked out the hidden message. I n s i x d a y s d r o p b o x h e r e 43.9781 N, 15.3836 E. Then she read it faster. "In six days drop box here." She looked up at him. "Those coordinates are about five hundred miles away from Spring Haven."

AJ nodded, slowing down as they approached a large open field. A sign in front of it read OVERNIGHT PARKING, PERMIT REQUIRED, NO OPEN FIRES. Two other RVs and a truck were already set up for the night.

"Impressive code-breaking, Daisy Bertha Dinkleman," AJ said as the in-dash computer spewed out a pink paper with PERMIT printed across it. AJ turned off the engine and slapped the fake permit onto the windshield. "Who needs computers when we have ol' D.B.D. on the team?"

Daisy rolled her eyes. "So you give me a middle name, and you can't think of anything better than Bertha? Is that even a real name?"

"Sure it is," he said, ducking out of the driving area so he could stretch. "I have an aunt Bertha. Or maybe she's a great-aunt."

"Hey," Daisy said, realization dawning on her. "That's right! You're eighteen now. You know who your real family is!"

AJ nodded. "Can't talk about it, of course. Except, well, now you know about Aunt Bertha. Or maybe her name's Mabel. Anyway, how about I whip us up something special for dinner now that we have our next plan? I'm thinking tacos."

Something clicked inside Daisy when he said *tacos*. Her mind began moving pieces around like a jigsaw puzzle. First, she had *just* been hoping for tacos, and then he mentioned them out of nowhere, like he'd read her mind, the way siblings do. Second, he couldn't tell her about his family. Maybe he couldn't tell her because it was also *her* family! Third, Grammy often stuck them together for assignments, maybe because she wanted them to bond. Fourth, he hung out with her parents when he could, often without her. Fifth, and perhaps the best evidence of all, they constantly annoyed each other, they were always competing, and she was often tempted to pinch him really hard and run.

AJ stood at the freezer, trying to pry out a box of frozen tacos from behind the bag of ice. It wasn't exactly the meal she'd dreamt of, but it was still tacos. She tiptoed up behind him, reached under his hat, and yanked a single hair out from his head. His other senses really must have increased after all, because he yelped and jumped, nearly hitting his head on the top of the freezer.

He turned to stare at her. "What was *that* for?"

"I'm going to prove it!" she declared, marching toward the bookshelves with the hair held firmly in between her thumb and forefinger.

"Prove *what*?" he asked, rubbing his head.

She pulled out the book on the left corner of the shelf, and the whole shelf flipped over to reveal a mini laboratory. It had been built into the RV so they could analyze any foreign material or create their own chemicals, if the mission required. But she would be using it for a different purpose.

"Daisy," AJ said, his patience clearly wearing thin, "can you please tell me what you're trying to prove?"

She placed the hair into one of three slots labeled SAMPLE and slid the cover over it. Then she looked him straight in the eye and said, "I'm going to prove you're my brother."

CHAPTER EIGHT

AJ stopped laughing long enough to say, "I knew this day would come. The pressure of your job has finally made you crack. We don't even look anything alike. Me . . . you . . . related . . . that's—how would you put it? A whole hat full of crazy!" Then he started laughing again.

The fact that she wanted to kick him hard in the shin just confirmed her suspicions that they were siblings. "You've never heard me use that expression."

"I'm pretty sure I have," he said, wiping his eyes. "But both of us saying the same thing doesn't make you my annoying kid sister, no matter how much you act like one."

"Said just like a bossy older brother," she snapped. "I'm telling you, it could be true. Maybe the family they told you about isn't real. Maybe they couldn't tell you about your real family until *I'm* old enough to know, too."

That shut him up.

She turned back to the lab and let a thin stream of saliva pool into the slot marked SAMPLE B.

"Lovely," AJ muttered. He left her to it and started on dinner.

She reopened the first slot to make sure the tiny white follicle was still attached to the end of the hair from where she'd pulled it out. That was the part with the DNA in it. Once assured that she wouldn't have to yank out any more, she keyed in the instructions and watched as the two samples descended into the machine to be analyzed. Both of their DNA strands would be replicated over and over, and then eleven genetic markers would be compared to obtain the results. Then to top it off, the results would go wirelessly to a real lab to be verified before they were sent back to the mini lab. "We'll know the truth in twenty-two minutes," she announced.

"Good," he said, pulling the tacos out of the microwave. "That will give us time to have dinner before you have to apologize for your temporary detour to Crazytown."

"Once it's official," Daisy said cheerfully, "you'll have to be a lot nicer to me."

His expression turned serious. "Look, don't be disappointed when you see we're not related."

"Don't worry, I won't." But as they sat down at the booth, she knew she would be. What was that expression Grammy used? *The devil that you know is better than the one you don't.* If they were a match, at least the mystery would be solved.

A frozen taco was better than no taco, but just barely. They ate in silence as they watched the sun take its final dive behind the horizon. The field was filling up with trucks and motorhomes, all of them keeping their distance from each other. A woman in the camper next to their RV stepped outside, right into their line of sight. She looked to be about fifty years old, wearing very white sneakers and an apron stamped with the words MOTORHOME MAMA. Daisy knew the RV's windows were impossible to see into. It didn't stop the woman from peering closer, though, until her nose was almost against the glass. Then she disappeared back into her camper, and when she came out again, her hands were full.

Daisy and AJ looked at each other, and then both jumped up from their seats. Daisy flicked the switch that would turn on the outside lights while AJ fumbled to open the door. They ran down the stairs to meet the woman, closing the door firmly behind them.

"Howdy, neighbors," the woman said as she approached. "Hope I'm not intruding."

"Not at all," AJ said, flashing her his brightest smile. "We just finished dinner."

"You two cooked for yourselves?" She looked around. "Or are your parents with you?"

Daisy shot AJ her best "See, I told you people think we're related!" expression and then shook her head. "Our parents are at work," she explained. "We're on our way back home from . . . a two-week camping trip." She was very good at lying when it wasn't truly lying.

"How lovely!" the woman said. "I can't get my own kids to go five minutes without bickering, let alone choose to spend two weeks together. Your parents must really have raised you right!"

"Yes, ma'am, they did," AJ said, tipping his cowboy hat. Daisy forced a smile.

The woman beamed at them. "Would you two like some home-made cherry pie?"

"Absolutely," AJ said, sounding as though he couldn't imagine anything better in the world at that moment. The woman beamed even more and handed him a large plastic plate with half a pie sitting on it. She pulled two plastic forks from her apron pocket and stuck them in the pie.

"Thank you very much," Daisy said. "I bet it's wonderful." She knew they couldn't eat it, no matter how good it smelled or how delicious it looked with the steam still rising through tiny Xs on the crispy crust. Basic rule of life as a spy—never take food from strangers.

"Well, we're just a hop, skip, and a jump away," the woman said, turning to go. "Stop on by if you need anything."

They assured her they would. As soon as she turned the corner, AJ dug into the piece of pie.

"Mmmm, delicious," he said, rubbing his belly with his free hand.

Daisy stared. "First of all, why are you eating that when you know it goes against our training, and second, I thought you said losing your sense of smell means you can't taste things."

He ate another bite, then said, "First, our training also allows us to judge the potential for harm. Since she arrived before us, I judged the likelihood that she would know our identities and would have some reason to serve us poisoned pie to be very low. And second, my brain still remembers what cherry pie tastes like, even if my tongue can only taste a vague sweetness. And my brain tells me this is some high-quality pie!" He held the plate out to her. "Want a piece?"

Daisy shook her head. "That woman might not know we're spies, but she could still be a crazy person who wants to poison innocent travelers on a lonely country road in the middle of nowhere."

AJ put his fork down with his next bite stuck to it. "Boy, you really know how to ruin a piece of pie for a guy."

"Just doing my sisterly duty."

AJ rolled his eyes and stood. "C'mon, time's up. Let's put an end to this crazy idea of yours."

Daisy grabbed his sleeve before he could open the door. "Wait. We should talk about this first. What if it comes out positive?"

"Nothing's going to change either way," AJ said firmly. "We'll go back to barely tolerating each other, but at least we'll know why we can barely tolerate each other."

She frowned. "Is that really how you feel about me?"

"C'mon, don't you think I know how you complain whenever your grandmother assigns us a mission together?"

Daisy stuck out her chin. "That's because you're always so braggy and know-it-all-ish."

"I'm only like that around you. You're so good at everything that I feel the need to take you down a notch." Then he grinned when he heard how that sounded. "Maybe you're right and we're siblings after all."

"Race you inside." She pushed him out of the way and darted up the stairs.

"Pretty sneaky, sis," he said, close on her heels. They hurried over to the lab. Twenty-four minutes had passed. The results were in. Daisy took a deep breath and tapped the screen. The words came up quickly.

Sample A and Sample B are not related.

"Well," AJ said. "Talk about getting straight to the point."

Daisy nodded but didn't meet his eyes. Instead, she reached for a jacket hanging by the door. "I'm going to go outside for a walk if you don't need me for anything."

"Are you okay?" he asked.

She nodded, too embarrassed to look at him. "It was a dumb idea. I don't know what I was thinking."

"It wasn't a dumb idea," he said. "We're a team anyway, right?"

"Sure," she said without enthusiasm.

"At least take your vid com so I can find you if I need you," he said.

She nodded and stuffed it in her jacket pocket. She had the feeling AJ wanted to say more, but he didn't stop her as she brushed past him and went out the door.

The air was warmer at night than it had been in the mountains at camp. It would be time for lights out in the cabin. She briefly wondered what the girls at camp thought had happened to her. Or to Ava, rather. She hoped they wouldn't take it personally that she'd left.

That one flicker of thought would be all she would give the girls she'd spent nearly every waking moment with for the past two weeks. And that's exactly how it should be, how it *should have been* after she left the factory. It was ridiculous to try to cobble a family together, and with AJ, of all people. She made her way between the parked vehicles, hands shoved deep in her pockets.

As she reached the far end of the field, she began to notice that all the parked vehicles had their outside lights off. It couldn't be much past nine thirty. Was everyone asleep already? If she hadn't had such excellent eyesight, she might have tripped right over the group of at least twenty people lying on blankets or leaning back in folding chairs. They were all looking up at the sky, many with binoculars.

"Oh, sorry!" she said, assuming she'd stumbled upon a private gathering. She turned to go.

"Wait, come join us," a kind voice said. "Pull up a chair."

She traced the voice to an older man at the end of the row of chairs. He patted the arm of an empty chair next to him. She was about to politely decline but then thought better of it. She wasn't ready to go back to AJ yet, and the group—a mix of young and old—didn't look too scary. Plus she could take them in a fight.

"Thanks," she replied, sitting down. She leaned her head back and looked up. Lots of stars, but not really any different from the ones at camp. "Um, what are you all looking at?"

"Wait for it . . . ," the man said. "There!" the crowd gasped and applauded. Daisy looked where the man was pointing but saw nothing unusual. "There!" someone else shouted. Again, applause.

"It's a meteor shower," the first man explained. "On account of the dust and ice left behind from that comet everyone's talkin' about that's heading toward Earth so fast. You know, the one that's bigger than the one that wiped out the dinosaurs? It's got such a long tail that we'll be seeing shooting stars for the next *week*!"

"Um, cool?" Daisy said, not about to admit that she hadn't heard any mention of this potentially apocalyptic, life-ending collision. She listened politely as the group explained that the comet nears Earth every seventy-five years. Once she knew what to look for, she did manage to spot a few bright streaks of light as they zoomed across the sky. Her heart wasn't in it, though. To stargaze, a person needed to focus on the heavens, and she couldn't pull herself away from her situation on the ground. She'd come to a decision. She would go back to being the best young spy in the world, and when she turned eighteen, she'd find out her name and whether she had a brother, and then she'd decide what—if anything—to do about it.

Unless this comet destroyed everything that walked on two legs.

Her vid com vibrated in her pocket. It wasn't AJ's frequency, or her grandmother's, so it had to be one of the three boys.

Daisy let it ring.

She let it ring the whole ride home the following day. AJ tried to engage her in conversation, but she only gave one-word answers. She didn't complain when he put on country-western songs and sang along at the top of his lungs. She only barely cracked a smile when he pointed to a sign in front of a Steak & Ribs Shack on the highway that read HORRIFYING VEGETARIANS SINCE 2002! And when the RV finally pulled into the long, winding driveway that led to the compound, she had AJ drop her off at the stables even though she still had enough time to make it to the Kickoff at the factory and surprise everyone.

She rode faster than usual through the fields and into the woods. On Magpie's back there was no room for error. Letting her mind wander could mean whacking her head into a branch. She couldn't think of anything other than where each hooved foot would land. She definitely couldn't think of everyone soon celebrating the first batch of Harmonicandies. How they'd all be cheering, and maybe Philip would teach everyone to play a song with it, and, like, a hundred people would all be playing the same tune at the same time on a chocolate harmonica, and they'd never forget that moment. Even if she could have made it there, what would have happened when people wanted to take her picture along with the other kids? She didn't even look the same now that she was back to her normal brown hair. The Daisy of the contest was a temporary Daisy, like a tattoo that comes off in the bath. They'd be taking pictures of a ghost.

Nope, she definitely couldn't think about any of that. She rode harder and faster, slowing down only when Magpie began to pant. She set the pace back at a trot so both horse and rider could cool down before stopping to drink.

When they arrived back at the stables, Courtney was on her way out. She wore a stained apron and a tall white chef's hat. She yanked it off and stuffed it in her apron pocket when she saw Daisy. "Don't ask," she said with a grimace.

"Wouldn't dare." Daisy always respected the need for secrecy when it came to going undercover for assignments. "Only you could look good in a chef's hat," she added.

Courtney followed them into Magpie's stall. "How was the gig?" she asked.

"Pretty good." Daisy began unhooking the saddle and bridle. "I'm excellent at making lanyards now. And picture frames out of Popsicle sticks."

Courtney laughed and stuck her chef's hat back on. "I can make a mean chicken Marsala."

Daisy smiled, which felt good. Grammy was right about one thing. It really was nice to be able to talk about her life with the girls, at least with Courtney. Even though they couldn't go into detail about their jobs, even this much made her feel a little less isolated.

"I had fun making your friend Philip squirm," Courtney said.

Daisy had nearly forgotten about that whole thing! She couldn't help smiling at the thought of him squirming. "Thanks again for that. I owe you one."

"No problem," Courtney said, taking the bridle from Daisy and hanging it on the post. "You know you could have done what he'd asked yourself, with your vid com."

Daisy smiled. "I know. But sometimes ya gotta make them work for it."

"Good one," Courtney said, nodding. "He was kind of cute, though. A little uptight, but not bad to look at. Now that I think about it..." She tilted her head and examined Daisy closely. "With your hair dark like this, you two kind of resemble each other. Maybe you have a secret brother out there!"

Daisy stared at Courtney, openmouthed. "Do you know something you're not telling me?" she demanded.

Courtney laughed. "I'm only kidding. I'm sure Philip Ransford the Third is not your brother."

Daisy shuddered at the thought.

"Your vid com's been buzzing since I got here," Courtney said, gesturing to Daisy's backpack on the bench. "Whoever's been calling you must really want to reach you. You're not wearing your transceiver?"

Daisy shook her head and reached for the bucket and sponge. "I'll check the messages later."

Courtney took the sponge from Daisy's hands. "I'll wipe down Magpie for you. You check your messages."

"Fine," Daisy grumbled, still not planning to do it. She had no interest in hearing how wonderful the Kickoff was.

"Oh," Courtney added, squeezing the water out over the bucket, "I almost forgot. A man called the house asking for Daisy Carpenter. I assume that was the name you used on one of your assignments?"

Daisy's voice caught in her throat. "Who was it?"

"He said his name was Henry. And that it was a chocolate emergency, whatever that means. I'm not sure what he thinks you can do about it."

"Me neither," Daisy said, trying not to let on that the message worried her. Maybe one of the boys had put him up to it. "When did he call?"

"Just a few minutes ago."

She pulled her vid com out of her bag. All the recent calls had AJ's face next to them, not the boys' and not Henry's. Reluctantly, she called AJ back. "Miss me already?" she asked.

"Hardly," he replied. "Have you unpacked yet?"

"No. I just finished my ride. Plus my bag is still in the RV. Why?"

"We read the coordinates wrong. The dead drop is much farther away than we thought. We've got to hit the road again."

"What, right now?"

"Not right now," he said. "That'd be crazy. I'll pick you up outside the barn in ten minutes."

Daisy groaned and slammed the cover of her vid com shut.

"Cheer up," Courtney said, plopping her chef's hat back on. "I'd go on a gig with AJ anytime. He's totally cute."

Daisy shuddered for the second time in five minutes. "Gross."

PART FOUR

PHILIP

CHAPTER ONE

Late Sunday night

Five Lies I've Told in the Last 24 Hours and Why I Told Them:

Lie #1. I told Marietta, our latest cook in a long string of cooks, that the pancakes she made me for breakfast did not taste like a brick.

Explanation: If I told her the truth, that I think one of them cracked a corner of my tooth, she might quit. Since between me, Reggie, and my father we can't boil an egg, she really has to stay or we'll starve.

Lie #2. I told Reggie that I would compete in the Nation's Most Talented Kid competition that Dad signed me up for, because I was afraid he'd tell my father that I had no intention of doing any such thing.

Explanation: After Dad found out that I could play the violin so well, he didn't make me stop...for about three days. Then he said I really needed to be spending my time on educational pursuits that have a chance of helping me succeed in the future, rather than indulging in a hobby like playing an instrument. In his words: *"Hobbies are just an excuse to waste time doing something other than what you're supposed to be doing."* And since I'm still furious about how he lied to me seven years ago and told me I was banned from the candy factory when I wasn't, I told him that my skills at the violin are almost unheard of at my age but that he didn't have to worry about my grades slipping. All he heard was the first part, though, about me having a skill others did not. He immediately found the information about the contest and has already arranged for me to fly out to it with Reggie.

Leave it to my father to find a way to make me hate the violin by making me compete against a kid who can solve a Rubik's Cube blindfolded and another who juggles fire, ALSO blindfolded. Not sure what kind of parents would let their kid do that and then sign him up for a contest, but if they're anything like my dad, and there's prize money involved, I have my answer. I have almost finished my original composition—half of the music I wrote before the contest, the other half since then—and I would play it at the contest if I were going. Which I'm not.

Lie #3. I told Logan I can't come to the factory tomorrow because I have a dentist appointment.

Explanation: While the potentially cracked tooth and the amount of candy I'm eating make a visit likely in the near future, I do not have one scheduled. After I froze up during a few post-contest-winning interviews, the publicity department gave me a training session on how to handle myself better with the press and with the candy industry bigwigs. Still, it has been a few months since I've had to deal with all that, and the hoopla about the Harmonicandy coming out makes me want to stay far away from the factory. I feel bad about lying to Logan, since he's so trusting, but my tooth was sore from the pancake and it was the first thing that came to my mind when he called to ask if I was coming.

Lie #4. I told myself I would stop eating so much candy.

Explanation: When getting dressed for the fund-raising dinner Dad dragged me to, I couldn't get my belt to close and had to loosen it by a notch. Still, I have seven candy-free years to make up for and a friend (I have a friend!) who owns a candy factory, so I know I'm not going to stop anytime soon.

Plus—and this may be the most compelling reason—I have the success of the Harmonicandy to consider. It would be a bad business move if I didn't have a full understanding of the candy industry, and that includes firsthand knowledge of the products. All of them. Especially the sour ones. Those are my favorites. And also taffy.

Lie #5. I let Daisy believe I didn't know where she was. This may count more as a lie of omission than a straight-out lie, but I'm including it anyway because five is a nice, round number. And now I sound like Miles. Ugh.

Explanation: I didn't want her to think she wasn't being a good spy, but she was wearing a Camp Tumbleweed sweatshirt. So basically, I boosted her confidence without her even knowing it or taking credit.

Philip closed his small notebook and slid it onto a high shelf. Some kids kept track of how many pogo-stick jumps they could land without falling off. Others counted how many lightning bugs they spotted at dusk. Philip tracked his lies. It didn't seem like that strange a thing to do. When his language arts teacher told the class they'd be expected to hand in a journal about their summer break, she probably didn't expect it to be quite like Philip's. This one was for his eyes only.

He turned to examine the contents of the next box, when the door to the room began to creep open. The door to the room did not ever, *ever* creep open. Philip froze. His heart wasn't pounding double-time because it was the middle of the night and he was scared, but because other than himself or his father's personal assistant, Reggie, no one else had walked into the room for nearly seven years. After Philip's mother had passed away, his father had stashed all her stuff in this room and locked the door. If the busy man even remembered the spare room existed, he never mentioned it. Philip doubted tonight was the night his father suddenly felt the need to visit.

The intruder couldn't be Reggie, either, because after driving Philip and his father home from the charity dinner that night, Reggie had complained of a headache and said he was going straight to bed. The maids never went farther down this hallway than his father's office, and anyway, they wouldn't be cleaning at this time of night.

Yet the door continued to open.

Philip's initial reaction was to hide. But when he got down on his knees and started to crawl toward the largest stack of boxes, he felt foolish. This was *his* room more than anyone else's. It was private. And somewhere deep inside him, he knew it was where he felt closest to the mother he barely remembered. He would protect the room, and its contents, even if he hadn't looked at most of his mother's stuff too closely until tonight. He felt bad that he'd made such a mess. And he hadn't found what he'd been looking for. He began to doubt it existed at all. But right now he had a bigger problem.

He scrambled to his feet. His eyes darted from Daisy's communicator, resting atop a shelf, to his violin and sheet music on the desk across from him. He'd only have time to cover one. Seeing no choice, he threw off his jacket and launched it on top of Daisy's vid com. He could claim that the violin was his mother's (his original one had belonged to her, after all), but Daisy's spy gadget couldn't fall into enemy hands. He didn't even know half the things it could do. He puffed out his chest and waited for the intruder to show him- or herself.

A jeans-covered leg came first, followed by a blue shirt. And then . . .

"Yo," his older brother, Andrew, said, stepping inside. "I figured I'd find you here." He looked around the room and grinned. "Love

222

what you've done with the place. You should probably air it out, though." He waved his hand in front of his nose. "Smells pretty ripe in here."

Philip's mouth hung open. Before Andrew could say something about how no one looks smart with their jaw hanging open, Philip snapped it shut. "When did you...," he sputtered. "How did you..."

Andrew shut the door behind him, making the room feel even smaller than it already did when Philip was alone.

"I decided to come home from college for the summer," Andrew replied. He then tried to lower himself onto the room's only chair, but a large stuffed panda was in the way. He pushed it off. That panda had been Philip's sole audience member for more than five years. He cringed when it hit the floor.

"You get to bask in my presence for two whole months!" his brother continued. "How lucky are *you*?"

"*So* lucky," Philip said, finding it hard to breathe. He wished he'd taken off the stupid tie that now felt like it was choking him.

As stealthily as possible, he sidestepped until he was blocking Andrew's view of the violin. One of his notebooks was open to a page full of musical notes, and he did not want to have to explain anything. Trying to keep his voice light, Philip said, "I thought you had a summer job lined up with one of Dad's friends out of state."

Andrew shrugged. "Didn't work out."

"Really?" Philip asked. Things always worked out for Andrew. He was the golden child, the one everybody wanted to be like. Clever, handsome, athletic. If the job hadn't worked out, it must have been the other guy's fault.

Andrew didn't elaborate, and Philip didn't ask again. Instead, he said, "But what are you doing here?"

Andrew yawned and leaned back in the chair. "Told you, I just drove in. Planning a summer of relaxation. Read, play tennis, see some old friends." Then he chuckled. "Guess we both know I never had time to make many of those. Can't win at everything and expect people to—"

Philip cut him off. "No, I mean, what are you doing *here*? In my room?" He backed up a few more inches toward the table.

"I didn't know this was *your* room," Andrew said. "Okay, I'm kidding. I know this is where you come to play that violin of yours." He scratched his head. "Don't understand that kind of music at all. Sounds like a wailing cat, no offense."

Philip's jaw hung open again. "You...you know about that?"

His brother nodded. "Not much gets past me."

Philip should have known. As clever and sneaky and manipulative as he himself was, his brother was the master. Of course he knew about the violin.

"You can stop guarding the table now," Andrew said. "I'm not going to pick up your violin and start playing. Trust me, you inherited all the musical talent."

Philip stepped away from the table. He felt his shoulders relax a bit. He'd hidden his violin playing for so many years it was a relief to get it out in the open with the final member of his family. "Dad knows about it now, too," he said.

"I bet he's thrilled," Andrew said, his voice heavy with sarcasm. "We all know what a fan of the arts he is."

"Yeah, he's never even asked to hear me play. If the violin can't win me anything, he's not interested. He's making me sign up for this Nation's Most Talented Kid contest. It's in a few weeks, but I'm not going to do it."

"Why not?" Andrew asked. "From what little I know of the violin, you'll win for sure. That's what we do, you and me. We win contests! Then we gloat and brag and frame our certificates and proudly display our trophies and medals!"

Philip shook his head. "I'm just not interested."

"Is there prize money if you win?" Andrew asked.

Philip nodded.

"And fame?"

"I guess."

"What's not to like? It's been a while since you've won anything."

"The candy contest was only four months ago," Philip reminded him. "That one had fame and money, too." He hoped Andrew wouldn't ask him about his plans for the prize money or his share of the future profits. He'd already written down his lies for the day and didn't want to add any more.

But Andrew's only question was "What candy contest?"

CHAPTER TWO

Philip waited before answering his brother, certain that Andrew would say he was kidding and that of course he knew about the candy contest. But Andrew's expectant expression hadn't changed. He really didn't know!

"You mean Dad didn't tell you I won the Confectionary Association's annual New Candy Contest?" he asked, his voice rising more than he'd intended. "That my name was in newspapers across the country? Well, candy industry newsletters mostly, but still!"

Andrew grinned. "Seriously? That happened?"

"Yes, that happened! I can't believe Dad didn't tell you!" Philip didn't know whether to be more disappointed or angry that his dad cared so little about his victory. He knew that once his father found out what he planned to do with the profits from the candy sales, he would be furious, but for now, at least, he should have been proud that his son won.

"You could have told me yourself," Andrew said.

Philip frowned. "You've called me once since you left for college, and that was to ask me to send you a shirt from your closet." Truth be told, the silence from his brother hadn't bothered him. The two of them were very similar, but the six-year age gap between them meant they had never been particularly close.

"You're right. I'm sorry," Andrew said. "College has been...busy."

"It's okay," Philip said. "I've been busy, too."

"Clearly you have! So how did it work? You just sent in some candy you made, and it won?"

Philip shook his head. "I actually spent three days at the **Life Is Sweet** candy factory working with—"

Andrew held up his hand. "Wait, the place where Dad took us on a tour and you got kicked out and banned for life? You were devastated. You never ate candy again after that day!"

Philip looked down at his feet. He dreaded having to tell Andrew this part of the story. It was so humiliating. "Yeah, well, it turned out they never actually kicked me out."

"What?" Andrew shouted.

"Shh!" Philip said. "You'll wake him!" He looked up at the ceiling, hoping not to hear Dad's footsteps above.

"What do you mean, they never kicked you out?" Andrew asked, his voice a little softer, but not much.

"Dad made it up, if you must know," Philip said. "He was planning on trying to take over the factory and didn't want me to be friends with the Candymaker's son, Logan. I guess it was easier for him to make the Candymaker seem like the bad guy by telling me I'd been banned from the place."

Andrew shook his head in disbelief, then burst out laughing. He laughed so hard he had to hold his sides.

Philip glared. "What part of that story could you possibly find funny?"

Andrew gasped for air. "Seven years!" he managed to get out. "For seven years you hated those people and swore revenge. I used to hear you muttering about it. And it never really happened!" The laughter started all over again. Andrew's reaction reminded him of another reason why they weren't very close. His brother was even more obnoxious than he was.

"Thank you for laughing at my pain," Philip said, slipping on his suit jacket. He turned his back and tucked Daisy's device into the inside pocket. "Very brotherly of you."

"I'm sorry," Andrew said, not sounding very sorry at all. "It's just classic Dad. Tell me the rest of the story. How'd you win? Obviously you cheated. Was it the bait 'n' switch? The distract 'n' conquer? Did you sabotage the other contestants' entries? I bet it was the last one, am I right? You switched out their sugar with salt! Or maybe the chocolate chips with raisins?"

Philip stopped buttoning his jacket midbutton. "Why are you so sure I cheated?"

"Come on, Philip. That's what we do. You're not going to try to tell me that out of nowhere, you suddenly became the best candy-maker in the country all by yourself. I've never even seen you butter a frozen waffle!"

Philip suddenly felt very tired. Obviously he couldn't have won by himself. But there was no way he was going to tell Andrew about Logan with his scars, or Miles with his head always somewhere else, and definitely not about Daisy the spy. He couldn't really blame Andrew for suspecting him. He would have done the same had the situation been reversed.

"It's late," Philip said. "I'm going to bed. Just so you know, there was teamwork involved, but I won fair and square. I didn't cheat."

Andrew stood up and patted Philip on the shoulder. "Doesn't matter to me if you did or didn't. You came out on top, and that's the Ransford way."

A few months ago Philip would have nodded in agreement, but now it felt wrong. Hearing his brother imply that their family was special, that they didn't have to follow the rules as long as they came out on top, made Philip realize how much he didn't want to be like that anymore. "What if I don't always want it to be the 'Ransford way'?" he heard himself ask. "People can change, right? Like Dad changed after Mom died. For the worse, I mean."

As soon as the words were out of his mouth, he wished he could take them back. Andrew knew Dad's faults, but he still worshipped him. As soon as college was over, Andrew would be joining the family business. And anyway, they never talked about their mom. Not ever.

"Never mind," Philip said quickly. "C'mon, let's get out of this room." He tried to step around Andrew, but his brother held up his hand.

"Wait, we should talk about this," he said. "What do you mean, Dad changed?"

Philip was too tired to think of a way out of the conversation, so he just said, "Reggie told me that Dad wasn't always so obsessed with work. That he was...nicer."

Andrew rubbed his chin again. "I suppose that's true," he said. "Probably because Mom was so nice."

Philip felt a lump form in his throat. "I...I don't really remember her that much."

Andrew looked away, letting his eyes stray around the room filled with their mom's old stuff. "You were only three. But she was great. She was funny and smart, and she used to play games with us for hours in the backyard."

Vague images flitted through Philip's mind. A swing set, a laugh, the smell of chocolate and mint. It wasn't enough, but it was something. "Did you know she grew up in an apartment in the old section of Spring Haven?"

Andrew nodded. "Reggie took me there before I left for college."

"Really? He took me, too," Philip said, stepping again toward the door. "I think he's afraid we're going to turn out too much like Dad."

His brother looked up at him sharply. "Would that be such a bad thing? Dad's rich and he's powerful. He doesn't let anyone walk all over him. He's a winner, Philip. We would be lucky to turn out like him."

The last thing Philip wanted to do right now was fight about their dad. "Sorry, you're right. I'm going to bed." This time Andrew stepped aside for him. As Philip slid by, his leg knocked into one of the knitting needles, and the ball of yarn fell off the shelf and landed on his foot. He bent to untangle himself from it. Andrew reached down to help.

"Purple's a good color for you," Andrew said, tossing it to him. "I didn't take you for a knitter." As it sailed through the air, the ball unwound a bit, and Philip could see that the yarn wasn't simply tangled, as he'd thought. He was now holding a half-completed scarf. It didn't get very cold in Spring Haven. No one wore scarves. Had his mom started it before she knew she was sick, or after? It felt like someone was physically squeezing his heart. He'd never know who she had been making it for.

"Very funny," he said, trying to keep his voice from breaking. "It's not mine. Obviously it was Mom's. Like everything else in here." He stuck the ball of yarn under his arm.

Andrew shook his head. "Mom didn't knit. That was Grandma's."

Philip stopped short. He'd never seen his dad's mom do anything remotely grandmotherly, like knitting. Their father had learned his "Work hard and win at all costs" way of life from his own parents, who still worked sixty-hour weeks managing three different international businesses. When they weren't on a cruise around the world.

"No way," Philip said. "Grandma would hire a team of people to knit for her. And then she'd stick the scarves in one of her walk-in closets and never wear them." He continued out the door.

"No, not Dad's mom," Andrew said, closing the door behind them. "*Mom's* mom."

Philip stopped again, this time right outside their father's locked office door. He'd never thought about his mom having a mom. Or a dad. Whoever they were, they must have died before he was born, since he'd certainly never met them. "Well, I guess there's no way to know if Mom's mother knitted or not." He hurried down the rest of the hall, anxious to be alone.

"Sure there is," Andrew said, bounding up the stairs ahead of Philip. Over his shoulder he said, "Just call her up and ask."

CHAPTER THREE

Monday

Are you awake?" Reggie called through Philip's bedroom door. It had been six hours since Andrew's offhand comment about a mysterious grandmother. Philip had grilled him as they headed back to their wing of the house, but Andrew said he had only been kidding.

He hadn't sounded like he was kidding.

"I never went to sleep," Philip mumbled. "Go away."

Reggie pushed the door open. "I've got a special delivery for you."

Philip felt the bottom of the bed sag as Reggie dropped something with a *plop*. A few seconds later, a second *plop*. Philip knew what they were. They'd been arriving for months.

"You should really think about opening them this time," Reggie said, pulling up the blinds on the window. "Your adoring fans want to hear from you."

Philip winced at the onslaught of sunlight and buried his face in his pillow. "You open them," he said into the pillow, only it sounded like, "Oo ooen em." Fortunately, Reggie was used to being muttered at and knew what Philip was trying to say.

"Sorry, not in my job description," Reggie replied. "And before you suggest I ask your father to *add* it to my job description, don't bother. He doesn't want anything to do with this. I have the post office hold your mail, and I pick it up once a week."

Reggie sat down on the edge of the bed. Philip could hear him undoing the metal latch on one of the large mail pouches. A rustling, and then a minute later came the sound of an envelope being ripped open. "Would you like to hear one?" Reggie asked. Philip grunted. "I'll take that as a yes," Reggie said. "So this is from Dylan, age ten. It says, 'Dear Philip Ransford, you are…'" Reggie paused and looked up. "Good choice for the Confectionary Association to drop that 'the Third' business when you won, by the way. Makes you more relatable to the public, less pretentious."

Philip only grunted again.

"You'd probably get a lot less mail if your fans knew how charming you are in the morning."

Philip finally turned over. "They're not my fans. They just like candy."

Reggie waved the card in his hand. "Let's see what young Dylan here has to say." He continued reading. "'Dear Philip Ransford, you are my idol. I read what you wrote in your application essay, and I just want to say I went through the same thing, and your family must be very proud. Next year I'm going to enter the contest, too. I hope I do as well as you! Long live the Harmonicandy! Your friend, Dylan Williams.'"

Reggie tossed the card to Philip, who was now sitting straight up, fully alert. "My *application essay*? How did he get a copy of that?" The application had been submitted electronically. You couldn't even print it out, as he recalled.

Philip reached over and grabbed the open mailbag. He dumped the contents onto the bed. Letters and card-sized envelopes fell all over, many sliding to the floor. "Are these all about my essay?" He tore one open, skimmed the contents, then tossed it aside and moved on to the next. The first three he opened were about the

Harmonicandy, like the others he'd read when they first started coming. They basically asked one of three things—how did he come up with it, did it really play, and when would they be able to buy it? He reached for the next one.

Reggie placed his hand on Philip's arm. "Breathe," he said. "You're getting yourself all worked up."

"You don't understand," Philip said, pulling away and tearing open a large purple envelope. "That essay was private. It was meant to get me into the contest and that's it."

Envelope number four contained only a crayon drawing of the Harmonicandy. The rectangular blob of chocolate had been drawn in different shades of brown. Musical notes of various colors drifted in the air around it. Pretty cute, actually, but Philip didn't have time for cute. He tossed it onto the floor. Reggie stood up and retrieved it, placing it gently on Philip's night table.

"I have to admit," Reggie said, "I always wondered how you got in. Not that I doubted you could do it. You've proved over and over you can do anything you set your mind to, and you always want to improve yourself. Even back in preschool you got excused from recess by claiming that your time would be better spent learning how to read. And yet...for someone who hadn't eaten candy in seven years, to convince the Confectionary Association that you deserved to be chosen over so many others—well, that may have been a bigger accomplishment than actually winning!"

Philip flung off his blanket, sending the letters flying, and began to pace the length of his room. How could this have happened? He'd written that essay almost a year ago and hadn't allowed himself to give it a second thought since then. It had one purpose—to get him into the contest at all costs. It was never meant for anyone other than the judges to see. It was private and personal, and it was full of lies.

He continued to pace while Reggie picked up the letters and put them back in the bag. He slung both bags over his shoulders. "Out of the goodness of my heart I'll open these for you. If any others mention your essay, I'll let you know."

"Thank you," Philip said, only half hearing him. His mind was too busy going through the possibilities. Had his essay been published in a candy industry newsletter? Had the boy hacked into the Confectionary Association's computer system? What if he'd hacked into *Philip's* computer? He couldn't imagine the last one being possible. His dad had all sorts of firewalls on their computer network to protect his top-secret business deals.

Philip's attention flipped back to Reggie, who now resembled Santa Claus, carrying the two large satchels over his shoulders. "I know you're freaking out," Reggie said, "but try to see the positive. Whatever you wrote obviously made an impression on this kid, so maybe it's not a bad thing that it's out there for others to read."

Philip considered that for about one second before shaking his head. "Trust me—it's a bad thing."

Reggie shrugged. "Try not to worry. You have exciting things coming up." He headed out the door, leaving Philip to pace alone.

"Wait!" Philip said, running into the hall. He'd been so blindsided by the boy's letter that he'd completely forgotten what had kept him up all night.

Reggie stopped a few feet away from Andrew's bedroom door. "What? Did I miss some letters?"

Philip shook his head. "No. I mean, maybe. I really don't know." He motioned for Reggie to come back to the room.

Reggie sighed. "I know I look strong with these broad shoulders. Who knew a bunch of letters could weigh so much?" But he came back to the room anyway.

"Sorry," Philip said, closing the door. "I just didn't want to wake up Andrew. He's home, you know."

"Actually, he's not. He left the house hours ago." Reggie adjusted one of the bags, which had started to slip. "I dropped him at the country club to find a tennis match."

"Figures," Philip muttered. Sure didn't sound like Andrew had any trouble sleeping.

"Is that it, then?" Reggie asked. "Heavy bags, and these old bones aren't as strong as they used to be."

"No," Philip replied. "I wanted to ask you…" He took a deep breath. "Do you know where my grandmother is?"

"Hmm," Reggie said, tilting his head in thought. "It's Monday today, so … pulling into port in Santorini?"

"Huh?"

"Greece," Reggie explained. "Their next stop on the cruise. Do you need to reach them? I'm sure they'll be checking their messages."

"No, no, I don't mean *them*," Philip said quickly. "I mean… my mother's mother. Andrew said something last night like maybe she's still alive."

Reggie blinked a few times, then shook his head. "He must have been messing with you, kiddo. Sorry. And you know, if this essay thing has you all worked up, why don't you just track down the kid who wrote to you?" Reggie hiked up the bags again and left the room.

Philip knew Reggie's suggestion was a good one. He would indeed track down the boy. But the thought crowding out all others in his mind was this: Reggie had never—in nearly thirteen years together—called him *kiddo*.

CHAPTER FOUR

Dylan Williams must have been absent the day his teacher taught proper letter-writing skills. He hadn't put his return address on the upper left corner of the envelope, nor did he write it in the letter itself. The only clue Philip had to go on was the postmark. Assuming the letter had been mailed from the city Dylan lived in, at least it was a place to start.

Unfortunately, Williams was a very common last name. An online search of the telephone directory for his city listed eleven. Seven told him they had no one named Dylan in the family, he had to leave three messages, and one woman hung up on him, claiming that she "gave at the office," whatever that meant.

He crossed the last name off the list and marched over to the kitchen drawer where he stashed his candy. After only a second's hesitation, he popped a piece of grape taffy into his mouth. He still remembered the shock and horror that had gone around the Taffy Room when he tossed that piece back to Max on the first day of the contest. Every time he ate it now felt like an apology.

His phone rang and he grabbed it quickly, assuming it was one of the families calling him back.

"Hello?" he said, pushing the taffy to one cheek so his words wouldn't slur.

"Philip?" a man's deep voice asked.

"Yes, this is Philip. Are you Dylan's father?"

"Sorry, don't know a Dylan," the man said. "It's Richard Sweet. Do you have a minute?"

Philip sat up straighter, even though of course the Candymaker couldn't see him through the phone. He wished he'd changed out of his pajamas! Usually he put on clothes right away. Only lazy people wore pajamas out of bed, and Philip had no patience for lazy people. He swallowed the taffy. "Of course, sir. Is everything all right?"

"Everything is wonderful," Mr. Sweet boomed cheerfully. "You all set for the big day tomorrow?"

Philip hadn't even thought about it all morning. He really needed to get his head straight. But he answered, "Yes, it's very exciting."

"It certainly is!" Mr. Sweet agreed. "Logan told me you had a visit to the dentist this morning. Everything go okay?"

"Yes, false alarm," Philip said, his stomach twisting. He'd have to remember not to lie to people he cared about. He knew he shouldn't lie to *anyone*, but that would be asking too much of himself. Cutting it down from five a day to four would be a good start.

"Glad to hear you got a good report," Mr. Sweet said. "Did you know it's not sugar itself that causes cavities but the bacteria that feeds on the sugar left behind on your teeth?"

"No, sir, I didn't." Philip hoped the whole conversation wasn't going to be about teeth.

"Yup. So make sure you brush and floss at least two or three times a day."

"Yes, sir, I will."

"Good! The reason for my call—I'm hoping you can come by

the factory after lunch today. The final contract is ready for you to sign, and we have a big announcement for you and the other kids."

Normally a surprise announcement would be fun, but he'd had enough surprises lately. He wasn't sure he could take many more. He wasn't sure about going to the factory, either. Even though after talking to Daisy last night he felt a little better about things, he still didn't want to be the center of attention. But Philip couldn't say no to a direct request from the man in charge, and signing that contract was important. "Okay," he said. "Reggie will take me."

"Can you bring your father this time?" the Candymaker asked. "He'll have to sign off on the paperwork, too."

"He will?" Philip asked, his heart sinking.

There was a pause on the other end. "Philip, your father does know what you're planning to do with your portion of the profits, doesn't he?"

Philip's silence gave him away.

The Candymaker's sigh was long and loud. "All right. I'll give you the contract to take home, and you can discuss it with him. When the first Harmonicandy goes on sale in a few weeks, this agreement needs to be in place."

"Yes, sir," Philip said, dreading the conversation he'd need to have with his father.

"Of course, you're welcome to change your mind. No one but us knows about it."

"No," Philip said firmly. "I'll figure it out."

"All right, son. I'll see you after lunch, then."

The Candymaker hung up, but Philip sat gripping the phone. *Son.* Mr. Sweet had said it with such affection. Philip knew nothing he could do would undo what had happened at the factory all those years ago. But now he could help make it better. He couldn't let his dad stop him.

He finished the omelet Marietta made him (it tasted a lot better than her pancakes, so he didn't have to lie when he told her so). He still had a few hours before he needed to be at the factory. He checked his phone one more time to make sure he didn't miss a call from Dylan. No luck.

On his way to get dressed, Philip stopped by Andrew's room. His brother must not have picked up any bad habits at college, because his room was as neat and organized as it had always been. A few more books filled the bookcase, and a college sweatshirt lay folded at the foot of his perfectly made bed, but other than that it looked the same as when he was away.

Philip stood there for a minute, deciding whether snooping around might give him any more clues about their mother's parents. He'd had all year to snoop through his brother's room without fear of discovery, and he hadn't needed to. Now Andrew had been home ten hours and here Philip was, debating right from wrong.

So on the "wrong" side, people deserved their privacy, and he wouldn't want someone digging around in *his* stuff. But on the "right" side, his brother had dangled this really big news about their family and then pulled it back. Or he'd made it up in the first place just to be mean. Either way, if anyone was in the wrong, it was Andrew.

Mind made up, Philip began to inch forward. He made it halfway to the desk before he stopped again. Did he really think he'd find years' worth of letters between Andrew and some probably imaginary grandmother? And what if he did? Would he want to know someone who clearly hadn't wanted to know him for nearly thirteen years? He took two steps toward the door, then pivoted, went right for the desk, and opened up each drawer. Nothing unusual jumped out at him among the school papers and old certificates. He hadn't really expected it to. He closed the drawers carefully. Well, at least now he could stop thinking about it. It wasn't even lunchtime, and he was totally stressed out! Even more than usual!

While he still was uncomfortable with the pull his violin had on him, Philip had to admit that when he played, all other thoughts and worries flew from his head. Since neither his father nor Andrew was due home soon, he decided to risk playing his violin in the middle of the day.

But when he got down to the storage room, it wasn't the violin that called to him. He walked straight toward his mother's boxes. Last night he'd gotten through most of them while searching for his mother's Chocolate Mint Squares recipe. Now that he had learned so much from Max and the others at the factory about baking, he wanted to make his mom's special recipe and bring it to everyone to sample. But the only recipe he'd found was one for homemade cucumber face cream, and that didn't sound very tasty.

He knelt in front of the last two unopened boxes and began sorting through them. Pretty much more of the same—books, clothes, a deck of playing cards, old makeup, some loose change. The last box contained two photo albums labeled OUR FAMILY. The living room walls used to display a few family photos of them doing regular family stuff, like playing at the beach and posing next to a fountain while on vacation. Over the years they had been replaced with pictures of him or his brother holding up a trophy, and a few of their father shaking hands with important people. If Philip closed his eyes, he could still see his mother in those old pictures, but his memory of her face had grown dim. He put the albums aside, definitely not ready to stir up old memories that had lain safely buried for nearly a decade.

Under the albums lay some art supplies—half-used tubes of paint, pencils with broken tips, a sketchpad. Reggie had told him once that when she first got sick, his mother took up art to keep her calm. If she'd ever actually completed any paintings, Philip had never found traces of them. He'd also never come across any sheet music for the violin she'd left behind. Maybe she'd only thought about playing it but never actually learned how.

After he lifted out a small plastic bin filled with Magic Markers and colored pens, only one item remained at the bottom of the box—a black fabric pouch. Judging by the shape and the length of the straps, it seemed made to attach around someone's waist. Philip started to toss it aside when a thin, dark blue pocket-sized notebook slid out. Could his mother have written the recipe in there? Or had she kept some sort of journal?

His heart thumped a little faster. What secrets would he uncover if he opened it? All he'd wanted was to find one chocolate recipe to impress his friends with his newly acquired candymaking skills. Now he had uncovered two photo albums and a secret journal. He really wasn't emotionally prepared for this.

He tried to slip the notebook back into the pouch, but his fingers seemed to have trouble letting go of it. Should he call Daisy again for advice? She hadn't been very helpful with the ball of wool, even though that wasn't what he'd really called about. He didn't know how to ask her to keep him company while he looked through his mom's stuff. That was just too weird. And anyway, there was that whole "on fire" thing, so he really shouldn't bug her again.

He decided he'd look at the cover to see what his mom had written there. It wouldn't mean he'd have to open it. He took a deep breath and flipped the notebook over to the front. To his surprise, it wasn't a secret, hidden journal after all. It wasn't even a notebook. He was holding his mother's passport. He'd never seen one up close before, or he'd have recognized it earlier. On the rare occasions when he and Andrew went along on a business trip, their father always held on to all the passports.

Did he need to know if his mom went to Rome for her eighteenth birthday? Or to Aruba on her honeymoon? He flipped the passport back into the box, picked up his violin, and played until his right elbow ached and all other thoughts flew away.

CHAPTER FIVE

Philip had just put the ice pack away in the freezer when his phone rang. "Hello?" he said, hurrying out of the kitchen, where Marietta was busy making lunch.

"Can I speak to Philip?" a girl's voice asked.

"Daisy?" he asked, surprised.

"No, I'm looking for Philip," the girl said. "Philip Ransford?"

"Huh?" he asked, confused. "Is this Daisy?" It didn't sound like her, but what other girl would be calling him?

"No," the girl said. "It's Dylan. Dylan Williams. You called my house looking for me?"

Philip sat down on the closest chair. Dylan Williams was a girl! "Oh!" he said. "Sorry! Yes, this is Philip. Thank you for calling me back. I got your letter."

"I wasn't sure you'd ever see it!" she said, suddenly sounding a little breathless. "You must get so much fan mail. I can't believe I'm really talking to you!"

"Um..." Philip didn't know how to respond to that. "Jumping right in, you wrote in your letter that you read my contest essay. How did you get it? I thought it was private."

"Oh!" she said, sounding surprised at the question. "Well, I guess it's sort of private. The winning essay only goes up after the contest has been over for a few months. And only members of the Confectionary Association can see it. My dad works at **Fudge on a Stick**, so I logged into the network one day when I went to visit him at the store."

"Fudge . . . *Fudge on a Stick*?" Philip repeated.

"He's worked there ten years," she said proudly.

"Do they sell other things on sticks? Other than fudge, I mean?"

"No," she replied. "Why would they do that?"

Philip filed the name in the back of his mind so he could tell the others. They'd get a kick out of it, for sure. But for now he had to get to the bottom of the situation. "Let's get back to my application," he said. "It's supposed to be private. Can you go back and delete it for me?"

"But it's so beautiful," she insisted. "I read the winning essay each year, and trust me, yours was the best I ever read. Why would you want to delete it?"

Philip, although flattered, blurted out loudly, "Because it's full of lies!"

The other end of the phone went quiet. Philip closed his eyes and leaned against the back of the couch. "I'm sorry," he said.

When she didn't reply again, he feared she'd hung up. He couldn't help thinking of something Andrew had warned him about once—that you should never meet your idols, because they will disappoint you. Guess he'd proved that one right.

"Only the Confectionary Association can take it down on their end," she finally said, her voice flat. "Why don't you call and ask."

And then she really did hang up.

Hadn't Dylan heard the expression *If you don't ask, they can't tell you no*? Philip knew immediately that asking was not an option. If he found a way to pull it down himself, the organization would assume it was a computer glitch. But if he pulled it down once they'd already said no, he would be the prime suspect. Of course, they might just say yes, but he couldn't take that chance.

He went back to his room and called Daisy. In the thirty seconds she allotted him, he explained as much as he could of the story and asked if she could hack into the system and delete all traces of his essay. She said he would need to be hardwired into the computer network, but she agreed to have her friend Courtney lend him some kind of gadget that would allow him to do it himself from **Life Is Sweet**'s central computer. "To be clear," she added, sounding very distracted, "I'm not advising you to do this, but I know how determined you get. At least this way I won't have to worry about what you might come up with on your own." The address of where to meet Courtney popped up on the bottom of Philip's screen. Daisy signed off by saying, "Don't get caught. And if you do, forget my name."

CHAPTER SIX

With five minutes to spare, the limo pulled into the empty parking lot at the rear of what used to be the Spring Haven High School before the school moved to a bigger location across town. "Can you give me a hint about what we're doing here?" Reggie called over his shoulder. "All you've given me so far is 'Reggie, essay, car, now!' That leaves room for a lot of questions."

Philip peered out the rear window. He could see the back of the school on one side and the football field on the other. "You don't want to know," he replied. He had given Reggie that answer dozens—if not hundreds—of times in the past. It kept them both safer when Reggie didn't know the details of Philip's schemes. Reggie didn't even know Daisy was a spy, and Philip planned to keep it that way.

"Fine," Reggie grumbled. "But it's not against the law, right?"

Philip shifted in his seat. "Define *against the law*."

Reggie sighed. "Is it likely to land you or both of us in jail?"

Philip shook his head and lied. "Definitely not."

Reggie pulled into the farthest spot in the lot and turned off the car. "Good. Let's wait outside. You could use the fresh air."

"I get plenty of fresh air," Philip said, not budging.

"No, you don't," Reggie replied. "Then we're getting out so we don't look so suspicious sitting in an abandoned parking lot."

"I told you we didn't need to take the limo," Philip grumbled.

"I have to pick up your father from his meeting soon. You know he prefers I pick him up in this car."

His dad certainly did like to impress. Philip climbed out and leaned against the car, staring at the entrance to the parking lot.

"What, you no longer wait for me to open the door for you?" Reggie joked, joining him.

"I can get back in again if you want me to," Philip replied tartly.

Reggie shook his head. "I'm good."

They waited for another minute, but no cars turned in. Philip decided if he was the nail-biting type (which he absolutely was not), he would be biting them to the quick at that point.

"I need to pick your father up from his meeting in a few minutes," Reggie said. "Any chance we can hurry this along?"

"She'll be here any second," Philip promised. He checked his watch. She was late. Or she would be in exactly forty-one seconds.

"I'm glad you're not swayed by current fashion trends," Reggie said, glancing at Philip's wrist. "Most kids today check their electronic devices for the time."

"I'm not most kids," Philip replied.

"No, you are not," Reggie agreed. "You haven't asked, but no, I didn't find any more letters that talked about your essay."

"That's good," Philip said. "Shouldn't be a problem after today anyway. Unless we're being stood up."

"You're not being stood up," a girl's voice said from behind them. They both whirled around to find themselves facing a teenage girl on a huge black horse. She must have ridden across the field and approached them from the back. He should have figured a friend of Daisy's wouldn't arrive in the normal fashion.

She swung down from the horse in one graceful move. She was

taller than she'd appeared, with long blond hair that she swept off her shoulders with one hand. He thought he smelled grapefruit.

He forced himself to stop staring at her hair, which fell in waves almost all the way to her waist. Reggie gave a little chuckle. Philip nudged him with his elbow. "Some privacy, please?"

Reggie held up his hands and backed away. Philip waited until the car door fully closed again before turning back to the girl.

"You're Courtney?" he asked.

She nodded. "Password?"

"Password?"

She took a rolled-up envelope out of her pocket. "I can't give you this without a password. You could be anyone."

"But I'm not anyone. I'm Philip. Daisy's friend."

She shook her head. "Daisy doesn't have any friends."

Insulted, he put his hands on his hips. "From the candy factory job a few months ago?"

She shrugged. "We don't discuss our gigs with each other. It's against the rules."

Philip glanced at his watch again. Mr. Sweet would be expecting him soon. He had to get moving. "Well, I'm who you're supposed to meet. Why else would I be waiting in this parking lot?"

She shrugged. "Who knows. You and your chauffeur could be out for a leisurely Sunday drive and pulled over for a bite to eat."

"It's Monday," Philip pointed out. "And we have no food. And Reggie hates the word *chauffeur*."

"Password," she repeated.

"Daisy didn't give me one," Philip insisted. Had she? He went over their brief conversation in his head. She definitely hadn't.

Maddeningly, Courtney closed her hand around the envelope.

"Candy?" Philip guessed, figuring Daisy would have come up with a password that linked the two of them together.

Courtney shook her head.

"Harmonicandy, then? Rowboat? **Life Is Sweet**?"

She shook it again. Hair everywhere, more grapefruit. He had to focus. "I don't know! Magpie?"

At the sound of her name, the horse whinnied and stamped her foot. Courtney smiled. "You got it." She handed him the small envelope. He could feel something hard inside it, about the size of a pack of gum.

"You will plug it into the central computer like you would a flash drive," she explained. "But it's programmed to allow you past any encryptions or password requests you might find when you get to the website. Whatever you delete will be permanently gone, including any other copies that may exist elsewhere on the Web."

"Great, perfect." He slipped it into his pocket.

"But the best part," Courtney continued as she climbed up onto Magpie's back, "is that if anyone has already printed out what you just deleted, those copies will instantly disintegrate, leaving behind nothing but ash."

Philip gaped, his head spinning with the possibilities of making papers disappear from a distance. "That's just—just amazing!" he stammered. "I can't believe such a thing is possible."

Courtney shook her head and picked up the reins. "Daisy warned me you'd be easy, but man, no, it's not possible. Do I look like Houdini to you? Thanks for making my day, though."

With another swing of her hair, she galloped off.

Philip grumbled. He bet he hadn't really needed a password, either.

You have to drop me first," Philip insisted. "I don't want to sit in the car with him."

Reggie turned off the crowded main street and headed for the fancy part of town, where Philip's dad usually held his business lunches. "You know your dad doesn't like to wait," Reggie replied. "I'll just pick him up and take you to the factory right after."

"Please, Reggie, it will take five minutes extra to drop me off first."

The car stopped at a red light. Reggie glanced at him in the rearview mirror. "Why does it matter if you get there a few minutes later?"

Philip knew if he had any chance of Reggie doing this for him, he'd have to tell him the truth. But until he signed those contracts, he didn't want anyone to know his plan. Even *after* he signed them. So he quickly decided to go with a close version of the truth. "I just...I just don't want him to know about the Harmonicandy debut tomorrow. When he sees all the cars in the parking lot at the factory, he's going to figure it out."

"Why don't you want him to know? It's a big day for you. I'm sure he'd want to celebrate it with you."

Philip frowned. Reggie drummed his fingers on the steering wheel. "Okay, maybe not celebrate exactly, but that's because this particular win of yours meant he lost a lot of money. You ruined his plans."

"I know," Philip said. "What if he tries to stop me from going or something? That would ruin the day for all the others, too."

"Oh, fine," Reggie said, making a U-turn and getting honked at from both sides.

Philip sank back, relieved. He had no idea how he was going to get his father to sign that contract, but he couldn't deal with it right then.

He tucked Courtney's device into his briefcase and went over the plan in his head. Arrive at the factory, sneak into the Computer Room (next door to the Cotton Candy Room), do the deed. Get in, get out, have some cotton candy. If anyone asked what he was doing in there, he'd say he had to fill out Harmonicandy paperwork and tax forms, and that would bore them into not asking more questions.

Reggie slammed on the brakes in the factory driveway. "Out," he commanded. Philip barely had time to grab his briefcase and close the door behind him before Reggie screeched off again. He wiped the dust off his pants legs and started toward the factory entrance.

Drat! Miles was sitting on the porch reading! Philip didn't want to lie to him, but he couldn't take him along. Philip ducked behind a tree just as Miles lowered his book. He counted to ten, then peeked out again. The book was back up in front of Miles's face. Philip took off at a run toward the tunnel where the delivery trucks dropped off supplies and the farmers stored their crops. He knew it would eventually lead inside.

The tunnel felt nice and cool, but he couldn't linger. He darted around barrels of nuts (cashews, peanuts, hazelnuts, and pista-chios), piles of damp soil earmarked for the various types of trees in the Tropical Room, and a huge bucket of blueberries (he stopped and grabbed a handful of those). He had almost reached the door marked FACTORY, HALLWAY B when he tripped over a knee-high bag of Leapin' Lolly sticks. Not the whole lollypop, just the stick. He managed to keep his balance and stay mostly upright, but the bag split open. The old Philip would have kept right on going. Actually, the current Philip would have liked to keep right on going, too. But he forced himself to gather up the sticks that had fallen out. He knew he couldn't put them back in the bag once they'd hit the floor. Not seeing a trash can, he opened his briefcase and shoved them inside. He'd have to toss them out later. Then he tied up the bag as best he could and dropped a fifty-dollar bill on top. He hoped that would be enough to cover the lost sticks. He had no idea what things cost. It would have to do.

Once inside, he knew there would be no way to fly under the radar, but he had entirely underestimated how many people would be crowding the halls. He wanted to shout that the Harmonicandy wouldn't be coming out until tomorrow. Still twenty-four hours away, people!

But "Congratulations!" and "Hey, it's him!" flew at him from all sides, mostly from people he had never seen before but who clearly knew who he was. Either they had been at the competition, or maybe they recognized him from the giant poster the Confectionary Association sent out each year to all the factories, candy stores, and distribution centers. He had a few extra posters rolled up under his bed. He'd have to remember to tack one up on Andrew's wall just to be funny. (Although if it also served to remind Andrew that only one Ransford boy had had a poster made for him, then so be it.)

He remembered what the publicity folks had taught him, and he smiled pleasantly at the visitors, thanking them as they gripped his shoulder or patted his arm in passing. The youngest of the visitors just stared up at him in awe.

Philip had never been inside the Computer Room before. He pictured it as the control center of the whole factory—walls full of state-of-the-art computer monitors, rows of techies churning data and calculating sales projections. What he found instead? A brown wooden desk with a three-legged chair in front of it, a half-empty bookcase, an oil painting of a tree on a beach, and a clunky old desktop computer that must have been older than he was. A worn piece of paper taped to the front of the desk said:

Username: LifeIsSweet
Password: LifeIsSweet

Clearly the Candymaker wasn't too concerned with security! Or decorating! Philip quickly sat in front of the computer and nearly fell twice before he figured out how to balance on the back legs of the broken chair. He typed in the username and password and waited. The computer beeped a few times and slowly crackled to life. An old picture of four-year-old Logan's smiling face stared at him from the background of the screen. His scar-free face brought Philip right back to the day they'd first met. He actually reached his hand out to touch the screen.

Conversation and laughter from the hall reminded him of his task. He unlatched his briefcase, and only the fact that the hinge momentarily caught saved him from chasing after a hundred lollypop sticks.

He unwrapped Daisy's device. Other than being heavy and made of what felt like solid silver, it looked exactly like the regular flash drives he always used to back up documents for school. He felt a moment of dread wash over him. Was this Daisy's idea of an elaborate practical joke? Could she be getting back at him for bothering her twice while she was on an assignment? Did this computer even *have* a USB port? Fortunately, he found one on the back of the hard drive tower below the desk. He stuck in the device and waited.

The screen jumped for a split second, but nothing else changed. Then Logan's face splintered into thousands of pieces and the screen went dark. Philip could actually see his own startled reflection mirrored in it!

A single empty text box appeared in the middle. The cursor flashed impatiently. Philip quickly typed in the address for the Confectionary Association's website. Instantly Daisy's device went to work trying password after password to get into the private areas that only the administrators of the network had access to. All combinations of numbers and letters flew across the screen until...

He was in! He wasted no time finding the applications for the competition and scrolled down through the names. Literally *thousands* of kids had applied! He had no idea the number was so high. He wondered briefly what he would have done if he hadn't been chosen and was thankful he'd never have to find out.

He found the section with the top thirty-two finalists and saw the group of names assigned to **Life Is Sweet?**. He had always been curious what the others' essays had said. The lies in Daisy's essay had to be even worse than his! Here was his chance to find out. His finger hovered over the keyboard, but in the end he went only to his own. The small text beside it told him it had been opened a few times around the time of the contest, one time two months ago, which must have been by Dylan, and then again within the last twenty-four hours. He hoped that last one was Dylan again, but there was no way to know. At least after today it would be gone.

He highlighted his name and hit the Delete button. A warning popped up, telling him this would be a permanent decision. Another warning box flashed on the screen from Daisy's device, reminding him that any other copies elsewhere on the Internet would also delete themselves. At least Courtney hadn't been kidding about that part.

For a split second he debated reading the essay again before deleting it, since this would be his last chance. But then Mrs.

Sweet's voice came over the loudspeaker, announcing the end to visiting hours, and startled him so much his finger flew down onto the key.

It was done. Gone. No more record of his lies. He shut down the computer, pulled out the device, and hurried out of the room feeling better than he had in days. He may have even whistled as he strode through the emptying hallways toward the Harmonicandy Room. The essay was gone for good, talking to Daisy last night had made him feel better about accepting praise, and having Andrew home for the summer would take some of his father's attention off him. Maybe they'd even have fun together. Stranger things had happened.

Philip could hear muffled laughter inside the Harmonicandy Room as he approached. Max hadn't allowed any of them even a tiny peek, so this would be his first time seeing it. He was eager to see his friends, too, even though Miles exhausted him. He might even let them drag him outside to play on the lawn later. He had to admit that Name That Cloud had grown on him. He could swear he saw a bowl of spaghetti and meatballs in the sky last time.

Then he opened the door and fell—head over heels—in love.

CHAPTER EIGHT

Emotions rushed at him from all sides—pride, disbelief, joy, and, most of all, a fierce need to protect what they'd built here. All of this existed because of his last-minute idea of a chocolate bar that played music. It hadn't truly felt real until he stepped into the room and saw how much effort had gone into bringing the Harmonicandy to life.

With a deep breath, he pulled himself together and got to work. He wanted to know everything about the processing and distribution of the candy. He'd learned a lot in the last four months of following people around, and he knew the right questions to ask.

When Mr. Sweet announced he was taking them on a tour to promote the Harmonicandy, Philip knew there was no chance at all that his father would give him permission to go. Then Mr. Sweet told him his father had not only said yes but had made a joke about bringing his knitting. His father had charm, ambition, intelligence, and guts. But he did *not* have a sense of humor. At least not that he ever let Philip see. And how would he know about the yarn? Only one answer made any sense.

Philip slipped away as soon as no one was watching and closed himself in the storage room by Max's lab. He'd spent a lot of time in that room during the contest, and he still went in there when he wanted to think, or play his violin, or do homework. Now he used the solitude to call his brother.

"Really, Andrew? Knitting?"

Philip heard a *thwack* in the background that could only be Andrew's racket hitting a tennis ball. "Sorry, bro, couldn't resist," Andrew replied, confirming Philip's theory. His brother was breathing hard. "You looked very attached to that ball of yarn last night." *Thwack*. "It worked, though, right? Just like when I used to call out sick for you in school so you could work on your spelling bee words, or a fencing tournament, or whatever other contest you were training for."

Philip began pacing around the small room, which basically meant turning one way, taking three steps, then turning the other. "Yes, pretending to be Dad fooled Mr. Sweet, but what good will it do? Our real father will never let me go when he finds out. I told you, he doesn't want anything to do with the factory."

Thwack. "I've got that all worked out. Reggie's supposed to take you to your Talented Kid contest, right?"

"Yes, but I'm not planning to go."

Thwack. "You'll have to go," Andrew said. "It's your excuse to be out of town. So instead of Reggie taking you, I'll tell Dad *I* want to take you. You know, to spend more time together."

"But he'll notice that you haven't actually left the house."

"So I'll go visit some college buddies. I have those now. Well, I have one, but who's counting?"

One last volley, and Andrew's opponent called the game over. "Good game," he heard the other guy say. "Good game," Andrew replied. "Meet you at the clubhouse in ten." There was some rustling in the background as they no doubt shook hands and put their rackets back in their sleeves. Philip knew that if his brother was trying to get something from the guy he was playing, he'd let him win. Andrew was all about strategy.

"We good?" Andrew asked Philip. "I've got a job interview to prep for."

Philip stopped pacing and stood in front of the sink. He looked in the mirror above it while he spoke. "Before you hang up, tell me what you meant about us having grandparents."

"Grand*mother*," Andrew corrected. "You're a smart kid. You'll figure it out."

Andrew hung up. Philip continued staring in the mirror. Figure *what* out? He shook his head. He could only focus on one problem at a time. Was he really going to sneak away? It wasn't like he hadn't done things behind his father's back before. He hadn't exactly asked permission to enter the candymaking contest, but his dad was never very involved in his plans anyway. This was a week, though. Could he convince his father he'd need a full week away for the talent contest? A lie that big would fill up his small notebook for sure. He needed guidance from someone familiar with sneaking around—someone who did it for a living.

He pulled out his vid com and called Daisy. He still wasn't on fire but felt that this counted as a big enough crisis to bother her. He was annoyed, although not surprised, when she didn't pick up and he had to leave a message. He led off by trying to convince her to come on the trip. He'd just started asking for advice on how to pull off the trip without his dad finding out when the knob on the storage-room door began to turn. He must really have been distracted, because he always locked the door behind him. He got out a quick "Call me back" before the door opened.

Henry walked in and kept walking, right past Philip! A sense of unease settled onto Philip as he watched Henry step squarely on a yellow rubber duck, which he then tossed back toward the open box full of ducks. The duck missed the box, but Henry didn't seem to notice. He reached up and slid a blue plastic bin marked OLD RECEIPTS off the top shelf. He wiped the dust off it with his sleeve, then tucked it under his arm. It wasn't until Henry was halfway out the door that Philip spoke up. "Um, Henry?"

Henry stopped and whirled around, clearly startled. It took slightly longer than it should have before his eyes landed on Philip, who raised his eyebrows. "Didn't you see me standing here?" he asked.

After an awkward silence, Henry finally sighed and waved Philip toward the door. "C'mon, let's talk."

Even though the halls were empty, neither of them spoke as they walked together to the Marshmallow Room. Henry shut the door behind them, then ducked into his office to stash the bin. Philip waited impatiently. "So?" he asked when Henry reappeared.

"You first," Henry said. "Why were you lurking around a storage room?"

Philip figured he may as well be honest. Henry knew all about his dad anyway. "Mr. Sweet didn't actually talk to my father about me going on the trip. It was my brother, Andrew, pretending to be my dad. He said he'd cover for me."

"I figured there was some explanation for your father's apparent change of heart," Henry said. "Are you still going?"

"I think I am," Philip said. "When will I have this opportunity again to be part of promoting a candy bar that I helped create? Let's face it. I'm not going to be a candymaker when I grow up. You won't tell, will you?"

"I won't tell what?" Henry asked innocently.

"Thanks, Henry. Okay, your turn. Something's going on with you."

After a slight pause, Henry admitted, "I'm losing my eyesight."

"What?"

Henry repeated it. "I'm losing my sight. I'm going blind. It came on suddenly, starting with my peripheral vision. In a few months my vision will be ninety-five percent gone."

Philip stared at his friend, the person who'd recognized him right away when he'd shown up for the contest. The only one who knew his whole story and still didn't give up on him. "When did you notice this? Is there anything you can do to stop it?"

"It crept up on me," Henry said, his voice matter-of-fact. "When my eyes got blurry, I thought it was from lack of sleep, or that staring at all those white marshmallows had finally gotten to me. But I went to the doctor, and then a specialist, and then three more specialists. They all came to the same conclusion. The pressure building up inside my eyes will soon disrupt my eyesight to the point where I will only be able to see the outlines of shapes."

Philip felt like someone had punched him in the stomach. He had very little experience feeling empathy. He was at a loss for words, an occurrence that seemed to be happening to him more and more lately. For someone who prided himself on being in control and having the last word in any situation, it was an awful feeling. He finally stammered out, "I'm—I'm really sorry, Henry."

Henry nodded. "I have to get back to work. I want to get a new batch done for tomorrow."

"Can I help with anything?"

Henry hesitated, then gestured with his thumb toward his office. "Well, I do have a lot of paperwork piled up. Could you enter some receipts into the computer for me? They're on the desk. A little messy in there, I'm afraid."

Philip nodded. He'd helped Henry with the nightly paperwork before, so he knew what to do. He took his time walking to the back room, though. He wanted to make sure Henry wasn't sitting too close to the burner while he stirred the marshmallow mix. "Maybe you should let the machine do that for you," he suggested from the doorway to the office.

Henry shook his head without turning around. "The first

Harmonicandy deserves a handmade batch of marshmallow. Trust me—I could do this with my eyes closed."

What could he say to that? Philip only nodded and went into the office. The desk was more than a little bit messy. Last time he'd been back here, it had been very well organized. But now papers and folders were strewn all over the desk. He saw all the pairs of thick glasses, and his stomach knotted up again. He'd seen Henry wearing them over the last few months, and while it had registered that they'd gotten progressively thicker, he never stopped to think why.

He forced himself to get down to the task at hand. He pulled out everything that looked like a receipt for a work-related purchase and sorted them. He then entered them into the spreadsheet on the computer and corrected some that had been entered in the wrong column. Henry was weeks behind, but the work went quickly. Philip looked around for some kind of tray system to put the leftover papers in to make it easier for Henry to find. He had to push away the thought that it wouldn't matter soon anyway. Henry wouldn't be able to do paperwork at all. He wouldn't be able to make marshmallows, either. The thought of that made tears rush to Philip's eyes, and he had to blink hard before he could see clearly again.

He opened the bottom desk drawer and found the bin marked OLD RECEIPTS that Henry had just taken from the storage room. Maybe Henry wanted him to put the receipts in there once they were entered into the computer.

But when he pried the lid off the box, there weren't any receipts in there at all, only old photographs and cards, some still in their envelopes. After unearthing more than he'd wanted to of his mom's old stuff, Philip had no interest in pawing through someone else's. He closed the lid and put the bin back in the drawer. Reggie would be here soon. He needed to get going.

When Philip stepped out of the office, Henry was waiting by

the door. The lights were off, and the fresh marshmallow mix was cooling in the fridge. "Thank you for your help," Henry said. "I would prefer that you didn't tell anyone about our conversation yet. Especially not Logan. He wouldn't go on the trip if he knew, and I believe it's really important for him to go. For all of you to go."

Philip nodded, then said, "Maybe there's some kind of experimental surgery or something like that. If money's the issue, I—"

But Henry shook his head. "Thank you, but I've come to terms with it. This condition doesn't get better no matter how much money I could throw at it. Now, let's stop with the sad stuff. Tomorrow is your big day. You should only be excited right now."

"I don't know what to feel anymore," Philip admitted. "This day has been a total roller coaster. You don't even know the half of it."

Henry patted him on the arm. "Hey, I've cried twice today, and neither time had anything to do with my eyes. Well, except as a source for the tears, but you know what I mean. Some days you control life; other days life controls you."

Philip wasn't a big fan of platitudes, but Henry was a wise man. He nodded as Henry headed off down the hall. Philip noticed he was weaving a little, trying to stay in the center of the hallway as he swiveled his head from side to side. Philip hurried after him, feeling like he should be close by in case Henry veered toward a wall or tripped.

Henry came to a stop outside the library when he noticed he wasn't alone. "Young man, I'm fine. I can still see straight ahead of me. You don't need to hover."

"Who, me?" Philip said innocently. "Can't a guy get a book from the library without people accusing him of hovering?"

"I am fairly certain I've never seen you step foot in that library," Henry said.

"Me? I practically live there," Philip said, pretending to be indignant. "Now, if you don't mind, I have books to read." He turned on his heel and pushed open the door. Henry chuckled and continued on his way.

Philip was glad to see Miles by the display table. Teasing him felt normal on a day when little else had. He was about to ask Miles if he was going for a world's record for Band-Aid wearing, but then a thought popped into his head. Did he *owe* it to his father to invite him to the Kickoff? Maybe once his dad saw the Harmonicandy and what a big deal it was, he'd get on board. Or maybe his dad planned to come anyway. Philip had never actually hidden the event from him. Whether his father had paid attention to the Harmonicandy's production schedule was a different matter.

But then Reggie arrived and told Philip his dad had left early for his trip, so the question of whether he'd show up at the Kickoff was moot. Between worrying about Henry and being angry at his father for making things so hard, he didn't have room in his brain to be annoyed when Reggie offered Miles a ride home, even though he still sort of was.

At first, having Miles in the car felt wrong. It was like two parts of his life colliding, and it made his stomach churn and his throat go dry. Maybe Miles would be quiet and Philip could be alone with his thoughts. But Miles being Miles, that wasn't likely to happen.

Sure enough, two seconds later, the questions began. Philip kept silent, hoping sooner or later Miles was bound to get the hint. But he didn't, and somehow Philip heard himself referring to Logan and Miles as his friends, and his throat tightened up again.

When the limo pulled up outside the O'Leary house, Philip couldn't look away. It was smaller than his house, of course—most in town were—but it looked so homey, with flowers around the edges of a small lawn, and bikes in the driveway, and a little garden gnome wearing a pointy hat.

Miles was talking to him again, apologizing for the ride or for talking or whatever, so Philip mumbled something back

263

halfheartedly. He was distracted by a dark-haired man headed away from the house. The man was leading a dog with a stuffed animal in its mouth. He must have been a friend or a relative who'd come to visit, and that sent Philip's mind thinking about how little he knew about his own extended family. If there was a grandmother out there somewhere, who else might be lurking in his family tree? Then Mr. O'Leary came out of the house, and Miles hopped out of the limo, and Philip pulled himself away from the window.

"You okay?" Reggie called back to him as they headed home.

Philip didn't answer, so Reggie kept talking. "Are you worried about the trip? I know you're in good hands or I wouldn't have told Andrew to say yes."

Philip looked up in surprise. "*You* told him?"

Reggie nodded. "He ran it by me first, and I agreed."

Philip felt relief flow through him. Having Reggie's approval to go was almost as good as his dad's. "Thanks, Reggie."

"Don't thank me too quickly. You can take those two mailbags with you. You'll have plenty of time to answer mail on the road."

"I thought you were going to do that."

"I only said I'd *read* it," he replied. "Plus I'll be too busy covering for you."

Philip chuckled. "Fair enough."

Andrew stepped into Philip's room at exactly 9:50 a.m. "We leave in ten minutes. What's with the tie?"

Philip finished adjusting the knot in the mirror and turned around. "A lot of big players in the candy biz will be at the factory today."

Andrew nodded appreciatively. "Gotta dress to impress, as I always say."

"You bet," Philip said. "What's with the tennis whites again? I thought you were looking for a job."

"I am," Andrew replied. "A few of the big power guys play doubles every Tuesday morning. Yesterday I overheard one of them say he was short a partner, so I volunteered. I figure I help him win with my awesome backhand, he gets me an interview with his company. It's a win-win!"

Philip nodded in approval. "Figured you had some strategy. I have to finish packing, so if you don't mind…"

"Eight minutes left," Andrew said. "Then Reggie and I leave without you."

"Why can't you drive yourself there?" Philip asked, placing a folded pile of clothes neatly into his open suitcase.

"When I can show up in a limo?"

He was right, of course. "I'll be ready."

Andrew ducked back out, and Philip began stuffing things into his suitcase with greater speed. Reggie had taken pity on him and only gave him a dozen letters to answer. He opened his briefcase to stash the letters inside, and a cascade of lollypop sticks fell out. "Argh!" He didn't have time to pick them up.

When he was done packing, he double-checked the list from Mrs. Sweet until he was satisfied that he'd gotten everything. He'd added a few things that weren't on her list, like a button-down shirt and a pair of dress shoes. He couldn't very well wear shorts and a T-shirt to meet influential candy shop owners, and certainly not to the Talented Kid competition. At some point he'd have to tell the others they needed to make an extra stop, but that could wait.

He put the suitcase outside his door for Reggie to take, then hurried downstairs to the room behind his father's office. He grabbed his notebook and sheet music and checked that his rosin, extra strings, and cloth were in their compartments in the case. Satisfied, he clicked the case shut. He closed his eyes and stood in the middle of the room. After a full minute passed, he reopened the case, tossed his mother's passport inside, and clicked it shut again. *Now* he was ready to go.

Instead of driving straight up to the factory's front door as usual, Reggie followed the stream of cars and parked in the rear of the parking lot. "All this is for the Kickoff?" Reggie asked. "Looks like a big deal. Perhaps you should have told your father about it."

"I was going to. But he took off early anyway, so it doesn't matter."

"You didn't even give him a chance."

Before Philip could respond, Reggie got out and headed toward

266

the trunk. Once it was clear that he wouldn't be opening the door for him, Philip grabbed his briefcase and got out. Reggie was already halfway up the driveway, wheeling the suitcase behind him.

"C'mon, Reggie. We both know he wouldn't have come anyway."

Reggie just kept wheeling. When he got to the door, he turned and asked, "Do you want me to come instead?"

"I'm fine, Reggie," Philip insisted. "Really. I'm used to it."

Reggie put Philip's suitcase down on the porch, and his expression softened. "All right. Have a good time today and safe travels. Keep in touch with me and your brother." He reached out his hand and Philip shook it, holding it longer than a normal handshake.

Philip felt an unfamiliar pang as he watched Reggie walk away and get smaller and smaller. The feeling followed him inside, where he left his suitcase and briefcase in a pile with all the others. It didn't worry him for a second that leaving them unattended could be risky. It just wasn't like that at **Life Is Sweet**.

When he stepped into the Harmonicandy Room and saw the way Miles's parents looked at their son, he realized what that feeling was. Reggie had looked at Philip the same way, with the same affection and pride. Maybe Philip didn't have the most traditional family, but Reggie really cared about him, and, in his own way, so did Andrew. He'd proven it now with the trip, and he'd proven it when he first left for college and gave Philip his private notebook with all his tips for success.

For a second he considered calling Reggie and asking him to stay after all, but then it was time to press the button and he had to focus on that. The Harmonicandy was about to be a Real Thing! Henry squeezed his shoulder and beamed at him through his thick glasses. There were plenty of friends around him, and that was more than enough.

Still, when Reggie showed up again, Philip's surprise quickly turned to gratitude. He was glad he'd left the violin in the car and even more relieved when he saw that his mother's passport hadn't fallen out. When everyone else had turned away, Reggie whispered to Philip, "Mr. Sweet just said something very strange. He said, 'You all must be very proud of Philip's decision about what to do with his portion of the profits.' What did he mean by that?"

Philip froze. He didn't want to talk about it. Reggie tried again, a little louder, but he must have seen Philip cringe, because he let it go with a gentle pat on Philip's shoulder. Philip relaxed. "Thanks," he whispered.

By the time Philip handed out candy bar after candy bar under the bright blue sky, he didn't remember ever feeling so happy. If Daisy had been there, it would have been a perfect moment. He looked over at Logan, who had swept away the hair he usually had hanging over the worst of his scars, and at Miles, who had changed so much from the kid with the slightly haunted look in his eyes when the contest first started. Miles saw Philip looking at him, showed a flicker of surprise, and grinned back. He held up a Harmonicandy and gave a thumbs-up.

"Are you going up there?" Reggie asked when Mr. Sweet began to address the crowd. Philip was about to say no when Mr. Sweet waved him up. He threw Reggie a startled look, but Reggie patted his shoulder encouragingly and whispered, "You got this. No one can make things up on the spot like you." They grinned at each other, and Philip squared his shoulders and walked to the front. As captain of the debate team at school, he'd given plenty of speeches before, and of course he'd accepted more than his fair share of awards. But this would be the first speech that really meant something to him.

He spoke too fast, trying to get out what he wanted to say. He knew everyone probably wanted to hear the Harmonicandy and not him, so he wrapped it up by saying, "Let's see what this thing can do!" For a minute it felt like he was back at the candy contest, praying that when the judge blew into the bar, notes would come out. He crossed his fingers and blew.

He couldn't tell which notes were his and which belonged to the hundreds of people blowing along with him, but the resulting music was one of the best things he'd ever heard. Hearing Logan say a few minutes later that there was something wrong with the Harmonicandy ranked as one of the *worst* things he'd ever heard. His stomach twisted into a tight knot. At least Reggie had just left and didn't have to see how quickly things had turned.

As they raced around to find Henry, Philip thought back to those two days when they were experimenting with the ingredients. He could remember making a few trips to the Marshmallow Room, and he was pretty sure Henry had come into the lab once or twice, but it was all a blur now. If Henry *hadn't* tasted it, then they were going to all this trouble for nothing.

Philip glared at Miles and Logan when they left him down at the pond as he posed for pictures, but they didn't even notice, which was typical of them. He knew his mean streak was sneaking in as his mood darkened, but he was too upset to do anything about it. He had to fake every smile as the moms snapped pictures. It seemed like hours before Logan and Miles returned and rescued him, even though it couldn't have been more than fifteen minutes.

When they finally found Henry by the marsh, Philip shouted at him for trying to ditch them. But as angry as he was, he was more scared that Henry could have fallen into the water and drowned!

He had no idea why Miles would say Henry was lying about not knowing anything about the chocolate mix-up (did Miles really think he couldn't understand his backward talk?), but at least they were still going on the trip.

Philip walked very close to Henry as they made their way through the fields toward the front of the factory. He was angry and confused, but he wouldn't let Henry fall. He kicked an ear of corn out of the way right before Henry would have stepped on it and maybe pitched forward onto his face.

"Are you all right, Philip?" Henry whispered.

"No," Philip replied. "You?"

Henry shook his head. "I'm sorry about all this. So, so sorry."

Something about the way Henry apologized brought back a memory. Philip had been in his cubicle in Max's lab and had all the ingredients laid out on the table. He was totally panicking about not knowing what to do, when Henry stopped by to check on how things were going. Henry made some waving gesture and knocked over a small bowl of chocolate that was on the table. He kept saying how sorry he was, over and over, as he replaced it with a new bowl he just happened to have with him. Philip hadn't given it a second thought at the time, nor in the four months since that day. But he was giving it a second thought now!

They reached the front of the building before he could find the words to question Henry about the incident. Whoever would be taking care of them for the next week would be waiting. Philip had a momentary hope that maybe it would be Reggie after all. But a battered old minivan sat idling in the driveway. Reggie would never drive a minivan. If it couldn't be someone from the factory—like Randall, or even Avery—then who could it be?

Philip's eyes widened when he saw AJ step away from the car, swinging a set of keys around his finger.

"Who's up for a road trip?" AJ called out.

Miles and Logan gasped in surprise, then raised their hands like they were in class. "I am!" they shouted at the same time, running toward the car. Henry smiled after them like an amused grandfather. Philip faced the man who had been the one person in the factory who really knew him, the man he had trusted with his secrets, who had always looked out for him. He tried to keep the shaking out of his voice as he said, "I remember where I got the chocolate from."

Henry took off his glasses, wiped them on his shirt, and put them back on. Then he patted Philip on the shoulder. "You can thank me later."

PART FIVE

ALL

CHAPTER ONE

I t wasn't easy for Logan to pry his parents away from all the guests at the Kickoff, but he finally got them to come with him. "This is AJ," Logan said when they reached the front hall. "He's Daisy's cousin and our friend."

"You look familiar," Mr. Sweet told AJ as they shook hands. "Have we met before?"

"I don't believe so, sir," AJ replied. "I must have one of those faces." He flashed a grin that managed to look both charming and sincere at the same time.

Logan tried not to squirm. If his dad recognized AJ from the candymaking contest—when he'd pretended to work for the Confectionary Association—it would be hard to convince the Candymaker that AJ was, in fact, Daisy's cousin. Which, of course, he wasn't. Oh boy, this was confusing. Logan looked around for Miles and saw him dragging his parents by the hands toward them.

"Since no one at the factory can take us, is it all right if AJ brings us on the tour?" Logan asked. "He's very mature. And, um, dependable."

"And you know that how?" the Candymaker replied, finally turning away from his examination of AJ's face. "Being a chaperone is a huge responsibility to take on."

Miles and his parents joined the group, and Miles echoed Logan's claim. "Yeah, AJ's totally responsible and an excellent driver. I would trust him with my life. I mean, not that my life would be in danger in a car with him. No, sir. Heh-heh, I mean—"

Logan threw him his best "stop talking" look. Miles clamped his mouth shut. He couldn't help his nerves. They *had* to go on this trip!

Mr. O'Leary placed his hand on Miles's shoulder. "Son, I know you want to go very badly, but we can hardly send three kids out on the road for a week with someone we don't know."

Mrs. Sweet squinted at AJ. "I've definitely seen you before," she said. Logan and Miles exchanged a worried look. But she only said, "You've dropped Daisy off a few times when she came to visit. Right?"

Both Logan and Miles relaxed a bit. AJ's cover was still intact.

"Yes, ma'am. I did."

"Why didn't you ever come inside?" Mr. Sweet asked, tilting his head at him. "Most people can't pass up a chance to see the inner workings of a candy factory."

Without missing a beat, AJ replied, "Daisy's parents aren't around a lot, and her time at the factory is so important to her. I didn't want to get in the way of that."

Whether the whole truth or not, AJ's response seemed to have the intended effect on Logan's mom, who patted AJ's arm kindly.

"You may well be an excellent cousin," Miles's mother said, "but that doesn't mean you're an excellent driver, or responsible enough to make sure that these kids are safe and fed and rested and that they get where they're supposed to go." She looked worriedly at Miles's father, who nodded in agreement.

"Maybe these will help alleviate your concerns," AJ said, pulling a large envelope out of the bag he had slung over one shoulder. He opened the envelope and slid out a stack of official-looking papers and badges. At a glance, Logan could see they were made out in the name of AJ Carpenter.

The parents began to look through them. "Very impressive," Mr. O'Leary said, nodding his head.

"You're only twenty-two?" the Candymaker asked. "And you're a black belt in three martial arts and a licensed mechanic and have a double graduate degree in child psychology and history?"

"According to this, he speaks six languages!" Miles's dad waved a page titled *Lists of Accomplishments* in the air.

"Five, really. My Klingon is a little rusty." AJ admitted this with a wink.

"That's the made-up *Star Trek* language," Miles whispered to Logan.

"Ah," Logan whispered back.

Henry stepped forward for the first time. "I think we can all agree that AJ is a fine lad. We've gotten to know each other over the last few months, and I trust him wholeheartedly." Miles risked a glance at Logan, who also looked surprised at that information.

Logan's father held up a finger, then gestured for his wife and the O'Learys to join him inside the Cocoa Room with Henry. Philip thought about following them but went over to the pile of suitcases and grabbed his notebook out of his briefcase instead. For the first time in weeks he felt the need to throw notes down on the page. It wouldn't complete his violin composition, but it would bring him closer.

Miles and Logan barely glanced over at him. As soon as the door closed behind the grown-ups, they crowded around AJ and eagerly peppered him with questions.

"Slow down, my young friends. One at a time."

"Speaking of young," Logan said, "I thought you were only eighteen."

AJ shrugged. "I'm whatever age I need to be for the assignment."

"So none of that other stuff was real, either?" Miles asked, disappointed. He'd been looking forward to helping AJ brush up on his Klingon.

"That information is classified," AJ replied.

Logan glanced back to make sure the door was still shut. "When Henry told us he found someone to take us, I never thought it would be you. No offense, but you didn't seem to like us too much since the contest."

"True, but it's nothing personal," AJ said, checking his watch. "Just because Daisy is willing to risk hanging around with people who know her true identity doesn't mean I am. Except now, I mean. And I'm only doing this because Henry begged me."

"He did?" Logan asked. He had a hard time picturing Henry begging for anything.

"If it makes you feel any better," Miles said, "I don't know your true identity at all. I don't even know if your last name is really Carpenter."

"It isn't," AJ said.

The door of the Cocoa Room swung open after what felt to all of them like a full day. The grown-ups came out and, one at a time, shook AJ's hand. The Candymaker was last, and he held on tight. "Against what is probably our better judgment, we are giving you permission to take the kids on the trip. There are rules we will need to trust you to uphold. Henry is vouching for you, and I expect you will not let him, or us, down in any way."

"Yes, sir," AJ said. "No, sir. I mean, I'll guard them with my life." The Candymaker gave a grunt of approval at that and finally let go of AJ's hand. The moms then spent ten minutes giving the boys instructions on how to behave in the car, at the hotels, and at the candy stores, where they would now have to represent **Life Is Sweet**.

While the boys loaded their suitcases into the minivan's trunk, the dads grilled AJ on how he would handle various situations if they arose—everything from a flat tire to the stomach flu. When the grown-ups were finally satisfied that AJ would send a full report every night, wasn't going to speed or let them subsist on only candy, and would remind them to shower once in a while, they were free to go.

Logan held on to his mom even longer than Miles held on to his. Over his shoulder, he saw AJ hand Philip some papers and Philip give them to Logan's dad. Logan watched curiously but then figured it was a copy of AJ's driver's license or some other travel document. Hopefully his dad wouldn't look too closely at it! After Logan's mom finally let go, she walked right over to Philip and hugged him tight, too. Philip stood very still, but he closed his eyes.

"Woo-hoo!" Miles shouted as the minivan pulled out of the factory's long driveway. "We're officially on the road, baby! No parents, no rules!"

Logan forced himself to turn away from his waving parents and quickly wiped his eyes. He'd accepted the idea of leaving the factory behind, but leaving his parents behind was a lot harder than he thought.

Philip—still feeling warm from his hug from Mrs. Sweet—glanced back at Miles from the front passenger seat. "We haven't even gone one block. Are you going to be like this the whole trip?"

Miles grinned. "I'm just excited. But I'd also like to point out that this van would have had plenty of room for Whaley." He gestured at the empty third row. "He would have made an excellent mascot."

Philip was about to tease him about still sleeping with a stuffed animal, but AJ suddenly swerved off the road into the parking lot of the old Spring Haven High School, and Philip forgot about teasing Miles. Was the girl with the horse going to be here again? Were they here so he could return the spy gadget she'd given him?

AJ drove past the school toward the overgrown field in the back. "Why are we here?" Miles asked. He waved the handout Mr. Sweet had given each of them. "The itinerary says we have to drive almost two hundred and fifty miles today to reach the first hotel by nighttime. And that's not factoring in stopping for meals and bathroom breaks."

"We won't need to stop for meals or bathroom breaks," AJ said. "You didn't think we were going to drive halfway across the country in this tiny thing, did you?"

Miles replied, "Um, yes? You know, considering we're in it right now? And it's not really tiny . . ."

AJ shook his head. "*That's* our ride."

Before them loomed the largest RV any of them had ever seen up close. Even Philip's jaw fell, and he wasn't easily impressed.

Logan and Miles gasped. "Are you *serious*?" Logan asked, not taking his eyes off the huge machine. The question came out more like a squeal, but he didn't care.

Miles began bouncing up and down in his seat. He'd never dreamt of riding in an RV! He couldn't even imagine what it would look like inside.

AJ stopped the car alongside the giant house-on-wheels. Miles and Logan immediately jumped out their respective doors while Philip hesitated for a second, then followed. As embarrassing as it was to admit, he'd been waiting for someone to open the door for him. Old habits died hard.

The RV had three doors—one by the driver's seat, one by the front passenger seat, and one in the middle that looked more like the door to a house than a vehicle. There was even a doorbell next to it! AJ rang the bell and stepped back, like he expected someone to answer.

"Um, why aren't we going right in?" Logan asked. "Or is this a big joke and it's not really yours?" He tried to peer in the windows, but they must have been made of some special glass, because all he could see was his reflection.

"It's mine, all right," AJ assured them. "I'm just being polite."

The door swung open and there stood Daisy, wearing baggy sweatpants, an oversized T-shirt, and a towel wrapped around her hair. "Can't a girl take a shower in peace?" she asked. The expressions on the boys' faces were priceless. Whenever she was in a bad mood in the future, she'd remember their shock and delight at seeing her standing there in AJ's hand-me-downs.

"Daisy!" Miles shouted, throwing himself up the stairs at her. She laughed and let herself be pulled into a hug. "Daisy, it's you! It's really you!"

Logan bounded up the stairs and joined in the hug. "Does this mean you're coming on the tour?"

She nodded. "AJ pretty much kidnapped me. First he lied to my grandmother and told her we needed to head out to a gig a week sooner than we did, and then he fed me the same line. I've been away from home for weeks, and he didn't even give me time to pack clean clothes." She pulled off the towel and combed her damp hair with her fingers. She suspected none of the boys would notice that her hair was brown now, and sure enough, none of them did.

Logan couldn't stop smiling. He felt *so* much better knowing that the four of them were together again. He wouldn't want to admit it out loud, but having Daisy there made him feel safer. "We have so much to tell you!" he blurted out instead.

"First, what's with him?" She gestured down the stairs at Philip, who stood alone outside the RV, looking up at it with a wary expression.

"You coming?" she asked. "No wait, you're actually a vampire and have to be invited into someone's house, right?"

"Funny," he said. "You're sure this thing is safe? Looks too big to fit on the road, in my opinion."

"It's very safe, I promise," AJ replied. "If I ever lose control of the wheel and we go careening off a bridge, the RV will turn into a plane and we'll fly to safety."

Miles's jaw fell open. *"Really?"*

Daisy kicked AJ in the shin. "It's not nice to tease the boys." She turned back to Philip. "C'mon. Trust me—everyone else on the road stays out of your way. Plus there's about two million dollars' worth of high-tech spy gear installed on it, so yeah, it's built to pretty much stand up to anything."

She clapped her hands. "This is going to be fun!" She grinned at the boys, who were listening with open mouths. "Who wants a tour?"

CHAPTER TWO

A J looked at each of his passengers in turn. He'd instructed them to sit in the large kitchen booth, since confining them to one spot was his best chance of keeping their attention. "Okay. If you guys are going to be living here for the next week, we need to get a few things straight." He held up one finger. "First, what I say goes, no exceptions." He held up another finger. "Second, as big as Big Bertha is, everyone has to keep it clean so we're not tripping over every—"

"I'm sorry," Miles interrupted, "but you named your RV Big Bertha?"

"You have a better idea?" AJ asked.

A name popped into Miles's head right away. "Harvey!"

"Harvey?" AJ repeated.

Miles nodded. "Harvey is a good, strong name, and it has *RV* right there in the middle!"

"I like it," Logan said.

"Me too," Daisy agreed. "Although it would be nice if it was a girl's name."

"Boats are named after girls," Miles said. "Cars are boys. Right, Philip?"

Philip abstained from comment. His parents used to have a boat named after his mother, but after she was gone, he never saw it again.

"Fine," AJ said. "As I was saying, *Harvey* is big, and even bigger when the slides are out, but that doesn't mean I want to see your stuff lying around everywhere. Number three—" He stopped and sighed. "What is it now, Miles?"

Miles lowered his hand. "Like a playground slide?" He hadn't gone down a slide in a long time, but he'd put many of them in the playgrounds scattered throughout the afterlife. He didn't know you could turn an RV into a playground, though.

AJ sighed. "Not that kind of a slide. Large sections of the vehicle slide out to make more space when we're parked."

Miles and Logan began chanting, "Tour! Tour!"

AJ ignored them and held up three fingers. "And last, Harvey is not a toy. Do not play with the shiny buttons and knobs. I know that will be hard for some of you." He stared pointedly at Miles, who flashed a "who, me?" face.

"All right, then. Now, this is what I meant by slides." He directed everyone to get up and stand in the center of the aisle while he walked past them to the climbing wall. After a last peek out the windows to make sure they were still alone, he reached for one of the plastic footrests—a blue one—and gave it a gentle but firm tug. "You may want to hold on."

A low hum filled the air. Then the booth where they'd been sitting began to move. Not just the booth—the whole side of the RV was sliding out! It was happening on the other side, too.

"Whoa!" Logan shouted. "Look at the roof!"

"Look at the floor!" Miles shouted.

The interior of the RV had just doubled—no, tripled! The ceiling, once only a few feet above his head, was now so high he couldn't reach it even if he climbed on the table!

Before they could fully absorb the fact that the RV had gone from basically a bus to an enormous one-story house, AJ pulled another toehold on the climbing wall. The cabinets along the top—the ones Daisy had assumed were for storage—opened up, and beds slid out of the walls! A rope ladder unfurled from each one, and the kids all had to jump out of the way to avoid being bonked on the head.

They gathered around as AJ rattled off a list of features of the RV, in no apparent order. He spoke quickly and pointed instead of leading them around. "First, the front section containing the dashboard and the driving area is called the Control Center. That is where I will mostly be and you should rarely be. Next, the laboratory, computer, laser printer, and 3-D printer are hidden behind the bookshelf. Off of the bedroom is the bathroom. There are two toilets. One has a fake bottom with an escape route. The other is, well, a toilet. Be sure you know the difference. Inflatable rafts will extend out from all sides of the exterior in the unlikely event that we're submerged in water." He pointed above their heads. "A long-distance periscope with a high-powered microphone rises from the sunroof, allowing us to see and hear very far away." He pointed behind him toward the kitchen. "That closet next to the oven converts into a holding cell in case we have to detain anyone."

The boys' heads swiveled fast from place to place, trying to take it all in. AJ pointed at the entertainment center. "A built-in satellite antenna lets us pull in television signals from around the world. Video games are all built into the system. The jump pad behind the couch doubles as a trampoline, which is off-limits while the RV is in motion. There is one shower, and I expect you will each use it once a day, turning the water off as you wash so we don't run out. I will post a schedule. The kitchen and laundry rooms are self-explanatory. Once we've stopped for the night, you can explore. Just remember not to touch anything if you don't know what it does."

"Is there a machine on the wall that can give you food whenever you want it?" Miles asked hopefully.

"There sure is!" AJ said.

Miles's eyes widened. "Really?"

"Yes. It's called a refrigerator."

Miles's face fell. "Not exactly what I meant."

AJ patted Miles on the shoulder. "When our Research and Development department figures out how to combine molecules in such a way as to create the perfect ham-and-cheese sandwich out of thin air, I'll make sure you're the first to know."

"Tell them about the safety features," Daisy prompted.

"Okay," AJ said. "In case of unexpected impact, air bags will inflate on both the inside and the outside of the vehicle. It will feel like being embraced by a very puffy cloud."

"Not that," Daisy said impatiently. "I meant how the tailpipe can release an oil slick or a stream of nails or a thick white smoke if someone's chasing us."

"Seriously?" Miles asked, wide-eyed at the thought of it. "Harvey is, like, a superhero!"

"Why would someone be chasing us?" Logan asked.

"Spies have to be prepared for any development," Daisy explained. "Which reminds me, this little trip isn't only to visit candy stores to promote the Harmonicandy. AJ and I have to complete a dead drop. That means we have to drop off a package and wait to make sure it's retrieved."

"Are you saying we'll get to go on a spy mission?" Miles asked, grabbing on to Logan's arm.

"Definitely not," AJ said firmly before Daisy had a chance to answer. "You shouldn't even know *that* much." He shot Daisy a scolding look. "But while we're on the topic of detours, if you have any other stops I'll need to make, let me know ahead of time so I can build them into the route."

With a push of the button hidden inside the climbing wall, AJ converted the bunk beds back into cabinets. They all held on as the sides of the RV moved inward and the ceiling lowered. It was just as cool in reverse.

Daisy watched AJ slide into the driver's seat. She'd begun to think she didn't know AJ as well as she thought she did. First he had agreed to help Henry—someone he barely knew at all— by taking on the huge responsibility of bringing four kids on a week-long road trip, and now he was offering them a chance to make other stops? What had gotten into him? Whatever it was, she liked it!

If she could do anything at all? She'd try to find the mystery brother. If he even existed. She had no idea where to begin, though, or how to explain it to the others. How could they understand not knowing your own family?

Miles plopped down at the table, his heart thumping. He glanced quickly at Logan and then down at the floor. He wanted to tell them about his hope that he could help with Logan's scars somehow, but how could he come out and say that? He also wanted to find out more about where his father came from. And he wanted to find some geocaches! But most pressing of all, he needed to find out what Samuel Sweet's contract meant.

Philip could tell by the way Miles was bouncing up and down in his seat that he was thinking about something exciting. Other than doing whatever it took to save the Harmonicandy, Philip couldn't help thinking of his brother's comment about having a grand-mother out there somewhere. Was this his chance to find her? He'd have to tell them about the talent competition, too. No one else said they had any other agenda. Could he really ask for two stops that only had to do with him?

Logan could practically see the gears turning in his friends' heads. What were they plotting? All he wanted to do was figure out how to save the Harmonicandy. That was more than enough for him.

Daisy cleared her throat. "So as I was saying, we'll have to make a small detour. For, um, the dead drop." She couldn't get out the brother part yet; it was too weird.

"I have one, too," Philip said, sitting down across from Miles. He couldn't bring himself to mention looking for his grandmother. It was just too random, and anyway, he never talked about his mother and didn't really feel like starting now. He'd tell them the easier thing. "There's this Nation's Most Talented Kid competition in a few days. It was the only way I could come on the trip. My father signed me up."

Daisy raised an eyebrow. "Will you be juggling fire blindfolded while speed-solving a Rubik's Cube?"

He sighed. "How could I use my hands to juggle and solve the cube at the same time?"

Daisy grinned. "That's why you'd be the nation's most talented kid! Okay, so we'll have two detours. That's not too bad."

"Make that three," Miles said. "I, um, have to find a few things, but I don't know where they are yet." If anyone asked, he'd just say he meant geocaches. He wasn't ready to tell them the other stuff yet.

"Four," Logan added. "We have to figure out where the chocolate came from that we used in the competition. How can we promote the Harmonicandy if there's something wrong with it? Not that I have any idea where to start."

Philip took a deep breath and closed his eyes. He couldn't keep it to himself anymore. In a voice nowhere near as steady as he wished it were, he said, "I might know something about it."

Miles stared at Philip. Whatever he knew was obviously hard for him to admit. He needed to come clean, too, even if it would upset Logan. He took a deep breath and said, "Me too."

Philip looked at him with surprise, and also a little bit of gratitude.

Logan plopped down next to Miles, unsure what to think. How could they know more about this than he did? They couldn't even taste a difference.

"Wait," Daisy said, looking at each of them. "What are you talking about? What's wrong with the Harmonicandy?"

CHAPTER THREE

hilip went up to the front to fill AJ in on the detours. He figured he'd get a hard time about having to be in that contest, but all AJ said was, "I bet you'll rock it." Philip thought he probably *would* rock it, but his bragging days were behind him. He dawdled up in the Control Center, not quite ready to go back and spill what he knew to the others.

"The view up here is pretty cool," he observed, determined to keep the conversation light. They were perched up high over the road, and the large curved windshield almost made him feel like he was outside. And seeing the great outdoors from *indoors* was his preferred way of seeing it. AJ looked at him out of the corner of his eye. "You really want to talk about the view?"

Philip gazed out the window. "Guess not."

"Well then, if you don't have anything else to say, this is my area, remember?"

But Philip wanted to stall a little longer. "Well, actually, I do have one more thing. Why did you agree to take us on the trip?"

AJ glanced in his side camera and expertly steered the RV onto the highway. He kept his eyes on the road, but Philip knew AJ had heard the question. Stretching his arms over his head, Philip leaned back in the comfy passenger seat. "Take your time," he said languidly. "I could hang out up here all day just enjoying the view. And the company, of course."

AJ gave a grunt of annoyance. "Fine. I'm still trying to figure that out myself. That's your answer. Sorry it's not a better one."

Philip shrugged and stood up. "It's not so bad."

"Logan's about to start," Daisy told Philip as he slid back into the booth. Her hands were poised over the screen on her vid com. "Unless you'd like to tell us what you know first?"

He shook his head. "Nope, I'm good."

Daisy looked up at Logan expectantly as she lowered her hands to the tabletop. A virtual keyboard lit up the surface. She began to type on it! All three of them jumped back.

"Whoa!" Miles exclaimed. "How long has it been able to do *that*?"

"It's a new modification," she said. "Yours doesn't have it yet." A few seconds later she had three vid coms piled in front of her. She sighed. "I'll load it on them later. Can we focus, please?"

Logan tried to think of the best way to explain it. Describing how something tasted was always difficult for him. In the end, they'd just have to trust him. "When I tasted the Harmonicandy this morning, it was . . . wrong," he finally said, trying not to be distracted by Daisy tapping on the tabletop. "The chocolate we used for the contest had a richer, deeper kind of taste to it."

"So what's the big deal?" Daisy said. "You'll just fix it for the next batch."

Logan shook his head. "There's no more of the original chocolate. The contest rules state that the final product has to be exactly the same as the one submitted to the contest, and all the ingredients have to be easily available to anyone."

Daisy tried to make sense of what he was saying. "I spent a lot of time in the Cocoa Room with Steve and Lenny. They make all the chocolate from the beans in the Tropical Room, right? And then the chocolate gets pumped into all the different rooms. So why would the Harmonicandy be any different?"

"The milk chocolate base that we use is always the same, that's true. But then most of our chocolate candies are mixed with some percentage of either dark, bittersweet, or white chocolate. Those come from smaller batches made in each individual room. But in this case, even the base was...wrong. That's just the only way I know how to describe it."

"Did you guys notice this, too?" Daisy asked Miles and Philip. Both shook their heads.

"But Henry did," Miles said. "He told us he'd tasted the original once before—like, decades before we made the Harmonicandy." That comment hadn't seemed too important at the time, but now it hung in the air, refusing to be ignored.

Daisy jotted down Henry's comment. A lot of drama had unfolded at **Life Is Sweet** while she'd been riding Magpie! "And no one else noticed?" she asked Logan. "Not Randall, or Max, or even your dad?"

Logan shook his head. "They hadn't tried the original one, remember? There wasn't time to share it with anyone."

"Well, Henry must have tried it, or he couldn't have noticed the difference," she pointed out.

"He *said* he did," Logan agreed. "But I can't picture when it would have been. As soon as the samples cooled down, we put them right into the van. And then there wasn't any left after the contest. It's all very strange." He looked at Miles and Philip. "Can you guys think of when Henry might have tasted the Harmonicandy?"

Miles and Philip looked down into their laps. Daisy knew they were both hiding something. She'd known it since they walked onto the RV. And the fact that they didn't glance at each other told her they each had their own secret. It wasn't lost on her that only that morning she had resigned herself to not being a part of the boys' lives anymore. And now here she was, putting clues together to help them, like she was on one of her missions. Except *unlike* her missions, working on this mystery was her choice.

"So that's pretty much all I've got," Logan said. "I don't know where the other chocolate came from or how we wound up using it, but if we don't find it again, the Harmonicandy is over before it even begins."

Philip knew Daisy would turn her laser-focused gaze on him next. He would be ready. He *was* ready. He'd tell her what he knew—or thought he knew. Simple as that. He drummed his fingers on the table. Once he had made up his mind about something, he didn't like to wait.

"All right, then," Daisy said, satisfied that Logan really didn't know anything more. "Let's let Philip talk before he explodes."

Philip took a deep breath and told them about his memory of Henry switching the bowls before the contest. When he got to the part where Henry had said, "You can thank me later," Logan and Miles audibly gasped. It looked as if the color leaked out of Logan's face, making the pink scars on his cheek stand out even more. Philip's stomach twisted. Should he not have told them? What choice did he have?

Logan stared at Philip as he tried to process what he had just heard. *Henry?* Henry gave them the chocolate that they used for the contest, but pretended not to have any idea what had happened? And at the end made it sound as though he was doing them a favor? A *favor*?

"But... but why would Henry do that?" he choked out.

"I have no idea," Philip said.

"Anything else?" Daisy asked Philip, who quickly shook his head.

Miles slid out of the booth and retrieved his backpack from where he'd tossed it on the couch. If he hadn't seen the scenery passing by on either side, he would swear they were standing still. But they weren't standing still. With every mile, they were getting farther from home and family and normalcy and heading somewhere entirely *other*.

He returned to the booth and pulled out the burned contract. Wordlessly, he placed it down in front of Logan.

CHAPTER FOUR

We, the four signers of this contract, do hereby
solemnly swear never to reveal the location of the
special beans, nor how Samuel Sweet came to be in
possession of them. If questioned, we agree to say
we don't remember any details about our time spent
there. We promise to uphold our vow to help keep
the valley hidden, whatever that might take in the
future. This contract binds us together for life,
both in friendship and in secrecy. We have been
given a great gift, and we hereby agree to repay
that debt whenever possible, anonymously, asking
nothing in return. Once this binding contract is
signed and sealed, it shall be destroyed.

They all looked up from the document. Daisy let out a long
whistle and shook her head. "That does not look good for Samuel
Sweet."

"Where did you find this?" Philip asked.

Miles had forgotten that Philip didn't know about the box.
"Randall found Logan in the Marshmallow Room and gave him a
bunch of old papers and journals from when his grandfather was

younger. I found this contract in the box with some other . . . interesting stuff." That other stuff would have to wait.

Logan felt sick to his stomach. "Did my grandfather really do something sneaky to get some special beans? Maybe even . . . illegal?" No one who had known his grandfather had ever said a bad word about him. *Smart, driven, kind, generous, funny.* Those were the words used to describe Samuel Sweet.

Philip knew a thing or two about being sneaky. "Don't jump to any conclusions," he warned Logan. "People do things for a lot of different reasons. Obviously your grandfather isn't around to ask, and without knowing whose names are under the scorch marks, we might never know what went on."

"But what would even make a bean *special*?" Logan asked. "So special it was worth hiding?"

Miles dug into his pocket. He held open his palm to show them the marble-shaped blue bean. "Maybe like this?"

The RV immediately filled with the scent of chocolate. Philip waved his hand in front of his face. The smell was overpowering. "I bet AJ can smell that up in the Control Center," he said.

"I wouldn't put money on it," Daisy muttered.

Logan inhaled deeply. The smell instantly calmed him, and he felt the tightness in his stomach loosen a little. He had smelled that exact smell before. But where? The factory had been gearing up for the Kickoff by increasing its candy production, so the smells had been pouring out of every candy room for weeks. It could have been any of them.

"It's obviously a cocoa bean," Philip said. "At least it smells like one."

"If you'd paid any attention at all during our tour of the factory," Daisy scolded, "you'd know cocoa beans turn brown in the roasting process. They don't turn bright blue."

"Okay, so maybe it's not roasted," Philip said.

Miles shook his head. "It has to be roasted, or else it wouldn't smell like chocolate yet."

"I know that," Philip snapped. Then he muttered, "Sorry."

Logan used the side of his hand to slide the bean from Miles's palm onto his own, where he cupped it so it wouldn't roll off. It felt heavier than he'd expected it to, which was a little weird. "Sometimes the wet bean might actually look a little purple," he told them, "but it's only that color right when it comes out of the pod and hasn't been processed yet. This one *must* have been fermented and dried and then roasted." He frowned. "But then why isn't it brown?"

"Maybe someone dipped it in paint," Philip said. "Or used food coloring to dye it blue."

Logan scratched it gently with his fingernail and shook his head. "You can tell the color goes all the way through. I've seen a lot of different cocoa beans, but never one this round, or this blue, or this strong smelling. Where did you get it, Miles?"

Miles hesitated before answering. He felt bad pointing another finger at Henry, but it was the truth, after all. "I found it in the Marshmallow Room."

Logan frowned. "That's strange. Henry never has chocolate in the Marshmallow Room."

"Well, it wasn't exactly *in* the room," Miles said. "More like I found it on his desk."

"It must not have been in there yesterday," Philip said. "I was helping him catch up on paperwork. I definitely would have seen it on his desk."

"Well, it wasn't so much *on* his desk," Miles admitted, "as it was inside an envelope with an old picture." He reached into his backpack and placed his copy of the Opening Day photograph on the table.

Even though Logan's stomach was still in knots, he couldn't help smiling when he saw the picture of his grandfather as a young man. He walked by a large print of this photo every day. It hung in the hallway of his apartment. "Why do you have this?"

"It was in the library display on the history of **Life Is Sweet**," Miles said. "After seeing all that stuff in Sam's box from when he was younger, it just sort of caught my eye, so I borrowed it and made a copy. Then I saw another copy in Henry's office with the bean, so I'm pretty sure it must mean something. You told me once you don't recognize anyone other than your grandparents, right?"

Logan nodded, tracing his finger over his grandfather's face. The original Candymaker couldn't have been more than ten years older than Logan was right now when the picture had been taken. Very strange to think about. Where would he be standing in ten years? Who would be standing beside him? Hopefully the same people who were sitting beside him right then.

"I asked Arthur to see if he can track down their identities," Miles continued, hoping Logan wouldn't think this was an invasion of privacy. He seemed to be in a trance, though, staring at the picture and not blinking.

Daisy looked up from her virtual keyboard. "So am I correct that we're all assuming there's some connection between this bean and the contract and the chocolate used to make the first Harmonicandy?"

"But the original Harmonicandy wasn't blue," Miles pointed out.

"True," Logan said, prying his eyes away from the photo and back to the bean. "But remember, the Harmonicandy was a mixture of dark and milk chocolate. If Henry had mixed it already, the blue would have been absorbed by the darker color, and we wouldn't have noticed."

"Can't you use that dog skill you have?" Philip asked. "If you taste the bean and it tastes like the original Harmonicandy, won't we have our answer? I mean, at least we'll know more than we do right now."

Logan picked up the bean (an act that took both hands), sniffed it, then with only a second's hesitation about where the bean may have been before, he licked it. His smile told the others all they needed to know.

His hands shook as he placed the bean back down on the table, where it kept trying to roll off. "This bean—well, one from the same harvest of cocoa beans—was used to make the original Harmonicandy. No question."

"And you're sure you've never tasted it before?" Daisy asked, tapping on the table. Her brain had been busy putting all the pieces together, and she was almost ready to lay out her plan.

"I've definitely never tasted it," Logan said. "I might have smelled it before, but I'm not sure exactly."

Daisy picked up the bean and watched as the sunlight through the window made it gleam. Most beans were dull and had no shine at all. She made one last notation, then stood up and began pacing in front of the table. It was strange to be able to walk normally in a vehicle going seventy miles per hour on the highway, but she wasn't complaining.

"All right. Let's go through what we know and what we don't know. We don't know why this bean was stuck in an envelope with that photograph, or whether the people in the picture are the same people who signed the contract. We don't know if this blue bean is one of the 'special beans' they talked about, either. But we *do* know that beans of the same type were used in making the Harmonicandy, and we know that they were used at least one other time, because Henry claims to have tasted it before, and Logan may have smelled it before."

"Is there something we can do to find out where else it was used?" Miles asked. "Other than tasting every chocolate candy out there? Not that I'd mind, I mean, if it came to that."

"I'm not sure good 'ol Harvey here can tell us that," Daisy said, "but we can get a lot of other information. We can use the lab to analyze the bean's chemical composition and to find out what part of the world it came from. The computer can find the identities of the people in the photograph, although that will take some time, and maybe Arthur will find them sooner."

"Wow," Miles said, shaking his head in amazement. "Harvey can do all that?"

"I'm telling you, R and D spared no expense with this baby."

"I'll try to remember where I smelled it," Logan said. He closed his eyes and concentrated on the chocolate smell still hanging in the air. Maybe he could narrow it down to a question of timing— had he smelled it recently, or years ago, or somewhere in between? He tried to clear his mind of everything else—a pretty impossible task at the moment—so he could focus purely on his sense of smell. He began to get an image of himself standing somewhere as he smelled it, but all he got was a sense of yellow. The sun? Had he smelled it outside?

Something about the bean was nagging at Miles, too. But it wasn't the smell; it was the color. When Daisy had held it up to the light a few minutes earlier, it glowed such an unusual, shiny bright blue. Not sky blue or baby blue, but almost midnight blue. He'd seen that exact shade before, except it had a shimmery look to it. He looked down at his hand. That's where he'd seen it—in his hand! But what had he been holding?

Miles stared into his empty palm, willing his brain to remember. Then suddenly he knew! He jumped up from his seat, nearly banging his head on the row of cabinets above it. But before he could say anything, Philip jumped up, actually *did* bang his head on a cabinet, and yelled, "We have to go back!"

"What?" Daisy said. "Why?"

Rubbing his head furiously, he said, "I left my violin in the Harmonicandy Room!"

"Can't you borrow one when you get there?" Daisy asked.

"Or we can rent one on the way," Logan added, slightly annoyed at having his concentration broken when he was on the brink of remembering.

"It doesn't work like that," Philip insisted. "I need my own."

Miles shouted, "He's right! We need to go back!"

Philip gave him a surprised look. He wasn't used to Miles being on his side for things. "Er, thanks. See? Miles gets it."

Miles shook his head. "No, I mean, sure, you totally need your violin, but there's another item we need to pick up."

"If this is about Whaley," Philip said, "you've gotta let it go. It's embarrassing."

"It's not Whaley," Miles promised.

Logan grabbed Miles's arm. "You figured something out, didn't you?"

"I think I know when Henry tasted that chocolate before," Miles said, trying to keep his voice steady. What he was going to say sounded crazy, even to him. "But to prove it," he continued, "we'll have to go back and get a sample."

"A sample?" Logan asked, confused. "But there isn't any left, remember?"

Miles shook his head. "There *is*. And it's locked in the factory's safe. We're going to have to steal it."

Logan's eyes opened wide. What could be so precious it would be locked in the safe? He heard Henry's voice saying he'd only tasted it once, a very, very long time ago. He stood up, banging his knee on the underside of the table but not caring. "The Magic Bar! You want to steal the last remaining Magic Bar!"

Miles nodded.

Daisy leaned back and smiled. "And the adventure begins."

bsolutely not," AJ said. "We can't possibly turn around now." He'd pulled off at a rest stop and was now doing a hamstring stretch on the climbing wall, which apparently also functioned as an actual climbing wall.

They tried to argue with him, but AJ only said, "We're due at **The Candy Basket** in the morning. If we miss our first stop, the Candymaker will pull the rest of the tour for sure."

That quieted them. "What if we got in and out really fast, and then you drove through the night?" Logan asked. "We could still get there on time, couldn't we?"

AJ shook his head. "No can do, not safe. Why do you need this particular candy bar so badly? Can't you just buy another one?"

Logan and Miles groaned in exasperation. "This is the *only* one," Miles explained. "The Magic Bar hasn't been made for *fifty years*."

"Fifty years?" Daisy repeated. "You never said that. How could the same chocolate have lasted long enough for you guys to use it in the contest?"

"It couldn't," Logan said. "Even if it were frozen. That's part of the mystery we need to solve."

AJ switched to the other leg. "So why try to use the same

chocolate now? If they stopped making the Magic Bar, that means it must have tasted pretty bad if no one bought it, right?"

Logan and Miles only stared at him, incredulous. Philip sighed. "Even I know the history of the Magic Bar. It was the first chocolate bar **Life Is Sweet** ever produced. It sold more units in one week than any other chocolate bar in the country. Then they pulled it from the market, and no one knows why."

"Balderdash!" Daisy said. "Someone knows why. Just not us."

"*Balderdash?*" Miles repeated, momentarily distracted from the current situation. He rolled the word around in his head, loving the way it sounded both harsh and soft at the same time.

"Nonsense," Daisy clarified. "Baloney. Hogwash. Hooey! All those things. Obviously there's a lot more going on here than we know, and I say we do whatever's necessary to figure it out. Otherwise everything we worked so hard for in the contest is out the window."

AJ grabbed a bottle of water and began to walk back to the driver's seat.

"So you see, AJ," Miles said, following him, "we have to get that Magic Bar."

"Plus I really need my violin," Philip added. "It's not like it can fly out of the factory and drop in through Harvey's sunroof and land in my lap!"

AJ stopped and turned around. "Are you thinking what I'm thinking?" he asked Daisy.

"The drone!" they exclaimed at the same time. Daisy laughed. "We haven't used that thing since the mission to—"

AJ held up his hand. "You've got to stop talking so freely."

"Sorry!" Daisy said. "But you've gotta admit it was cool! Coming down from the sky in the middle of—"

"Daisy!" AJ said again, exasperated.

"Oops, sorry! But we could totally use it now, right?" Her brain began working overtime. "Okay, we could get Courtney to break into the safe and get the Magic Bar, then scoop up the violin, then pack them into the drone and program it to track our signal!"

AJ nodded. "Don't see why not."

Miles and Logan stared at them, open-mouthed. "Are you... serious?" Miles asked AJ, hardly daring to believe his good fortune. "A drone might land on Harvey? While we're *driving down the road*?"

"Well, it could arrive when we're parked for the night, but theoretically, yes, it could arrive while we're driving. It will track our current GPS coordinates, alter its speed and direction accordingly, and find us wherever we are."

Since Logan and Miles were too busy whooping and jumping up and down, Philip figured he had to be the voice of reason. "Am I going to have to point out that my violin is very, very fragile? And if that Magic Bar is the last one in existence or whatever, do we really want to trust its safety to a hunk of thrown-together electronic parts that has to fly hundreds of miles to reach us?"

"Yes!" Logan and Miles shouted.

"But what if people notice it and yank it down?" he asked. "Then we've lost both!"

"Don't worry, Philip," Daisy said. "It's big enough to keep everything sealed against the elements, and small enough to look like a hawk. The drone is a very safe way to transport important items."

"And you know this because you've used it how many times?"

Daisy paused. "Well, only once, but you can trust me."

He looked at her skeptically. They both knew that statement wasn't always true.

"Well, you can trust me *this* time," she corrected herself.

"Fine," he grumbled. "Now what?"

"Now we get back on the road," AJ said, returning to his seat. "You guys need to figure out how to get the violin and the Magic

Bar to the drone in the first place. Don't bug me about it until it's time to call the drone into service."

"Yes, sir," Miles said, not even sarcastically.

Daisy pointed all the way to the back of the RV. "Let's spread out in the bedroom and make the plan."

Miles and Logan led the way, eager to explore that part of Harvey. By the time Philip and Daisy got into the bedroom, Miles and Logan were nowhere to be found. "I know this place is big," Daisy said, "but it's not *that* big. Unless they already jumped into the fake getaway toilet!"

Philip pointed at the closet. "Pretty sure they went in there."

"Huh?" Daisy stepped past the shelves and ducked her head between the firefighter uniform and the tuxedo hanging from a wooden rod above her head. She knew the closet was deeper than it appeared, but when she stepped all the way in and extended her arms and still didn't hit the wall, she realized how much she'd underestimated it. "Miles?" she called out, her voice muffled by the clothes. "Logan?"

"Turn left at the cheerleader outfit!" Miles called back, then giggled. "You have to see what Logan's wearing."

"Hope it's not the cheerleader outfit," she muttered. "What the—?" A narrow tunnel ran what looked like the whole length of the RV! She could see a faint light up ahead and quickly deduced it was the lamp on a miner's hat, which was currently on top of Logan's head. She pushed past the scuba suit, the camouflage bathrobe, the doctor's scrubs, and a frilly purple bridesmaid dress that must have been selected by a very mean bride. She caught up with the boys just past the fake mailbox large enough to hide in, and stuck her hands on her hips.

She was about to remind them about the seriousness of their current assignment, but they both had fake mustaches stuck above their lips, and she couldn't scold them with a straight face.

"At least now we know we won't go hungry," Miles said, tapping giant cardboard boxes of canned peaches, tuna, and tomato sauce with the tip of a cane he'd found. "Yum!"

AJ's voice burst into Daisy's ear as the transceiver she'd forgotten she'd stuck in there switched on. "Do you have the plan yet? Courtney is about to leave the compound." Daisy lowered the volume. After a month without wearing it, she'd forgotten how it felt to hear something no one else could.

"I thought she finished her gig for the day," Daisy said, motioning for Logan to take off the hula skirt. "Where is she going?"

AJ paused. "She has a date."

"A date?" Daisy shrieked.

"Ouch!" AJ said. "Volume!"

"Sorry," Daisy whispered. "How do you know she has a date? Isn't that against policy?"

The boys stopped clowning around to listen to this one-sided conversation.

"Officially, yes," AJ said. "But your grandmother looks the other way as long as it doesn't get serious."

Daisy didn't know what to say to that. She wasn't sure what that really meant, and she decided she didn't care all that much, either. "Okay, I'll let you know in a few minutes."

Daisy turned off the transceiver. "C'mon, guys. Let's get back to work."

Logan held out the bright purple bridesmaid dress with frills and lace all around the edges and said, "I bet this would look great on you."

"What's going on?" Philip asked, appearing at the scene a minute later. He looked from Miles to Logan to Daisy, where he stopped, closed his eyes, and them reopened them. Nope, he hadn't been seeing things. "Did you lose a bet?"

CHAPTER SIX

With a few keystrokes Daisy linked her vid com up to the security system at the candy factory, a feat that both impressed and scared the others. The four of them were lying across the bed, watching the screen intently.

"There she is!" Miles cried out. They could now see Courtney approaching the delivery tunnel on the side of the building. Logan thought that would be the best way to get inside without being seen. Daisy and Philip agreed, although neither mentioned they'd snuck in that way before.

Courtney kept to the shadows of the trees, darting between them so fast they could barely see her go. She wore dark clothes and a cap pulled down over her face. When she reached the entrance to the tunnel, she pressed herself against the wall and disappeared from the screen.

"Switching to the camera in my baseball cap," she whispered. They heard a soft *click*. The view narrowed and became brighter once the video stream wasn't coming secondhand through the security camera anymore.

"Thanks again for doing this," Daisy said to her.

"It's okay," Courtney replied. "I'll just add it to the growing list of favors you owe me."

"Fair enough," Daisy said. "Okay, let's get to it. You shouldn't encounter any activity in the tunnel. Most people are gone for the day. The door at the end will lead to Hallway B. At that point you'll be about halfway between your two destinations."

Courtney made her way around the crates and boxes stacked in the storage tunnel. "Smells kinda rank in here," she muttered. "Like wet cows or something."

"They must have gotten a recent shipment of soil for the Tropical Room," Logan said. "It can smell a little if it's already been mixed with fertilizer."

"You have to bring in *soil*?" Miles asked. "There must be tons of it just outside the factory's door. Can't someone just dig it up?"

Logan shook his head. "In order to grow here, the trees need soil from their natural habitat. My grandfather was able to tell which soil went with which kind of tree just by the smell."

"They all smell pretty bad to me," Courtney grumbled. "And I'm around horses' stables all the time."

"You're almost there," Daisy said.

Courtney approached the door. She stopped, and they could hear her fumbling for something. When she tilted her head down, her hat camera revealed she was holding a thin metal tool.

"You won't need to break in," Daisy said. "The door's never locked. They really need to improve their security."

Logan harrumphed. "Why? The only people who sneak in are you guys!"

"Which way am I headed first?" Courtney asked, slipping through the back door into the (thankfully) empty hallway. "In case I can't get both for some reason."

"The Magic Bar," Daisy, Miles, and Logan replied at the same time.

"Hey!" Philip complained.

"Is that Philip with you?" Courtney asked with a wink. "He owes me something, too."

Miles and Logan whipped their heads around toward Philip. "How do you two know each other?" Miles asked.

Philip felt his cheeks redden. "Long story."

"We've got time," Miles replied.

Courtney snapped her fingers at them. "Hello? Kind of in the middle of a heist here?"

"Sorry," Miles said. "Keep on heisting." But he gave Philip a look that made it clear he wasn't about to let it drop for long.

Logan directed Courtney down the hall to the Computer Room, where the safe was in full view on the back wall. Daisy shook her head. "You guys seriously need to up your game. Ever heard of hanging a picture or mirror over a safe?"

"That's weird," Philip said, peering at the view on the screen. "There actually *was* a picture there just yesterday. A palm tree, I think." He really should have picked up on the fact that the picture would be hiding something. His father had pictures and mirrors covering safes all over the house.

Logan turned to him in surprise. "You were in the Computer Room yesterday?"

Philip hesitated, then nodded. "Part of the same long story."

"Sounds like a good story," Miles said. "I'd love to hear it one day."

"Wouldn't we all," Daisy agreed, making Philip wish he'd used his "filling out boring paperwork" alibi instead.

"I'm pretty sure no one uses this safe much," Courtney declared, bringing their attention back to the screen. They could all see the dust on the surface of the safe's door.

Daisy turned to Logan. "Your grandfather didn't happen to tell you the combination when he showed this to you, did he?"

Logan shook his head.

"Seeing how no one cares much about security over there," Daisy said, "it very well might be unlocked. Try it."

Courtney pulled on the knob, but the safe door didn't budge. "It's possible they didn't reset the lock after it was opened last," Daisy said. Courtney twisted it clockwise, pulling as she went around, but it didn't open. "Try some obvious combinations," Daisy suggested. Courtney twisted the knob clockwise, then counterclockwise, then clockwise again, trying different patterns and checking over her shoulder in between to make sure no one had come in.

"You won't have to blow it open with dynamite or anything, right?" Miles asked. "I'm pretty sure someone would notice that."

"You've seen too many movies," Courtney said. "I'll just have to crack it." This time she turned the knob very slowly in a full rotation while pushing her ear up against the side of the safe. "The hum from the computer makes it too hard to hear the drive pins clicking," she said. "I don't want to shut the computer down in case that triggers an alarm in the system. I'm gonna have to drill into it."

Logan paled at the thought.

Seeing his distress, Philip said, "Wait. Look around first. The password for the computer is written right beside it. What if the combination for the safe is somewhere nearby, too?"

"Let me guess," Miles said. "Long story how you know that?"

Philip nodded.

"It's a good idea," Daisy said. "Do you see anywhere between three and six numbers near you?"

The image on the screen tilted as Courtney looked under the table and around the sides of the tall bookshelf that held the factory's awards. She examined the walls and shelves and desk closely and shook her head.

Daisy asked Logan, "Can you think of any favorite numbers

your dad or grandfather might have had? A birthday or an anniversary or something?"

Logan suggested some birth dates, but nothing worked. "I'm sorry," Logan said. "That's all I can think of. Do you really have to drill into it, though? What if it hurt something inside?"

"Pretty sure there aren't any puppies and kittens living in there," Philip said.

Miles's head began buzzing the same way it had when he was trying to bring back the memory of the blue Magic Bar wrapper. He'd seen a string of numbers recently. Was it at the factory? Suddenly he sprang off the bed. "I'll be right back. Don't do anything yet."

"That was weird," Philip said as Miles ran out.

"So, Courtney," Daisy said while they waited. "Who's this big date with?"

Courtney checked her watch. "The one I'm an hour late for? A guy I met riding one day at the park. You should get out into the world more, too. When you're not on a gig, I mean. It would do you good."

Daisy smiled. "That's exactly what I'm doing."

Miles returned and with a shaking voice said, "Four three one two seven."

They stared at him. "Really?" Daisy asked.

He nodded.

Daisy turned back to the screen. "The lock only goes up to thirty-nine, right?"

"Yes," Courtney confirmed.

"All right. Then that leaves only one option. Try four, thirty-one, twenty-seven."

She did. "Bingo!" The door swung open.

They all turned to stare at Miles as they waited for an explanation. Miles reddened. "Um, lucky guess?"

"We'll get back to you later," Daisy said, pointing her finger into his chest and leaving Miles no doubt that she wouldn't forget. On the screen, Courtney was shining a flashlight into the safe. They all instinctively leaned closer to the screen. They could see stacks of papers, jewelry boxes, some keys, a roll of cash. Typical stuff people would keep in a safe. "Do you see the Magic Bar?" Daisy asked.

Courtney pulled out one Magic Bar and held it up to the camera. It looked exactly like the fake one Miles had seen in the display. "That's it!" he shouted.

She stashed it in her bag. "Anything else you need, or can I get outta here?"

"Let's close it back up," Logan said, feeling really uncomfortable. The sense of invading his family's privacy had gotten stronger once they could see inside.

Courtney had just closed the safe when they heard voices coming from the hall. "Hide!" Daisy shouted. Before the word was even out of Daisy's mouth, Courtney had launched herself to the other side of the bookshelf. The voices grew louder until they could tell the sound was coming from directly outside the room.

"It's Henry and Max," Logan whispered.

"Maybe they'll keep walking," Miles whispered.

"Why are you guys whispering?" Philip asked. "The only person who can hear you is Courtney."

"Shh," Daisy said. "Courtney, is your position secure?"

"I can't tell from this angle," she whispered. "I doubt it, though."

"See, now *she* has a reason to whisper," Philip pointed out.

"See if you can adjust your camera angle," Daisy said. "I'd like to be able to see you."

In a flash, Courtney yanked off her hat, and the screen blurred as the hat (and the camera) flew across the room. Judging from the angle of the image now on their screen, it had landed directly on the doorknob. "Good aim," Philip said, impressed.

They could clearly see Courtney pressed up against the wall.

The side of the bookshelf did almost nothing to hide her, but there was truly nowhere else to go. Under the table wouldn't be any better.

"Hopefully Max won't come in," Miles said. "He spots everything. He noticed that the right wing on one of my Bee Happys had one more black licorice spot than the left."

"No one usually uses this room, since all the departments have their own computers," Logan said. "I don't think we need to worry."

"I hope you're right," Miles said. "Someone would have to be blind not to see her."

"A great day for the factory," they heard Max say.

"Always is," Henry replied. "I'll see you in the morning. I just need to look something up real quick."

The door to the Computer Room swung open. So much for Logan's theory. They saw Courtney press her back against the wall, but it hardly mattered. Miles's hands flew up to cover his eyes. He watched through his fingers as Henry bumped gently into the desk chair. He assumed Henry would then pull out the chair and sit down at the computer station. Instead, he pushed the chair out of the way, walked right past the desk, and went straight to the wall safe. He was now close enough to Courtney to stretch out an arm and touch her. No one breathed.

And then...nothing. He didn't turn toward her at all. He just stood in front of that safe, as Courtney had less than a minute before.

"Why isn't he saying anything to her?" Miles asked.

No one had an answer.

"I thought you said no one uses this safe," Philip said.

"I didn't think anyone did," Logan said, not taking his eyes off the screen. What was Henry up to?

Henry's back was to them now, but they could see the door to the safe swing open. His arm began rooting around inside. Was he putting something in? Taking something out? Then they heard a chuckle, which grew until it became a full-blown laugh. Four jaws hung open—five, if you included Courtney's. Just as quickly, Henry's laughter turned into tears.

Logan recovered first. He was familiar with how this worked. "This could go on for a while," he said with a sigh. But Henry squared his shoulders and pulled himself together. By the time he passed the hidden camera on his way out, he'd already popped a marshmallow into his mouth and was chewing happily. The door clicked shut behind him.

For a few seconds nobody spoke. Then Philip said, "Um, what was *that*?"

"It was like he was glad he couldn't find something," Logan suggested. "And then he was sad. But then happy again? Really hard to tell."

Miles just shook his head in confusion.

Then Courtney asked, "Why didn't he say anything to me?"

"Maybe Daisy put up a force field of invisibility around you," Miles suggested, only half joking.

"I wish," Daisy said. "Spies have cool gadgets, but we can't make things magically go invisible."

"Not yet, maybe," Miles said.

"He must have wanted to pretend he didn't see you," Logan said. "That's all I can think of."

"That marshmallow man is becoming more and more of a mystery," Daisy said.

Philip debated explaining that Henry wasn't pretending not to see Courtney standing only a few feet to the side of him. He really *didn't* see her. But he'd managed not to let Henry's secret slip before, so he'd do it again. "C'mon," he said, "my violin isn't going to fly here on its own, remember?"

Why are we slowing down?" Miles asked. They'd just finished eating the rest of the sandwiches from the fridge, and he and Logan were about to pull out some video games. With all the excitement about Henry and Courtney and the drone, everyone seemed to have forgotten about asking him how he'd guessed the combination for the safe. He'd like to keep it that way for a while and figured the more distracted they were, the better the chance of that.

"We're stopping for the night," AJ announced.

Miles looked out at the busy highway with a frown. "But the drone hasn't come yet."

"It will find us at the campground," AJ said, taking the exit just past a blue sign with a white tent painted on it.

Miles was pretty sure that his own face matched Logan's disappointed expression. Having a drone land on top of your vehicle while you were parked wasn't nearly as exciting as having it happen while you were driving!

"This will cheer you guys up," Daisy said at their frowns. "Come see." They followed her back to the bookshelf-turned-spy lab. "Look." She pointed down at the monitor. She'd scanned in the copy of the old photograph Miles had given her, and the facial-recognition software had added names above the heads of the first two people—Samuel Sweet and Florence Sweet, Logan's grandparents. They'd known the identities of those two already, of course, but it was a good test of the program. "At this rate we might have all of them by morning," she said.

"This is great," Miles said, rubbing his hands together in anticipation. He didn't know how the information would actually help, but it would be one more piece of a very large puzzle.

Philip heard them talking about the photo from the bedroom, but he had to admit it didn't interest him much. He wanted to finish putting his clothes in the drawers. He would feel more settled that way. He'd already sent Andrew and Reggie a message telling them that he was doing fine. Andrew had replied that he would be expecting to see a knitted sweater when he got back. Reggie only said to keep his mind open to new ideas, whatever that meant.

He hung his suit in the disguise closet and placed his dress shoes beneath it. He wasn't sure he quite believed that this drone of Daisy's would actually show up with his violin. He'd likely have to rent some third-rate model instead of playing with the violin he'd found in the candy factory. It had quickly replaced the one he'd found in his mother's stuff. As good as that one was, it couldn't compare with a Stradivarius. Nothing could, really.

He heard the low groan of the brakes, which was the only indication the RV had stopped. He hurried out to join the others before they complained that he'd taken up all the drawer space.

He found everyone with their faces pressed up to various windows. One glance and he could see why. He knew they were stopping at a campground, but he'd pictured a dirt field with a few trees, some tents, maybe a handful of other RVs or tents. This was pretty much the opposite of that.

AJ went out first, and they all ran after, eager for a closer look. The sun had already dipped below the valley, but campfires blazed in every direction, lighting up the night. RVs and tents lined up as far as they could see. (Well, Daisy could see farther, but even she would admit they went on really far.) People were laughing and cooking on grills; kids were biking and running after balls, dogs, and each other. Music played, lights swung from RV awnings, and the smell of burgers and toasted marshmallows hung heavy in the air.

"Wow," Miles said, eyes wide. "This place is awesome!"

"Remember," AJ said, returning from the other side of the RV, where he'd been hooking up the water and electricity. "No one brings strangers inside the RV for any reason. If you leave the immediate area, bring your vid com with you. I'll go to the campground's general store and pick up some food and supplies."

"We can do that for you," Miles said, holding out his hand for money.

AJ shook his head. "No offense, but I wouldn't trust you to come back with anything other than donuts and toys."

Miles shrugged. "Yeah, that makes sense."

"I'll go with you," Daisy said. "Maybe they have some clothes I could buy, since *someone* didn't let me pack clean clothes before we left."

"C'mon, Oopsa," AJ said, putting his arm around her. "Let's go get you some of the campground's finest attire." Over his shoulder he said, "You boys behave. And don't put out the slides any farther than I already did. We don't want to attract attention."

Once they were gone, the three boys looked at each other and then around them. They were in a totally foreign environment with no parents or guardians, and they didn't know a soul. "What do we do first?" Miles asked.

Logan said, "I have an idea." He ran back inside the RV, then came out with something slung over his shoulder. "What better way to make friends, right?" He held open the pillowcase to show all the candy he'd collected from the factory.

When Daisy returned twenty minutes later, she found Logan and Miles playing flag football in a nearby clearing with eight of their new best friends. She ducked inside the RV to drop off a bag of the least stylish clothes a thirteen-year-old girl would ever want to wear and checked the photograph for any new matches. There weren't any, so she headed back out to the game.

"Where's the tall one?" she asked, looking around for Philip.

Miles held his hands down by his flags to protect them from being grabbed while he answered. "He heard someone playing a violin really badly and stormed off to demand they stop."

"That sounds right," Daisy said with a nod. She activated the locator on her vid com, overlaid a 3-D map of the campground, and saw the red dot marked PHILIP flashing about fifty yards away. She decided that was close enough that she didn't need to worry.

Logan waved to her. "Wanna join the game? You can have one of my flags!"

She shook her head. "I need to stretch my legs." What she really needed to do was resume the training she hadn't been able to do at camp. She disliked feeling that she wasn't in peak physical condition. What if she suddenly got a mission that required her to scale a mountain or canoe through raging rapids?

She headed toward the central path, which divided the tents from the RVs, looking around to get the lay of the land. One of the bike paths ran along the outskirts of the campground, but she would have too much company there, even at night.

"Are you lost?" a girl's voice asked from behind her. "It's easy to get turned around here. All the tents and RVs start to look the same."

Daisy had heard the girl's footsteps approaching, her flip-flops smacking the ground. But anyone in flip-flops wasn't likely a threat, so Daisy hadn't turned around. She did now, though.

Even in the dark, she could tell the girl had purple hair. It took Daisy a few seconds to remember that her own hair was back to the brown she'd been born with. Seeing the girl, she suddenly felt the desire to change it again. She'd never dyed her hair just for fun, only for a job. She was pretty sure this girl didn't have a job that required her hair to be the color of an eggplant.

The girl tilted her head at Daisy, clearly waiting for an answer. She was a few years older, probably AJ's age. "I'm sorry if I startled you," the girl finally said. "Are you here with your family? Me and my brother and sister are all sharing one tent, so I needed some space, ya know?"

Daisy stared. This girl was talking to her like she was a regular person on a camping trip, not a girl in a totally tricked-out mobile spy unit waiting for a secret drone to find her and deliver stolen goods so she could solve some long-hidden mystery and save a candy bar and maybe a man's reputation. But even with all that going on, right at that minute she really was a regular person! She wasn't pretending to be anyone other than herself. She didn't remember the last time she'd been out in the world as simply Daisy. It felt really, really good.

Daisy smiled. "I'm here with friends. But I was kind of looking for somewhere to be alone, too."

"Yeah," the girl said, "you'd think with all this nature, privacy would be easier to find."

"Totally," Daisy agreed.

"I heard they're doing night yoga down at the activity center," the girl said. "Wanna check it out?"

Yoga certainly wasn't the endurance training she was used to, but staying flexible was important, too. Plus, purple-haired girls in campgrounds never asked her to hang out with them. Who knew when it would happen again? "Sure," she said. "I just have to tell my friends where I'll be." Daisy turned a little sideways, pulled out her vid com, and fired off a group message.

"Do you want to invite them?" the girl asked as they headed toward the activity center.

Daisy tried to picture any of the boys doing yoga and giggled. "They're not really athletic types."

Philip heard his vid com ding with a message, but he didn't bother to look at it. He had found the tent where the music was coming from (although the last thing he would call that noise was music). It was near the edge of the campground—one of the last campsites, in fact. Beyond it stood a wall of darkness. He couldn't imagine why someone would pick such a distant spot. He'd be creeped out. It was hard enough to be out in this field in the dark where he couldn't see what was crawling around at his feet. He wanted to get back to the RV, but he'd come all this way, and the sound *really* had to stop. It was an affront to all violins.

Now that he'd found the right place, was he just supposed to knock? How could you knock on a tent? What was the proper campground etiquette? He should have brought a flashlight.

He heard a groan behind him and turned to see a girl a little older than him sitting by a campfire with her hands over her ears. Without uncovering her ears, she said, "Let me guess, you're here to beg my brother to stop playing his violin."

"Oh, is that what he's doing?" Philip asked. "I thought he was dragging his nails down a chalkboard while sitting on a cat."

The girl's mouth twitched. "Yeah, that's a pretty accurate description." Her accent placed her from somewhere in the Midwest. She raised her voice and called, "Zack! You're killing me here. Please take a break."

The sound finally stopped, and the girl tentatively lowered her hands. She rubbed her eyes for some reason and blinked a few times. "Ahh, much better."

Her brother came out of the tent, his beginner's violin hanging at his side. "Not my fault. I think this thing's broken."

"I could take a look at it," Philip offered. "I know a little about violins." Truthfully, he was itching to hold one in his hand again, even one like this, which wasn't too many steps up from a toy.

The boy hesitated, glancing at his sister. She nodded. "Might as well give it to him. If he turns out to be a violin thief and runs away with it, then you'll have an excuse not to practice."

Philip adjusted the pegs until it was as tuned as it was ever going to be. He handed it back to the boy. "You were right. The violin *was* the problem."

The boy lifted it up and drew the bow back and forth on the strings. This time both the boy's sister *and* Philip covered their ears.

"Okay, so maybe not the *whole* problem," Philip corrected.

"That's it," the boy said, laying the violin and bow down on a nearby picnic table, where the remains of dinner were piled up. "When I get home, I'm totally switching to the triangle. No one can stink at the triangle." He scooted back into the tent.

Philip looked at the girl. "I hope I didn't hurt his feelings."

"Nah," she said, waving her hand. "The violin's, like, the worst."

Philip bristled at that comment. "No, it's not."

The girl stood. "I didn't mean it like that. I'm sure it's not the worst for everyone. I mean, um, it's kind of hard to explain."

Philip checked his watch. "I've got nowhere to be."

She sighed. "I've got this thing called synesthesia. It means when I hear sounds or music or whatever, I see colors and shapes in the air. When my brother's playing the violin, I see these sharp, jagged lines, and it makes me dizzy."

"Oh," Philip said, not expecting that.

"It's not always bad," she was quick to add. "The shapes and patterns I see, I mean. Usually it's really cool. Just, you know, not when he's playing."

"So if someone were to play the violin really well, would you see something else?" he asked.

"Maybe. I don't know anyone who plays it really well."

Philip went over to the table and reached for the violin. "Mind if I give it a shot?"

"I guess not," she said uncertainly.

Philip tested the strings one more time, then began to play. First Zack came out of the tent to listen. Then people started wandering over from neighboring campsites. He closed his eyes and tried not to focus on how much worse his original composition sounded on this compared to his own violin. Something about being outside in the night air, with the crackling of the fires and the eyes of strangers on him, sent him into some kind of trance. He kept playing until he'd performed the whole piece, something he'd never done in front of anyone before, not even Reggie. It was good practice for the contest. He knew something was missing from it—just the last few notes now—but his audience wouldn't.

As he drew his bow across the last string, he opened his eyes.

The crowd had grown large. It now included Logan and Miles as well. Philip lowered the violin to his side, and everyone broke out in applause. He glanced over at the girl. She was wiping away a tear and wasn't covering her ears, so those were good signs. Her parents had returned, and they had their arms around her. He felt a tug of different emotions—pleasure at being able to move her like that, and jealousy of their seemingly perfect family.

She came toward him. "I saw the most awesome things while you were playing. You should always do that. I mean, like, seriously, never stop doing that."

He laughed and handed the violin to Zack, who looked at it

like he couldn't believe it was the same instrument he'd been playing. "Maybe you should keep it," Zack said, trying to push it back at him.

"That's okay," Philip said. "I'm all set."

"My name's Mia, by the way." The girl stuck out her hand.

"Philip," he replied. Her hand felt warm when he shook it.

When the crowd realized he wasn't going to play anymore, they began to disperse. Her parents joined them. "That was outstanding," her dad said, shaking Philip's hand. "You have quite a gift."

"Thank you, sir," Philip replied.

"Would you and your parents like to join us for s'mores?" Mia's mom held up a bag of marshmallows in one hand and a giant chocolate bar in the other. "I bet Zack would love to hear about the years of practice it must have taken to get that good."

"Triangle, Mom," Zack said. "I'm switching to the triangle."

Philip swallowed hard. Before he could think of an explanation as to why his parents weren't there, Logan and Miles rushed up. "We're with him," Miles said, wiping away his own tear but pretending he was pushing hair out of his face. "Our parents are all back home."

"We have a chaperone," Logan added.

"Well then, you're all welcome to join us."

"Hey, look, Aurora is back!" Mia suddenly shouted.

Miles craned his neck back. "Oh my gosh, where?" he said, spinning in circles. "I don't see it."

"Don't see what?" Philip asked, following Miles's gaze. More stars filled the sky than he'd ever seen, but truthfully, he didn't look up all that often at home.

"The aurora borealis!" Miles exclaimed, still spinning. "The northern lights?" At Philip's blank expression, he said, "When charged particles from the sun pass through Earth's magnetic field, they hit gases and dust and make these green and red lights that dance in the sky." He was looking in every direction but still couldn't find them.

Logan pulled on Miles's arm and pointed to Mia, who wasn't looking up at the sky but rather was kneeling down next to the picnic table, holding her hand out to what at first looked like a very large, fat squirrel. At closer inspection, it turned out to be a cat. A very small, very fat cat.

"This is Aurora," Mia told them by way of introduction. "She doesn't belong to anyone. The campground owners said she just showed up one day. Isn't it sad? There's no one to take care of her."

"Clearly she hasn't gone hungry," Philip noted.

"Let me guess, not a cat person?" Mia asked.

"*I* am!" Miles said. "I'm totally a cat person." He fell to his knees and started making kissy noises. "Here, kitty, kitty." The cat took one look at him and said, *Woof!* Miles sat straight up. "Did that cat just bark at me?"

Logan laughed. "Totally."

"Yeah, she does that," Mia said. "Weird, right?"

Philip sat down on the picnic bench to wait for the others to get bored of the cat. After a few minutes of trying and failing to coax it out from under the table, they finally gave up. "C'mon," Mia said. "Let's go make the s'mores before my brother eats all the ingredients."

"Be right there," Philip said, still tired from his performance.

Logan and Miles followed her to the fire pit, betting each other whether real s'mores would taste better than Some More S'mores. Philip doubted it. Some More S'mores were *really* good. Mia returned to hand him a stick with a marshmallow on it. It was a real stick. It had only recently been lying on the ground, and before that, it was part of a tree with birds landing on it and who knows what else. And he was expected to eat something impaled on it? He hardly thought so. When she turned back around, he tossed it over his shoulder into the woods.

A few seconds later something furry landed on his lap. He wouldn't want to admit it, but he may have squealed a little as he jumped off the bench. The little cat flew a few feet into the air, twisted around, and landed gracefully on its paws. It barked again, then headed right back to him. It began to rub up against his legs, purring loudly as it weaved in and out between them.

"Where's your marsh—" Mia started to say, then noticed that the cat had come out from under the table, and talk of marshmallows slid away.

"She likes you!" Mia said in a hushed voice. "She *chose* you. It's very special when a cat chooses you."

Daisy picked that moment to show up. "A cat chose Philip?" she asked, clearly amused at the scene. "Why?"

Mia raised her eyebrow at Daisy. "Why wouldn't she?"

"I'm sure I could come up with ten good reasons off the top of my head."

The two girls assessed each other warily until Mia's mom said, "There you are, Beth." A girl with purple hair arrived a few feet behind Daisy.

Philip looked from the girl back to Daisy. "Daisy! You made a friend!" he said.

She kicked him in the shin. He kicked back.

"You're sure you're not here with your family?" Beth asked Daisy, watching this. "This kid totally seems like an annoying little brother."

"Hey, I resent that!" Zack called out.

"Nope," Daisy assured her. "Not a brother."

At the same time their vid coms all beeped. None of them reached for the devices, though. They might look like regular tablets, but not enough to take a chance this close to people.

Daisy tilted her head. Philip could tell AJ must be speaking to her through the transceiver. Excitement flickered in her eyes. "We need to go," she suddenly said, snapping her fingers. "I'll go grab Logan and Miles away from the s'mores."

Mia watched Daisy go. "Your friend sure is bossy."

"You don't know the half of it."

Mia lifted up the cat, holding her only inches from Philip's face. "Take me with you," she said as though the cat were speaking. "Please take me home, Mr. Music Man."

He laughed, something he immediately realized he didn't do enough of. "Not a chance."

She moved the cat's paw until it was on his chest. "Pretty please?" she asked in that little cat voice again. The cat stuck out its nose and nuzzled Philip's chin! He wiped at his chin with his hand. Nothing had ever nuzzled his chin before! "If you like it so much, why don't you take it?" he asked.

"Believe me, I would. But my cat, Mustard, is very territorial. He doesn't get along with other cats well. Plus she didn't choose me, she chose you."

He had to admit the cat was pretty cute, as far as animals went. The firelight wasn't bright enough to show him what color she was, but he could see a few different patterns on her back and head.

Mia's mother came over to them, followed by the rest of the family. "Mia, leave the boy alone. Not everyone sees a cat in a field and wants to take it home." She turned toward Philip. "Are you sure you all can't stay a bit longer? We're about to do some stargazing. The meteor shower will reach its peak tomorrow night, but we'll still get a pretty good show tonight and for a few days after. Even though it's very rare to see the aurora in the summertime, we might get lucky and spot it." Then she added, "Not the cat."

"Thank you for the invitation," Philip said, "but we've got to leave early in the morning. We should go." The excuse sounded lame even to him, but Daisy was mouthing the word *picture*. Their database must have matched another face.

"We're here another day," Zack said. Graham cracker crumbs fell from his lips as he spoke, and he wiped them away. "Mom's an astronomy teacher, and we're going to see the dedication of a new telescope."

"Really?" Miles said, stopping midchew. "That's so cool. Where is it?"

"A few hundred miles from here," Mia's mom replied. "First light isn't until Thursday."

Zack nudged Miles with his elbow. "First light is when a telescope first gets turned on and the light from the universe starts streaming in." He got a dreamy, faraway look on his face. "This new scope will be able to spot life on other planets! I entered a contest from the Planetary Society to name an exoplanet that a group of kids found last summer, and they're announcing the winner at the dedication!"

Miles's first thought was *rats*, he wished he'd known about that contest. Naming a candy bar and a puppy was nice and all, but a planet? That was surely the coolest thing a human being could name. His second thought was to begin calculating in his head whether they could build another stop into their trip. Daisy gave him a quick headshake. That girl could read his mind way too well!

"This scope won't be able to detect *life*, Zack," his oldest sister corrected. "It can only try to find planets with Earth-like conditions."

"Same difference," Zack said.

"No, it's not," Beth insisted.

Mia's mother smiled. "If my kids have to argue about something, I'm glad it's astronomy."

Mia's father clasped Philip on the shoulder. "Thanks again for the unexpected concert. I'm sure you have a bright future as a violinist ahead of you. Your parents must be very proud."

Philip felt that queasiness in his stomach again. This time it was

Daisy who came to his rescue. She put her arm around him, even though she had to reach up to do it, and said, "Yes, everyone's very proud of young Philip here. Besides his skill with the violin, he invented the award-winning Harmon—"

He lifted her arm off and quickly said, "That's enough about me. Thank you all again for welcoming us. Have a great trip." Before anyone could protest, he headed away from the campsite, wishing again that he had brought a flashlight. Many of the campfires had gone out by then, and it was unbelievably dark. The others caught up with him quickly, and Daisy showed them how to use the light on their vid coms to guide them.

"Why didn't you want me to tell them about the Harmoni-candy?" she asked Philip as they crossed over to the RV side of the campground.

"Until we know if there will even *be* a Harmonicandy," Logan said, "we shouldn't talk about it more than necessary."

Philip grunted in agreement.

"Hey, cheer up," Daisy said, bumping him with her hip. "You made a friend tonight, too. That's huge for you. What does that make, four in about thirteen years now?"

"Sounds about right."

AJ had pulled down their beds for the night and was lounging on the couch, chomping on a sandwich when they filed in. He gestured to the computer screen in the lab. Another name had indeed popped up on the photograph. Evelyn Sheinblatt, the other woman in the photo.

They all looked at Logan, who peered more closely at the picture. "I don't remember meeting her," he said. "But her name sounds familiar. I think my grandpa mentioned his friend Evy once or twice. That must be her." He wished he'd paid more attention to everything his grandfather had ever said.

Unable to hold it back, he yawned, feeling the weight of the long, insane day catch up with him. Had the Kickoff really only been that morning? Some days went by in the blink of an eye, and others felt like they lasted for a month. Today had lasted for a year.

Daisy was about to suggest heading to bed, when they heard a dog barking outside the RV. It was too dark out to see anything.

"Maybe the drone has arrived!" Miles suggested.

AJ cautiously opened the main door and peered out. In a flash, a small, fat multicolored cat ran up the stairs and down the aisle before leaping into a stunned Philip's arms.

Daisy grinned. "Make that *five* friends in thirteen years."

CHAPTER EIGHT

It felt like he'd only been asleep for five minutes, but when Logan checked the clock, it said 3:00 a.m. He wasn't sure what had awoken him until he heard the scratching. It sounded like it was coming from the roof above him. His first, sleep-addled thought was...*Santa?* But he dismissed that one quickly.

He peered over the side of his bunk bed to check whether Philip's cat was scratching the furniture. But the cat lay curled up in the crook of Philip's arm, both of them sound asleep.

The light in the back bedroom flickered on, and AJ walked out a few seconds later. Logan sat up and saw that Daisy was also awake and standing in the middle of the RV. She was fully dressed. He had the feeling she slept with one eye open. She switched on a flashlight.

"What's going on?" he whispered, blinking.

She pointed the beam of light at the sunroof over her head. "The drone is here."

"The drone is here?" Miles repeated, suddenly wide awake. He hopped out of bed.

AJ pulled one of the levers on the climbing wall, and the sunroof slid open. Seconds later a steel-gray robot-bird thingy with four octopus-like tentacles flew inside and descended silently toward the floor. Logan thought it was about the size of one of the warming ovens in the Some More S'mores Room. Or maybe he just had s'mores on the brain!

Philip woke up last and groggily propped himself up on one arm. The cat stretched and pushed her paws on his chest. Startled, Philip scooted backward in his bunk before looking down to find Aurora. Why had he allowed the others to talk him into letting the cat sleep in the RV with him? Then he saw the drone.

"My violin?" he asked, squeezing himself around the cat and out of the bed. He ignored the rope ladder and landed on the floor at the same time as the drone.

They all knelt around it. Instinctively, Logan and Miles reached out to touch it. "Warm!" Logan said. "Smooth!" Miles said at the same time.

"Yes," AJ said. "It is warm and smooth. It's also worth more money than any of us—well, except maybe Philip—will ever earn in a lifetime, so let's not touch it. Or, you know, breathe on it too much."

The boys backed up an inch. AJ turned the drone over and slid open a hidden compartment to reveal a small keypad. Daisy leaned over and typed in a series of numbers and letters. For a few seconds nothing happened, and then a whirring sound came from the drone's belly, followed by a single click. Daisy could now easily lift the top off. She reached in and took out the candy bar, which Courtney had wrapped in tissues. She unwrapped it and handed it to Logan, who, out of all of them, was the closest to its rightful owner.

Logan let the Magic Bar rest in his palm. It weighed more than he'd have expected—about as much as two Harmonicandies, and those had cookie harmonicas in the middle. He hadn't seen a real Magic Bar since he was very small, in Spring Haven's only candy shop. Miss Paulina of **Miss Paulina's Candy Palace** had kept one as a souvenir on a high shelf. That one looked pretty banged up, and he hadn't been allowed to touch it. Now that he thought of it, she must have gotten rid of it, because he hadn't noticed it there in years. This one was in much better condition. Its shiny blue wrapper still shone, the edges only slightly frayed.

He raised the Magic Bar to his nose but couldn't smell anything. Not that he'd really expected to. Even though the wrapper had held up so well, after fifty years the chocolate itself would have long ago turned bad. The fat and sugar would have separated from the cocoa, covering it all in a dried-up gray-white slime called bloom. Any nuts inside would have gone rancid, and the bar would have crumbled into pieces. Keeping it at a cool temperature inside the safe would have protected it in the beginning, but at this point, the tight wrapper would be the only thing holding the bar together. He laid it gently on the laboratory counter, where he and Miles could admire it from afar.

Philip grabbed for his violin. He turned his back to the others and opened the case. He slipped the passport into the waistband of his pajamas, then inspected the instrument and gave a grunt of satisfaction when he didn't see any obvious injuries. He handed the case to AJ, commanded, "Put this somewhere safe," and climbed up the rope ladder into bed. The cat climbed right up after him, turned in a tight circle, then lay down on Philip's back. A few seconds later, they were both breathing steadily.

"Wow," Daisy exclaimed. "He's even *more* charming in the middle of the night. Who'd have guessed it?"

"Can we start analyzing the candy bar and the bean right now?" Miles asked.

Daisy shook her head. "It'll be delicate work, and waiting five more hours isn't going to change anything."

Reluctantly, Logan and Miles returned to their beds. It took a while before either of them could stop thinking about that Magic Bar just sitting there on the counter, holding all its secrets inside.

Miles woke first and headed straight for the Magic Bar. Daisy had put it on a paper plate, covered the plate with a plastic bowl, and stuck a sticky note on the side that read:

> Do not touch or the
> Magic Bar will self-destruct.

He grumbled when he saw it but had to admit it was probably a good idea. The candy bar had to be incredibly fragile after all this time.

Plus he was pretty sure Daisy could actually make it self-destruct if she wanted to.

Aurora started pawing at the door to be let out. She turned and rubbed against Miles's ankle. "Oh, I see how it is," he whispered, bending down. "You're only going to pay attention to me when you need something." She let him scratch under her chin for a few seconds, and then when she'd had enough, he could swear she began glaring at him.

"Okay, okay," he said, pushing the door open wide enough for the cat to squeeze out. The fresh morning air blew in the open door like an invitation. He glanced back at his sleeping friends and reached over the side of the booth to grab his backpack. He hurried outside before he changed his mind.

Even though the sun had already risen, most of the campground was still asleep. He knew AJ would have a cow if he wandered off, so he sat at the picnic table beside Harvey and pulled out Arthur's geocaching book. The red envelope peeked out from inside the cover, and he realized that in all the excitement yesterday he'd never opened it.

He traced the curves of the Aramaic letters that spelled out his name, then tore open the envelope. He smiled as he pulled out the handmade card. Jade had drawn a picture of the two of them. (He knew it was them because of the arrows pointing at their heads, with their names written alongside.) Fluffernutter, whose name she'd shortened to FN, sat between them on a rock. They were all eating Pepsicles. It was the best picture anyone had ever made him. Probably the only one, too.

Inside Arthur had printed a short poem:

> WE SHALL NOT CEASE FROM EXPLORATION
> AND THE END OF ALL OUR EXPLORING
> WILL BE TO ARRIVE WHERE WE STARTED
> AND KNOW THE PLACE FOR THE FIRST TIME.
> —T. S. ELIOT
>
> We are happy to know you and your family, and will look forward to hearing about your journey. Arthur, Tina, & Jade (& Fluffernutter)

Miles read the card over again, then slipped it back in the envelope and carefully slid the envelope into the book. He wasn't sure he fully understood the poem, but he liked the way it sounded.

Aurora jumped onto the table and got right up in his face. A second later came the barking. Then she ran over to the RV door, looked over her shoulder, and waited.

"Did anyone ever tell you you're not actually a dog?" Miles asked Aurora as he opened the door for her.

"There you are!" Logan said, pulling Miles inside. "You're not going to believe this!"

"What is it?" he asked, trying not to stumble on the steps as Logan dragged him.

"You've got to see the Magic Bar!"

"It didn't self-destruct, did it?" Miles said, only half kidding.

"No," Logan said, "it's, like, the opposite of that."

"It *un*-destructed?"

"Exactly!" Logan said.

"Huh?"

Logan held up the plate with the unwrapped Magic Bar on it. "It looks like the day it came off the belt!"

"How is that possible?" Miles asked. "I've found many a Halloween candy bar a few months later, and they'd already turned wonky." He looked at the wrapper, which had been taken off in one piece and laid beside it. Inside the shiny foil lay a thin sheet of wax paper. Miles pointed to it. "Could the wax paper have helped it stay fresh?"

"To a degree, yes," Logan said. "But maybe it would have given it an extra five months of freshness. Not five *decades*."

"Maybe it's not real," Philip suggested. "It could be a rubber prototype, or just some kind of material made to look like chocolate."

Logan had to admit that made sense. After all, he'd never seen a real Magic Bar before. Maybe they had never really looked this shiny and smooth. Philip's theory would certainly explain why it didn't even have any bloom on it.

He brought it to his nose and sniffed. The faint chocolate smell rose up. "It's real," he said. "I can't tell what's in it from the smell, though."

"We'll find that out when we analyze it," Daisy reminded them. She reached for the plate, but Logan was gripping it tight.

"But how can the lab tell us if the Magic Bar used the same chocolate as the original Harmonicandy?" he asked.

"It can't," Daisy said. "There's only one way to do that."

Logan shuddered. "I'm going to have to taste a fifty-year-old candy bar, aren't I?"

"'Fraid so," Daisy said.

Miles nodded gravely. "If you keel over and start frothing at the mouth, we'll save you."

"Good to know," Logan said, meaning it. "Okay, here goes." He took a deep breath and lifted the Magic Bar. Never in his life had he thought he'd get to even see a Magic Bar, let alone taste one. Even a fifty-year-old one.

AJ joined them, placing a metal first-aid kit at his side. "Just in case," he said when they all turned to stare at it. "If you have a bad reaction, we can give you an injection that will destroy any dangerous bacteria. I warn you, it is not a small needle."

Logan gulped but nodded.

"Stop freaking him out," Daisy said, but she looked worried, too.

Logan pushed away the image of a needle as long as his arm and took a small bite. He was aiming for a big enough sample that he'd be able to fully taste the ingredients, but not so much that he wouldn't be able to spit it out if it was awful.

The group moved closer as Logan chewed, swished the chocolate around in his mouth, and swallowed. When his expression froze, Daisy grabbed the metal kit, ready to flip it open.

"Well?" Miles shouted.

Logan only stared straight ahead, his eyes unfocused. Philip held his hand in front of Logan's mouth until he felt warm air. "He's still breathing."

"Are you okay?" Daisy asked, gripping Logan's arm and giving him a shake.

Calmly and carefully, Logan formed his words. "I know why they stopped selling the Magic Bar."

CHAPTER NINE

After Logan's cryptic comment about knowing why the factory stopped making the Magic Bar, he'd asked for privacy and had been holed up in the bedroom ever since. Once AJ was convinced Logan wouldn't implode, pass out, or sprout wings from eating something made in the middle of the last century, he got them back on the road. They had two hours to get to **The Candy Basket**, and if he didn't prove he could get them there on time and in one piece, he had no doubt their trip would be cut short.

"Can't this giant hunk of metal go any faster?" Philip asked, coming up to bug AJ for the third time in thirty minutes.

AJ groaned. It turned out they couldn't run the lab tests while the RV was in motion—some sort of safety precaution shut down the power to the sensitive equipment. The kids weren't being very patient about having to wait. In fact, they were being totally *im*patient and, frankly, highly annoying. "Can't you entertain yourselves for a little while longer?" he asked.

Philip leaned on the arm of the passenger seat. "Did you know the cat from the campground is currently curled up on your pillow?"

"What?" AJ said, tightening his grip on the wheel so they

wouldn't swerve. "I told you this morning to leave her at the campground."

"Yes, you did," Philip agreed. "The cat apparently had other plans. She refused to leave the RV." A more accurate explanation would be that she'd refused to leave *him*, but Philip couldn't bring himself to say that.

"We don't have any cat food," AJ pointed out. "Or a litter box."

"The outside world is her litter box," Philip said. "And Miles found some canned tuna in that giant hidden closet. It stinks, but the cat likes it. Surprised you can't smell it." He waved his hand in front of his nose. "It reeks."

"Has Logan come out yet?" AJ asked, changing the subject. The last thing he wanted to talk about was his inability to smell.

Philip shook his head. "Don't worry, though. We've been taking turns checking on him. He's deep in thought."

"Go," AJ said. "Now go play a game. Enjoy the scenery. Read a book."

"Fine," Philip said, getting up. "But you drive like an old lady."

AJ ignored the insult. He knew plenty of old ladies who drove very fast. Well, one, anyway. Daisy's grandmother could beat anyone in a drag race.

Philip was only gone a minute before Miles plopped down in the passenger seat. AJ groaned again.

"Is it true Harvey will float if we go into a body of water?" Miles asked.

"Yes," AJ replied with a sidelong glance.

"Cool." Miles looked out the huge windshield. "If we fall off a cliff, would we fly?"

"Of course. There are jet propulsion rockets next to the wheels. If the wheels sense we've lost traction with the road, the rockets will kick in."

"Seriously?" Miles asked, his eyes widening.

"No. You really are too gullible."

Miles grumbled in response. But he bounced back quickly. "Can we play video games while Harvey's moving?"

"If I don't say yes, will you continue to ask me really annoying questions?"

"Very likely," Miles said.

"Fine. Just use the seat belts on the couch."

Miles jumped up and patted AJ on the shoulder. "You're a very good guardian. Chaperone. Whatever you call yourself."

AJ muttered something about the RV being a pet-free zone as Miles left to join Philip and Daisy.

It turned out Daisy had only played spy-training video games that tested coordination, and Philip had never played any video games at all, which pretty much blew Miles's mind. But they found a role-playing game called *Role with It* that everyone could agree on. They got to scan in their heads to become part of the game. Miles's head went onto a cowboy's body, Daisy became a rock star, and Philip got stuck as a half man, half goat. Miles had to work hard not to cry from laughter when he saw how seamlessly their heads melded together with their animated counterparts.

The three of them spent the next hour trying to save their Wild West city from an alien attack. Miles and Daisy giggled whenever Philip had to use one of his goat legs to kick an alien in its large, squishy head. "Sorry," Philip grunted each time. He might be competitive to a fault, but he wasn't the violent type. As much fun as the game was, they couldn't help glancing at the bedroom door every few minutes.

Finally, just as Miles thought he couldn't stand the suspense anymore, Logan came out and joined them on the couch. They laid down their gaming devices.

"The Magic Bar contains only two ingredients," Logan announced. "The majority—at least eighty percent—is pure cocoa. That's a mixture of cocoa paste and cocoa butter. The only other ingredient I can taste is sugar, and only a pinch."

"That's it?" Miles asked, surprised. "No caramel, marshmallow, nougat? Nuts? Wafer? Fruit?"

"No vanilla to add depth?" Philip asked. "No lecithin to keep it smooth? Don't all chocolate candies need those?"

Logan still had a hard time accepting the fact that Philip knew a lot about the chocolate-making process now. "Most do," he agreed. "But trust me, this didn't need anything else. The best word I can think of to describe the taste is *pure*. Like I was eating the soul of chocolate itself." He reached over to the counter and picked up the blue bean. "Like I was eating the soul of *this*." He placed the bean in his palm and held it out to them.

"Wow," Miles said, carefully lifting the bean from Logan's palm as though it were the most precious item in the world. "That's powerful stuff."

Logan nodded. "I know."

"What does this mean for us now?" Philip asked. No use pretending that the Harmonicandy wasn't his first priority. "Even if this was the same chocolate used for the contest, we don't know where to get more beans. I'm pretty sure we can't make thousands of Harmonicandies out of *that* one." He pointed to the small bean Miles was rolling around in his hand.

"It was definitely made from the same chocolate," Logan said. "But even if we found the beans, we couldn't use them."

"Why not?" Philip demanded.

Logan knew his explanation wouldn't be good enough, but he had to try. "Because the beans themselves are too...special. It's like they're almost not supposed to be in a chocolate bar. I think I didn't pick up on it in the original Harmonicandy because there were so many other ingredients, and some of our own dark chocolate went in there, too."

Philip scoffed. "We can't use it because it's too *good*?"

Logan knew he wasn't making much sense. But how could he explain the feeling he got when he ate it? He looked to Daisy for help. She'd been very quiet through all this.

"Let's wait to see what the results are from the test," she said. "For all we know, the beans came from Timbuktu, and there's no way we'd find the source anyway."

Philip scoffed again and crossed his arms. "That's not even a real place."

"Sure it is," Miles replied. "It's in West Africa at the southern edge of the Sahara desert."

"No cocoa trees in the desert," Logan reminded them. "To grow properly, cocoa trees need to be within ten degrees of the equator in a humid, tropical environment."

"People say Timbuktu when they just mean a really faraway place," Miles explained. "Nothing to do now but wait, I guess."

Logan patted down his pockets, wishing he'd brought some poems to stock in there. He could use some inspiration right then. Miles saw him frown. "Everything okay?" he asked.

He'd long ago told Miles about his tradition of keeping a poem in his pocket. "You wouldn't happen to have a poem lying around, would you?"

Miles placed the bean back in its bowl on the counter and retrieved the card Jade had made him. He tore out a piece of paper from his notebook and quickly copied down the poem Arthur had written. He handed Logan the paper. "This is sort of poem-ish."

"It's perfect," Logan said. He read it over twice and then stuck it in his pocket. He actually felt a little calmer.

The RV pulled into the parking lot of a giant superstore, and AJ took up eight spots along the edge of the lot. As soon as the engine cut off, the four of them jumped up and raced over to the lab.

"Hold on," AJ said, popping up and stepping in front of it. "We

341

have fifteen minutes until we're due at the candy store. Before you do anything else, you need to change into your clothes, and it wouldn't kill anyone to brush their hair." When no one moved from the counter, he said, "Seriously. You're still wearing your pajamas. And I think Miles has honey on his chin that's two days old." AJ peered more closely at Miles. "With cat hair stuck to it."

Miles covered his chin. The rest grumbled but followed AJ's orders. Five minutes later they were back, dressed in their finest, hair quickly brushed or combed. Then they had to wait another three minutes because Philip had put on his suit and tie, and they told him he was way overdressed and made him change. He insisted on keeping the tie. He didn't expect them to understand.

With only seven minutes left, they had to work fast. Daisy pulled out a drawer beneath the bookshelf that the others had assumed was just storage. They should have known better. The "drawer" contained ten slots of various sizes along with a keypad. Daisy had already sliced off a piece of the Magic Bar, and now she placed it inside one of the slots. She dropped the bean into the next one. She relayed the commands to the computer to both analyze and compare the two objects' chemical compositions and to trace their origins. Plastic covers slid over the slots, and the objects disappeared from view.

"And now we wait," she said, sliding the drawer carefully back into place.

"For how long?" Miles asked. All this waiting for answers did not come naturally to him.

"For about two hours," she said, looking at her watch. "That gives us exactly one minute and sixteen seconds for you to tell us how you knew the combination to the safe."

Miles puffed up his cheeks and blew out the air. The others waited expectantly. *Rats.* Of course they hadn't forgotten.

"One minute, nine seconds," Philip noted.

"All right, all right," Miles said. He stepped over to a small drawer in the wall next to the laundry machine. Since this drawer was an actual drawer and not a high-tech laboratory in disguise, he'd been using it to hide the materials he'd taken from Samuel Sweet's box. He returned to the group with the map.

"Thirty-eight seconds," AJ warned.

"Hold your horses," Miles said. "This is delicate work." He carefully unfolded the map and laid it down on the counter. The others gathered around. "There," he said, pointing to the rock. "Look at these lines. They're not cracks in the rock. They're really numbers."

"I don't understand," Logan said to Miles. "It's really cool, but why would you have painted numbers on a rock, and then how could you possibly know they'd open the safe?"

Miles shook his head. "I didn't make the map. It was in your grandfather's box. I don't know why he had it, but he must have decided to use the numbers hidden in the rock when he chose a combination for the safe. I'm sorry I didn't just show it to you sooner. I don't know what to think about any of this."

"It's okay," Logan replied. "None of us know what to think."

"Speak for yourself," Philip said. "I think plenty of things, like that this Map of Awe doesn't look all that *awe*-inspiring...a little water, a few trees, a couple of rocks? And there's no *X*."

"No *X*?" Logan asked.

"You know, *X* marks the spot, like where you'd dig for treasure. There's no *X*."

"Not all maps are treasure maps," Miles said as patiently as possible. "Most just show you where you are, or how to get there."

Philip shrugged. "This one doesn't seem to do either of those things."

Miles felt himself getting angry and started to silently count backward from ten, the way his mom had taught him when he was younger and frustrated at not understanding a word in one of the books he was reading. Why was he defending Sam's map? It's not like he knew any more about it than Philip did.

"Hey, I realize not much is cooler than a mysterious map," Daisy said to AJ, who had been leaning over their shoulders. "But don't we have to go?"

AJ forced himself to stop studying the map on the counter and turned around. He frowned. "Not with you looking like that."

The boys didn't see anything wrong with the way Daisy looked, even though they were still getting used to seeing her with her normal brown hair. Daisy rolled her eyes, but she marched to the back room and closed the door. They heard her open the disguise closet. When she emerged five minutes later, she wore a soccer uniform, complete with cleats and a ball under one arm. The raised letters on her shirt spelled out CHESTERFIELD CHEETAHS.

The boys all opened their mouths, but Daisy held up a hand. "Before you ask, this way I'll look like a normal kid from"—she looked down at her shirt—"Chesterfield, who came to the store before her soccer match. This *is* a publicity tour, after all, and there's nothing a spy hates more than having people take their picture and publish it."

"Why does AJ still get to look like AJ, then?" Logan asked.

In response, AJ pulled a baseball cap out of his back pocket and stuck it on his head. A mass of brown curls spilled out from under the cap, totally hiding his short blond hair. He stuck a pair of large mirrored sunglasses on his face.

"Nice," the boys said, nodding in approval.

"But wait," Logan said as they filed down the stairs. "How did you get the name of the town on your shirt so fast?"

"Easy," AJ said, locking the door behind them. "I used the 3-D printer to make the letters and then glued them on last night."

"How domestic of you," Philip said. "You can add those skills to your long list of accomplishments the next time you need to convince someone to trust their kids with you."

"And I shall!" AJ said with a grin.

The tinted one-way windows of the RV filtered out a lot of the sunlight, and it took everyone except AJ (who had his sunglasses) a minute to stop squinting. Actually, Daisy only pretended to squint because she didn't want the boys to feel inferior.

"We never really talked about what we're going to tell people today," Logan pointed out as they followed AJ in the direction of the candy store. "Aunt Rosie, the owner of **The Candy Basket**, is really nice, and—"

"Wait, the owner is your *aunt*?" Miles asked.

Logan shook his head. "She just calls herself Aunt Rosie."

"I know someone like that," Daisy muttered. She didn't miss Aunt Jess at all. And she was pretty sure Aunt Jess didn't miss *her*, either.

"As I was saying," Logan continued, "she's supported the factory since the early days. How can we promote the Harmonicandy when there might not be one?"

"That's easy," Philip said. "Haven't you heard the expression *Fake it till you make it*?"

"Um, not really?"

"It's about creating your own reality," Daisy explained. "Take it from someone who lies for a living. When you want something to happen for you, pretend it already has. The more committed you are to the illusion, the more real it starts to feel. Others believe it, and then *you* start to believe it yourself."

Philip nodded in agreement, but Logan and Miles exchanged a doubtful look. Anything that felt like lying would be hard for them. Logan made a decision. "How about we stick as close to the truth as possible, and lie more by what we *don't* say, rather than what we *do* say."

"You're giving me a headache," Philip said. "But whatever. We can try it your way." *Lying by not lying*, he thought. *Interesting!*

"One more street," AJ said. "Then we turn left at the corner and we should see it." They found themselves in a little town square not much different from downtown Spring Haven. Large trees lined the streets, their branches forming a canopy of leaves over the road. For Logan, that canopy was his favorite thing about visiting Aunt Rosie's store. He hadn't been in a few years, but seeing the branches reaching toward each other as if they were embracing always made him feel like he was in some amazing storybook. His pace slowed as they neared the final corner. Could they really pull this off?

"You know what?" Philip said. "I bet we're making a much bigger deal about this whole thing than the stores are. They're used to salespeople and factory owners coming by to hype their products. Our visit is probably like any other day for them."

That thought lifted Logan's spirits. "Maybe you're right. We can just be friendly and chat with Aunt Rosie and her staff while they eat the Harmonicandies that Max shipped yesterday. We'll get in and get out and move on."

"Sounds good!" Miles said, relieved. He and Logan high-fived. Then they turned the corner, and any hope that the visit wouldn't be a big deal flew from their heads.

CHAPTER TEN

I magining a larger-than-life cardboard cutout of yourself propped up on a sidewalk in a strange town is a lot different from actually *seeing* one. Since before that moment Philip had done neither, the whole thing was quite a shock. Someone had used the picture from after he won the contest—the same one on the posters under his bed—blown it up, and mounted it on thick cardboard. The cutout version of Philip held a sign that read COME MEET ME AND MY FRIENDS AT **The Candy Basket** TODAY AT NOON!

"Who's that handsome fella?" Daisy joked, trying to lighten the mood.

Philip only stared. His own eyes stared back at him. The person in the picture felt all too familiar and like a stranger at the same time. Even though he was smiling in the picture, it gave him the creeps.

"Look, someone drew a mustache on you!" Miles said. "Just kidding, they didn't."

"So there's a giant cardboard cutout of you," Daisy said, pushing him forward. "Just brush it off. It doesn't mean they're going to make a big deal about you inside the store."

"Pretty sure *that* does." Philip didn't have to point out the crowd of excited kids hovering outside. It was impossible to miss.

"That's him!" a little boy shouted. "The inventor of the Harmonicandy! He's here!"

AJ put his arms out protectively in front of Philip just as the little boy flew at him. Philip stumbled backward. Logan and Miles watched the whole thing with wide eyes. Word of their arrival must have reached inside the store, because Aunt Rosie ran outside, her long white hair flowing behind her, arms wide open.

"Children! How lovely to see you!" She gave Logan a big hug and shook hands with everyone except Daisy, who hung back and blended into the crowd. "We're so very happy to have you here!" AJ kept the crowd at bay while Aunt Rosie led them into the store. Harmonica music played through the speakers. Everywhere they looked, towers of candy displays nearly reached the ceiling. Logan easily spotted every one of **Life Is Sweet**'s products, with a whole section reserved for different colors of Sour Fingers. For whatever reason, **The Candy Basket** sold more of those than any other store in the country. They still had their plaque on the wall for selling the very first Snorting Wingbat, too. This was a special store, and being there gave Logan a warm feeling all the way to his toes.

The store also stocked a hundred different varieties of nuts, and candies from other factories that he hadn't seen before, like an anatomically correct frog that you dissected and then ate! He spotted a display marked SCHOOL SUPPLIES that consisted of candy pencils, notebooks, and erasers. Pizza-flavored bubble tea swirled around in a giant pitcher. The wrapper on a candy bar simply named HOT boasted that its jalapeño filling would make smoke come out your ears. Logan wasn't sure he believed that, but he'd have to bring one home for Max to sample.

"Hey, try this," Miles said, pulling Logan over to a table marked

FREE—TRY ME. He popped a caramel-filled pretzel into his mouth. "Yum!" Logan tried one, too, followed by three more.

Daisy broke away from the crowd that surrounded Philip and found Miles and Logan. No one was taking pictures yet, so she figured it was safe. "I've never been in a store like this!" she told them, her eyes darting around in wide circles.

"Have you ever actually been in a candy store at all?" Miles asked.

She thought for a minute and shook her head. Before she could say anything else, a girl with two long braids and braces came running up to Logan. "Do you ever see Daisy Carpenter, from the candy-making contest?" she asked in excited bursts.

Daisy began inching away toward a rack of foot-long strands of multicolored licorice.

"Um, yes, she pops up now and again," Logan said, trying hard not to glance in Daisy's direction.

The girl's eyes sparkled. "Can you tell her I think the 3G's should have won!"

"Um, sure," Logan said.

"Thanks!" The girl giggled shyly and ran back to her mom.

"You have a fan!" Miles said when Daisy sidled back toward them, licorice draped around her shoulders.

"How'd she know about my Green Glob of Goop?"

"Word in the candy business travels fast," Logan said. "And the 3G's was pretty legendary in its awfulness."

"Hey, it wasn't that bad!" Daisy said. "It tasted like a summer's day, remember?"

"We'll have to agree to disagree on that," Miles said. "At least you know your disguise works."

"My disguises always work." She took a bite of the licorice. It tasted like she imagined a rainbow would taste—airy and soft and sweet. It would go well paired with the 3G's.

Aunt Rosie's voice came over a microphone. "Greetings, every-one, and welcome to our very special guests! In a moment we'll be handing out samples of the Harmonicandy, winner of the annual New Candy Contest! You'll get to try it weeks before it hits stores!" She gestured at the table behind her, where two employees were using gloved hands to unpack the candy bars from the cooler, since they weren't wrapped.

The crowd cheered.

"But first I'd like to invite Philip Ransford to say a few words, if he doesn't mind." She stepped aside and held the microphone out to him.

Philip figured this was coming. He'd have to do better than at the Kickoff. As he walked up and the kids cheered and the parents clapped politely, he knew that the crowd would be expecting him to talk about the Harmonicandy—how he came up with it and how excited he was for its upcoming release. But they were supposed to avoid talking about it. He looked around the store at all the loving parents holding their kids' hands or bouncing their kids on their knees, and he knew just the right story for the occasion. It would mean making up lies worse than many he'd written in his notebook, but lying to *avoid* lying about the Harmonicandy made it seem less bad.

He took the microphone and looked out on the happy crowd, the brightly colored candies that filled the room, and Aunt Rosie herself, who had pink and blue cotton candy strands stuck in her hair. He took a deep breath.

"Candy makes people happy," he began, letting his eyes sweep the room. "It adds a little touch of sweetness to our days, when sometimes life really isn't all that sweet. I want to share a story with you, about the part candy has played in my own life."

Out of the corner of his eye he saw Logan stiffen. He was sure his friend thought he was going to talk about what had happened when they were younger, when he thought he'd been banned from the factory. But Logan didn't need to worry. Philip had a different version of his life story in mind.

"When I was a little more than a year old, my mother took me to the **Life Is Sweet** candy factory for its annual picnic. I don't remember this, of course, but the family photos from that day show a blue sky dotted with puffy clouds, acres of green grass and trees, rowboats on the pond, fields of grains and berries, and a farmhouse with cows and chickens roaming free behind a white picket fence. Then add in boxes of chocolate pizza, cotton candy the size of your head, rubber-duck races, and the Candymaker in his chocolate-smeared apron shaking my hand. When I'm an old man—if I get lucky enough to *be* an old man one day—that is how I'll picture the perfect day."

The crowd smiled up at him, nodding in agreement, but he was just getting warmed up. He didn't dare glance at Logan again, or he might lose his nerve. He continued. "Then it got even better. According to family lore, I took my first steps that day, out on the great lawn, while the ducks watched from the pond. My mom was able to catch it on video."

Murmurs of "aw" and "so sweet!" trickled through the crowd.

"The next year we went back, and the next. Our duck even finished in second place that year! I won two bucks!"

The crowd cheered and giggled.

"But that was my last visit to **Life Is Sweet** with my mom," Philip continued, his voice cracking in just the right place. "She died a few months later from cancer."

A shocked hush fell over the group.

"But here's the thing," he said after a respectful pause. "Thanks to the Candymaker, my new friends, the amazing teachers at the factory, and the judges of the candymaking contest, I get to go back there every day now, and every day I get to remember my mom out on that grass, cheering for me not to fall on my face, and every day I get to be grateful for being part of a business whose job it is to add sweetness to people's lives." He paused for a second as people wiped their eyes. "I'd like to dedicate this to her." He reached over to the tray of Harmonicandies and picked one up. He brought it to his lips and blew a strong, clear note that rang through the whole room.

Then he smiled and said, "Thank you."

The room erupted in applause, and Aunt Rosie hugged him for a long time until he wished she would stop. The Harmonicandies were handed out, and from across the room his friends stared at him as though they'd never seen him before. He wasn't looking forward to hearing what they had to say.

"Okay, dude, that speech was awesome," AJ said to Philip on their way back to the RV. "If you ever want a career as an undercover agent, you let me know. You could sell honey to a bee!"

Miles and Logan weren't quite as complimentary. Sure, they told him what a great speaker he was, how he'd captivated the room, but Philip knew they were a little scared of him now for how easily he'd lied—mostly because Miles actually said, "I'm a little scared of you now." They knew his mother had no part of his experience at the factory.

Logan followed a few steps behind the others. He didn't know how to explain to Philip how it had felt watching him make up a story in front of a hundred trusting kids and parents. While it definitely took the heat off the Harmonicandy for a little while, how could Philip have played with the crowd's emotions like that? Hadn't anyone taught him right from wrong? Maybe they hadn't.

But on the other hand, Philip really *had* lost his mother when he was three, so that part of it wasn't a lie at all. How could Logan confront him in light of that cold, hard truth?

At least the speech had everyone focusing on Philip, so he was grateful for that. The bright fluorescent light, which was great at making the candy wrappers sparkle, had made Logan's scars show even more than usual. Many of the younger kids had looked longer than necessary, until their parents grabbed them away. He knew they weren't being mean. They were just curious. Still, he'd pushed his hair further over his face than he had in a while.

He had to admit that some parts of the visit were exhilarating. He'd loved sampling the store's candies, of course, and meeting grown-ups who told him how the Neon Yellow Lightning Chew or the Oozing Crunchorama had been an important part of their childhoods. The highlight was when Aunt Rosie led the crowd in a rousing rendition of "Row, Row, Row Your Boat" on the Harmonicandy. It pained him to think that there might only be two more Harmonicandy concerts.

As they were leaving, Aunt Rosie had pulled him into another of her tight hugs. "I hope you won't give up on the Bubbletastic ChocoRocket," she'd told him. "You've got a lot of people rooting for you." He'd nodded and promised, but he wasn't so sure. He didn't want to risk letting people down again if he was never able to make it work. Her last words to him were to tell Henry she was sorry to miss him and that she was looking forward to seeing him at the next Confectionary Association convention.

"Yeah, a lot of us are looking forward to seeing good ol' Henry," Philip had said under his breath as he passed by.

AJ reached the RV first, but a frantic barking and growling made him stop before he could punch in the final number on the keypad to unlock it. "Everyone stay still," he warned, looking around for what sounded like a big, scary dog.

Miles didn't want to laugh at him, so he calmly told AJ that he didn't need to worry. It was just their new cat. AJ looked skeptical but unlocked the door anyway. The cat sat at the top stair, barking and narrowing her eyes at whoever dared approach her home.

"Who needs a guard dog when we've got a little fluffy kitty to protect us?" Miles said with a grin. He leaned in to pet her, but she darted past him and down the stairs.

"She probably just needs to go to the bathroom," Logan said, but instead of heading to the patch of bushes next to their RV, the cat went right up to Philip and began weaving in and out of his legs.

"Sorry," Philip said to Miles with an apologetic shrug. "It's nothing personal, I'm sure."

"Easy for you to say," Miles replied with a pout. "C'mon, Logan, let's check whether the results are in."

Daisy held Philip back until they were the only ones still in the parking lot. She led him a few feet away from the RV. Aurora stood at Philip's feet, watching Daisy very carefully.

"That was some story you told back there," Daisy said. "So full of emotion and details, one might even think it was true."

He laughed. "I assure you, it wasn't. But thank you for the compliment."

She kept eye contact, waiting for him to blink. She'd been trained at an early age to tell if someone was lying. "I'd be inclined to believe you," she finally said. "Because you are certainly an accomplished liar. But I've heard that story before."

He shook his head. "I've only told that story once before. And there's no way . . ." His voice trailed off. "Unless . . ."

"That's right," she said. "I read your essay."

"But—but," he sputtered. "If you could get into the system to read it, you could have just deleted it for me!"

She shrugged. "You need to learn to work for things," she said. "Don't change the subject. The more important issue is why you told that story today after going to all that trouble to hide your essay."

He had to admit, it was a fair question. "I honestly don't know," he said. "That story got me into the contest, so I figured it would take the focus away from the Harmonicandy, which, you'll have to admit, it totally did."

She nodded. It had been a brilliant move. "But then why did you care so much if your essay got circulated?"

"Before I answer that, let me ask you a question. When you read the essay and heard the story today, did you think it was true?"

"Well, I would have if I didn't know your real story. With Logan and the truck and your dad and everything."

"But even for a minute, while you were reading it, what were you feeling?"

"I don't know," she said. But she did know. And he did, too.

"You felt sorry for me," he said firmly.

She paused, then nodded.

He stepped around her to board the RV. "I never want anyone to feel sorry for me except when *I'm* the one pulling the strings."

Aurora sniffed at Daisy, then marched inside after Philip.

"I don't think that cat likes me," Daisy muttered. She lingered by the door another minute to let Philip have the satisfaction of storming off properly. When she got inside, one glance told her that the computer was still analyzing the bean and the bar. This surprised her, especially since Logan had said there were so few ingredients. Must be because the items were so old.

Miles burst out of the bathroom door. "Yuck!" he shouted.

"I'm afraid to ask," she said.

Miles pointed at Aurora. "Now I know why she didn't do her business in the woods by the parking lot!"

"Why?" Daisy asked.

"She did it in the *toilet*! And left it there!"

"Impressive!" Logan said. "Now she just needs to learn how to flush!"

Daisy laughed. "Hey, Philip, your cat is toilet trained!"

Aurora was currently curled up on Philip's lap, gazing at him adoringly. He absently scratched her under the chin as she purred. "Good kitty," he said. The others watched in surprise. That was the first time they'd seen him show any affection toward the cat. Something must be wrong.

"Are you okay?" Miles asked.

"I'm not sure," he said, a puzzled expression on his face. "I think . . . I think my grandmother had a cat."

"So what?" Daisy said. "Mine has a ferret, two donkeys, and a pelican. Well, sort of a pelican."

"How can someone have sort of a pelican?" Miles asked. "You either *have* a pelican, or you *don't* have a pelican."

"Ah, Miles," Daisy said, patting him on the head. "If only life were that simple."

Miles's brow furrowed, but he turned back to Philip. "So what's the big deal about your grandmother's cat? Was it toilet trained, too? Did it bark like a dog? Did it ignore everyone who actually liked cats and only come to you?"

Philip shook his head, still petting Aurora with a faraway look in his eyes. "I don't know. When I walked in just now and the cat looked up at me, I got this quick memory of another cat looking up at me, and I think it was my grandmother's. But I don't remember knowing my grandmother at all. If she was alive, wouldn't I know it?"

No one had an answer. Finally Miles said, "I might have grandparents I don't know about, too."

They all turned to look at him. Daisy was the only person who knew what he meant. "Did you talk to your dad about them?" she asked.

"A little," he replied, "but the conversation didn't get very far." To Philip and Logan he explained, "My dad was adopted. We don't know anything about his birth family. Or at least *I* don't."

Before anyone could comment on what Miles had just said, Daisy blurted out, "I might have a brother."

Philip stopped petting the cat as their heads swung from Miles to Daisy. "Seriously?" Logan asked.

Daisy nodded, glancing down the aisle to see if AJ was in hearing range. He was fiddling with the computer in the lab, so she waved them to the bedroom. Once the door slid shut behind them, she told them what she knew. Which, essentially, was nothing more than the one tossed-off comment from her mom.

"Can't you find him?" Miles asked. "With all your high-tech spy stuff?"

"I don't know," she admitted. "I wouldn't know where to start. It's not like I have a photo to match up, or anything really to go on at all."

"Maybe a memory will come to you like it did for me," Philip said.

"Maybe," Daisy said, not sounding too convinced.

The door to the bedroom slid open. AJ stuck his head in. "We leave in ten minutes." Then, almost as an afterthought, he added, "Oh, and the computer is done analyzing your chocolate."

The four of them squealed and lunged toward the door. AJ held up a hand. "I warn you. You're not going to like it."

Four hours had passed since the computer spit out its results, and they'd spent most of that time pacing up and down the aisle in various stages of shock and confusion. According to Daisy, the computer had analyzed the Magic Bar and the bean three times. All three times it had come up with the same results.

But the results were impossible. So now they were sprawled on their bunks, staring at the ceiling. AJ had recently parked at the campground where they'd be spending the night, but no one paid much attention. They were only vaguely aware that the sky had turned dark and that the scenery outside their small windows had stopped changing.

"All right, zombie children," AJ called out as he opened up the slides. They grabbed onto the edges of their bunks as the walls moved.

"Time to stop zoning out," he ordered, piling frozen meat, burger buns, and paper plates on the kitchen counter. "We have to deal with the facts at hand. First fact—we need to eat. Second fact—your parents and/or legal guardians will want to hear from you, so tell them something short and sweet about your wonderful event at **The Candy Basket**. Third fact—we have the next candy store visit tomorrow, and then we will have two days on the road. During that time, Mr. Violin Prodigy over there will try to prove he's the most talented kid in the nation. One dead drop to complete, one last store to visit, then the long drive home."

"But what about the Harmonicandy?" Miles said, leaning over the side of his bunk.

"What about it?" AJ said. "We're at a dead end. Even if we wanted to track down those beans, it's impossible. You know Harvey doesn't *actually* have rocket boosters by the wheels."

"C'mon, AJ," Daisy said, dropping lightly to the floor. "You don't really think that report is correct, do you?"

"I don't know what to think," he said. "Our computer system is the most accurate in the world. It's never been wrong."

"Until now," Philip said, still lying flat on his back, eyes squeezed shut. "Unless you believe this is actually what's inside that bean?" Without opening his eyes, he thrust out his arm, the report clutched in his hand.

AJ sighed, taking it. "Okay. Let's go over this one more time. The analysis of the Magic Bar confirmed exactly what Logan had tasted. It contains two active ingredients—cocoa and sugar. On an elemental level, it is made of magnesium, iron, chromium, anandamide, theobromine, manganese, zinc, iridium, phenylethylamine, and tryptophan, plus glucose and fructose from the sugar." AJ looked up from the page. "Does that sound like the right chemical composition for a chocolate bar?"

No one answered. Logan cleared his throat. "I kind of tune out when Max starts talking about the periodic table."

"Don't look at me," Philip said, even though no one was.

Miles pointed an anxious finger at the last item on the list. "You're leaving out the big one."

AJ let his arm drop to his side. "C'mon, let's go outside, get some fresh air. Maybe this will make more sense with clear heads." No one moved. AJ narrowed his eyes. "That was not a suggestion."

Logan followed the others out. While their last campground had been very spread out, this one had trees between each campsite, which provided a lot more privacy. Each site had its own picnic table, fire pit, and grill, and Logan could smell the campfires around them, even if he couldn't see them through the trees. He hoped AJ had stocked up on marshmallows.

AJ flipped on Harvey's outside lights and began heating up the grill while Daisy made a fire with some logs that she'd piled in her arms as if they weighed nothing. Miles was rereading the test results for the billionth time by the light of a headlamp. He'd taken the miner's hat from the closet and felt ready to go underground to dig for copper or iron or whatever people looked for in mines. Philip sat hunched over the picnic table, scribbling in his notebook. It was the first time Logan had seen him writing in it since they'd left the factory. He'd thought Philip had finished his original violin composition, but maybe not.

Logan watched the activity from the steps of the RV. Since learning the test results, he'd kept pretty quiet. If he had to be completely honest, he'd started to miss his parents on a level so deep that it felt like a physical pain in his stomach. The wave of homesickness had begun when Daisy first read the results out loud. He couldn't help thinking how his parents and Max and Henry should be a part of this—especially when Daisy got to the last line of the results. At first she'd stumbled over the words, clearly not believing them herself. Then she cleared her throat and tried again. "The final ingredient in the bean is . . . is . . . a microbe not found on Earth."

Stunned silence had followed her words. None of them could suggest any theories that made sense. Miles thought aliens must have brought the beans to Earth; Daisy proposed that the microbe might have been created in a lab; and Philip even dared to suggest that if it had been created in a lab, it couldn't have been by Logan's grandfather, so Sam must have stolen it.

Logan hadn't really thought the results would show them exactly where the beans came from, but he'd at least expected they would have narrowed it down to their own *planet*.

"Are you okay?" AJ called over to him.

"Not entirely," he admitted.

Wordlessly, Daisy handed him a stick with a marshmallow, and he instantly felt better. He joined her by the now-roaring campfire and held it over the flames.

"Dinner is served," AJ announced, flipping the last sizzling burger. While the boys chowed down and debated, Daisy took the opportunity to slip back into the RV. She didn't particularly enjoy sneaking around behind her friends' backs, but she didn't want to get their hopes up in case her plan didn't work.

Bending down, she pressed a nearly invisible button below the lab table. A shallow drawer slid open, breaking the airtight seal and revealing the half-burned contract. It had been easy to find where Miles had stashed it. She'd liberated it from its hiding spot the previous night while everyone else had slept. She should probably teach the boys her sleeping-with-one-eye-open trick. She could have danced on their heads in high heels and they wouldn't have awoken.

One light touch with her fingertip told her the starch she'd sprayed on it had done its job and hardened the paper. Step one, complete. Working quickly, she spritzed the paper with a solution of glycerin and water and sealed it back up in the drawer. It shouldn't take long for the solution to do its job. Unless it turned the contract into a soggy mess, which she still couldn't rule out.

When she rejoined the boys by the fire, Miles handed her a burger and said, "AJ told us not to bug you about why you went inside because girls need privacy and we should be respectful of that."

"And don't you forget it, mister," she said, throwing AJ a grateful look. "So what'd I miss? Miles still arguing in favor of his little-green-aliens theory? Philip find any more girls to serenade?"

"No on both," Miles said, "but we saw four shooting stars."

"Oh yeah, I saw some the other night," Daisy said, her arm darting out to easily catch the water bottle AJ tossed to her.

"I saw them, too," Logan said. "Supercool."

"You did?" Miles asked. "I figured you'd have been asleep. I took a video to show you."

"I drew a picture to show *you*," Logan replied.

The boys grinned at each other while Philip rolled his eyes without looking up from where he was recording the lie from the candy store in his notebook. Making up that speech had maxed out his lying allowance for the day—maybe even the *week*.

"I wandered outside to get something," Logan said, "and just stumbled across it. Henry was there, too, but he couldn't see them."

Philip's head snapped up when he heard that. He stuck his pen into the notebook and closed it. "You ran into Henry outside the factory in the middle of the night?" he asked.

Logan nodded. Now that he mentioned it, he could see how odd it sounded. "He said he was out for a walk or something. At least I think that's what he said."

Philip shook his head. "He couldn't have been out for a walk."

"Why not?" Miles asked. "Lots of people actually enjoy being out in nature, remember?"

"Yes, I know that," Philip said. "But since Henry can't..." He trailed off. What could he say that would make sense now? He'd cornered himself.

"Since Henry can't see," AJ said from behind them. "Not well enough to walk around on his own in the dark."

All four heads wheeled around to stare at him. Philip's surprise quickly turned to anger. Who was AJ to reveal something like that? How had he even known? Logan jumped up so fast he almost toppled forward into the fire. Daisy quickly blocked him.

"What do you mean, Henry can't see?" Logan demanded, his voice a little shaky.

"He still didn't tell you?" AJ asked. He looked around at their surprised faces and realized they truly didn't know. Everyone except Philip, that is, who was throwing daggers at him with his eyes. "Sorry," AJ said. "I'll stay out of this." He backed away toward Harvey.

"Not so fast," Daisy said, instantly appearing in front of him. When had she gotten faster than him? The boys hurried over. "Spill," Daisy demanded.

"Please tell us what you're talking about," Logan pleaded.

AJ sighed. "Henry told me he was going to tell you," he said. "That's why he couldn't drive you on this trip."

"How long have you known?" Philip asked.

"A few months," AJ replied.

"*Months*?" Philip repeated.

AJ nodded. "I ran into him at a doctor's office where I was... getting a checkup." He didn't dare glance at Daisy. He had no intention of revealing his own health issues. He hadn't planned to reveal Henry's, either. "Occasionally I would drive him to his appointments when he couldn't drive anymore. That's really all I know." He turned to Logan, who had begun running his fingers through his hair at a fitful pace. "I'm sorry you didn't know. And I'm sorry he's losing his sight. There's nothing to be done anymore. It won't be long now till it's all gone."

"I've got to call him," Logan said, turning away from the group.

"Wait," Philip said, grabbing Logan's arm. "He doesn't want you to know yet. This is hard enough on him."

"But *you* knew?" Logan asked. For the first time, jealousy really did begin to bubble up in him.

Reluctantly, Philip nodded. "It wasn't on purpose. I figured it out."

"I should have figured it out, too," Miles said. "His glasses were getting huge."

Daisy remained quiet. She hadn't been around the factory enough to have seen any change. But it sure did explain why Henry hadn't said anything to Courtney yesterday by the safe. He hadn't seen her!

Logan's head swam. Memories of Henry bumping into things or being unable to read small—and not so small—print. The way he swiveled his head all the way around to see something that wasn't right in front of him. His frequent absences and the paperwork piling up on his desk. There were probably more signs, too. How had he missed all of them? His shoulders sank. He knew how. It was because all he'd been thinking about was himself and his own problems, which seemed very small and insignificant at the moment. His eyes filled with tears. "I need to talk to him."

Miles grabbed Logan's other arm—the one Philip wasn't holding. "Don't call him. That's not what Henry wanted for you on this trip."

"Then what was?"

Miles hesitated, then replied, "He wanted all of us to have an adventure."

"Hard to do that when he's home getting blinder every day," Logan insisted.

Miles shook his head sadly. "I know."

"I have something that will make everyone feel better," Daisy said. "Don't go anywhere." She ran back into the RV. AJ followed. Miles didn't let go of Logan's arm, in case he tried to make a break for it. But Logan wasn't thinking of running, or of waking up

Henry, or even about being homesick. He was thinking about the Magic Bar, and about what his friends didn't know about how it made him feel, and about how he could maybe help Henry.

"Guys," he said, in a low whisper, "I know Daisy wants to help us with the Harmonicandy, but as you know, she can't get too involved because she can't risk blowing her cover."

Miles nodded. "So?" Philip asked.

"So I need you two to promise me something." His voice took on an urgent tone. "Maybe the organism found in the bean just isn't in the database, so the computer can't match it with anything on Earth. Or maybe it really is from outer space, as unlikely as that sounds. But either way, promise me we won't give up on finding the beans."

Philip's eyebrows rose. "But you said we couldn't use them, even if we could find them."

"I might be changing my mind."

Miles and Philip exchanged a look of surprise. Then Miles stuck his hand out in front of him, palm down. Logan gratefully placed his on top. They both turned toward Philip, who, after a second's hesitation, added his own. "No giving up," he said.

"No giving up," Logan and Miles repeated.

"But where do we even start?" Logan asked.

"We should start by asking Henry what he knows about that bean," Miles said.

It was at that moment that Daisy emerged from the RV, holding two things that they couldn't make out in the dark. "We *can't* ask Henry," she said.

"Darn those supersonic ears of hers," Miles muttered.

"Why not?" Philip asked. "It's the best plan. He obviously knows more than we do."

She joined their circle. "We can't ask him because he's sworn to secrecy."

"Huh?" the boys asked.

She lifted one hand, and they could see she was holding a pair of rubber tongs with a piece of paper clipped to the end. "It's still a little damp," she explained. Miles snapped on his headlamp. They all crowded around when they realized what they were seeing.

The burn marks on the contract were completely gone. Four names appeared on the bottom in faded ink, one below the other, first names only. They scanned them hungrily. Sam was first, then someone named Frank, then Evy from the picture outside the factory. Their heads jerked up when they read the last name on the list. "Henry?" Logan asked, feeling dizzy.

"*Our* Henry?" Miles asked, stepping backward until he could lean against the picnic table for support.

Daisy nodded. "It has to be. Unless you know another Henry?"

"Logan," Philip said, turning quickly, "you were with Henry when that box came for you, right?"

Logan had to push through the fog in his head in order to focus on his words. He nodded and choked out, "Yes. He helped me open it. Actually, he cried when he saw what it was."

"He *cried*?" the others repeated.

Logan nodded slowly, thinking back to the other day. "He never told me why he was crying, so I didn't really put it together with the box. But it must have been that. Or, wait, it was after I read him the letter."

"You said an old friend of your grandfather's sent you that stuff," Miles said. "But I didn't see a letter in there."

Logan was glad the fire had nearly completely died out, so no one could see his cheeks redden. "Yeah, I took it out before I gave you the box. It's probably in the shorts I was wearing that day. It was kind of...embarrassing, I guess. Stuff about not feeling bad about losing the contest, that sort of thing."

"Did you know the person who wrote it?" Daisy asked.

Logan shook his head. "It was from a guy. I remember thinking it sounded like he had two first names."

Daisy pointed down at the name below Sam's on the contract. "Was it Frank?"

Logan thought back and quickly nodded. "Yes. He signed it Franklin, though. Franklin Griffin."

Miles sprang off the table as though he'd been pushed hard by an invisible hand. "Franklin Griffin?" he repeated. "Franklin O. Griffin?"

Logan took a step back, surprised by the outburst. "Um, yes? I think so. Do you know him?"

"Oh wow, oh man, no, I don't know him personally, just... wow." Miles flapped his arms around and bounced on his heels while the others stared at him. "Franklin O. Griffin is only one of the most famous mapmakers in the world! I have *three* copies of his maps on my bedroom wall at home. When I grow up, I want to be just like him. No, I want to *be* him! I wanted to write him a fan letter when I was little, but I couldn't find a place to send it. He's, like, a recluse or something. I used to imagine that he'd crawled into one of his own maps and was living there." Miles collapsed back onto the table.

"So you've heard of him, then?" Philip joked.

Miles just sighed happily.

"Oookaayy," Daisy said, patting Miles gently on the head, "that was extreme." She got out her vid com and opened the file she'd named *The Case of the Missing Chocolate*. "We've made some good progress. Time to update."

Philip began ticking things off on his fingers.

"One: Henry knew this guy Frank, so he must have known what was in that box, including the contract and the map, which, if I had to bet, was made by none other than Frank himself." He raised another finger. "Two: Henry was in possession of one of the beans mentioned in this contract. Or at least we can assume the bean came from the same batch, especially since he had that photograph with it. Three: He gave us chocolate made from the beans. It is unclear if he knew that it would be impossible to actually *get* more of it, since, according to our analysis, at least part of it is not found anywhere on this planet. That said, as Daisy no doubt overheard, we promised Logan we wouldn't stop looking. Four: Henry must have gone to the safe for the Magic Bar and realized we'd found it. He somehow persuaded AJ to drive us, so he clearly wanted us to go on this mission. His strange reactions both on the day we left and in front of the safe seem to confirm that. I say if we have any chance of finding the source for the beans, we will have to ask him to break the contract and tell us. Did I leave anything out?"

Daisy smiled. "Between your deductive reasoning and your ability to lie to large crowds, you really should take AJ up on his offer and consider spy work someday. You know, if the violin gig doesn't work out."

"I just might," Philip said. Something in Daisy's other hand caught his eye, and he suddenly backed away and pointed at it. "Um, Daisy, what is that?"

"Oh, right," Daisy said. She'd forgotten she was still holding the item from the dead drop. "This is what I went inside to show you. I thought you'd think it was funny." She held her palm closer to Miles's headlamp. He and Logan leaned in to get a better look at the absolute last thing in the world they expected to see. They scrambled backward, almost knocking Philip over.

"That's a pile of poop!" Miles exclaimed, eyes wide in horror.

"I know!" Daisy said, grinning. "Isn't it cool?"

CHAPTER TWELVE

Miles, Daisy, and Logan learned that the single best way to relieve the stress they were all under was to take turns hiding the fake plastic poop in various places around the RV. Under Philip's pillow as he slept that night. On AJ's shoulder as he drove toward their next candy store. On Aurora's back. Judging by her snarl and hiss, she was the only one who didn't seem to appreciate the joke. Philip had to pet her for ten minutes before she'd stop giving the others the stinkeye.

Logan called Henry at home six times, getting an answering machine each time. When the factory opened for the day, Betty, the main receptionist, told him Henry had gone on vacation.

"Vacation!" Logan said, hanging up. "Henry hasn't taken a vacation since I've known him. He chooses now?"

"Pretty sure it's not a coincidence," Daisy said. "I figured he wasn't going to be any help." She got up to check the computer. The last man in the photograph still stubbornly refused to be identified.

"He wrote back!" Miles said, checking e-mail on his vid com. "Arthur wrote back."

They gathered around the table as Miles read the note out loud.

Hello, young traveler, I hope you're having a
grand adventure and that you'll have plenty
of geocaching stories for me and will be
ready to hide your own when you get back.

Miles looked up. "Hmm. Haven't done any caching yet. Mr.
Sweet promised we could. And I told Arthur I'd teach you guys."

"We've been a little busy," Daisy reminded him. "You know,
trying to track down little blue beans from space."

When Miles continued to stare off, eyes unfocused, she said,
"Oh, fine, how about I give you the poop container. You can use it
to stuff some trinkets inside, and we can hide it when we get home."

Miles brightened. "It's a deal. The perfect cache!"

"Philip," she said, "can you grab it for me?"

He stood up. "Where is it?"

"In your underwear drawer," she said, keeping a straight face.
Logan and Miles giggled.

Philip sighed deeply. "You all may have serious problems." But
he went to fetch it anyway.

Miles continued reading Arthur's letter when Philip returned.

The first thing I did when you gave me
the photograph was try to contact the
photography studio that took the original.
By the way, I saw the original at the factory
when I delivered that old box of candy
wrappers to the librarian there. The factory's
library is a beautiful place. I can see why you
speak so highly of it. Anyway, oftentimes
photography studios will keep records of
each person in the photos they take in case a
copyright issue ever arises and they're asked

> to prove they own the image. But to cut to
> the chase, there are no records of the names,
> because Spring Haven Photographs & Fur
> does not exist. It never *did* exist.

Miles looked up again, brow furrowed. "That's weird!"
"Keep reading," Philip said, pointing back down.
Miles continued.

> All is not lost, though. I was able to figure
> out three of the people by perusing the
> other old photos in Mrs. Gepheart's display
> that did have names on them. See attached
> scan below. I will continue to venture forth.
> Say hello to your friends. I look forward to
> meeting them one day.

Miles scrolled down until a picture appeared. Above three
heads, Arthur had scribbled the names *Sam Sweet, Florence Sweet,*
and, for the last man on the left, *Henry Jennings.* That had to be
their Henry!

"It doesn't look anything like him," Logan said, "but that's his
name, all right."

Philip peered more closely at the picture. "Look how skinny he
was. Shame what eating a pound of marshmallows every day will
do to a guy."

Daisy kicked him under the table. "Let's see how good *you* look
in fifty years!"

"I hate to say it," Logan began, sliding the contract to the middle
of the table. "But we have to face the fact that the computer is wrong.
Wherever these beans came from, we know it wasn't outer space. The
contract talks about a hidden valley, and I'm sure it's not in the sky."

Daisy sighed. She knew he was right. But if the computer was wrong when it analyzed the bean, what if it was wrong when it analyzed her and AJ's DNA? What if he really *was* her brother? It looked like further testing would be required. "This is going to sound strange," she said, "but I have an idea. Let's give the lab more things to analyze, things we know the content of."

"Like what?" Logan asked.

"Well, it can't be too easy, or else it's not a good test," she said. She looked around at the group. "We all know we're not related to each other, right?"

"Trust me," Miles said, "if I was related to someone who lived in a candy factory, I'd be living in a candy factory!"

"Agreed," Daisy said. "So let's gather some stuff to test all our DNA against each other's."

"What kind of stuff?" Philip asked. "Is this really necessary?"

She nodded. Although truthfully, it probably wasn't. But she wasn't going to be able to think straight if she had to worry about AJ all over again. She handed out Q-tips to the boys and instructed them how to run the swabs over the inside of their cheeks. "Do one for the cat, too," she said. "I want to make sure the computer can tell the difference."

Philip stared at her. "Seriously? You want me to swab a *cat*?"

"I'd do it myself, but that cat hates me."

"I'm beginning to see why," Philip grumbled, but he went back to his bed to find Aurora anyway.

"And if anyone has an item they know someone else sneezed on or bled on or licked, bring it up, too. I can get DNA off of it."

"Something someone *sneezed* on?" Logan asked, scrunching up his face. "Why would we have that?"

"Who knows what boys carry around with them," Daisy said. "Lots of DNA in snot."

"Gross," Logan muttered.

Miles handed her the envelope his card had come in. He'd been using it as a bookmark. Might as well donate it to the advancement of science.

"Perfect," Daisy said. Then she called back to Philip, "Hey, bring some of those envelopes your fan letters came in."

Philip paused. He hadn't known the others knew about those letters. "Wouldn't hurt to have some privacy in this place," he grumbled, grabbing them from under his mattress.

"Hey, being adored by the candy-loving public is nothing to be ashamed of," Daisy said, plucking the envelopes from his hand. She tossed the letters back onto his bed and stacked the envelopes on the table.

One by one, the boys handed her their swabs. She placed them into the slots, just the way she'd done with her and AJ's samples previously. Aurora wasn't giving it up easily, though, even for Philip. Daisy could hear them wrestling as she carefully sliced off a section of each envelope's seal. She didn't bother with the envelopes that had premoistened, self-sealing flaps. Once the samples had been deposited into their slots, she had one thing left to do.

"Ouch!" AJ said as Daisy stepped behind the driver's seat and yanked out more hairs. "Are you kidding me?" He rubbed at the spot furiously as his other hand gripped the wheel harder. "You're going to make me bald before my time!"

"Quit complaining," she said. "I totally took it from the other side this time."

She returned to the lab and examined her work. "Okay," she announced, "we have five envelopes, three boys, one girl, one grouchy teenager—"

"And one pissed-off cat," Philip said, handing her the swab. She in turn handed him a Band-Aid and a tube of antibiotic ointment for his scratched-up hand.

"AJ," she called up to him. "When's our next stop, so we can run this test?"

"Right now," he replied, switching off the engine.

"Now?" she repeated. They all turned to face the front windshield and were surprised to find themselves in the back of a crowded parking lot. The lone building at the far end of the lot looked like an old theater, with thick white columns in front and a marquee across the top. It was too far away for anyone other than Daisy to read the name on it.

"Are we parking here for *Ain't She Sweet*?" Logan asked. "I thought our visit wasn't until later this afternoon."

"We're not here for the candy store visit," AJ said, stretching his legs. "We're here to see a show—more specifically, we're here to go backstage after the show."

"Say what now?" Daisy asked. "You're taking us to see a *magic show*?"

Logan and Miles lit up. "A magic show?" Miles shouted. Logan was already slipping on his shoes. "You're the best chaperone a kid ever had!"

Daisy crossed her arms. "You want to take us to see a magician who calls himself the Great Shoudini? He's obviously trying to rip off Houdini. We have a mystery to solve, remember?"

AJ grinned that grin of his that made all the girls (except for Daisy) swoon. "That's why we're here."

"What do you mean?" she asked.

AJ reached over to the table, picked up the contract, and pointed at the names. "Sam is gone. Henry won't talk to us. This Frank fella is clearly antisocial. That leaves this one." He tapped the paper over Evy's name. "That's who we're going to meet right now."

Their eyes widened. Philip dropped the tube of ointment he'd been clutching. "You found out Evy's going to see the Great Shoudini?"

AJ shook his head. "I found out Evy *is* the Great Shoudini!" He laughed at their shocked expressions. "You should see your faces!"

"I get it!" Miles shouted. "The word *she* plus *Houdini* equals *Shoudini*! Evy is the female Houdini!"

"How did you find this out, AJ?" Daisy asked, admittedly impressed.

"I did a little research on her from the back bedroom last night."

"Looks like *some* of us have privacy," Philip muttered.

Ignoring the comment, AJ said, "It turns out she recently came out of retirement to do a few shows. Had to drive two hours out of our way, but we'll still make it to the shop on time."

"Does she know we're coming?" Daisy asked.

"She does not."

"How will we get backstage, then?" Miles asked.

"Please, you're with me. Of course we'll get backstage."

Daisy rolled her eyes, but it was true. AJ could talk his way into or out of practically anywhere.

"What are we waiting for, then?" Logan asked, standing by the door. "She knew my grandfather! She has answers—I just know it!"

"Easy, tiger," Daisy said. "She did sign that contract to keep quiet. Getting information out of her is going to require a delicate touch."

"*Your* delicate touch, I suppose?" Philip asked.

"Yes. I can talk to her woman to woman."

"Who's the other woman?" Philip asked, then immediately backed out of range of Daisy's kick.

"We've probably missed two more tricks by standing here," Miles said. "Let's go!"

Daisy turned back to the lab. "You guys go watch the show. I'm going to stay here and run these tests while I have the chance. Let me know when the show's over, and I'll meet you backstage."

"Me too," Philip said. "I could use the quiet to practice."

"Suit yourselves," AJ said, closing the door behind him. Logan and Miles were already halfway across the parking lot.

Daisy turned to Philip. "Don't like magicians, eh?"

"Just wanted a break," he said, grabbing his violin case and notebooks. He saw no need to tell Daisy that magicians freaked him out. He didn't like feeling tricked.

AJ hadn't made up the bed in the back, so Philip did that first and then sat down to think. A bark outside the door let him know the cat wanted in. He slid it open and watched as Aurora went straight for the bathroom. Lovely. He closed the bathroom door to give her privacy. He'd tried to bring back the brief memory he'd had of a woman with brown hair streaked with gray, and an orange cat, but it kept slipping away. The trip was going quickly. He knew if he had any chance of finding her, he had to act soon. Finally alone, he pulled his mother's passport out of the violin case and opened it.

On the other side of the door, Daisy double-checked that she had written a number on each envelope and that each one matched the correct slot. She had rebooted the entire system, so if there had been a glitch before, that should no longer be the case. Satisfied that everything had been set up correctly, she pressed the button to start the processing. The screen began counting down from twenty-two minutes. Not too long to wait at all. She pulled out her vid com to see where they were on the map, then tucked it back in her pants.

"I'm going for a run," she called out to Philip. When he didn't answer, she added, "There's a park across the street. I'll let you know when it's time to go into the theater." She waited for a reply but didn't get one.

Philip heard the door close but barely noticed it. His mother must not have updated her passport when she got married, because it still had her maiden name on it. *Karen Rickman.* His parents had only been together for nine years before she died, after all.

He couldn't take his eyes off the passport picture. He'd only given it a quick glance when he'd first found it. She looked so young. Not much older than Andrew, although of course she was, even when the picture had been taken. He looked below the picture, expecting to see the address of the apartment Reggie had shown him. But the address wasn't in Spring Haven at all. It was in River Bend, a larger town about an hour away.

He pulled out his vid com and did a search for the address. In seconds, the sales records for the last four people to own the property came up. Mr. and Mrs. Marshall Rickman were first on the list. He stared at the screen. He'd found them so quickly. Well, not *them*, but a record of them. The name, at least. He called out to Daisy, remembering a second later that she'd left.

He bet he could track them down. It might not even take more than a few minutes. Instead, he closed the vid com, took out his violin, and began to play.

"Mom?" Daisy said, stopping short. A guy biking behind her had to swerve to avoid colliding. "Sorry!" she called out to him. When her vid com had buzzed, she figured it was AJ. Her mom's face on the screen came as a shock. They'd spoken a few times when she was on the camp gig, but not since.

"Hi, honey!" her mom said, waving from a corner booth in a restaurant. "Enjoying your road trip?"

"Um, just doing a dead drop with AJ," she replied, not sure what to say.

"Uh-huh," her mom said with a slow nod. "Look, I only have a second, but I just wanted to tell you I miss you and I'm proud of you. Did Grammy tell you we have a family gig coming up next month?"

Daisy shook her head.

"Yup. Heading out west, all of us."

"All . . . meaning you and me and Dad and . . . my brother?"

Her mom frowned. "Are you still on that?"

"Just tell me!" Daisy insisted.

"Honey, listen." Her mom pulled the screen closer to her face. Daisy could see some new thin lines that she wouldn't dare point out. "In a few more years you'll find out everything you want to know. Until then, for your own good, can't you forget I said anything?"

Her mother looked so earnest and vulnerable that all Daisy could do was nod. "I can try. Not promising anything, though. Might help if you told me some other secret so I don't feel so bad."

Her mom looked thoughtful, then said, "I've got one! When AJ was little, he used to sleep with a stuffed unicorn named Corny. He would sing to it before he fell asleep."

Daisy laughed. "That's pretty good."

"Now, get back to those friends of yours. You look stressed. Have some nice hot tea with cinnamon to relax."

Tea? How old did her mom think she was? Sixty?

"And be careful crossing the street. That's a blind curve."

"Hey! How do you know where I am?"

Her mom smiled. "You're my baby girl. I always know where you are. That, and the GPS I implanted under your fingernail when you were born." Daisy's horrified expression made her mom laugh. "I'm kidding! I picked up the map from your vid com coordinates. Plus I can see over your shoulder." She waved one more time, and the image winked out.

Daisy smiled at the dark screen. No matter how many miles were between them, her mom always made her feel loved. She hurried back to the RV (careful to look both ways before she crossed). She meant what she'd said. She really would try to put the brother thing aside. She'd check the test results just to complete the project, and

378

then would put it to rest for four and a half more years. But after that all bets were off.

She checked the time. Still six minutes left. Her vid com buzzed again, and a message from AJ popped up. *D & P, show just ended. Tell box office lady you're Evy's great-niece and nephew. They'll let you up to the dressing room, where we will meet you in the hall.*

Philip hopped out of the RV, clearly having gotten the message, too. "Ready to solve the mystery?" she asked.

At first he seemed surprised by the question, then recovered quickly and nodded. "I've decided something," he said as they hurried across the parking lot toward the theater. Daisy would have come back with something silly, but he sounded so serious that she didn't dare interrupt.

"I've decided that even if my grandmother is alive, I don't want to find her. Anyone who would just drop out of her grandchildren's lives after they lost their mother isn't someone I want to know."

Daisy didn't say anything at first. Then she admitted, "I just let my brother go, too. Or the idea of him. If there even *is* one." She sighed. "Relationships are hard."

"They shouldn't have to be," he said. And it may have been a gust of wind, or the fact that the pavement wasn't entirely level, or that Daisy tried to avoid a pothole to her left, but for a second their hands brushed against each other, and they both felt better.

CHAPTER THIRTEEN

You wouldn't believe it!" Logan gushed as Philip and Daisy joined him and Miles outside the door with a big silver star painted on it. "Evy was amazing! She pulled these doves out of nowhere, and then she put them in this cage, one by one, and then—"

Miles, his face flushed, jumped in. "And then she made the whole cage disappear right into thin air! With all the doves inside!"

Logan pushed forward again. "And she had a guy assistant! You know, instead of how the magician is usually a man with a female assistant?"

"She's one of the only professional female magicians," Miles added, waving the show's program. "Isn't that amazing?"

Daisy agreed that it was, in fact, groundbreaking.

"Man, it was great," Logan said, shaking his head. "You guys should have seen it."

The door opened just as Philip said, "I don't really like birds."

AJ stuck his head out. "Come on in. She'd like to meet you."

Miles and Logan rushed in, clutching their programs in sweaty hands. Vases filled with flowers covered every flat surface. Assistants rushed around packing up crates and boxes with colorful scarves and sparkly things, and Daisy was pretty sure she spotted a plastic skull.

The Great Shoudini sat at her makeup table in front of a large mirror with lights all around it. She looked up when they entered, but her hands continued shuffling a deck of cards so fast the kids could barely follow it. She wore a sequin-covered dress and a black cape pinned at the neck with a red rose. Her white hair flowed halfway down her back, and she'd kicked off a pair of high-heeled shoes at her feet. She still wore her stage makeup, which made her look even more otherworldly. Daisy couldn't take her eyes off the woman.

Evy's eyes roamed over their faces until they landed on Logan and settled there. If it were anyone else, he would have thought she was staring at his scars. And maybe she was a little, but she was see- ing other things, too.

A slow, broad smile spread across her face. She tossed the cards onto the table and held out her arm for him to approach. He hurried forward. "Dear boy," she said, putting her hand on his arm. "When your friend here told me Samuel Sweet's grandson was at my show, I could hardly believe it. Seeing you makes me believe Sam found some kind of time machine and returned to me."

Logan beamed. "When I knew him, we didn't look that much alike!"

She laughed. "No, I wouldn't think so. But you have his eyes, and his spirit. I can see it bursting out of you."

Daisy knew what she meant. She'd felt the power of Logan's spirit the first time she touched him.

One of Evy's assistants approached the chair. "I'm sorry to interrupt, but we only have twenty minutes to clear out before the next performers show up. And our train leaves in an hour."

Evy nodded. She leaned closer to Logan as if to tell him a secret.

"That's show biz for you. The stage isn't even cold yet. But I don't do this for the glory. I do it for the wonder on people's faces." She waved a hand in front of the rose at her neck, and it turned from red to white!

Logan and Miles gasped and clapped joyously. She leaned back and smiled. "Yes, like that!"

Behind them Philip cleared his throat. Logan knew he had to act quickly. "Um, Ms. Shoudini, I..."

"Please, we're old friends. Call me Evy."

"Um, okay, Ms. Evy...these are my friends Miles, Philip, and Daisy, and you met our chaperone, AJ. We have a favor to ask you."

Miles pulled out the contract from his back pocket and handed it to her. "Please," he said, "we need to know where to find the beans." As she took the paper from him, he blurted out, "And you were amazing on the stage. I still can't figure out where those doves came from!"

No one spoke again as they watched Evy slowly realize what she was holding. Her hand shook as she rested it in her lap. "I... I thought this was destroyed. I saw Sam put it in the fire myself."

"It looked a lot worse before," Daisy said, speaking for the first time. "I was able to recover most of it. Modern technology, right?"

But Evy wasn't amused. She frowned. "I don't suppose you can forget you saw this?"

They shook their heads. "It was in a box of my grandfather's old papers," Logan explained. "Franklin Griffin sent it."

She blinked hard. "Frank? Frank sent this to you?"

Logan didn't seem to know what to say, so Miles came to his rescue. "It was tucked in the back of a small notebook," he explained. "He may not even have known it was in the box."

Evy stood and began to pace the room in her stockings. "Can you please give us a moment?" she asked her assistants. They protested and pointed to the clock, but Evy shook her head firmly.

"Polly's Prancing Poodles can wait. And if we miss the train, we'll catch the next one." When they were alone, she took off her cape and draped a sweater over her shoulders. "I'd like to know why you want the beans."

Philip launched into an explanation about the candymaking contest, and the Harmonicandy, and the rules, while Miles filled in the parts about the Magic Bar.

She took it all in and nodded slowly when they'd finished. "Thank you for sharing your story. I wish I could tell you where we found the beans, but I can't." When they opened their mouths to protest, she held up her hand. "But I can tell you that you wouldn't be able to make your candy bar with them anyway. Sam learned that the hard way. It was heartbreaking for him to launch the Magic Bar and then to have to pull it a week later."

"But why?" Philip pleaded. "Why did he have to pull it?"

She sighed. "You know how magicians are never supposed to reveal the secrets of their tricks?"

They all nodded.

"I'd tell you all I know about the art of magic before I tell you the answer to that question. I'm so sorry."

Logan looked around at his friends' disappointed faces. They'd promised to help him find the beans, and he hadn't been completely forthcoming with them. He had to get her to change her mind. "Henry's going blind," he blurted out.

His friends all turned to look at him, no doubt wondering why he'd chosen that moment to bring up the topic. Evy didn't say anything for a minute. When she finally spoke, she simply said, "I know."

"You do?" Logan said, his turn to be surprised now.

She nodded and waved the contract in her hand again. "Bound for life, remember?"

"But that's why we need it," he said. "To help him."

Miles, Philip, and Daisy called out variations of "What?" and "Huh?" and "We do?"

But Evy didn't ask any questions. She only tilted her head at him thoughtfully. This time he got the distinct impression that she was looking at his scars. "You tried the chocolate," she said confidently. "But your friends don't know what happened." It was an observation, not a question. He didn't know if he was supposed to nod or say yes or say no, so he just stood there.

"Don't know what?" Philip demanded. Miles and Daisy just looked confused. AJ leaned against the back wall, checking his messages.

Her face softened as she shook her head. "My dear boy. Henry would not take the beans, even if you were to offer them." She held up the contract again. "Never for ourselves."

Philip threw up his hands. "What are you guys talking about?"

Daisy had watched the exchange carefully. Suddenly she knew, or at least thought she knew, something. "It's his scars," she said, coming forward. She reached out her hand and gently touched his arm. She felt that same warmth, that aliveness. But the scar under her fingers was just the tiniest bit flatter against his olive-colored skin. Years of training allowed her to see what others would miss.

He looked down at his arm. "What do you mean, my scars?"

"Don't you notice a difference?" she asked.

Logan hesitated, then shook his head. Miles ran up and looked at Logan's arm, turning it this way and that.

Evy laid her hand lightly on Logan's chest. "You felt it inside, right?"

A lump formed in his throat at the memory of his one bite of the Magic Bar. He nodded, feeling his heart beat faster. She gave a little nod and lifted her hand.

Philip was about to explode. "Will someone please tell me what's going on?"

Logan took a deep breath. "When I ate the Magic Bar, I felt something I've never felt before, or at least I don't think I have. It was like...the cells in my body kind of...pulsed? And then I felt...stronger. Like, better." He looked at Evy. "Is that how you'd describe it?"

She smiled, but it was a sad smile. "I never felt it. None of us did."

"None of you ever tasted a Magic Bar?" Miles asked. "How is that possible? Sam must have tasted it a million times while making it."

"Oh, we all tasted it, all right, but none of us ever felt what Logan's describing. A few days after it was on the market, we started getting calls and letters from people who reported feeling better, or healthier, or healed in some small way after eating it. It didn't cure cancer or make the deaf suddenly hear, but for people with an illness or an affliction of some sort, it did *something*. The four of us always knew the beans were...special...but we didn't know why. To us it tasted like the best chocolate you'd ever had, but that's all. It looked like the Magic Bar was living up to its name." She gave a small regretful chuckle.

She turned to Logan and sighed. "I guess I'm going to reveal some of my secrets after all. It took only days before the government got involved. Claims of miracles tend to get the attention of people in high places. Your grandfather made the decision to withdraw the Magic Bar from the market immediately. Without understanding what was happening, we couldn't be sure it was safe. We all agreed it was best to keep it out of the news. Today, of course, that wouldn't have been possible."

Miles couldn't believe he was finally learning the mystery of the Magic Bar! He hung on her every word.

"You have to understand," Evy continued, "**Life Is Sweet** was in the business of making candy, candy *without* surprises, even good ones." She rubbed her temples, then sighed wearily.

"And honestly, we knew that we weren't supposed to use the beans to make the chocolate. But who could resist when they tasted that good? We were all to blame, really. Sam and Frank and Henry and me—we were a team." She looked at the four of them. "Like you are." She focused on Daisy. "Not easy being the only girl, am I right?"

"You know it, sistah." Daisy held up her hand for a high-five. Evy gave her an awkward one.

"So that was it?" Miles asked. "You just shut down production and moved on?"

Evy nodded. "Essentially, yes. Sam had an offer from a man who'd just opened a cocoa bean–processing plant to buy out the remaining stock of beans, but of course he turned it down."

"So you never investigated the beans?" Philip asked. "You never tried to find out what made the Magic Bar so special?"

She shook her head. "Remember, this was a long time ago, without the benefits of modern technology. We weren't doctors or scientists. Heck, we couldn't even say for sure it was the beans causing these side effects. Life moved on. Frank was hiding in his parents' basement drawing his maps all day, Sam had his hands full with his new business, and all Henry wanted to do was make marshmallows and watch over the factory."

Logan smiled at her description of Henry. "He still does."

"I know," she said. "Getting to spend your life doing what you love is a gift. At that time I was just a young girl making sneezing powder out of black pepper, dreaming of bringing people unexpected moments of wonder and surprise, of making grand illusions onstage one day."

"Hey, I read an article about you!" Miles said.

Logan grinned. "My grandfather loved that sneezing powder. And the itching powder. And the handshake buzzer. That was you?"

"Here, have a brochure," Evy said, reaching over to grab a thick pamphlet titled *Hocus Pocus Gags & Novelties* out of one of the piles of boxes. "Order anything you want, on the house."

Miles and Logan took them eagerly.

But Philip wasn't ready to let it go. "So you don't know that there's a micro—"

AJ chose that moment to rejoin them. Cutting Philip off midsentence, he began gently rounding them up and pushing them toward the door. "We've taken up more than our fair share of Ms. Shoudini's time."

Philip got the message that AJ didn't want him to talk about the test results, but he needed to know one very important thing, even though he felt ridiculous asking it. "Just tell us this—did the beans come from outer space?"

She burst out laughing. "Where did you get that idea?"

Philip reddened, then glared at Daisy and AJ. It was their laboratory, after all. "Nowhere," he muttered. "Never mind."

"I'm sorry," she said, walking them to the door. "I don't mean to tease you. But no, we may have gotten lost on that camping trip, but we didn't wind up off the planet."

Daisy made a mental addition to her file—two clues to follow up on. First, the friends had been on a camping trip when they found the beans, and second, Evy said Sam knew they shouldn't use the beans to make the chocolate, but she didn't say *how* he knew.

Logan wanted to hug Evy goodbye but didn't want to be too bold. Luckily, she made it easy by holding out her arms. He went in for the hug, and she held him tight. "You smell like sugar," she said, breathing in deep. "Just like your grandpa." They stayed that way for a long minute. "There was only one more time Sam used those beans," she whispered into his ear. "He got our permission first, of course. I think we made the right choice."

Logan had no idea what she meant; he was just enjoying being held by someone who cared about his grandfather so much. Plus it made him a little less homesick for his mom's hugs.

When he pulled away, they both had tears in their eyes. She ushered him back to the door, where the others were waiting. AJ opened it, and Evy's relieved and annoyed assistants rushed back in and began attacking the boxes and props again.

"Thank you," Miles said, pumping her hand fervently. "For your time and the show and the brochure. Hey, since you won't tell us where you found the beans, maybe you can tell me where you hid those doves?" Then he added, "Ow!" as Daisy pinched him.

Evy stood at the doorway as they filed past her into the hall. "I'll tell you this much. The magic doesn't happen in the magician's hands. It happens in the mind of the spectator. It's about misdirection. Making you look over there so I can do something over here. And remember, more often than not, the best place to hide something is in plain sight." Then she winked, pulled a giant silver dollar from Miles's ear, dropped it into his hand, and closed the door behind them.

CHAPTER FOURTEEN

S nacks in the lobby on me!" Miles declared, holding up his silver dollar.

"I don't think that's gonna cover it," Daisy said.

Miles dug into his pocket. "I also have this fifty-dollar bill! I found it in the factory."

Philip, who had been silently brooding, turned his head at that. "Where exactly did you find that?"

Miles told him about the guy spilling the big bag of lollypop sticks. Philip opened his mouth to comment but then shook his head. "Never mind," he snapped. "It doesn't matter. Nothing matters anymore." He turned away and began running down the steps of the theater.

The rest of them looked at each other. "Was it something I said?" Miles asked.

Daisy shook her head. "It was something Evy said. She basically gave the Harmonicandy the death knell."

"The death knell?" Logan asked.

"It means the last hope is gone," AJ explained. "Philip knows for sure the factory can't use the chocolate, and now he knows why."

"I'll go after him," Daisy said. "We'll meet you back at Harvey."

She'd expected to find Philip halfway across the parking lot, but instead he was sitting on the curb in front of a pizza place two doors down. Most of the crowd from the theater had already left.

"I know you're upset," she said. "But—"

He cut her off. "Logan could have told us what happened to him when he tasted it. He didn't need to hide it."

"Maybe he *did* need to," she said. "It must have felt really, I don't know, *personal*. You of all people should know about keeping stuff inside. You do it more than anyone I know."

"Except for you," he pointed out.

"Okay, anyone who isn't a spy."

"Whatever," Philip said, kicking at the ground with his heels. "I guess I just didn't believe it was over until now."

"I know," she said. "But you don't have to take it out on Miles or Logan. The Harmonicandy is as big a loss for them as it is for you. For the whole factory, really. And the whole candy-eating community!"

Philip shook his head. "It's worse for me, much worse. You don't understand."

"*I* understand," Miles said from behind them. Philip and Daisy turned to see the others standing there on the sidewalk. "You think it's worse for you because you'll lose the money you would have made on the sale of every Harmonicandy."

"That's not really fair," Logan said to Miles. "Philip tried to insist that we split his share of the profits, but the three of us agreed he should have it."

Miles didn't answer. He was too surprised that Logan had taken Philip's side in an argument over his. Plus he still thought he was right.

Philip didn't answer, either. He just glowered at everyone. AJ finally spoke. "You're right," he said to Miles. "Philip *is* upset about the money. But it's not for the reason you think."

Philip tried to protest, but AJ went ahead. "He was planning to use his profits to provide a mobile burn unit for communities without one. I know because he asked me to sign the contract for him right before we left the factory."

Everyone's head swiveled back to Philip. "Is this true?" Logan asked.

Philip didn't know what to say, which was not a position he enjoyed being in. He stood up and headed toward the RV, not looking back. Logan glanced at the others, then ran after Philip.

Miles and AJ started to follow. Daisy pulled them back. "Let's give them a few minutes to be alone."

"I feel bad," Miles said. "I should apologize."

"You didn't know," AJ said. "It's not your fault."

They watched across the parking lot as Logan and Philip went inside the RV. "It sounds like his plan would have helped a lot of people," Miles said, "but not Logan, you know? I was reading about things you can do for scars, like honey, or maybe we can find some specialist he hasn't seen before, or—"

Daisy stopped him. "I know, but there's nothing we can do. When he was younger, there wasn't enough undamaged skin to use for skin grafts. That's why he has so many scars. The problem is that sugar retains heat very well, and it sticks to the skin. That caused his burns to go really deep. I don't think he even knows how bad the accident really was."

Miles stared at her. "How do you know all this?"

"I may have hacked into his hospital records," she admitted.

Miles was quiet. Then he said, "Now I know why he made us promise last night to still look for the beans. Maybe he thinks he can use them to get better?"

Daisy shook her head. "More likely he wanted to use them to help *Henry* get better."

"That does sound more like him," Miles agreed. "But there's no reason he can't use them, too, right?"

"I don't know," Daisy said. "He'd probably come up with some excuse not to."

"That's why *we're* here," Miles said. "To let him know it's okay."

Logan suddenly burst out of the RV and waved for them to hurry up. "Guys!" he shouted. "You won't believe this!"

They started running.

"What?" Daisy asked when they got closer. "Is everything okay?"

"The lab results!" he said, stepping aside so they could run in. "We got a match!"

Daisy's eyes almost bugged out of her head. *"What?"*

"You were right before," he said. "The computer *is* broken! That's why it gave us that alien reading, and that's why it says there's a match when we know there can't be! It's good news! I mean, it doesn't tell us where the beans are, but at least we know for sure that Evy was telling the truth."

Daisy shook her head. "No. It means that AJ and I are brother and sister after all!"

The others gasped.

Daisy's heart pounded. She didn't know how to feel. Relieved to have the mystery solved? Ashamed for not being nicer to AJ all these years?

"What?" AJ said, pushing his way through to see the screen. "No, we aren't! I know who my parents are, and they are *not* your parents." He skimmed through the report on the screen. "This doesn't say we're related," he insisted. "It just says the computer found one match. It doesn't say who matched whom. Daisy! Are you even listening?"

"Huh?" she said, thinking that she should have gotten him better birthday presents.

He shook her until she focused on him. "Daisy! The computer is matching each sample against every other sample. It says it's found a match, but we don't know which pair it is."

Finally hearing him, Daisy ran over to read the screen herself. "Okay, so in theory, you're right. But c'mon, who else would the match be? Philip and the cat?"

"Hey now!" Philip said. He put his hands over Aurora's ears. Truthfully, he was glad for the change in everyone's focus. Logan had thanked him for what he'd tried to do, and that felt good, but not as good as actually being able to do it would have felt. It would have helped a lot of people, and it would have proven that he'd changed. "How long will it take to finish all the tests?" he asked.

Daisy looked at the screen and groaned. "There are fifty-five combinations. At twenty-two minutes a pair, that's over twenty hours from when we started, and it pauses while we're driving! Ugh!"

"I can tell you the results right now," AJ insisted. "Maybe the equipment was damaged when we went over a pothole or something, but it is giving inaccurate readings."

"Look at the two of them," Miles said, shaking his head. "Fighting just like siblings would."

Daisy glared. "I'm glad you're enjoying this, Miles O'Leary!"

Miles grinned. "My money's still on Philip and the cat."

"C'mon, sis," AJ said. He put his hands on Daisy's shoulders and guided her toward the couch. "Sit, relax. Enjoy the three-hour drive." He wrinkled his nose. "Maybe do a load of laundry and put on some clean clothes."

A knock on the door made all of them jump. They hadn't had any visitors yet on this trip.

"Maybe we're not supposed to park here," Logan said.

"Maybe it's the Great Shoudini!" Miles suggested. "She's decided to tell us where the beans are after all!"

AJ calmly looked out the window. "Neither one. Our pizza just arrived!"

The drive to **Ain't She Sweet** felt like forever to Daisy, even though the boys did their best to keep her entertained. Philip read them his fan letters as he wrote the replies, Miles and Logan put on a fashion show with half of the disguises in the closet, and even Aurora pitched in by chasing her tail for a full five minutes. Doing her laundry provided an unexpected laugh, as Logan pulled her Camp Tumbleweed sweatshirt out of the dryer and exclaimed, "You really *were* at camp!" and she got to tell them about her exciting last day.

After beating the boys at *Role with It* (Logan didn't really have a chance—his face had been morphed into a chess piece and could only move in certain directions), she turned to updating *The Case of the Missing Chocolate*. "Hey, Logan," she said when she was done typing. "Do you know what Evy might have meant when she said Sam knew he shouldn't have used the beans to make the Magic Bar in the first place?"

Logan set down his controller. Next time he'd ask to be made into a character that had arms and legs so he could do more than simply hurl himself at the aliens. He shook his head at the question. "The only thing I can think of is that the Magic Bar had failed the quality-control tests, but that's impossible. I mean, it's still good after fifty years."

"If the chocolate in the Magic Bar really had healing powers," Miles said, "think of all the people they could have helped since then."

The rest of them nodded. It seemed like such a strange choice to have hidden the beans away, no matter what reasons Evy had given.

Philip finally decided to lighten the mood. "Who's up for a rematch?"

Although no one said it, they were all thinking the same thing as they grabbed their controllers. As much as Evy had told them, there was a lot more she hadn't.

When Harvey finally stopped down the street from the next candy store, Daisy got to work immediately, making sure the tests were still running. AJ left to check out the situation at the store. "Good news," he told Philip when he returned. "No life-sized cardboard cutouts of you outside the store."

"Bummer," Miles said. "Then I'd have a matched set."

"Very funny," Philip said, checking his hair in the bathroom mirror. "I know you didn't take that one with you."

"Maybe I did, maybe I didn't."

"Good-size crowd, though," AJ reported. "But not everyone is there for you guys. The store is holding some sort of mutant-candy contest. There's a huge display of all these weird-shaped candy things."

"Weird-shaped candy things?" Logan repeated. "Like NQPs?"

"Am I supposed to know what that means?"

"'Not Quite Perfects,'" Logan explained. "A Gummzilla with three arms and no hind legs, or a Sour Finger with two colors instead of one. Or an Oozing Crunchorama with the ooze on the outside instead of the inside. Or—"

AJ held up a hand. "I get it, I get it. Like I said, weird-shaped candy things. Now let's get going." He pointed at Philip. "You. No speeches about first steps and rubber ducks and all that. Brilliant as it was, I don't want to leave a second store with everyone in tears."

"I don't know what you mean," Philip said innocently as he slipped past AJ and out the door.

Logan felt around in his almost empty pillowcase of candy to see whether any NQPs had slipped in. The closest he found were two Icy Mint Blobs stuck together, but that wasn't really contest-winning material. As eager as he was to see Harvey's 3-D printer in action, he knew using it to make one would definitely be considered cheating! His hand closed around one last piece of candy. It was the one from Randall. He held it out to AJ. "Want this?"

"What is it?" AJ asked.

"It's a Fireball Supernova. Just have a lot of bread handy when you eat it. Most people can't keep it in their mouths for more than a second or two their first time."

AJ popped it into his mouth. Logan and Miles—who still remembered his only encounter with that candy, when Max had let him sample one in the lab—stared as AJ continued to suck on it.

"Why isn't smoke coming out of his ears?" Miles whispered.

Logan only shook his head slowly. "I've never seen anything like it."

AJ shrugged, chewed, and swallowed. "No biggie. Now c'mon, we've gotta go."

Miles and Logan backed down the stairs, looking at AJ like he could walk on the moon. "Wow," they kept saying as they joined Philip, who was already outside. "Just...wow."

Daisy shook her head at AJ. "Are you gonna tell them someday that you only ate that because you have no sense of smell or taste right now?"

AJ grinned and stuck his fake hair/baseball cap on his head. "We'll see. Now let's go."

Daisy hesitated, reluctant to leave the lab. "Let's go!" Philip called up.

"Fine!" Daisy grumbled. She grabbed a pink hoodie sweatshirt from the dryer. (She recognized it as belonging to a girl in her cabin at camp. Oops.) A pair of oversized sunglasses later, and she was as disguised as she was going to get.

Aurora sat at the top of the steps as though deciding if it was worth going out. She sniffed at the air, then turned in a circle and lay down. Daisy had to climb over her. Aurora gave a small bark, but it didn't sound as if her heart was really in it. "I think she's warming up to you," AJ said, closing the door behind her and locking up.

Ain't She Sweet was located in a medium-size city, but to anyone who'd grown up in Spring Haven, the buildings might as well have been skyscrapers! Miles and Logan walked with their heads tilted back, hoping they didn't bump into anything. Philip tried to act cool, but he kept sneaking glances at all the businesspeople with their suits and briefcases.

The store was on a corner, next to a sandwich shop, which meant they all knew what they'd be having for dinner. "Short and sweet," AJ reminded them. "Same as last time, try to steer the conversation away from the Harmonicandy." They could see large groups of kids and parents crowded around a long rectangular table in the center of the store and at one of the many candy counters. Everyone looked like they were having a good time.

Logan took a deep breath and pushed open the door. His nose immediately filled with the most delicious smells. Abe, the owner, came running up when he saw them. "Welcome!" he boomed, opening his arms wide. "We have been cooking for you!" He pointed to a section of the store that had been turned into a mini fudge factory. "Free fudge for everyone!" he said, laughing. "This has been keeping the crowd at bay until they can try a Harmonicandy later!"

"Smart," Logan said. They shook hands warmly, and then Abe turned to the others. "Abe Sweet," he said, "but call me Abe."

"Your last name is Sweet, too?" Daisy asked Abe, looking between him and Logan. "Any relation?"

"Sure!" Abe said. "Logan's great-great-great-grandfather's second cousin three times removed married my great-great-grandmother's half niece."

"So basically, no relation," she said.

"Nope!" he replied. He nudged Logan. "I like this one. She's spunky!"

"You don't know the half of it," Logan said, grinning. He'd always liked Abe. "My parents are really sorry to miss seeing you," he said. "They've got their hands full getting ready for all the new **Mmm Mmm Good** products."

Abe rubbed his hands together excitedly. "Do you know which ones you're getting yet?"

"I think it's still supposed to be under wraps," Logan said, lowering his voice. "But one of them is the EnchantMints!"

"Excellent!" Abe boomed. "We love those here, as you can see." He pointed to a mostly empty display case. Only three boxes remained. "Better hurry up with production!" he joked. "Although I'm sure you've got your hands full with the Harmonicandy." He turned to Philip. "And this must be the man himself!" He shook Philip's hand vigorously. "Congratulations! So tell me, what are your marketing plans? I have some ideas for shelf displays, if you want to hear them."

Without missing a beat, Philip said, "I'd rather have a tour of your amazing store. Talking business can wait, right?" He put his hand on Abe's elbow and steered him away.

"He's smooth," Miles said, edging toward the fudge. Logan grabbed his sleeve and pulled him toward the long table in the center of the room. "Let's check out the mutant-candy contest first." Daisy flipped up her hood and went off in search of more multicolored licorice.

The contest table was so full of misshapen and miscolored candy and chocolate that Logan literally felt his mouth water.

"That's him!" a young girl at the table squealed. "The Harmoni-candy kid! Congratulations on winning!" She was pointing at a tall, dark-haired boy across from her. He could see the resemblance between him and Philip, but this boy looked older by about a year and had a sticker on his chest that read FIRST PLACE! Logan could understand the girl's confusion.

"Um, thanks," the boy said. "But I didn't make the Harmoni-candy. I just, um, won this mutant-candy contest."

"Oh," the girl said, shoulders sagging. Then she brightened. "But that's cool, too!" Her mother pulled her away.

A short, red-haired girl next to the mutant-candy winner laughed and poked the boy in the ribs. "Your first fan! Sort of!"

"I guess the contest is already over," Logan whispered to Miles.

The winner must have overheard, because he said, "It ended last month. You had to send a picture of your mutant candy, and the finalists were invited to show up with the real ones."

"Congratulations on winning," Logan said. "Which one is yours?"

The boy pointed at what looked like a whole pack of Starburst blobbed together in one long row. "All the wrappers were missing, too," he explained. "It's kind of the pride of my collection." He blushed a little and said, "I don't usually talk about my mutant candy collection, but"—he waved his arm across the table at all the entries—"you know."

His friend laughed and said, "Yeah, these are your people."

"I think it's awesome!" Logan said, nodding in appreciation. "The winning entry *and* the collecting! Once we forgot to let a batch of High-Jumping Jellybeans go through the cooling phase, and a blob the size of my head came out. That was one big NQP!" At their uncertain looks, he explained what it meant for the second time in an hour.

The boy's eyes widened. "You're Logan Sweet!" he gasped.

"Your dad's the Candymaker at the **Life Is Sweet** candy factory!"

"Now you've done it," the girl said to Logan. "You've officially blown his mind."

Since neither boy knew what to say next, the girl took over. She gestured with her thumb to her friend. "This guy with his tongue hanging out is Jeremy Fink," she said. "I'm Lizzy Muldoun. We're from New York City. We didn't come all this way for the contest, though. We're on a road trip to find my mom. She's not, like, missing or anything, but last summer I helped Jeremy with this really big project—I mean, *really big*—so now he's helping me."

"I'm sure they don't want our whole life story," Jeremy told her. Lizzy pushed him in response, and he knocked over an inside-out Snickers. He scrambled to straighten it as Logan smiled. Lizzy reminded him of Daisy, although Daisy was more of a kicker.

"I'm Logan Sweet," he said, "as you know already. And this is my best friend, Miles O'Leary. We're on a road trip, too. Not to find any missing moms, but . . . well, lots of other missing stuff." He pointed across the store. "We're here with the real Harmonicandy guy, Philip Ransford, and . . ." He felt bad leaving out Daisy (who he could see skulking around a display marked VEGGIE CANDY), but he had to protect her identity. "And our chaperone," he finished.

"We have one of those, too," Jeremy said, gesturing at a man in a limo driver's hat and coat. "We told him he didn't have to wear that outfit," Lizzy added, "but he insisted. He thinks it's funny. Which it kinda is, I guess."

"So what did you get for winning?" Miles asked. He kept stealing glances at Lizzy, who he thought was really pretty. Daisy was pretty, too, of course, but Daisy was like a sister to him, so she didn't count.

"I get to choose a month's supply of any candy I want. I'm planning to choose the Harmonicandy!"

Miles and Logan exchanged a look. "Um," Logan said, "you may want to choose something else."

Jeremy tilted his head. "Why?"

"It's a long story," Logan said, and he was relieved when Jeremy didn't push it.

Miles didn't want the conversation to end, though, because that meant Lizzy would go away. So he blurted out, "We can't get any more of the chocolate that we used in the contest, and the rules say it has to be the same, even though it still tasted really good, as you'll see when they get passed out in a few minutes. Also, the ingredients have to be easy to get and ours aren't. So…no more Harmonicandy." He swallowed hard. Saying it out loud made it finally sink in. All that work building the machines and the molds, and no one would get to hear his slogan.

"Wow," Lizzy said after a few seconds of quiet. "That bites."

Logan nodded, his stomach flipping like it did each time he thought about it.

Jeremy looked out over the table, at all the candy that wasn't quite right but was still awesome. "What if…," he said. "What if you could still make it, like if you withdrew from the contest? That way you could use whatever chocolate you wanted."

Logan and Miles stared at Jeremy, then at each other. "Do you think that's possible?" Miles asked Logan.

"I have no idea," Logan said, his mind racing with the possibility. "It never even occurred to me. No one has ever backed out after they won."

"But maybe it's possible?" Miles pushed.

"Maybe!" Logan said, feeling the knot in his belly loosen a bit. "It would be up to the Confectionary Association to decide." He stuck his hand out toward Jeremy. "Thanks for the great idea!" The boys grinned at each other as they shook hands. Logan didn't even flinch when Jeremy's hand gripped the scars on his palm. He felt like he'd just made a new friend.

"It's go time," Lizzy said, turning them toward the front of the store. The fudge-makers had laid out all the Harmonicandies on a long strip of wax paper. Abe and Philip stood behind the counter, handing them out to eager hands. "Come one, come all!" Abe shouted. "Try the hottest new musical candy before everyone else!"

Abe didn't make Philip give a speech but suggested he blow the first note. Philip did, and everyone cheered and started blowing into their own. No one led them in a song, but it sounded beautiful nonetheless.

"I'm definitely going for the month's supply of these," Jeremy said, holding up his Harmonicandy, which he'd bitten clear in half.

"You're supposed to *play* it first, *then* bite into it," Miles pointed out.

"With my month's supply, I can eat it thirty different ways!" Jeremy joked. "I really hope you still get to make it."

Lizzy—her arms full of assorted candy—dragged Jeremy away. "Gotta go!" she said as they waved goodbye. "Our driver promised to take us to the world's smallest wax museum. I think it's in someone's basement! Gotta love road trips!"

"Make sure not to bring any matches!" Miles called after her. She gave him a funny look, then a salute. Miles gave a goofy grin in response.

Daisy and Philip approached as Jeremy and Lizzy headed out the door. Daisy pushed her glasses onto her head. She looked amused. "Miles O'Leary, was that flirting?"

Miles blushed. "Maybe. Did you know less than two percent of people in the world have red hair?"

"I did not know that," Daisy replied.

Philip was gnawing on what looked like a piece of celery. "You've gotta try this," he told them. "It's candy, but shaped like a vegetable! And it has your daily supply of vitamins!" He handed

Logan a carrot and Miles an onion. Miles wrinkled his nose. Even though it smelled like peppermint, it still *looked* like an onion.

"You were talking to those two kids for a long time," Daisy said. "Who were they?"

"He's the mutant-candy winner," Logan said, chomping on his candy carrot, which had a refreshing orangey-grapefruit taste. "And he had the *best* idea!"

CHAPTER FIFTEEN

P hilip dug another can of tuna out of the storage room and spooned it into Aurora's bowl. He was pretty sure the cat was eating better than *they* were. AJ had made them all eggs and sausages for breakfast, but the sausages were dry and the eggs were wet and it didn't make a good combination.

The others had talked late into the night about the possibility of still getting to make the Harmonicandy even though it would be stripped of its award-winning title. He mostly just listened and nodded occasionally. He didn't know how he felt about it. They all agreed they wouldn't be able to tell anyone the real story about the beans—not that they knew much of it anyway—but they knew enough. Without that explanation, why would the Confectionary Association agree to the plan? After a while, he shut himself in the bedroom to practice. He fell asleep on AJ's bed and woke up back in his bunk. Apparently AJ had carried him there, which was embarrassing.

Daisy didn't have the same problem with breakfast. She ate every bite superslowly in the hopes of delaying their getting back on the road. It hadn't worked. Now she was counting down the minutes until they parked again. Fortunately, she didn't have long to wait.

AJ pulled off the road into a rest stop. "Anyone need to use the restroom?" he asked.

"Isn't the point of having an RV so that we don't have to use public bathrooms?" Philip asked.

"I was just kidding," AJ said. "This is the dead-drop location."

"Really?" Miles said with interest. "Such a public place?"

"Not here. We're headed into the woods across the street. Now, here are the rules. Rule number one—you wait here. Actually, that's the only rule."

Miles threw up his arms. "Seriously? You bring us this close to a real spy mission and we have to watch out a window?"

AJ nodded. "Trust me, a dead drop is not very exciting. We leave the package, and tomorrow another spy comes to pick it up. That's all there is to it. Normally I'd want to wait to verify the pickup, but because of *someone's* need to be crowned the most talented kid in the nation, it works best to do it this way so we don't need to backtrack."

Philip held up both hands. "Hey, it's not my fault I'm crazy gifted."

Miles rolled his eyes. "You got part of that right."

Birdhouse under her arm, Daisy climbed out of the booth and over to the lab. AJ groaned. "We're only going to be here for probably a half hour or so. Do you really need to start that up again?"

"That's enough time for one more pair," she said, flipping the switch. "Why, you afraid that once we confirm the truth, you'll have to start being nicer to me?"

"I'm plenty nice to you," AJ said, snatching the birdhouse. "Now let's go before I pull your hair or hide your toothbrush."

"Is that what you think siblings do?" Philip asked. "As the only one here who actually has one, I can tell you Andrew has never pulled my hair." He paused and added, "He did bite me once."

"Stay out of trouble," AJ warned them as he left the RV with Daisy on his heels. She knew Miles and Logan were disappointed not to go, but AJ was right. Just bringing them along this far was already breaking ten different rules. She turned around once they got to the other side of the street and saw the boys watching from the window. She nearly lifted her hand to wave but stopped herself. Even though they were a day early for the drop, spies didn't wave to their friends on a mission.

AJ used his GPS to lead them into the thick trees and to the drop-off point. They passed a few other people on the trails, either hiking or jogging. Daisy had expected the coordinates to be deep in the woods, but AJ stopped after only a few minutes. He pointed to a tree with a lot of low branches, perfect for tucking the birdhouse in securely. He adjusted some leaves to cover as much of it as possible.

"Well, that's that, then," he said.

"Yup," Daisy said. "May whatever's in there finally reach its destination on the road of life."

"Very poetic of you," AJ said. He stepped back to snap a picture of the birdhouse's position in the tree, and a wider photo showing the whole tree. It was always wise to have proof of a drop. He counted out ten paces, then drew a red slash mark on the side of a birch tree.

When they returned to the RV, they found the boys outside, sitting on top of a picnic table in front of the rest stop. "Aurora needed some fresh air," Miles explained, pointing to the cat, currently brushing up against a nearby tree trunk.

AJ raised his eyebrows. "Aurora did, or you did?"

"Well, you have to admit, it's not normal for growing boys to be cooped up inside so much," Miles pointed out. "It's summer, after all. Can we just get some fresh air for a little while?"

Daisy checked her watch. "Or for the next six hours and nineteen minutes until the tests are done?"

"I'm thinking more in the fifteen-minute range," AJ said.

"Plenty of time for snacks, then," Logan said. He and Philip went to check out the vending machines along the outside wall of the rest area while Miles entertained Daisy and AJ by describing the people who passed by.

He pointed at a man in a business suit who was getting out of his car. "That guy's on his way to closing a big business deal. But he ate a bad burrito at a drive-through on his way to the meeting and doesn't want to use the bathroom at the office."

"Fascinating!" Daisy said. "What about her?" She pointed at a middle-aged woman in a purple sweat suit walking a fluffy white dog.

"She's a professional dog walker," Miles replied. "She secretly wants to keep this dog because she thinks if she dyes it purple, they will be matching."

"And them?" AJ asked, tilting his head toward two college-age boys emerging from the woods across the street. They wore hiking boots and backpacks and high-fived as they headed toward the parking area.

"That's easy," Miles said. "They're geocachers. Just found a really hard cache and are proud of themselves. Hey! Maybe there really *are* caches in there!" He scrambled to pull the vid com out of his backpack at his feet. He'd figured out from Arthur's book how to search your nearby location for caches. In less than a minute he had a list of five, all within two miles! He switched over to the map view and pointed to two green flags that indicated locations in the woods across the street. "Please, please, please, can we try for these two?"

"Why not," AJ said. "I'm in a giving mood today."

"Yay!" Daisy said, jumping off the table. Miles knew she was more excited about having the extra time for her tests, but he didn't care.

"C'mon, guys!" he called out to Philip and Logan. "We're going geocaching!" He dug around in his backpack some more and pulled out the small yellow plastic compass, a blue swirly marble, a plastic spider ring, and a pencil to sign the logbook. He shoved them all in his front pocket, leaving the candy coupons in the bag in case there wasn't a candy store nearby. "Let's go!"

"You sure you've got everything now?" AJ asked, clearly amused. Miles gave a thumbs-up and waited impatiently until Logan and Philip joined them, their arms full of salty snacks, which they passed around.

Chomping on chips, they headed into the woods. Philip kept swatting at invisible bugs. "How do we know there aren't bears in here?"

"We don't," Daisy said.

"Well, that's comforting," Philip muttered.

Logan started whistling. He loved being in the woods. Everything felt so alive, and it reminded him of the Tropical Room at home. Plus he'd never been on a treasure hunt before.

Miles looked up from his vid com and turned west. "The first one is over this way. It's supposed to be a small green box."

"It's right there," AJ said, pointing at the base of a tree.

"What?" Miles said, twisting his head to see. "We haven't even started looking!"

AJ pointed at the ground. "Those two leaves are crushed, those three rocks are piled at an angle not likely to have happened naturally, and there's a green M&M a foot away."

Miles exhaled loudly. "You are banned from geocaching."

"Wait till Mom and Dad hear about this," Daisy said, shaking her head.

AJ pinched Daisy on the arm. "We are *not* related! And it's not my fault I got a perfect score in tracking class."

Miles grumbled but pulled out the container anyway. "I'm not claiming this find," he said. He still hadn't come up with a name for himself anyway. He snapped off the lid, and Daisy and Logan eagerly bent down to see what was inside. Philip was too busy scratching imaginary bites on his shin.

"Hey, Philip," Daisy said, reaching in. "This was meant for you." She handed him an individually wrapped bug-repellent wipe. He ripped it open and rubbed it up and down his legs and arms.

"And this is for you, Miles," Logan said, digging under the logbook to pull out an eraser in the shape of a blue whale. "It'll be like Whaley is with us after all."

Miles grinned. "This is what I love about caching. You hope that what you put in will be just what someone finding it will need."

"Not sure anyone *needs* a Whaley eraser," Philip said.

"You're just jealous," Miles joked, sticking Whaley in his pocket and pulling out the swag he'd loaded. He placed the compass and the ring in the box, sealed it back up, and hid it just like he'd found it. Or rather, like AJ had found it. Miles was still a little bitter about that.

"On to the next!" he said, brushing off the leaves from his legs. "You can trail behind," he told AJ. The compass built into the GPS said the next cache was only a tenth of a mile away, the minimum distance allowed between caches.

"What are we looking for this time?" Logan asked.

"The description says it's a handmade container, so I guess it could be anything." He scrolled down the recent logs, careful to watch where he was going. Arthur had drummed into his head the importance of not looking down at your device while walking. You could walk off a bridge that way. "Hmm, it doesn't look like it's been found in a while. It might not be here anymore."

Miles stopped a few minutes later. "Okay, it's somewhere within a twenty-foot circle from here. The name of the cache is "Look Up," so I'm guessing that means it's hanging from a branch."

Daisy started to laugh.

"What's so funny?" Miles asked. "Has AJ found it already?"

She shook her head. "You're almost right on top of our drop!"

Miles and Logan checked out a few of the closest trees, spotting the birdhouse easily. "You guys didn't do such a great job hiding it," Philip said.

AJ stepped closer. "I thought it was covered better than that." He pushed a few leaves away and lifted the birdhouse out of the nook made by the branches. "Whoa, look!" He showed it to Daisy, who gasped as she lifted off the chimney, which had been put back on upside down. She hadn't even known it opened!

She hurried over to check the signpost and then ran back. "If they came for it already, they didn't make the *X*!"

AJ pulled out his vid com and fired off a message. If the spies had picked it up early, they'd have sent word to headquarters. They also would have taken the container with them—or at least that's the way it usually worked. You didn't leave any evidence behind.

Daisy shook the birdhouse, turning it over in her hands. She heard the same clink as the contents bounced against the sides, so that was a relief.

AJ's vid com beeped. He frowned as he read the message. "Nobody has been sent to the area yet."

"Maybe a really fat owl landed on it," Miles suggested. "When the bird couldn't get inside, it broke the chimney in frustration?"

"Stranger things have happened," Daisy said, trying to reach her fingers into the chimney hole. "I don't think we need to worry, AJ. Whatever was in here is still here. Got it!" She pulled her hand out to reveal a tiny green turtle with a mask across its face. What looked like an engraved dog tag hung from a chain attached to its foot. "What the—?"

"That's a Teenage Mutant Ninja Turtle!" Miles exclaimed.

Logan nodded and grinned. "It sure is!"

"It's a what?" Daisy asked.

"Come on," Philip said, "even I've heard of the Teenage Mutant Ninja Turtles, and I don't get out much. You never saw the cartoons? Movies? Action figures?"

Daisy shook her head.

"Turtles trained in the Japanese art of ninjutsu?" Miles added, crouching in what he hoped looked like an intimidating ninja-warrior pose.

Daisy turned to AJ, dangling the object from her finger. "To think, this strange thing was in there the whole time." She brought the dog tag closer to read it. All it had on it was a string of numbers.

AJ shook his head, his tan skin going pale. "No, it wasn't."

Daisy looked up from the tag. "What do you mean?"

"The birdhouse had a microdot camera in it. It didn't have a dog tag and a cartoon character in it."

"Why would you know what's inside but Daisy doesn't?" Philip asked. He didn't say it in a mean way; he was truly curious.

"If you must know, it's safer if only one of us has that information. Spy protocol."

"So why is this toy in here now?" Daisy asked. Right as the words came out, she knew the answer. She wheeled around to face Miles. "Those guys really *were* geocachers, weren't they? And they thought this was the cache! They took our camera and left this behind!"

Miles nodded. "Either them or someone else."

"Time to use those famous tracking skills, right, AJ?" Philip asked.

But AJ was already on their trail. Flattened grass, footprints in dirt, another M&M. Bent branches revealed their heights, but he'd already seen what they looked like, so he didn't need those kinds of clues. It frustrated him to no end that he couldn't use his sense of smell. They might have eaten something or been wearing some strong deodorant or cologne or bug spray that he could follow. He glanced at Daisy, who put her finger on her own nose and shook her head. Okay, he felt better that his sense of smell wouldn't have helped there. The trail led them back to the paved path, where it went cold.

AJ turned to Miles. "So tell me, how do we find who broke into our dead drop?"

Miles froze for a minute. AJ had never asked him for advice. He wished he'd read more of Arthur's book. He tried to think of the timeline of events. "Okay. We'll go back to the first cache and check the logbook. Then we'll know their caching identity. I think it's safe to assume that if someone was caching in the woods, they would have gone for both caches listed there. Then what we can do is hide our own cache—we can use the fake poop as a container—get it on the official list and hope the same people come back to find it and leave the camera thingy. A lot of people can't resist being the first to find a new cache. You usually get a really good prize in it. We can make sure to put something really great in there, so they'll for sure have to leave something. Hopefully the camera."

"That sounds complicated," AJ said. "Too many loose ends, like what if someone else finds the new cache first? Simplify."

Miles thought again. "We go back to the first cache, get their names from the logbook, contact them, and get the camera back by using your good looks, charm, and gentle persuasion?"

AJ nodded. "Much better."

But when they pulled out the logbook, they saw that the last cachers had only written initials—*BM & CB*—and the date. "This isn't going to help us much," Miles warned. "Usually people write the nicknames they're listed under in the geocaching registry." He typed the initials into the search box of registered cachers. As he'd expected, nothing came up. "Our only other hope is that they went online to log their find," he said, packing the box up and tossing the rocks back on top. He showed them his screen with the listing for the cache. "Once they claim the find, the log will appear here. It could show up any minute."

AJ wanted to be nearby on the off chance the cachers returned, so they headed back to the RV to plan their next step. Miles kept refreshing the page to see if a new listing popped up, but there was nothing yet.

Daisy began to pace in the parking lot, nervously turning the plastic turtle over and over in her hands. Logan and Miles exchanged a worried look. They'd never seen her like this. She was usually the calm-under-pressure type. The fact that she hadn't rushed inside to check her test results meant this was really serious. "Are you going to be okay?" Logan asked.

"That camera could have really sensitive information on it," Daisy said. "We could be in really big trouble."

"What is a microdot camera, anyway?" Philip asked.

"That's classified," AJ said, out of habit.

"If we're a team here, we should know what we're looking for," Miles pointed out.

"Oh, fine," AJ said, barely able to believe it had come to this. He couldn't stand the thought that his perfect track record of successful missions was going to be derailed by some random guys trying to find trinkets hidden in the woods. "Spies use these special cameras to take a picture of a large amount of information," he explained. "The image is then shrunk down to the size of a tiny dot, which would need to be put under a microscope to read. You could hide detailed instructions or secret maps in a period at the end of a sentence. No one would know a microdot was there unless they knew to look for it."

"But these guys aren't going to know what they have," Logan said. "They'll probably just think it's a toy."

"Maybe," AJ said. "But we still need to get it back, since we don't know what's stored in that camera right now. And preferably before the real spies show up to collect it. So far all we know about the people who took it is their initials. It's something, but not a lot to go on."

Daisy held up the turtle. "We know they like turtles."

"Or that they don't like turtles," Logan pointed out, "so when they found that one in another cache, they decided to pass it on the first chance they got."

"Wait a minute," Miles said. "Let me see that." He snatched the turtle from Daisy. "I think this is a travel bug! Arthur told me about these. Each tag has a number on it that you use to track the bug's progress from cache to cache. Some of them wind up on the other side of the world!"

AJ took it from him and held it up. "If we enter in this number, will it tell us who had it last?"

"I think so!" Miles said. AJ read off the numbers while Miles typed them in. A few seconds later a page popped up:

MUTANT NINJA TURTLE MADNESS!
GET THIS BUG TO ANY TOWN WITH THE NAME TURTLE IN IT!

What followed next was a map of where the travel bug started and a description of its mission. So far it had gone three hundred miles and been in sixteen different caches, none of them in a town called Turtle. Miles scrolled down with his finger until he found the most recent entry. The nickname of the last person to have found the travel bug was TwoDudesCaching, who reported taking it from a cache a week prior. He clicked on the name, and a profile popped up. Underneath a cartoon rendering of a twenty-something guy, it said, *Brennan McCabe, geocaching for five years. Personal motto: Not all who wander are lost.* Miles jabbed at the screen and handed it to AJ. "That's our guy! I don't know how you'll find him, though. He could be anywhere by now."

"Leave that to me," AJ said, slipping the vid com into his pocket. "I'll have that camera back in an hour. Daisy, you're in command now." He tossed her the keys. "And, Miles, if this works, anything you want, it's yours."

"Wait," Daisy said as AJ began walking away. "I know you're fast, but you're planning to hunt this guy down on foot?"

AJ shook his head and continued to the rear of the RV. They all watched as he reached underneath, pressed a few buttons, and then stood back as a previously invisible rear hatch opened up. "Stay back," AJ said, stepping inside as four mouths hung open.

A minute later he came out wearing a leather jacket and a helmet and wheeling what looked like a cross between a motorcycle and a scooter. He slid the vid com into a slot on the dash, and it clicked into place. "I started a trace on Mr. Brennan McCabe's license plate. It won't take long to track him down. Go get yourselves some sandwiches, and pick me up a ham-and-cheese." He flipped down the visor on his helmet, revved the engine, and zoomed off.

"Man, he's good," Logan said as the bike disappeared around a bend.

"He has his moments," Daisy agreed. "Here, lunch is on me." She handed them a fifty-dollar bill.

"Hey, isn't this mine?" Miles asked.

"Maybe you shouldn't leave money under your pillow like you're the tooth fairy," she replied. "I'll have a veggie sub, extra mayo."

"I'll take that," Philip said, plucking the bill from Miles's hand. "Pretty sure it's really mine."

"I'll let you boys work this out," Daisy said as she climbed into the RV. Now that AJ was handling their current problem, she couldn't wait to get inside. According to her calculations, the tests should be done!

When the boys returned with their bags of sandwiches and chips and soda and pickles, they found Daisy sitting cross-legged on the couch, the cat purring in her lap. Miles wasn't sure which was more disturbing, the fact that Aurora had suddenly decided to like Daisy, or the look of shock on Daisy's face that he was pretty sure didn't have anything to do with the cat.

CHAPTER SIXTEEN

When AJ returned, he found them all sitting on the couch playing *Role with It*. "Mission accomplished," he reported, slinging his jacket over a seat. "The camera is safely back at the dead drop where hopefully no more cachers will stumble across it before we leave."

"Awesome!" Miles said, laying down the controller. "How'd you do it?"

"Let's just say I can be very persuasive when I need to be."

Philip stood and stretched. "So basically you told them they took the wrong thing and they gave it back to you."

AJ grinned. "Essentially, yes." He turned to Miles. "Thanks, kid, for your help back there. I'm going to inform the powers that be that dead drops aren't as secure as they used to be."

"I'm happy to help," Miles said. "Did you really mean I could choose anything I wanted?"

"Within reason," AJ said, washing his hands at the kitchen sink.

"Well, the kids we met at the first campground told us about this telescope dedication happening tonight. I know it's taking us out of the way, but Philip's contest isn't until the day after tomorrow, so maybe we have time?" Miles tried to give him his best hopeful puppy-dog look.

"I'll look up the info," AJ said. "If it's doable, we'll go. It would be good to add something educational into the trip."

Miles and Logan high-fived.

"By the way," Philip said, eyes still on the game, "if you're thinking about talking to Daisy, don't bother. She hasn't said a word since you left."

AJ unwrapped his sandwich and began wolfing it down. With his mouth full, he asked Daisy, "If bis bue?"

Daisy just kept petting Aurora with one hand while her rock-star alter ego blew up aliens with the other.

"Yes, it's true," Philip answered for her. "I checked the lab results, and from what I could tell, she wired them to another lab to check them over. I don't know if she heard back yet or not, but she's in full-on zombie-ate-my-brain mode. As to why the cat is her new best friend, I'm guessing bribery was involved."

AJ finished his sandwich and slid into the driver's seat. "She'll bounce back. I'm not too worried." He pulled out some maps and began plotting their course. "Hey, the country's largest ball of twine is on our way. Should we stop?"

"That might be good for you, Philip," Miles said, "you know, as a knitter."

Philip grunted. "I am *not* a knitter. Plus you don't knit with twine."

"A fact only a true knitter would know," Miles replied.

Daisy allowed herself a tiny smile. On the screen, one kick from Philip's goat leg knocked Cowboy Miles off his horse.

By the time Harvey began climbing the mountain that would lead to the Phyllis E. Glorian Radio Telescope, the sky had darkened considerably.

"We're going to be entering a radio quiet zone," AJ announced as the road got steeper. "That means no electronics. Everything's gotta be shut down. We won't get any outside service at all."

"Not even the vid coms?" Logan asked.

AJ shook his head. "Any slight interference could ruin the readings from the telescope."

A look of relief crossed Daisy's face.

"Is no electronics a good thing for some reason?" Miles asked her.

She shook her head. "It's just that if everything's turned off, I won't hear from the outside laboratory tonight. I can put it out of my mind."

"Glad to have you back, then," he said.

After climbing for another twenty minutes, they began going downhill again, until the road flattened out. They were in some kind of valley. AJ pulled off into a huge, gravel-covered parking lot full of cars and trucks and a few other RVs. The only lights breaking up the darkness were the headlights blinking off as cars pulled into spots. They could see out the window that most people carried flashlights, a lot of them with red lenses, which were supposed to help your eyes see the night sky better.

AJ handed them each a flashlight that hung from a chain. "Cool," Miles said, slipping the chain over his head

"You are easily impressed," Philip noted.

"I also have two pairs of night-vision goggles," AJ said, holding them up. "We can take turns. Now, stick together. We don't know what to expect, and you can already see how dark it is up here." Philip took one pair and AJ kept the other. Then they grabbed sweatshirts and headed outside.

Miles was last off the steps, and as the door swung shut behind him, his jaw fell wide open. He could only stare up at the clearest, widest, most star-packed sky he'd ever seen. The Milky Way arched overhead in a long streak of dazzlingly bright stars while the last of the sunset left orange, yellow, and purple blasts of light behind. It was literally the most beautiful sky he'd ever seen. Every few seconds, a meteor zoomed across its path.

"Great Galileo's ghost! Look at that!" a boy shouted as he got out of the car next to them. Miles couldn't help glancing over. The boy stood with his mouth open, staring straight up. Miles smiled, knowing exactly how the kid felt. He turned back to the sky and would have stood there forever if Logan hadn't pulled him off the steps.

It was cold, much colder than any summer night had the right to be, but he barely registered it. His chest felt both heavy and light at the same time, so overwhelming was the beauty of what lay above him. Miles remembered from his research that telescopes were usually built in areas known for having especially clean, dry air so electromagnetic signals could pass through the atmosphere easier. The air here sure was clean! No wonder the stars were so bright. *Nothing exists except atoms and empty space.* In that moment, he understood exactly what the line meant that he'd copied before the trip.

The crowd—old and young alike—began to move toward a square building at the end of the parking lot, where a podium and rows of chairs had been set up in front of a flat, grassy field. The enormous telescope was impossible to miss. The curved dish was about a thousand times bigger than a TV satellite dish on someone's roof. As they got closer, more and more lampposts flickered on—still dim, but they could clearly see each other now.

They chose seats in the last row, feeling a little like they were crashing someone else's party. A tall man in jeans and a long white lab coat climbed up to the podium. The excited crowd hushed. "Friends, fellow scientists, members of planet Earth!" He shouted in the absence of a microphone. "I am Dr. Ian Randis, the director of this fine observatory. Welcome to a historic evening. Our a-little-too-close-for-comfort comet friend is treating us to the year's best meteor shower! There goes one now!"

The crowd whistled and laughed as the shooting stars zoomed overhead as if the timing had been planned.

"We live in a grand age, an era when we can see nearly to the beginning of time itself with the help of little guys like these." He gestured behind him, and the crowd laughed again. The structure was anything but little.

He beamed and continued. "Just a few weeks ago NASA's *Juno* spacecraft reached the orbit of Jupiter. Soon we will know all the secrets this baby sun that never ignited has been hiding in the far reaches of our solar system. The Phyllis E. Glorian Radio Telescope you see behind me will peer much, much farther than that to teach us about the energy released from black holes and to enable us to watch the evolution of far-flung galaxies. But perhaps most exciting of all, it will be at the cutting edge of extrasolar exploration—the discovery of planets around other stars. Maybe it will take a day or a decade or ten decades, but we will find life out there in this vast universe—of that I have no doubt. Thank you for being here tonight to help celebrate the dawn of a new era in space exploration."

The crowd clapped and hooted and cheered. Miles leaned over to AJ. "Thank you for bringing me here," he said, wiping his eyes. AJ nodded and blinked fast.

Dr. Randis motioned for six kids to come onto the stage. They stood on either side of him, looking excited and nervous. One of the girls clutched some kind of pouch hanging around her neck. Miles recognized the boy who had shouted out in the parking lot. He and one other girl were the youngest in the group, probably about eleven or a little older. The others looked to be about thirteen or fourteen.

"This must be the naming contest!" Miles whispered to Logan.

Logan nodded absently—he was too busy staring at one of the girls. She had long dark hair and dark eyes and was easily the prettiest girl he had seen in real life, ever.

"I have the honor of introducing a group of very special kids who call themselves Team Exo! With a little guidance, they used a telescope, a computer, and some excellent math skills to confirm a suspected exoplanet around a distant star last summer. Please welcome Ally and Kenny Summers, Bree and Melanie Holden, Jack Rosten, and Ryan Flynn." The audience applauded.

Miles spotted Zack and his family from their first campground, the ones who had told them about this event. "Hey!" Miles called out to them, waving until Daisy gently pushed his arm down.

Dr. Randis put his hands on the two nearest kids' shoulders. "Now, the right to name the exoplanet would have rightfully been theirs, but I'm going to turn the floor over to Ally Summers, who's going to explain why they chose to have a contest to name it instead."

The girl with the pouch stopped clutching it and stepped forward. "Wow," she said, pushing her thick hair away from her face and looking out at the crowd. "This is so exciting. When you grow up on a campground, like my brother Kenny and I did, you spend a lot of time looking up at the sky at night. I used to pretend I had friends on other planets, and maybe one day that will really be true! We wanted to open up the naming to all kids in the hopes that they'll get as excited about astronomy and science as we are. Jack and Bree are going to announce the winning name."

She stepped back, and the girl with the long, shiny hair and the boy next to her stepped forward. The boy squeezed Ally's hand as they switched. "We received over five thousand submissions," the boy, Jack, said. "Five *thousand*. From all over the world. It really blew us away. A lot of people wanted us to name the planet after their dog or cat or favorite candy!"

Daisy giggled. "We could have voted for Aurora."

"Or Oozing Crunchorama!" Logan whispered back, glad that Daisy's weird mood had at least temporarily lifted.

Bree opened an envelope and pulled out a sheet of paper. "But in the end," she said, "we wound up choosing one that worked for us on a lot of levels—the name reminds us of kids discovering new worlds, of friendships being made and tested, of possibilities and wonder."

The other kids in the group lifted a large white poster up over their heads. It showed a map of the galaxy with an arrow pointing to Earth and one more pointing to the new planet, around a distant star. Together, all six of them said, "Let us introduce you to... Planet Narnia!"

The crowd clapped and cheered, especially the portion of it that contained a whole lot of eleven-year-olds who had just won for naming the planet after their favorite book series.

Jack shouted over applause. "So if Mr. Denberg's fifth-grade class from Lake Mohawk Elementary will please come up, we have something for each of you!"

About twenty kids ran out of the audience and up to the platform. Dr. Randis put a pouch like Ally's around each of their necks. The kids, of course, immediately opened the pouches to see what was inside.

"What do you think it is?" Logan asked.

Miles shook his head. "I can't tell."

"It looks like a rock," Philip said. "I think it *is* a rock."

Ally stepped to the front again. "We'll almost certainly never get to see Planet Narnia, or Kepler-438b, or Gliese 832c, or any of the other exoplanets that might harbor life. They are millions and millions of miles away and impossible to get to in person. But sometimes pieces of outer space come to us." She lifted up her own pouch and held it out. "In here is a meteorite—a tiny piece of a comet or asteroid—that my grandfather found. Or rather, it found him. Now you each have a meteorite of your own."

The fifth graders all started talking excitedly and holding up their space rocks.

Dr. Randis took the stage again. "Inside the observatory, the button has now been pressed. Radio waves are streaming toward us and landing right there!" He pointed to the face of the dish. Everyone stood up to get a better look. It didn't help. They couldn't see anything happening.

"Hey, you guys made it!" Zack said, jumping in front of them. Mia and Beth were with him, too.

"Pretty stellar up there, right?" Zack said, pointing up.

Miles laughed. "Stellar!"

Daisy rolled her eyes. "Vocabulary humor."

"Any of you want to go meet those exoplanet kids?" Zack asked. "Even though they didn't choose my name?"

Daisy and Beth chose to get a closer look at the telescope while the boys made their way through the crowd toward Team Exo. "What was the name you entered?" Logan asked.

"Planet Mango," Zack said a little sheepishly. "After a very special cat. Guess it wasn't too original."

"It's not that bad," Miles said.

"Narnia is better," Zack admitted.

"Yeah."

They'd expected Team Exo to be swamped with people, but most of the crowd was gathering around the telescope. They came upon Bree first. Logan hung back a few feet behind the others. He couldn't make himself go any closer to her.

"Hi!" Zack said cheerfully. "Was it this clear out the night you found the planet?"

She shook her head. "Rain, misery, drama. Even the best night at the campground isn't clear like this. Dr. Randis said this whole

423

area is some weird microclimate or something. Like, the weather's totally different on the other side of the ridge."

"You know what else is weird?" Zack asked. "That all these stars are still here during the day but you can't see them."

Bree smiled. "Just wait for the next eclipse. You'll see them, all right." The oldest of the Team Exo kids pulled Bree away with a simple "Sorry, need to steal her." Logan was relieved. Zack went to join his family, and Miles went up to Ally.

"Hi," he said shyly. "I think it's really cool that you wear that." He pointed to the pouch. "I never knew either of my grandfathers, but if I did and they gave me that, I'd wear it, too."

"Thanks," she said. "Sometimes kids at my new school look at me a little weird, but I've got these guys, so I'm okay." She gestured to her exoplanet friends.

"And it looks like you're starting a trend," Miles said, pointing to all the little kids running around with their meteorites bouncing on their chests.

Ally laughed. "It's true! Do you want to see it?"

"Sure," Miles said, holding out his hand. She pulled out a small, craggy-looking rock and dropped it into his palm. Logan inched closer to take a look. The silver-gray rock was only about half an inch long.

"Wow," Logan said, touching it with one finger. "This was in space!"

Even Philip couldn't help sneaking a peek at it.

"It almost looks more like a magnet than a rock," Miles said, handing it back. "Is it magnetic?"

She nodded. "It's made of iron, nickel, aluminum, and silicon. And iridium, of course. At least that's all I know of."

Philip had been doing his best to seem bored, but he was really silently blaming Mrs. Sweet for not putting warmer clothes on the packing list. At the sound of the word *iridium*, he perked up. "Excuse me," he said politely. "I've never heard of iridium before. I mean, not until recently. But what do you mean by 'of course'? Why is it 'of course' made of iridium?"

She seemed surprised by the question. "I guess I just meant that iridium is one of those minerals that they think came to Earth from space in meteorites. Like when that asteroid or comet wiped out the dinosaurs, one of the ways they figured it out was by dating all the iridium found buried at this huge crater site, and it was the same time period when the dinosaurs went extinct, sixty-six million years ago."

Philip felt his heart begin to beat faster. Logan grabbed on to one of his arms, and Miles the other. "Are you saying," Philip said slowly, "that if a plant or something has iridium in it, that plant would have had to grow somewhere a meteorite had landed?"

She nodded. "I think so. You can find an impact site with—"

"A metal detector!" Miles said.

Ally nodded.

"Thank you for the science lesson," Logan said. "We should let you go. You have lots of fans." He pointed behind them at the line of fifth graders holding autograph books and pens.

Ally blushed in the dark when she saw them. "Okay, that's a little weird."

Unable to help himself, Miles threw his arms around Ally. Logan and Philip joined in. "Um, thanks, guys?" she said, peeling herself out of the group hug. "It was great meeting you, too."

Philip straightened up first, and they all hurried back toward the rows of chairs. "I'll deny that hug happened if questioned."

"Me too," Logan said.

"Not me," Miles said happily.

AJ and Daisy were walking toward them. "That girl Mia told me to tell you good luck at the competition," Daisy told Philip. "She said if any of the judges have synesthesia, you'll win for sure once they hear you play."

"That's nice, but listen," Philip said. "We have to tell you something really important."

Daisy felt a shiver run through her. Had the boys picked up the final test results while she and AJ weren't looking? She felt like it was her job to tell them what she found, and they knew already? She searched their faces. They seemed flushed, but in an excited way, not a totally freaked out way. And anyway, the results couldn't have arrived, since they'd had to turn off everything that carried an electric current. She relaxed a tiny bit. "What is it?" she said cautiously.

Logan answered. "Do we happen to have any metal detectors lying around?"

CHAPTER SEVENTEEN

I know it's back here somewhere," AJ muttered, digging through the storage room. Since it was too late to find a campground, they were parked for the night in the back of a giant superstore that allowed RVs to stay over, probably in the hopes that the passengers would go in and buy stuff. Which, if AJ couldn't find the metal detector, was exactly what they'd have to do.

Aurora wandered in with one of AJ's socks in her mouth and plopped it at Daisy's feet. "Seriously?" Daisy said. "You want me to play fetch with AJ's smelly old sock? Didn't anyone tell you you're a cat?"

"My feet do not smell," AJ said without turning around.

"I can smell them from here," Daisy said.

"Hey, why do you have a pair of stilts?" Miles asked, pulling out anything that might be shaped like a metal detector. "Planning on going undercover in a circus?"

Daisy glanced at the stilts fondly. "AJ once had to shoot me out of a cannon at the state fair."

AJ nodded, his head stuck in a box filled, oddly enough, with sock puppets. "Good times."

"Yes, they were," she agreed.

"I found it!" Miles shouted. He held up the very high-tech-looking metal detector with a computer screen by the handle and a gold coil on the end. It had been wedged between a skateboard and an inflatable pillow in the shape of a sun. This was a strange room.

They rejoined Philip and Logan, who were currently arguing over what their next step should be. They were comparing Daisy's notes with the information on iridium and meteorites that Philip had jotted down in the margins of a brochure he'd picked up at the ceremony. It advertised something called a Messier Marathon at the campground where those Team Exo kids lived.

"So, what have you got?" AJ asked. "And I don't need to point out how far past your bedtimes it is."

Philip answered first. "We need to look for meteorite impact sites within a hundred miles of their hometown of Brookdale, which is likely where they would have gone camping. Then we go there, use the metal detector to pick up any traces that might be left, find the hidden valley, and find the tree. The end."

"You make it sound so simple," Daisy said, hopping onto the trampoline for some much-needed exercise. "But if cocoa beans grow only in tropical weather, how could the tree be anywhere within even a thousand miles?"

Philip shook his head. "I don't know. But Evy definitely didn't make it seem like they traveled to the equator."

"What about that microclimate effect Ally was talking about?" Miles asked. "Where the telescope was located had a cold and clear microclimate, but what if there could be a tropical one, and that's where the beans grew?"

"I may not know a huge amount about the world," Logan said, "but Brookdale is only about an hour away from Spring Haven. If there was some kind of tropical oasis anywhere nearby, I think we would have heard of it."

"I'm sure you're right," Miles said, "but Evy mentioned hiding things in plain sight. Maybe that's what she meant? It's right in front of us, but we don't notice it?"

"I never really agreed with that theory," Philip said.

"Wait a minute!" Miles suddenly shouted. "What if the tree has been in the Tropical Room all this time? Doesn't get more 'in plain sight' than that!"

Logan shook his head. "Not possible. I know every inch of that place. Plus Henry wouldn't have sent us on the road."

Miles sagged. "Yeah, I guess you're right."

Logan patted him on the shoulder. "Good thinking, though."

AJ stood and stretched. "Look, we all need to get some sleep. It's been a long day." He plucked the brochure from Philip. "I'll do some research tonight."

Daisy started laughing. "Look at your cat, Philip. She wants you to play fetch."

"For the millionth time, she's not *my* cat. What is that in her mouth?" He reached down and wrestled what appeared to be a small twig from between Aurora's sharp teeth. He held it up and turned it around. The bark had come off, and the smooth wood beneath looked like it had been carved, with small humps and indentations along one side.

"Strange," Miles said, taking it from him. "It almost looks like a big key. Where did she find it?"

"How am I supposed to know?" Philip said. "Outside, I guess."

"She hasn't been outside in a while," Miles said, mesmerized by the odd stick.

Logan wasn't paying much attention to the discussion about the stick. He was busy thinking about the only thing he hadn't told the others—the information Evy had whispered to him when she hugged him, about Sam's use of the beans one other time. It probably didn't mean anything, but then why did she whisper it just to him? Should he tell them anyway, though? Was his loyalty to her and to the memory of his grandfather, or was it to his friends? Couldn't it be to both?

Logan shifted his attention back to his friends, and that's when he finally took a real look at the stick. "Hey, that looks familiar," he said. "I thought it was in my suitcase."

"You carry sticks in your suitcase?" Philip asked.

"Just the one," Logan replied, taking it from Miles.

"I must have missed that on your mom's packing list," Miles joked. "It's cool, though. I can see why you wanted to bring it."

"Actually," Logan said, turning the stick over in his hands, "I just grabbed it to have something from the factory grounds. I didn't get a chance to look at it too closely. She can play with it, though." He tossed the stick back down to Aurora, who reached for it with her paws. AJ snatched it up first, though.

"This isn't a stick," he said. "It's a map!"

"What?" they all replied. Daisy stopped jumping.

"Where did you find this?" AJ asked Logan.

Logan thought back to his search. "I think it was by some trees, down by the picnic tables. Yes, it was right before I ran into Miles."

"Strange place for something like this to turn up," AJ said. "Primitive people used to carve maps of their local geography onto wood—coastlines, usually." He held the stick up for them. "On this one, these bumps look like hills or some other natural formation, and these two long lines indicate the edges of the property, and then this little nick would mean water, like a stream or a brook."

Miles gasped. "Could it be a river?"

"I don't see why not," AJ said.

Miles flew over to the drawer where he'd stashed his stuff and dug to the bottom to find the Map of Awe. "Look!" he said, spreading it out next to the stick. Now it was everyone else's turn to gasp. The features on the map lined up exactly with the carvings on the stick!

"I don't understand," Daisy said. "Logan found this random stick, and it happens to match this map perfectly?"

Miles shook his head. "The stick isn't random. When I was going through Sam's box, a few kids were playing around there and they tossed in some sticks and rocks. I must have tossed that one out with the others, and Logan found it!"

As they looked from one item to the next, there was little doubt that must have been what happened. Daisy asked what they were all wondering. "Could this be where the beans are?"

"There aren't any cocoa trees on the map, though," Logan said, peering at it. "And really, that picture could describe anywhere."

"I'll compare the geography to satellite photos," AJ said, "and then cross-reference it with reports of meteorite findings. Although if I had to guess, most of those aren't noticed or reported. There didn't happen to be a return address on this box, did there?"

Logan and Miles looked at each other. "There was," Logan said. "I don't remember it, though."

"I didn't even look," Miles admitted. "But I'll ask my parents to check. No, wait—they're away for a few days, celebrating not having to take care of me!"

AJ turned to Logan. "You said you did get a look at the address?" Logan nodded.

"Okay, if you're willing, I can help you remember. Everyone get ready for bed, and then we'll give it a try."

"You expect us to sleep when all this exciting stuff is happening?" Miles asked.

"I do," AJ said. "I plan on running for chaperone of the year."

"I'd vote for you," Logan said, patting him on the shoulder.

Half an hour later they were all tucked into their bunks, showered, teeth brushed. The cat had been fed. AJ turned out the lights, then sat on the floor between the bunks. The streetlights from the parking lot glowed yellow through the window shades.

In her upper bunk Daisy rolled over to face the wall. She threw her noise-canceling blanket over her head and turned on her vid com. The message light from the outside lab had been blinking for an hour, but she'd been ignoring it. She couldn't do that forever, though. It was time to hit Play.

"You're not going to hypnotize him, are you?" Miles asked. "This kid in my class's friend's brother once went to a birthday party in River Bend, or Willow Falls, where a hypnotist made this boy cluck like a chicken every time he heard the word *balloon*. That kid's probably *still* clucking!"

"No hypnotizing," AJ promised. "I just want you to think back to when you first saw the box. Of all the senses, smell is a very strong memory jogger. What did the room smell like?"

"I hope you weren't in the bathroom when you got the box!" Philip said. AJ shushed him, but the others giggled.

"Marshmallows," Logan said. "And butter and vanilla."

"Good," AJ said. "Focus on the smell, and put yourself back in the room. Feel the seat you were sitting on, feel the box in your hands, see the color of the ink on the address. Do you remember what you were thinking when you saw it?"

Logan nodded in the dark. "I remember thinking that it was strange that Henry claimed it was too smudged to read, because it wasn't. Guess now I know why he said it. He really *couldn't* read it."

"See yourself looking at the address and thinking about what you just told me. What else do you remember?"

Logan thought. "I remember thinking that I didn't know anyone who lived near there. And then I thought maybe it was a present from Daisy."

"Great, okay, we're getting close. Now try to put yourself right back inside your body when you were looking down at the address. Pretend you're reading it for the first time."

Logan squeezed his eyes tighter and tried to focus on each line of the address. There were only two. He tried to glide his eyes past the numbers. It was the town and street that mattered most. Suddenly it was right there in front of him. He could see the address! It wasn't a street—it was a post office box! He lurched up in bed, his head skimming the bottom of Philip's bunk. "I've got it!"

Miles shouted, "Yay!" Philip snored. Only silence came from Daisy's bunk.

Without talking, AJ turned on his vid com and handed it to Logan. The screen lit up, so he could see well enough to type in the dark. He typed in what he remembered, hoping it was accurate.

"Great job," AJ said. "You get some sleep and I'll get to work." He tucked away the vid com and headed toward his bedroom. As he passed by Daisy, he saw she had a noise-canceling blanket over her head. Even though he couldn't hear anything, he had the distinct impression she was crying.

CHAPTER EIGHTEEN

Daisy stumbled up to the Control Center and crawled into the passenger seat. "What time is it?" she asked, rubbing her eyes. "Why are we driving in the dark? Did you sleep at all? Did you find out anything? Where are we going?"

"Are you going to just keep asking questions," AJ asked, "or do you actually want me to answer any of them?"

"Answer."

"Okay, then. The time is five thirty in the morning. We're driving in the dark because we have a long way to go, and we'll have the road to ourselves for a little while. I slept about four hours. Yes, I found out lots of stuff. And as for where we're going, we're going to find those beans, and we're going to cure Logan's scars and restore Henry's eyesight."

Now Daisy was wide awake. "We are? You believe it, then? You're such a skeptic. I saw you roll your eyes in Evy's dressing room."

"Saw that, did ya?"

She nodded. "What changed your mind?"

He pointed to his nose. "I took a bite of the Magic Bar. I can smell now."

Her hand flew to her mouth. "No! Really?"

He nodded.

"That's amazing!" she said. "And a relief. I was afraid I'd have to send you off to a farm where all the broken-down spies go."

"Funny," he said.

She grinned. "I try. But seriously, that's great."

He glanced sideways at her, then back to the dark road. The sky hadn't yet begun to lighten. AJ took a deep breath. "Daisy, I need to say something. I know you got the official test results back last night, and you learned for sure that I'm not your brother. I know you were crying about it, but you don't need to worry. I'll always have your back, and you can always hide my toothbrush."

Daisy focused on the white lines on the road. A minute passed before she spoke. "You're right," Daisy said. "You're not my brother. And you're right, I was bummed about it. But that's not why I was upset last night. One of the pairs I tested really *did* turn up a positive match. The computer didn't give us false information."

AJ let up on the gas. "Are you serious?"

Daisy nodded. "Trust me, I freaked out, too. I have news that will literally change the lives of people I care a lot about. Maybe you and Grammy and my parents were right. Getting involved with friendships outside the mansion is dangerous."

"Well, it's too late now, Oopsa. You're in deep. When are you going to share the results?"

Daisy sank down in the seat. "I was thinking maybe you could? You have that whole charm thing going on."

AJ laughed. "Nice try."

"Yeah, figured that was a long shot."

They rode in comfortable silence for another half hour. The rearview mirror gradually began to glow with reds and oranges as the sun rose behind them. Daisy read a book, did some yoga in the back bedroom, wrote to Courtney and Grammy. The boys didn't start waking up until close to nine, by which time the highway had turned to back roads and then to dusty lanes that spit up brownish-red dirt at them. They didn't pass many other cars or people walking, but those they did pass always did a double take. Daisy had rejoined AJ upfront. "Um, Harvey's kind of attracting a lot of attention, ya know?"

"I agree," AJ said. "I'll pull over soon. We're almost there."

Miles shuffled up to the front and plopped down in the seat behind Daisy. They'd just entered a small downtown area with a few shops, a gas station, and a restaurant or two. He shaded his eyes from the sun. The colors looked muted in this town—the awnings over the shops, the posters in their windows. Maybe it was the bright sun that did it, but everything looked old. He could swear a tumbleweed rolled by. "Where *are* we?"

"We're at our first stop of the day," AJ said. He made a right turn past a tiny post office and drove a few blocks down the street before pulling into the parking lot of a small playground with a pond, two ducks, and a rowboat moored to a metal pole.

"Hey, Miles," Daisy said, "remember when you were allergic to rowboats?"

When Miles didn't reply, she said, "Still too soon for jokes?"

"Maybe a little," he admitted.

"What's going on?" Philip asked. He and Logan had already gotten dressed.

AJ parked the RV as far away from the road as possible, then turned to face them all. "Welcome to the official middle of nowhere. Otherwise known as the post office where Frank Griffin receives his mail."

Everyone started talking at once, Philip the loudest. "What? How?"

"I was able to remember part of the return address!" Logan said. "If we find Frank, we have another chance at finding the beans!"

"I get that," Philip said. "But when people don't want you to know where they are, they don't put their real return address on a package." He turned to AJ. "Surely you would know that."

AJ nodded. "Indeed I do. I didn't say we were at the address he wrote on the package. When people who aren't in the lying game have to do something shady, they tend to do it only in small increments. Like in this case, they might change the name of the state or lose one number of the zip code. Frank did both. He likely made up the P.O. box number, too, but we won't know that until we get inside. We'll arrive before the mail is distributed and hope he shows up." He looked at his watch. "We have twenty minutes."

"Wow," Logan said. "How did you figure out where to go if the return address wasn't real?"

Daisy chuckled. "Entry-level spy work. You treat it like a secret code. We've been figuring this stuff out since before we could tie our own shoes. Plus the clues about the camping trip and the meteorite crash would have made it easier to narrow down." She turned to AJ. "I could have helped, you know. Remember how good I am at deciphering codes?"

"You needed your beauty sleep," AJ replied.

"I'm beautiful enough already." She knew AJ's competitive streak had kicked in. He'd wanted to be the one to figure it out.

"So I guess this isn't where the tree is, then?" Miles asked. He peered out the window. "Everything looks very flat here. No big hills or rivers or fog. I don't think that pond is the River of Light."

AJ shook his head. "I checked all our satellite and topographical records and don't see any geography that fits. Still, this town had a definite meteor strike about a hundred years ago. If we don't find Frank today during our stakeout, we'll take out the metal detector and get to work."

"We're on a *stakeout*?" Logan and Miles asked, grins spreading across their faces. "Does that mean we get to use the disguise closet?"

"It does," AJ said. "Within reason." He had to call out now because they'd already started running down the aisle. "I don't want to see any firefighters or clowns. No stilts!"

Daisy shook her head at AJ. "You know we don't really need those disguises for this. Maybe Logan, but that's it."

"I know," AJ said. "But look how happy it made them."

"You're turning into an old softy," she said, elbowing him.

"I have a strange feeling about this, Oopsa," he admitted, lowering his voice. "I think this Franklin guy is hiding more than he's letting on. He's been out of the public eye for a very, very long time. People don't do that without a good reason."

"Let's go find out," she said. "I'd better check on them back there."

When Daisy got to the disguise closet/storage room, she was pleased to see the boys dressed in matching Scout uniforms and baseball caps. Sure, they wore wigs under their hats that looked totally unrealistic on them, but no one had a fake mustache or a pillow stuffed under his shirt, so she was grateful for that. She was able to talk all but Logan out of the wig. He showed her how it covered a lot of his scars and said that Franklin might know about them. Evy hadn't been surprised when she saw them, or if she had, she'd hidden it well. Daisy couldn't argue with his logic.

As they headed out of the room, Daisy noticed Miles was limping. She stopped. "Did you hurt your foot?"

He nodded. "I was working on my explorer badge, and my compass broke, and I turned the wrong way and stepped into a rabbit hole. These guys tried to stop me, but they were busy fending off a swarm of wasps. I think I twisted my ankle."

She tilted her head at him. "I'm sorry, what?"

Miles grinned. "I'm in character as a Scout. That's my backstory."

"Nice," she said appreciatively. "You could put a rock into your shoe. That would change the way you walk without you having to remember to limp."

"Good one!" Miles said. "I'll try that next time I'm in disguise on a stakeout."

"What are you going to be, Daisy?" Logan asked.

"I'll be Girl Mailing Letters," she said, snatching the pile of fan-mail replies from the end of Philip's bed. "These ready to go out?"

Philip nodded. The only good thing about having to give up the winning title for the Harmonicandy was that maybe the fan mail would stop.

Miles insisted on limping the few blocks to the post office. Actually, he only limped when he remembered, which was about every six steps. AJ had a backpack with him, and Daisy had the letters, but the boys only brought plastic canteens filled with water, which they slung over their shoulders to complete the look.

"Okay," AJ said when they got to the corner. "You three stay outside, sit on the curb, and look innocent while Daisy and I go inside. Come in if you see anything suspicious."

"Like what?" Miles asked.

"Like anyone who looks like he could be Frank," Daisy said. Bells tinkled over the door as she pushed it open. The small crowd inside talked pleasantly to each other while they waited for the postal worker to finish loading the mail into the metal boxes. A quick scan told them that no one of the right age and gender was among those picking up their mail.

Since they weren't picking up any mail, they had to stall, or else people would wonder why they were hanging out there. Daisy spent much longer than necessary deciding which of the ten different designs she wanted for her stamps. One of Philip's fans had been thoughtful enough to include a stamp and return envelope, but she still had three more to buy stamps for. Should it be the yellow flower stamp, the cartoon teddy bear, or the flag? She chose one of each so it would take the clerk that much longer to get them all.

Meanwhile, the boys busied themselves by drawing in the dirt with sticks and trying to guess each other's pictures. Logan's were always candies, so they were the easiest to figure out. So far they hadn't seen anyone who looked grandfather-aged. An actual Scout walked by with his dad and saluted them. They gave an awkward salute back.

Inside, AJ searched the numbers etched on the doors of the boxes. The number Frank had written for his return address didn't even exist at this post office branch. AJ tried to see if he could spot Frank's name on any of the envelopes the mailwoman was sorting, but she kept her back to them.

"Hey," Daisy whispered, "what if he gets his mail delivered to his house instead?"

AJ shook his head. "In rural towns they usually don't deliver to people's homes. Plus, judging by how secretive he is, he likely wouldn't give out his real address. If he shows up today, we've got him."

In the end, it went down differently. Once the mail had been sorted and the tiny mailbox keys spun in their locks, the crowd gradually slipped out to the street with their mail. "Okay," AJ whispered to Daisy. "He didn't come in the first wave. We'll have to stall longer."

"Is there anything else I can help you with?" the clerk asked them when everyone else had left.

"My sister and I are considering opening a post office box here," AJ said, flashing a warm smile. "Could you explain to me all the steps to do that?"

"Certainly," the woman replied. "I'll go get you the paperwork." She disappeared from view, and they were alone.

"We'll just have to watch the place from across the street," Daisy said. "He could come anytime, right?"

AJ nodded as the bells tinkled and an older woman with a baby rushed in, followed by a younger woman in dust-covered jeans and a flannel shirt that seemed too warm for the weather. The older woman just dropped some letters in the mail slot in the counter and left. The younger one lifted a key from her key chain and tried to get it to fit inside one of the P.O. boxes. She turned the whole key chain upside down and tried again. It wouldn't turn. "Do you want me to try?" AJ asked, bending down.

"Sure, give it your best shot," the woman said, handing him all the keys. The mail clerk came back with a form and a pen. When she saw them trying to get the box open, she laughed. "Maggie, that was last month's. He's up here now." She pointed to a box on the top row. Maggie sighed and took the key from AJ. "Thanks anyway. My boss changes P.O. boxes like most people change their ... actually, I don't know anything people change as often as he changes boxes!"

Without waiting for a response, she inserted the key in the lock of the correct one and opened it to find it empty. She didn't seem surprised and swung it closed. "See you tomorrow," Maggie called out to the clerk and gave a wave as she pushed open the door.

Daisy snatched up the form and showed it to the clerk. "We'll bring it back if we decide to open one." They hurried out. "Turn on the charm," she whispered to AJ.

"I'm on it," AJ replied, thrusting his backpack at her. "Juice, tape, screwdriver."

"Got it."

"What's going on?" Miles asked. Daisy swung the backpack onto her shoulder as AJ took off after the woman in the dress.

"C'mon," Daisy said, ushering the boys farther down the street in the direction the woman was walking. AJ had just caught up with her. They could tell the two were chatting, but they couldn't hear their words. "Did you see her get out of a car?" Daisy asked the boys.

Miles nodded. "It's that tan one over there." He pointed across the street at a parking lot with two cars in it. He'd seen the woman cross the street and go into the post office, but he hadn't paid much attention. They'd moved on from Name That Dirt Picture to Name That Cloud, and Miles had just been about to suggest that the large one overhead looked like a cross between Philip and a dragon.

AJ and the young woman suddenly turned to go into a sandwich shop. "That guy's good," Daisy whispered. "Okay, follow me. Don't do anything weird."

The four of them crossed the street, Philip whistling, Logan humming, Miles limping. Daisy just sighed. They reached the car and she ducked behind it, pulling them down with her. Fortunately, the rear of the car faced a brick wall, so they didn't have to worry about anyone coming up behind them.

The boys watched as Daisy pulled a fairly large silver pouch out of the backpack, followed by duct tape and a screwdriver. Before they could even ask, she'd taped the bag underneath the rear of the car, completely out of view unless you were crouching like they were. "Good," she said after testing to make sure it held firm. "One more step. Just let me know if they're coming."

Philip peered around the side of the car. "All clear," he reported.

Daisy gave a nod, then used the end of the screwdriver to poke a tiny hole in the very front of the bag. A thin pink liquid trickled out onto the pavement, then stopped as the liquid settled in the bag. Satisfied, Daisy put the tape and tool away. "When she drives away, we'll be able to follow the trail on the road without sticking too close. This is a great tailing method when you think you've been spotted or when you're driving an enormous beast like Harvey."

"Why not just stick a tracking device under her car?" Philip asked. "You must have them."

"Of course we do, but sometimes low tech is better than high tech. Especially when you don't know what kind of descrambling or cloaking devices the suspect has."

Philip looked doubtfully at the old car. "She doesn't seem too high tech. There's still a cassette player in her car."

"Oh, all right," Daisy snapped. "Sometimes low tech is just more fun, okay?"

Philip put up his hands. "You're the boss."

Daisy smiled. "That's what I like to hear. Now c'mon, AJ's charm isn't going to hold her forever."

"But why are we following her, anyway?" Logan asked as Daisy hurried them all back across the street. "Unless she's much better at disguises than we are, that's *not* Frank."

"We think she might work for him," Daisy explained. "Hopefully she'll lead us to him."

AJ joined them back at the RV ten minutes later. "Her name is Maggie Bellush," he announced. "She works as an assistant curator for a museum. That's pretty much all I got. But since there are no museums within a hundred miles, I figure she's here on temporary assignment."

Daisy tilted her head at him and tapped her foot expectantly.

"Fine," AJ said. "Her accent tells me she's from the South but has lived here at least five years. She likes her new job, but the bags under her eyes tell me she is stressed out and not sleeping enough. And judging by the number of sandwiches she just bought, she's expecting it to be another really long day."

"That's it?" Philip joked.

"Well, she used to be a swimmer in college—the broad shoulders told me that—and her birthday is in April."

"Let's just go," Miles said, "before AJ tells us her dog's name and

443

her shoe size." AJ could do in real life what he'd only pretended to do with Daisy at the rest stop. Although he'd been right about the geocachers!

"Pogo and size seven," AJ said, and then shrugged. "What can I say? It's a gift."

They gave Maggie a ten-minute head start and then rolled out into the street. The pink juice left a nice, clear trail to follow, and in the places where the dust had already blown over it, Harvey's heat-detecting sensors picked it up. The juice contained the same chemical as the heat dots AJ had left for Daisy to follow in the woods at the camp. "Oh yeah, don't drink that stuff if you see it again," she warned the boys.

Logan and Miles kept checking out the back, half hoping someone would be following *them* as they followed *her*. Then maybe they'd get to see how well the oil slick or thumbtacks or plumes of white smoke worked! They could tell by the glances between AJ and Daisy that they were worried the juice might run out soon.

The houses they passed began to get farther and farther apart until eventually all they saw were fields dotted with weeds and patches of dried grass. After another five minutes the road made a wide curve, and when it straightened out again, they found themselves facing a dead end. "Hold on, everyone," AJ said as he pressed hard on the brakes. They came to a quick halt without even feeling it.

A small, plain house sat at the end of the street. It reminded Logan of what a house would look like if a kid drew a picture of one with a crayon but forgot to put in windows. The car they'd been following sat in the short, narrow driveway, the only indication that the house wasn't abandoned.

"Do you really think Frank Griffin lives here?" Miles asked. "I mean, this guy's famous—like, superfamous. He should live in a huge mansion on the ocean."

"He's a famous *mapmaker*," Philip said. "That's not like being normal famous."

"I think we're about to find out," Daisy said. "Look." They watched as the front door of the house swung open. Maggie from the post office stepped out, hesitated only a second, and then began walking over to the door of the RV. They all jumped up, not knowing what to do with themselves.

"We can't let her in," AJ reminded them, as if they needed reminding.

"Should we hide?" Miles asked.

"I know!" Logan said. "Escape route through the fake toilet!"

Philip shook his head. "Aurora used it by mistake. I haven't had a chance to clean it yet."

Logan and Miles wrinkled their noses.

"I'd better go talk to her," Daisy said. "We'd be having this conversation sooner or later."

Daisy pushed the front door open just wide enough for her to slip outside. Before she could shut it, Aurora sprang off the top step and barreled through it. The door swung wide open before Daisy could do anything without risking hurting the cat. The timing couldn't have been worse. Maggie looked straight up into the RV and saw all of them gaping at her.

Her gaze swept over each of them, and then she asked, "Is one of you Logan Sweet?"

Chapter Nineteen

ogan looked at Daisy. She seemed as surprised as he was, but she gave him a nod. He squared his shoulders and said, "I'm Logan."

"Mr. Griffin would like to see you," Maggie said. She began to walk back toward the house. Logan didn't move. When she realized he wasn't behind her, she turned around. "Your friends can come, too."

"We'll be right there," Daisy said, hurrying back inside. She closed the door without waiting for an answer. "Okay, guys, listen up. This guy is clever; we knew that already. He's managed to avoid detection for decades, yet he knew we were coming—or Logan, at least. We don't know why he chooses to live all the way out here, away from everyone, or why he changes his post office box number every month, or why he sent Logan that package in the first place and whether he knew all it contained. My advice is to let him do the talking. See what he reveals about the past before asking him about the beans. AJ and I will be able to tell if he's lying."

Everyone nodded in agreement. "He seemed friendly in his letter," Logan pointed out.

Daisy nodded. "And we'll hope he's friendly in person."

Miles grabbed the map, contract, and bean and put them in

his backpack. It didn't feel safe to leave them behind, and they might need them for proof. He grabbed the Magic Bar, too, just in case. Daisy had sealed it in a plastic container that supposedly could withstand the weight of an elephant standing on it. Maggie was waiting by the front door for them. Up close Logan could see she was younger than he'd first thought. Probably not more than twenty-five. She gave AJ a pointed look. He simply smiled and said, "Small world."

"Indeed it is, Mr. Dinkleman." She pushed open the door, and they walked into the strangest house any of them had ever visited. Logan didn't have much to compare it with, since he'd only been to maybe four other houses in his whole life, but he knew this was unusual. Philip hadn't been inside many people's houses, either, but he had stayed at a lot of hotels. Daisy and AJ were not easily surprised by anything, but even *they* couldn't help turning in circles, trying to absorb it all. Miles literally had to hold on to a wall. His legs shook, and everywhere he looked, something amazing appeared. It was like the feeling he got when stepping into a bookstore, or a library, or a candy shop. Only multiplied by a hundred. He'd just stepped into a map-lover's dream.

Maps of every size, color, and dimension surrounded them. Paper maps hung on windowless walls; three-dimensional maps and globes sat on shelves and tables, and others hung, suspended by wires, from the ceiling. Miles could see maps of countries, cities, mythological worlds with made-up names; of palaces, gardens, and underground tunnels. His eyes landed on a giant full-color map, spread on the floor, of someplace called Smoranthia. In the center of it, islands with jagged coastlines dotted an ocean so vivid that Miles felt like he could swim in those turquoise waters. He knelt before it, his finger almost unconsciously tracing a journey around the islands and toward a mountain peak that rose majestically from the water.

"Do you want to know how I made those islands?" a man's voice asked from behind Miles. Immediately following the question, Miles heard his friends begin to talk all at once, almost shouting. But entirely unable to tear his focus away from Smoranthia, Miles made his head move up and down in response.

"An old pipe broke and left some water stains on the ceiling tiles in the basement," the man said with a chuckle. "I took down the tiles and traced the stains."

Miles stared at the coastlines of the utterly realistic islands, imagining them as simple water stains. "Brilliant," he whispered reverently. He slowly turned around, expecting to see an older version of the man in the Opening Day photograph, the one who the computer couldn't identify. Instead, he got another huge shock.

He was looking at Henry—a thinner, taller, glasses-free Henry. He realized why his friends had been reacting so strangely. He scampered backward, knocking into things and trying desperately to right them while still moving. His backpack softened the blow as he slammed against a wall.

"You'll have to forgive the mess," the man who was Henry—but not Henry—said. "I don't get many visitors."

Maggie chuckled. "That's an understatement. I was the first visitor. You guys are the second. Before you ask why it's so cold in here, it protects the maps."

Daisy collected herself and stormed over to the man. "Who *are* you?" she demanded.

"Forgive me," he said. "I thought you knew. I'm Frank Griffin."

She crossed her arms. "Then tell me, Frank Griffin, why is it that you look just like our friend Henry Jennings? Well, minus fifty pounds."

"Fifty pounds?" Frank said, shaking his head. "Henry should really cut down on those marshmallows."

"That's what I said," Philip called out.

Daisy tapped her foot at the man. "Well?"

"Henry's my brother. My younger brother, to be more precise. People used to think he was the older one, though. He always wants to take care of people, you know?"

"Yes," Logan, Miles, and Philip said at the same time. Daisy ignored them and continued to look Frank up and down. Surprises on missions made her irritable. "Why the name change?" she asked. "Running from the law?"

"Daisy!" Miles admonished.

Frank chuckled. "That's okay, it's a fair question. When I was a kid and reading my fantasy books, I used to take on the names of the mythological creatures. I wanted a last name that would look cool on maps. Frank Griffin sounded better than Frank Pegasus."

Miles thought Frank Pegasus sounded even cooler, but he didn't want to be rude by mentioning it.

AJ stepped forward. "His change of name must be why the computer couldn't find him, or Henry, for that matter. Maybe it couldn't decide which was which. Plus neither of them got out much." He looked around at the house. "Obviously."

Maggie suddenly clapped her hands and said, "All righty! Not sure what any of you are talking about, but let's get this show on the road. We've got a lot of work to do. Frank told me you need him to update a map of your town or something? A school project, was it?"

"Um . . . ," Logan said, stumped.

Frank jumped in. He put his hand lightly on Maggie's shoulder. "Why don't you take the rest of the day off. We can continue cataloging the collection tomorrow." He started leading her toward the door.

"But there's so much to do," she insisted. "I need to finish sorting the road maps, and the climate maps are a mess, and you still won't tell me if you have more in the basement, and—"

"It's all right," he said, opening the front door. He grabbed her purse and sweatshirt from a hook on the wall and put them in her arms. "Thank you for your dedication, but it'll all still be here in the morning."

She stood there, clutching her stuff. "But the museum is expecting me to—"

He closed the door before she could finish. "She'll be fine," he assured them. "She works too hard anyway. Museums don't pay nearly enough to have to deal with eccentric old cartographers like myself. Now, Logan, come, let me see you."

Logan hesitantly stepped forward. Frank knelt down and peered at Logan carefully. This close up, Logan could see subtle differences between the men—Henry's skin had more of a pinkish tone to it, while Frank's was tanner, with more wrinkles. His white hair didn't stand up in the air quite as much as Henry's. But still, the resemblance was freaking him out. He made a mental note to talk to Henry about leaving out important details of his life, like the fact that *he had a brother*. At least his crying over the letter made a little more sense now.

"Are you and Henry in a fight or something?" Logan asked.

"Why would you say that?" Frank asked, still peering at him like he was a specimen in a museum.

"He was in the room when your box came, and when he saw it was from you, he started to cry. So I thought maybe you guys weren't in touch or something. I don't know. We're confused about a lot of things."

Frank shook his head. "Henry and I aren't in a fight. He cried because of what the letter meant."

"Didn't it mean what it said?" Logan asked.

"Yes, of course. But it also meant what it didn't say."

Logan heard Daisy groan from the other side of the room. Her plan to let Frank explain things wasn't going very well. Logan knew it wouldn't be long before that plan went out the window. Before he

450

could ask Frank to explain, Frank spoke again. "You don't look as much like Sam as I'd heard."

Logan didn't know how to respond to that. He'd never thought he looked much like his grandfather in the first place. But of course he hadn't known him as a kid. Logan remembered the wig and yanked it off, along with the cap. "Not really blond," he said.

"Ah," Frank said, clasping his hands together. "There's my old friend!"

Logan couldn't help gloating a bit. "See, Daisy? The disguise worked."

"Nah, I knew it was a wig," Frank said.

"You did?"

Frank nodded. "You three aren't Scouts, either, I'd bet."

"How do you know that?" Philip said. He looked down at the badges on the sides of the vest he wore. "I may have just earned my wood-chopping badge." He paused and twisted the vest to see it better. "Or my outdoor-survival badge."

"Did you, now?" Frank said. "Good! You may need that skill. Not the tree-chopping one."

Daisy finally couldn't take it anymore. "Speaking of trees, Mr. Griffin," she said, "I know you all promised never to reveal the location of the beans that Sam used to make the Magic Bar, but Henry tricked Philip into using the chocolate, and you sent that box to Logan, so we're hoping that means you're going to tell us." She crossed her arms. "But you can start with how you knew we were coming here."

Frank raised an eyebrow. "Is she always this bossy?"

The question got a resounding *yes* from all the others in the room.

Frank got to his feet. "Let's talk outside. It's a bit stuffy in here." He headed toward the front door. Miles lagged behind, reluctant to leave.

Frank noticed his hesitation. "I'm sure a budding cartographer such as yourself would have a keen interest in my home. But don't you want to join your friends? Daisy might have exploded already."

Miles wondered how Frank knew things about them. He *did* want to go outside and hear what Frank had to say, but his feet had become rooted to the spot. He'd never felt more drawn to a place in his whole life. He was afraid that if he walked out of this house and got swept up in whatever would happen next, he wouldn't get back here. He couldn't leave yet.

Frank held his gaze another second, then walked back to the door and called out, "Give us a few minutes in here to talk maps." He grabbed the bag of sandwiches that Maggie had left on a front table and tossed them out to AJ, who was closest. "Have a snack. They were always meant for you." He closed the door and turned back to Miles.

"I knew I wanted to make maps since I was a boy and my father read me *Gulliver's Travels* and *Treasure Island*. I would stare at the maps for hours, days even, losing myself entirely in them."

Miles nodded, wide-eyed. "For me it was the maps of Middle-earth in *The Hobbit* and *The Lord of the Rings*. I'd like to make maps like that one day, like you do. Yours are amazing." Miles stopped short of telling Frank about the prints of his hanging in his room. He was already fanboy-ing enough.

"You would think the maps I make for the fantasy novels would allow me more creativity than the regular geographic ones, right?" Frank asked. He began strolling around the room, straightening out one map, rolling up another. Miles kept almost tripping over himself as his feet went faster than his eyes.

As they neared the giant Smoranthia map, Frank continued. "That is not always the case. With the fantasy novels, authors usually have very specific ideas for how their imaginary worlds should look. My job is to try to make them look real, so the reader gets

452

more immersed in the stories. But a traditional mapmaker still has great power. When drawing a map with limited space, it's up to us to decide what to put in and what to leave out. Life is like that, too. We just hope we make the right choices as we go along." He ran his fingers through his hair, making it stand up just the way Henry's did.

Frank seemed momentarily lost in his own thoughts, so Miles allowed his eyes to dart around again. His gaze landed on a small copper globe, and he stepped forward on shaky knees. "Is that the...Hunt-Lenox Globe?" He held his breath for the answer.

Frank nodded. "It's on loan. I was hired to make a replica. I actually made three." He chuckled. "Don't tell anyone."

Miles squinted to read the now-famous Latin words. In an awed voice, he recited, "*Hc Svnt Dracones*," adding in the vowels so it sounded like *hic sunt dracones*. "Here be dragons," he said reverently.

"Very good," Frank said. "You know Latin?"

"I know a little. I like languages."

"As do I," Frank said. He gave the globe a gentle spin. "Imagine a time when mapmakers really didn't know what was beyond the place they were mapping. Now we can get accurate maps of anywhere in the world from satellites, radar, and even sonar. Not many places remain truly hidden."

"But some still are, right?" Miles asked.

Frank gave a small smile. "Maybe one or two. Are you ready to go outside now?"

Miles nodded, took one last wistful gaze at the globe, and let Frank lead him out. "Thank you for your time," Miles said. "I can't tell you how grateful I am."

As soon as he stepped out the door, his friends came running from the side of the house, their faces flushed. Logan was holding the metal detector. Maybe they'd found something!

"Hi!" Miles said. "Did you find a meteorite? You guys won't believe all the cool—"

"Hold that thought," Daisy said. She turned to Frank. "We'd love it if you could tell us why we just watched our cat disappear into thin air."

It took Miles a few seconds to process what she'd said. Aurora had *vanished*?

Frank let out a deep sigh. "Evy warned me about that possibility. Cats are never fooled."

"*Evy?*" Daisy said, not expecting that answer.

Frank nodded. "Who else do you think could hide Paradise?"

CHAPTER TWENTY

A number of strange things had happened in the fifteen or so minutes when Frank left Daisy, Logan, AJ, and Philip out on the lawn while he talked all things maps with Miles. Daisy's first reaction to being essentially banished from the house had been to be really, really annoyed. That was her second and third reaction as well. But calmer minds prevailed (Logan's), and she eventually decided to be useful and distributed the sandwiches.

Philip, for one, didn't mind the break. The clutter in the house had caused a vein to throb above his left eye.

They sat on the curb across the street so they could get a clear view of the door when it opened. To the left and right a few evergreen trees added a tiny bit of warmth and life to the place, but from what they could see of the sides and the backyard, it was just more dirt and patchy grass. It was the type of house you'd drive right by and barely remember having done so. The perfect place to live for someone not wanting to be noticed.

They ate their lunches and watched the door. For entertainment, they watched Aurora run across the lawn, chasing something only she could see. To keep herself from storming back into the house, Daisy stood up for a closer look.

"It's like a ball of light or some kind of reflection," she said as a tiny light winked out in front of her and then appeared again a little distance away. It took a minute, but they eventually figured out that when Philip turned his wrist, the reflection of the sun caught the face of his watch and bounced off it. They'd all seen this effect before, of course, with other reflective items, but the resulting beam of light had to hit a surface—usually a wall—in order to become visible. This wasn't hitting anything.

"Maybe it's doing that because of the meteorites that you said fell in the area?" Logan suggested to AJ. "Like, there are strange metals in the ground attracting the light? Or maybe it's buried pirate gold! Can we take out the metal detector now?"

AJ glanced at the still-shut front door. "Not sure what Frank would think about us searching his lawn, but I'll go get it. If we find buried pirate's gold a thousand miles away from any ocean, we'll split it with him."

"No, we won't!" Daisy called after him. Clearly she hadn't fully recovered.

AJ brought the metal detector back from the RV and handed it to Logan. He also brought the stick map. If anyone knew about odd maps, it would be Frank.

Logan flipped on the switch and hadn't even pointed the coil toward the ground when the screen started flashing and beeping. "Whoa." The whole thing bucked like it was about to jump out of his hands! It turned sideways, toward the house. He felt like he was walking a very strong dog that was trying to catch a cat!

He looked to his friends for help, but they were running to the side of the house, in the same direction the metal detector was pointing. Surprised that they'd walked away, Logan's grip loosened. The detector flew out of his hands and began slithering along the ground like an awkward metal snake.

Logan gathered up his strength. Too bad he didn't have any

Gummzillas with him. Wrestling with a sugar dinosaur and then eating it always made him feel powerful. He ran after the bucking and squawking detector, tackled it, and, after fumbling for a few seconds, managed to switch it off. He picked it back up and joined the others. Out of breath, he asked, "Did you guys see that? This thing has a life of its own!"

In response, Philip pointed a shaky arm at a spot a few feet in front of one of the evergreen trees. At first Logan couldn't tell what he was supposed to be looking at. He squinted. *Aurora?* The back *half* of Aurora? They heard her give one final *woof-woof*, and then she was gone. *Poof.* Empty space.

Random sounds flew from their throats as they all instinctively scrambled backward. Philip and Logan actually fell and sat there, stunned and breathing hard. Logan still gripped the metal detector in one hand. Holding something solid helped keep his brain from screaming.

Daisy started forward again. AJ grabbed her arm. "Don't," he said. "Not until we know what's going on."

"I won't get too close," Daisy promised. A good spy always tested her environment carefully before leaping into the unknown. She picked up a stone and tossed it in the direction where they'd last seen Aurora. Daisy didn't want to throw it exactly where the cat had been, in case she was still there and just invisible. The stone landed with a *plop* on the ground. They all stared at it. "Hmm," Daisy said, her mind buzzing as it tried to make sense of what was happening. "Okay, I'm done waiting. It's time for Frank to answer some questions."

AJ and Daisy helped a shaking Philip and Logan off the ground, and they half ran, half stumbled to the front of the house. That's when they first heard Frank use the word *paradise*, but it wouldn't be the last.

"I don't know what you mean about paradise," Daisy said as

they rounded the corner of the house. "But we just watched an entire animal slowly disappear. Where is our cat? Is she all right? I don't want to hear that it was just a trick of the light."

"But that's exactly what it was," Frank said calmly. "A trick of the light. Only a very complex, well-thought-out, state-of-the-art trick of the light." He took a breath. "Understand, I've never told anyone any of this. Not ever. In the beginning we were much more low tech with our camouflaging techniques. Planting fake foliage, putting up fences. We experimented with painting huge canvases, but they couldn't stand up to the weather for long. Eventually, with the satellite technology these days, we knew we had to protect it from the eyes in the sky as well, so we had to get more creative."

A memory of a lesson on camouflaging taught by one of the experts her grandmother had brought in flitted around the edges of Daisy's mind, but she couldn't bring it into focus. Philip and Logan were still trying to get their hearts to stop pounding. Miles hung on every word. "I just want to be sure—are you talking about hiding the place where the beans grow? The one the contract said you would protect?"

"Of course," Frank said. "How many paradises do you know of?"

"None," Miles admitted. "Well, Logan's candy factory is as close to paradise as I ever thought I'd get."

"You're about to get closer," Frank said.

"Wait, what?" Philip said, coming out of his stupor. "It's right *here*? And you're actually going to show us?"

Frank nodded. "Henry made that inevitable when he gave you the chocolate to use for the contest. Right or wrong, he set you on this path. That decision gave him many sleepless nights over the last five months, I'll tell you that. He did it without asking Evy or myself first, which went against the contract. But that's my little brother for you, always looking out for me even when I'm not looking out for myself."

They all stared at him, struggling to make sense of it all. He looked from one confused face to another and sighed. "Guess I'm going to have to start from the beginning. Come, show me the exact spot where you last saw your cat."

They walked to the side of the house, and Logan pointed a few feet in front of them. "It was right around there."

Frank walked over to the area, kept walking, and disappeared.

"Taerg s'oelilaG tsohg!" Miles shouted, and he fell to the ground as his legs gave out under him. A symphony burst into Philip's head. That used to happen to him when he was young and something upset him and he needed to escape his thoughts. His brain was protecting him from having to process this. Logan's legs wobbled, but he leaned on the metal detector like a cane and managed to stay upright.

Then Frank's head appeared. *Just* his head. "Well?" he asked. "Aren't you coming?"

They all gaped at the floating head until the rest of Frank's body appeared. "Okay, that wasn't very nice of me," he admitted. "Couldn't resist. I've never had an audience before, you understand."

Frank held out a hand to a shaking Logan. "Let me show you. Everyone hold hands, and then, Logan, you take mine." Although reluctant to let go of the security of the metal detector, Logan lowered it to the ground. He helped Miles up, gripping his hand tightly. Philip took Miles's other hand. Then Daisy took Philip's and AJ's.

Frank led them toward the backyard. One by one they each gasped as the person in front of them vanished. Then they were in darkness. Utter, complete darkness.

"Hold tight," Frank instructed as they stumbled forward and

slightly downhill. They were already holding on so tightly they'd lost feeling in their fingers.

"Where are we?" Philip choked out. Fear—not only of the whole disappearing thing but of the oppressive darkness—squeezed his throat muscles together.

"Don't worry. We are only a few steps from where we were on the side of my house," Frank assured them as the downward slant grew steeper. "An elaborate system of mirrors bends the light around objects in my yard. Your cat didn't disappear. She simply walked between two of the mirrors. As did we. Houdini made an elephant disappear this way—we're hiding something a little bigger than that."

"Mirrors!" Daisy exclaimed. "Of course!" Now she remembered what that expert had spoken about—the art of hiding large objects in plain sight. She'd never seen it done in real life, though.

Logan felt relief wash over him, knowing that his entire view of reality—a reality where cats and people were *not* able to disappear—would not need to be revised. His breathing slowed down for the first time since Aurora vanished.

"We're in an underground tunnel," Miles said. "Right? The ground is slippery, and the air smells like it does on a rainy day, but much stronger."

"You are correct," Frank said. "I love the smell, don't you? So earthy and rich. All the silica and minerals in the dirt here make the odor even stronger. The high humidity in the air releases oils in the stone. That's what you're smelling."

"But there's barely any humidity in this part of the country," AJ said. "Even your grass doesn't grow."

"That's true," Frank said. "You can see the effects of the infrequent rain in the front yard. But in the backyard, things are a little different."

As he said the word *different* and took one more step, a blast of heat made them suck in their breath. It must have been at least forty degrees hotter now. It felt hotter than the Tropical Room, hotter than anyplace any of them had ever been.

One more step forward and the darkness faded as abruptly as it had fallen upon them. Walls of rock and sandstone rose up high on either side of them to form a narrow valley or canyon, the far end of which only Daisy could see. They blinked as blinding sunlight reflected off the powder-white sand that covered the ground. A stream of blue water flowed like liquid glass down a narrow riverbed, and the smell of chocolate filled their noses.

Frank spread open his arms. "Welcome to Paradise!"

CHAPTER TWENTY-ONE

I n the years to come, whenever they talked about that first moment, they found they couldn't raise their voices above a whisper. For Logan, the image that always came to his mind had to do with the tree. Not the lone cocoa tree itself, which stood in the center of the valley with its lush green leaves and low-hanging blue pods and branches as wide as he'd ever seen. No, what first caught his eye were the hundreds—or maybe even thousands—of butterflies perched on the branches, gently flapping their red wings. He had a feeling a few of these had followed his grandfather back home to the factory once and started families.

The butterflies made a big impression on Miles, too. When he spotted them, he knew for sure that he never needed to look for another sign. All those times during the contest he'd hoped to see a red-winged butterfly, hoped it would tell him if he was on the right path, if he had made the right choices. And now here they were. *All* of them. One of the sentences he'd copied before the trip floated back to him. *Be where you are.* A sense of great peace unfolded inside him. He was *exactly* where he was supposed to be.

For Philip, the butterflies—which he assumed had stopped in this hidden valley on some kind of migratory path—didn't hold much interest. The blue pods underneath them did, though. He dropped Daisy's and Miles's hands (which he was embarrassed to admit he'd still been clutching) and stumbled toward the tree. He was unused to walking in sand, thanks to his lifelong distaste for the beach, and he couldn't get the hang of lifting his feet high enough. The sand covered his shoes and weighed him down. His knees and palms landed over and over again in the soft, hot sand, but he didn't really mind. An almost childlike glee had fallen over him. The beans really existed, and he had an idea. He counted ten ripe pods on the tree, and maybe more underneath the dense piles of butterflies. Ten pods would yield about four hundred beans. Plenty.

As for Daisy, while the cocoa tree and the butterflies and the tall cliffs and the sand made her very happy, she found herself drawn to the water. She kicked off her sneakers and ran. A pro at running on sand, she sprinted past Philip and the cocoa tree, past the hammock strung between two clumps of palm trees, past a sitting area complete with a circle of wooden chairs, each with its own striped umbrella, and straight to the river's edge. She quickly understood that the water only appeared blue because it reflected the thin gash of sky above. Up close it was completely clear, allowing her to see all the way to the moss-covered pebbles on the bottom.

"Wait till you see that in the dark," Frank commented as he walked past her. By the time she tore herself away from the water to question what he meant, he was gone. She turned from side to side but didn't see him anywhere.

"He left," AJ said, strolling up to her, his shoes dangling from one hand.

Logan and Philip hurried over, both barefoot and carrying cocoa pods under each arm like oversized blue footballs.

"Frank's gone?" Logan asked, fearing the answer.

"He walked past Daisy toward the mouth of the stream," AJ said, "and then he just did that disappearing thing."

"Should we try to find him?" Logan asked. "I bet if we threw some sand around, we'd hit the mirrors, right?"

Daisy thought for a minute, then nodded. "We could do that. But I don't think we should. I think he's testing us."

AJ nodded. "I think so, too."

"Testing us to see if we'd take the beans?" Philip asked. He'd expected the pods to be heavy, but they couldn't weigh more than a pound each. "I think we may have failed already, then."

Logan shifted uneasily. He was so used to helping harvest ripe cocoa pods from the trees in the Tropical Room that he honestly hadn't thought twice about it. And these just twisted right off the trunk. At home Avery had to cut them off with a very sharp knife.

"I don't know if you're supposed to take them or not," Daisy said. "But I think Frank wants to see if you can follow in your grandfather's footsteps. If you have what it takes to protect this place."

Logan lost his grip on both pods, and they slipped from beneath his arms. Daisy's hands flew out and she caught the pods easily.

"Not exactly right," Miles said, joining them. "I don't think Frank wants to see if Logan can protect this place. He wants to see if *all* of us can protect this place. Together." Then he added, "Well, maybe not *all* of us. Sorry, AJ."

AJ tilted his face to the sun. "Hey, I'm just here for the ride. I mean, the drive. You know what I mean."

"How do you know that?" Philip asked.

Miles leaned back again and spread his arms wide. "Look around. We're the only people he's let in here. A mapmaker's job is to reveal the world, right? And here he was, all these years, hiding something so amazing, keeping it safe from the outside world for reasons that we don't entirely know yet. That has to mean something."

"It doesn't have to mean that he's handing the place over to four kids," Philip argued.

"I think Miles is right," Daisy said. "Frank's leaving. He's donating his maps to Maggie's museum. In his head he's already gone."

Philip was suddenly struck with a thought so outrageous that he momentarily swayed on his feet and sank onto the wet sand by the riverbank. "Are you okay?" Daisy asked, looking at him with concern. Philip Ransford the Third *never* intentionally sat in dirt. The others huddled around him.

"Logan," Philip said, trying to keep his voice from shaking, "do you know whose idea it was for your father to host a group for the candymaking contest? Had he ever done it before?"

Logan shook his head. "I know my grandfather had hosted kids a few times before I was born, but my dad never did till you guys. Why?"

"I think your grandfather was trying to find replacements even back then. The right combination of four people. But they never worked out. We proved we could work as a team when we made the Harmonicandy, and that's why Henry gave us the chocolate. He knew our individual skills, and he knew what we could do together. He was just doing what Sam would have wanted."

They all knew he was right. They felt it in their bones. It was their destiny to be there together. Figuring out what that meant for each of them would have to wait, though.

"What if we could move the tree?" Philip suggested. "Like maybe bring it to the Tropical Room and even grow our own beans there. And then this could be, like, a tourist destination. Isn't it kind of selfish that they kept it to themselves all these years?"

No one had an answer to that. But Logan could speak to the part about the tree. "We can't move the tree. Cocoa tree roots go really, really deep. You can only replant a seedling, and then it would take between three and five years before the first crop. We'd also need to move the soil." He turned to gaze at the magnificent tree.

He was able to see more of the tree itself now, since many of the butterflies had flown off and were either flying lazily around it or sitting along the riverbank. Besides its unusual height and width and fullness and bright blue pods, something else was just… *different.*

"I expected there to be more cocoa trees here," Daisy said. "I wonder why whoever planted it just planted one."

"Yeah," Miles said. "And whoever did plant it, we know it was growing cocoa pods at least fifty years ago, when Sam and the others found it."

"That's it!" Logan said. "That's what's been bugging me that I couldn't put my finger on. The tree is way too old! Cocoa trees only grow fruit for, like, twenty-five years." He grabbed for one of the pods Daisy had laid on the sand. He needed to know if the cocoa beans were still good. They couldn't possibly be. The pod slipped right through his hands, and he gave a little groan of frustration before kneeling down in front of it instead.

He ran his hand over the long ridges. The skins of cocoa pods were usually thin enough to break open with just a stick. This one was thick, though, and they would need a knife. Daisy realized what he was trying to do, grabbed it, and broke it right in half.

"Thanks," he said. The milky-white film that covered the beans looked normal and healthy. They all reached into a section and began pulling and scraping the outer layer off the beans. It didn't take long until they had their answer. Out of the forty-six beans in the pod, forty-five of them looked like normal brown cocoa beans, except they crumbled as soon as they hit the air. The forty-sixth bean was bright blue, firm, completely round, and smelled like chocolate.

In unspoken agreement, they repeated the process on the other three pods, with exactly the same result. Only one surviving bean in each—the blue one. "All that work to grow a pod," Miles said, "for only one bean to live."

"I don't understand how it's possible to smell like chocolate if it wasn't roasted," Philip said, rolling one of the beans in his hands. "It wasn't even fermented yet, and that's when the chocolate flavor first starts to come out. Right?"

Logan nodded.

"It must be the microbe in the beans," Daisy said. "Like it roasts it from the inside out?"

They all stared at the bean in Philip's palm, imagining that process. "I'm starting to see why they felt they needed to hide this place," Philip said, glancing back at the tree. There wouldn't be four hundred beans in the harvest; there would only be forty. He pressed the bean into Logan's hand. "Eat it," he said fervently. "Go on, eat it, hurry."

Logan stared at him. "What do you mean? Why?" He caught the others exchanging glances. "I don't understand."

"Your scars," Daisy said. "They faded a little. I mean, a few of them did. After you ate some of the Magic Bar."

Logan was stunned. "They did?" He knew the bar had made him feel different, and he knew Evy could tell, but he thought that was just from his reaction about it.

"On your arm," Daisy clarified. "But we think if you eat these, maybe all your scars will get better."

His head spun. Could he do this? *Should* he do this? All that trouble the tree went to in order to produce only a few beans. Other people needed this much more than him, like Henry. These were supposed to be for *Henry*.

As much as Miles wanted to help Logan, he needed to say something first. "Before you decide, remember what Evy said. They stopped making the candy bar partly because they couldn't be sure it didn't have other side effects. And as we know, they haven't used them since then."

Logan hesitated, but the time had come to tell them what Evy had whispered. "They did use the beans once more. Evy told me they'd given Sam their permission, but she didn't tell me what he wanted them for...." He suddenly blinked. A memory sliced through his head of a stick figure drawn with crayons and the strong smell of chocolate where there wasn't any chocolate. More memories hit him, ones long buried and forgotten.

"Are you okay?" Miles asked with concern.

Logan nodded. He swallowed hard. "I know what he did with them. He gave them to me when I was in the hospital, after the accident. He made a game out of it. He made me a get-well card and told me every night to eat a magic bean and I'd get better. As bad as my scars might be, I think he saved my life."

Daisy reached out and squeezed his hand tightly. "I think so, too." The medical reports made more sense now, but she didn't see the need to tell him that.

Tears filled Logan's eyes. "But then why didn't he use them to save himself when he got sick? He could easily have gotten more of the beans."

"Because they'd agreed not to," Miles said. "In the contract, remember? You can't protect something if you're using it for selfish purposes. And you know, maybe it's not so powerful that it can keep someone from dying when it's their time. Henry obviously didn't use it for his eyes, either."

"You're right, he didn't." Logan blinked away his tears and pressed the bean back into Philip's hand.

"Are you sure?" Philip asked. "It would make your life so much easier and..." He trailed off. He couldn't tell Logan that it would also make *him* feel better. He'd probably never stop feeling guilty about what had happened that day, even though he knew it was an accident. If Logan's scars were gone, maybe Philip would finally be able to let it go.

"I'm sure," Logan said. "But thank you." He smiled. "If Frank really does ask us to be the new guardians of this place, that means we'd be bound by the same rules. And you know what it also means?" His eyes glinted. "It means Henry *wouldn't* be anymore."

CHAPTER TWENTY-TWO

The only way Logan knew he'd fallen asleep in the hammock was that Miles was now shaking him and saying, "Wake up! You fell asleep in the hammock." Logan, disoriented in the darkness as he tried to sit up, found himself unable to stop from spinning over into the sand. "Oomph," he said, spitting out a mouthful of sand and grinning. "It's real. We're still here. Did Frank come back?"

Miles pulled him to his feet. "No, but look at the aurora!"

Logan's eyes hadn't adjusted yet to the darkness, which had an odd reddish-green glow to it. "I don't see her. Is she still curled up under the tree? She's probably hungry. I'm hungry. Are you hungry?" He patted down his pockets, hoping for a stray Icy Mint Blob, but they were empty except for that lollypop stick he'd stuck in there when he was cleaning up the hallway at home. It must have gotten stuck in his pocket when he'd emptied them that night.

"Not the cat," Miles said, tugging Logan's sleeve excitedly. "The *real* aurora! The northern lights!" This time Logan tilted his head back, then farther back when he saw something in the sky he'd never seen before or even dreamt could be real. A green glow shimmered and undulated above them, as if someone were shaking a picnic blanket out in the wind or pouring a bucketful of chocolate on the stars (if the chocolate happened to be green!). Every few seconds a smudge of red would peek out from behind it. "But didn't that astronomy lady say they're hard to see in the summer?" Logan asked Miles, who stood transfixed next to him, grinning from ear to ear.

"It must be something about this weird microclimate," Miles replied. He couldn't wait to tell his parents and Arthur and Jade about it. He pulled out his vid com to take a video, but it wouldn't work. That was odd. Well, it wasn't like he would ever forget it anyway. He tucked the device away and set about fixing the image in his mind so he could play it back for himself as he lay in bed at home.

"Did part of it hit the ground?" Logan asked a minute later. "And turn blue?"

Miles forced himself to look away from the sky and down at Logan. "What do you mean?"

"Look at the stream. It's glowing." Miles turned around and squinted in the dark. His jaw dropped when he saw the water. For a second he thought maybe the lights actually *had* come down to the ground, although he was pretty sure that was impossible. As they got closer, they could hear Philip, Daisy, and AJ laughing.

"Look at your legs!" Daisy shouted at Philip.

"Have you seen your hair lately?" he replied. "Blue is a good look for you!"

Miles stopped short. "Is that Philip...in the *water*? Well, his legs, anyway?"

Logan rubbed his eyes. Daisy and AJ were floating in the stream, fully dressed, while Philip sat on a rock and dangled his legs in the water. The scene would be bizarre enough if the water wasn't glowing bright blue, but it *was* glowing bright blue.

"Hey, guys!" Daisy called out to them, waving a blue arm. "There are tiny glowing things floating all around us!"

"We can see that," Logan replied, hurrying to the edge. The water looked alive, pulsing with thousands of points of light. In the midst of it, Daisy and AJ resembled some kind of ethereal race of people with glowing blue skin and hair. Aurora walked by, the tip of her nose glowing. She must have tested out the water.

"They're called dinoflagellates," AJ explained. "Tiny single-celled creatures that make their own light."

Miles pointed to Philip. "You realize you're basically wearing fish right now." Philip jumped up faster than they'd ever seen him move. He slapped at his legs in an effort to wipe off the invisible sea creatures.

"Do you think it's the River of Light from the map?" Logan asked.

Miles nodded. He'd been thinking the same thing. "It has to be." He ran back to get the map from his backpack and returned. The river shined a good amount of light on it, but the flashlight on the vid com would have helped a lot more. "Hey, Daisy," he called into the water, "did you notice our vid coms don't work?"

Tiny blue lights glittered on her skin and hair as she climbed out onto the sand. "Vid coms always work," she said confidently. But Miles was right; nothing happened when she tried to turn hers on. "AJ?"

AJ shook his head. "They must be blocking the signal somehow. Kind of like the radio quiet at the telescope."

Daisy frowned as she pressed the button repeatedly. She didn't like feeling so cut off. "Frank has the tech to scramble our signals? Doesn't seem possible."

"Maybe it's not Frank," Philip said, picking the last glowing dot from his knee. "It could be whatever's in the ground—those microbes that hitched a ride on the meteorite that landed here. Maybe they're supermagnetic or something."

Logan looked from the river to the tree. "Are they the same thing that's in the water?"

AJ shook his head. Blue lights flew out from his hair. "If our equipment can't pick it up, whatever arrived on that meteorite is a thousand times smaller. Like on the subatomic level."

"Frank might not know exactly what makes the beans different," Miles said, tilting the map toward the blue light, "but he knows a lot more than we do. I say we try to find him." His stomach growled. The others had eaten lunch, but he hadn't eaten since breakfast. "No one has any food on them, do they?" he asked.

"Sorry," AJ said, feeling like a bad chaperone. "I should have planned better. Next time we get trapped in paradise, I promise I'll be more prepared."

"I know it's hard to believe," Logan said, "but we're still behind the house, right?"

A line from Frank's letter came floating back to him. Frank had said something about "smelling it from here." That must have been a reference to how close he was to the source of the beans! Frank could definitely smell the chocolate from his backyard—and this whole thing actually *was* his backyard! Logan leaned over and tapped the map where it said *FOG to the North*. "*FOG* doesn't stand for real fog. It stands for Franklin O. Griffin's initials!"

Miles laughed, his hunger momentarily forgotten. "You're right!" He loved it when maps surprised him! He turned around in a circle, trying to get his bearings. "Frank's mapmaking skills have come a long way since he made this one. He didn't label which way is north. I knew I should have kept that plastic compass."

Daisy tried her vid com again, but it still didn't work. She looked up at the sky and shook her head. "Too narrow a swath of sky for me to see the North Star. Time to go old school. Philip, hand me your watch."

He hesitated a second, then undid the clasp and laid it in her hand. "Reggie gave this to me for my tenth birthday. You're not going to smash it, right?"

"Look on the bright side. At least we're not teasing you for still wearing a watch that doesn't do anything except tell time." Then she said, "No one happens to have a toothpick on them by any chance?"

No one did. She turned to Logan. "Do you think it's okay to take a really thin stick from the tree? I haven't seen any branches lying on the ground."

Logan hesitated. "I don't know. . . . It kind of feels weird to break something off."

Daisy figured he would say that. She knew what he meant.

"Too thick?" AJ asked, holding up the stick map.

"Yes."

"Would this work?" Logan asked, pulling the Leapin' Lolly stick from his pocket.

She grabbed it. "That would be perfect."

Philip and Miles both did a double take when they saw the lollypop stick, but before they could ask about it, Daisy began walking away, and they scrambled after her. She placed the watch on a rock next to the map, where the light shone the brightest, and held the stick straight up from the center of the hands. She turned the watch slowly until the resulting shadow cast by the stick lined up with the hour hand. She knelt in front of it and pointed in the air at the halfway mark between the shadow and twelve. "North," she declared.

Miles took the map and adjusted it accordingly until the path of the river lined up with what they could see in front of them. Something jumped out at him that he hadn't noticed before. The *W* and *E* of the word *AWE* were now lined up with where *west* and *east* would go on the compass. He sat back on his heels. "Frank *did* label the directions, right in the title!"

They all turned to face where the house should be. Basically sand as far as they could see. "Remember," Daisy said, "it's only an illusion. We know the house is there. Somewhere. Follow me and stay close."

Daisy did a variation of the rock throwing when the cat disappeared, except this time she tossed sand ahead of her. When it didn't hit a mirror, she took a step and waved the others forward. Miles's stomach growled louder with each step, but he didn't complain. They kept doing this until Daisy got frustrated and called out, "Franklin O. Griffin Jennings, if you can hear us, Miles is about to gnaw off his own foot!"

"I figured you might be getting hungry," said a voice. Frank appeared out of the darkness only a few feet ahead of them. One more toss of sand from Daisy and they would have found the way in! He carried a tray piled high with something delicious-smelling.

"Where did you go?" Philip demanded. He was never one for small talk.

"I hope you'll forgive my disappearing act," Frank replied with a tentative smile. "I wanted you to experience this place on your own. And I wanted to see your famous teamwork skills for myself. Well done!" He looked at Daisy and AJ, who were still glowing blue. "I see you've found the bioluminescent water. Isn't it marvelous?"

Daisy would have agreed that the water was awesome, because it totally was, but she was annoyed to have come so close to finding their way out. Just for spite she tossed some sand in the air in front of her. It *still* didn't hit anything. She grumbled.

Frank chuckled. "Don't feel too bad. You got much farther than I'd ever expected you to. Now, I know you must have a lot of questions." He motioned for someone to grab the blanket tucked under his arm. Daisy grumbled but took it and laid it out on the sand. Frank set the tray down and Miles pounced on the food. "Chocolate pizza!" he said in amazement.

"Sam gave me his recipe years ago," Frank said. "I thought you might appreciate a taste of home. And don't worry—I didn't use these beans to make the chocolate. Got it from the supermarket, like anyone who *didn't* have a blue-cocoa tree growing in their backyard would."

They dug in gratefully, even Philip, who had passed it up during the contest.

"Only the right combination of people could have landed on my doorstep," Frank said while they wolfed down the food. "If I didn't think you had what it took, I wouldn't have let you in." He paused before saying, "We were barely twenty. Sam had been working for years on his chocolate recipes, never finding the exact right thing that would allow him to open the factory. Then suddenly we find this amazing tree in this wondrous place that's the closest thing to paradise any of us has ever come across. It felt like destiny. It felt like the beans were waiting for us. It still feels that way. Only now they're waiting for you."

The four of them paused in their chewing and exchanged looks. They'd been right. He really *was* going to ask them to take over. If they hadn't been so hungry and it hadn't tasted so good, they'd have put down the food.

Frank continued. "We thought protecting the tree would be a twenty-five-year commitment at most, but as you can see, the tree is still going strong. Those butterflies? They're here *all* year. I've been the caretaker almost fifty years now. It's ironic, really. The only place on Earth I could never map is in my own backyard."

Logan pointed to the map Miles had laid on the blanket. "Other than this one, you mean?"

Frank shook his head. "I didn't make that one. Your grandfather did. We couldn't risk taking photographs of the place, and Sam loved to draw." He pointed to the rock with the numbers. "Instead of signing his name, those are the house numbers where we all grew up."

"Those numbers came in handy," Daisy said under her breath.

To Logan, Frank said, "I hadn't expected to send it until you were eighteen, but Henry moved the timeline up when he gave Philip chocolate made from the beans for your contest." Frank sighed. "He may have been looking out for me, or he may have been looking out for you. I don't know. Maybe he worried that if he didn't give you a reason to stick together, you might have drifted apart by the time I was ready to show you."

No one said anything for a minute as that thought sank in. Would they have drifted? Daisy couldn't meet anyone's eyes. If anyone pulled away, it would have been her. She'd come so close already. She swallowed hard and said, "Evy told us Sam knew he shouldn't be using the beans to make the Magic Bar. What did she mean by that?"

"*Tantum ad tempus*," Frank said solemnly. "It's Latin for 'only at the right time.'" He got a faraway look in his eyes, then said, "Those words are carved on the base of the cocoa tree. Over time the soil has grown over them, but when we arrived, they were clear as day. The only other sign that anyone else had ever been here was a carved stick we found below the words."

AJ held up the stick map. "This one?"

Frank smiled. "That would be the one. To the others, it was just a carved stick. Finding it gave me the confidence to believe I could be a mapmaker."

"Do you want it back?" AJ asked, holding the stick out to him.

Frank shook his head. "I had it for fifty years. That's long enough."

Miles cleared his throat. "If it's up for grabs, can I keep it for my collection?"

Frank nodded. Miles wrapped it carefully in some napkins and tucked it into his backpack. He couldn't wait to show it to Arthur.

"You have no idea who carved the words or why?" Daisy asked. "In all this time, no one ever came back?"

Frank shook his head.

Philip was busy running the words *only at the right time* over and over in his mind. How were they to know when that was? Who had the right to determine it? "What do you do with the pods when they ripen?" he asked.

"Nothing," Frank answered. "We learned early on that if we didn't pick them, they just hung there on the tree forever. They never rot or drop."

Logan shook his head in bewilderment. He'd spent his life around cocoa trees. This one sure was different. He started to say, "Philip and I op—" but Philip cut him off by asking, "Does the aurora come out every night?"

Frank tilted his head back to admire the sky, as did Miles. Logan shot Philip a questioning look. In response Philip just shook his head and mouthed the words, "Don't tell him."

"Why?" Logan mouthed back, but Frank had started talking again. "The aurora does come almost every night. We figured it has to do with all the magnetic energy in the valley."

"There's a microbe from space in the beans!" Miles blurted out. Frank seemed stunned as Miles shared what little they knew.

When Miles was done, Frank took a long breath. "You've learned more about our little tree in a week than we did in five decades. I knew you were the right four—sorry, AJ, hadn't really factored you in."

AJ held up his hand. "It's all good."

"I don't expect an answer right now," Frank was quick to assure them. "What I'm asking of you is too much. I need you to come to it on your own. When you are eighteen, I will pass you the keys to the kingdom, as the expression goes, and then it will be up to you to do as you please."

"You're getting ready to leave," Daisy said. She didn't frame it as a question.

"I am," he admitted. "Not today, though, and not tomorrow. I am old now, and I've been blessed with this view for a long time. It's time for me to go see the world I've been mapping all these years. The mirrors are very challenging to maintain, even with Evy's help, and with all the new technologies, it's getting almost impossible to keep my life hidden from outside eyes."

"You've done an excellent job in that department," Daisy muttered under her breath.

"What if you didn't have to wait?" AJ asked suddenly. "I'm eighteen. I can check on the place when you leave. I have access to certain . . . equipment. I can set up cameras inside the house and outside in the backyard, as you call it. With twenty-four-hour surveillance and early-warning alarm systems, you won't need someone to live here full-time."

Daisy jumped in. "And I can improve on those trick mirrors of yours. Not that they aren't impressive. They're truly a work of art. But I know someone who has developed a very special hologram projection technology. We can program it so that this whole area looks like anything you want it to. The scene can change each season."

Frank's eyes filled with tears, making him look even more like Henry. "You would do all that?"

AJ and Daisy nodded. Daisy turned to her friends. "I mean, if we're really all in?"

Logan's heart thumped. So much for not having to decide yet. He'd never been much of a planner. But here he was, sitting in Paradise, a place of such natural beauty that it filled him up inside and threatened to burst out. And whatever that tree was meant to do, even just knowing of its existence was a gift that only a few people had ever gotten. He knew his grandfather had trained him early on for this task. And Henry had faith in them as a team. But did that make him brave enough to take on this responsibility?

Instinctively, Logan and Miles turned toward each other. They both recognized the mixture of fear and excitement in each other's faces. They turned to Philip. His face showed only determination. Wordlessly, Philip stuck out his hand, palm down. With a glance at Logan for reassurance, Miles leaned over and placed his hand on top of Philip's. Logan looked to Daisy. They locked eyes as he added his hand to the pile. Daisy laid hers on top. They stayed like that for a long time.

Then Philip blurted out, "We opened four of the pods!" and broke the spell. They all pulled their hands away, laughing.

Philip told a surprised Frank how only one bean survived in each pod, and it was one of the blue ones. He described how easy it was to pull them off the tree, but Frank zoned out for a minute, totally lost in his thoughts. He didn't ask anything else about the beans, just smiled wide and said, "Well. This has been quite a day! Anyone have to use the bathroom?"

Four hands shot up. They all turned to AJ, who was gnawing on a pizza crust. He looked up and shrugged. "I'm trained to hold it in. I can go days."

Daisy shook her head at him. "I'm glad I missed that class."

A little over an hour later, Frank waved one last time, closed his front door, and turned the lock. Miles carried away an armful of maps, an expertly crafted replica of one of the world's most famous globes, and a smile a mile wide. Daisy carried a bag with the four newly picked beans so they could study them, and Philip carried a sleeping cat, which he pretended to be annoyed at having to do.

Logan and AJ had already returned to the RV to send off the nightly messages to everyone's families. Frank had given permission for the kids to tell their parents everything if they wished, but they'd have plenty of time to figure out how to approach that in the years to come. For now they wanted to keep it to themselves.

AJ made them take showers while he planned the route to Philip's Talented Kid contest. He'd have to drive well into the night, so the coffeepot was on. Daisy joined him in the Control Center, her damp hair pulled back into a braid.

"Thank you," she said. "For what you did back there. It's a huge commitment to something outside of our spy lives, which I know goes against what you believe in."

"You made an even bigger commitment," he pointed out.

She glanced out the front window at the house. The lights had gone out for the night. "I know." She turned back to him. "Are we crazy?"

"Probably. But these kids grow on you, don't they?"

Daisy nodded. "They do. But you must have a better reason than that. I know! It's so you can have a free vacation under a palm tree anytime you want—am I right?"

"That's it," AJ agreed. "You found me out."

"Seriously, though. Why?"

AJ glanced behind them to make sure the boys couldn't hear. Miles was shouting about Philip hogging the shower, and Philip was shouting back about finding glowing things in places that shouldn't glow, so Miles would just have to wait.

AJ leaned closer to Daisy. "I did it for Henry," he said, registering her surprise. "He told all the parents that he and I have been spending a lot of time together these last few months. He wasn't lying. After we kept running into each other at different doctors, we decided to start keeping each other company at our appointments. We had some good talks. He didn't tell me about any of *this*, of course." He gestured out the window at the completely invisible slice of Paradise only a few hundred feet from Harvey.

"Even though he knew I wasn't really your cousin, he never let on about my job. He treated me as *me*, and you know how rare that is for us. And he confided in me that he thought of Logan and you and Miles and Philip as his family. I could tell he'd spent his life protecting the people and places he loved. So when he asked me if I would take you all on this road trip, I couldn't say no."

Daisy laid her hand on his arm. "You *could* have said no. But you didn't. That's a big difference." She gave a squeeze and stood up. "Make sure to pull over if you get tired. There's one more thing I have to do before I go to bed."

AJ held up his giant coffee mug to show he was well caffeinated. "Plus you don't have to worry. If Harvey senses the driver drifting off, a blast of water sprays up into my face."

Daisy smiled. "Why am I not surprised?"

She waited until the boys had gotten settled into their bunks before she climbed into hers.

"Look," Miles whispered, pointing up to the skylight. "You can't see the aurora from here at all."

At the mention of her name, the cat gave a little meow. "Hey!" Logan said, opening his eyes. "The cat made a cat sound!" He'd just finished going through his gratitude list in his head—which had gotten a lot longer in the last few days, with all the new people they'd met and once-in-a-lifetime experiences they'd had. He quickly tacked the cat to the end of the list.

"Did she finally realize she's not a dog?" Daisy said, propping herself up on one elbow.

"It's not just the cat who's different after today," Miles said.

"Between the view of the Milky Way last night, and all the amazing things we saw today, and what we know is in our future, I feel more a part of the world now. Do you know what I mean?"

Philip's only response was a snore that shook his bunk.

"I think it's because now you know places like Paradise exist," Logan said, his voice slurring with impending sleep. "Or at least that *this* place exists."

"Exactly," Miles whispered. He lay back on his pillow contentedly. "I feel like a whole new Miles."

Daisy took a deep breath. "Hold on to that feeling," she said, "because I have to tell you something that's going to be a shock." She glanced over at Philip and Logan. They were both asleep.

Miles rolled over and leaned his head over the side of his bunk. "Lay it on me," he whispered. "New Miles can handle anything."

"Okay," she said, lowering her voice. "Here goes." She took a deep breath and let it out steadily. It was now or never. "You know your friend Arthur?"

Miles raised his eyebrows. He hadn't expected Arthur to be brought into the conversation. "Sure. What about him? Is anything wrong?"

Daisy shook her head. "Not wrong. Just . . . well, to put it bluntly, he's not just a friend. According to Harvey's computer and an independent DNA-testing laboratory, he's also your father's brother— or, you know, your uncle." She felt the relief wash over her. "Phew, it feels good to finally tell you!"

Miles gaped at her and whispered, "Taerg s'oelilaG tsohg! Niaga!" Then he rolled right off his bunk and onto the floor.

AJ glanced in the rearview mirror. "I knew I should have put seat belts on those things."

CHAPTER TWENTY-THREE

After he recovered enough to climb back into his bunk, Miles made Daisy explain three times how the DNA from where Arthur had licked that envelope matched Miles's own DNA from the cheek swab. Once the computer found the match, it analyzed it further. Twenty-five percent of their DNA turned out to be the same, indicating an uncle-nephew relationship.

Further, they shared the same Y chromosome, which is only passed down from the paternal line. That proved Arthur was related through Miles's dad. Arthur didn't share any of Miles's X chromosome, which would have come from his mom's side. Miles had read a book about genetics a few months ago, so once his brain was able to focus on the explanation, he pretty much got it.

"Do you think Arthur knows?" he asked Daisy.

"Yes," she said without hesitation. "He's probably waiting for the right time to tell your father."

Miles thought about how Arthur always invited the whole family on their geocaching outings, and how well the men got along when he visited the house. But now that he really thought about it, Arthur did seem a little nervous each time. Miles had just thought he was shy. "I wonder how he found us in the first place."

"Well, I'm only guessing now, but maybe his parents—your dad's biological birth parents—finally told him they'd given a child up for adoption, and Arthur went through the adoption records and found him. Or maybe Arthur came across some old paperwork and questioned them. Either way, I don't think it was a coincidence that he moved to Spring Haven. He wants to get to know you guys."

"Thanks, Daisy," Miles said. "For telling me, and for doing the test." He leaned over the side of his bunk to see her. "Wait, are you sleeping with the bag of beans?"

She slid the bag under her pillow. "What beans?" Then she flipped over to face the wall. "'Night, Miles, sleep tight! No falling out!"

Miles awoke in the morning to Daisy's face two inches away from his.

"Yikes!" he cried, groping around for his glasses. "Personal space! How long have you been watching me sleep?"

"An hour," Daisy replied casually.

"An hour!"

"Quite fascinating, really. All the breathing and the tossing and the turning."

"You need to get more hobbies." He glanced up and down the aisles. He and Daisy appeared to be alone.

"I just wanted to make sure you're okay," she said. "This is going to change a lot of things for you and your family. Hopefully in a good way, of course. Anyway, it was a pretty big bombshell to drop on you last night. Even in your super-Zen-like state."

"Yeah, New Miles seems to have gone away," Miles admitted. "I'm worried about how my dad will take the news."

"I bet Arthur knew it would be hard and figured it'd be easier on your dad if he got to know him first. It was a good idea. And you'll get your Zen back," Daisy promised. "When you get stressed, just close your eyes and picture yourself in Paradise, and you'll start feeling relaxed again. By the way, we totally need to come up with a better name for that place. Calling it Paradise doesn't do it justice."

Miles grinned. The idea of getting to name a place like that would be the highlight of his naming life. It would have to be something ancient and exotic and hidden, like Shangri-La or Atlantis. When they got home, he could ask Arthur to help him with the research. Or rather, *Uncle* Arthur!

"How crazy is this whole thing?" Miles said. "I thought I had to go on the road to find my father's family, but they were right there in front of me in Spring Haven!"

"Ah, but you wouldn't have found out about it if you hadn't gone on the road. So I am officially taking all the credit. Well, most of the credit."

"I'd expect nothing less," Miles replied as he stood up to stretch. "So where is everyone?"

"AJ's asleep in his room. He had to drive all night to get here, and after the competition we have a long drive to the last candy store. Logan went inside with Philip to check in."

Miles hurried to the window. Sure enough, they were parked in front of a high school. A huge banner above the front door asked,

Are YOU the Nation's Most Talented Kid?? Come find out TODAY!

"We've gotta go!" Miles shouted. He slipped into his sneakers and began running down the aisle.

Daisy grabbed him by the back of his sleeve. "Um, I think you're forgetting something?"

He turned around. She pointed at his superhero pajamas. He reddened. He needed to have a talk with his mom about more appropriate sleepwear now that he was entering the teen years. He quickly dressed and brushed his hair and teeth and was halfway out the door before he noticed that Daisy wasn't behind him.

"I'll meet you in there," she said. "I just need to finish something up first."

The front lobby looked exactly as Miles would have hoped. Everywhere he turned, competitors practiced their talents. He spotted lots of kids playing musical instruments. Identical twins twirled fire-tipped batons. A boy deftly twisted a Rubik's Cube blindfolded, and another pulled a live rabbit out of a hat. One girl tap-danced, one did backflips down the hallway, and someone in a rainbow wig sang "Old MacDonald Had a Farm" while juggling eggs. Miles hoped they were hard-boiled.

"Isn't this great?" Logan asked, appearing at his side. "All this excitement reminds me of the candymaking contest. But without all the candy!" And with a lot more strangers. He didn't say that last part out loud, though. He didn't want Miles to worry about him being uncomfortable.

Miles nodded enthusiastically as he took it all in. "Where's everyone's favorite violinist?"

"He went to practice somewhere he could hear himself think. Those were his words, not mine."

"Figured that." He wanted to tell Logan about the stuff with Arthur, but right now was about Philip. The news could wait until after the competition.

"Wow," Daisy said, joining them, "this place is crazy!" She held a large poster at her side.

"What's that?" Logan asked.

She flipped it over and held it up. The poster said **GO, PHILIP!** in sparkly gold marker.

Miles stifled a laugh. "You're not cheering him on at a hockey game."

"Good one," Logan said, giving Miles a high five. "Like Philip would ever play hockey!"

Daisy rolled up the poster, slid a rubber band onto it, and bonked them both on their heads. "Everyone can use a cheering section. Look around. All the other kids have their families with them. He just has us."

"Oh, sorry," Miles mumbled, feeling stupid.

"Yeah, sorry," Logan added.

"C'mon, let's just go find him." Daisy tilted her head, straining to pick up the sound of a violin among all the other noises. She pointed toward the auditorium at the far side of the lobby. "He's in there."

"Hold the door," an older woman in a blue-and-white-striped dress called out as Daisy swung open one of the auditorium doors. She wore a badge with the word JUDGE on it around her neck. The boys stepped aside to let her pass. The woman nodded at them as she headed inside, carrying a plate covered in aluminum foil. The smell wafted behind her, and they couldn't help inhaling the chocolate-peppermint dessert that must be underneath. All three stomachs growled.

"Guess we forgot to have breakfast," Daisy said.

When they got inside, they didn't see Philip, only a bunch of grown-ups running around with folders and microphones and stressed-out expressions. Long tables full of desserts covered in foil, wax paper, and plastic covers had been set up along the back wall. "Philip didn't eat, either," Logan said. "We should get something for him."

"Everything is still covered up," Miles pointed out.

"I'll take care of it," Daisy said. She waited a few seconds until all the adults' backs were turned, then sidled up to the table.

They expected some covert spy maneuver, but all Daisy did

was casually lower her rolled-up poster and slide it up to the first plate. She used the edge of the poster to pull up the foil a bit, then tipped the plate forward until an item slid out and dropped into the poster. Actually, it was pretty impressive. With her hand firmly on the bottom so nothing fell out, she repeated the move four more times on different plates before stepping back like nothing had happened.

"We could probably have just asked for some," Logan pointed out.

Daisy shook her head. "Where's the fun in that?"

Logan lowered his voice. "Did you get one from that plate the lady was carrying? The one you let through the door?"

Daisy glanced back at the table. "I think so, yes."

"Well, okay, then," Logan said, satisfied.

"It's almost time for the contest to start," Miles said. "Where's Philip?"

"I know where to find him," Daisy said. Less than a minute later they slipped through a door around the corner that led backstage. They fought their way through the crowd of kids and moms until Daisy found another door, marked JANITOR'S CLOSET. She opened it to find Philip on a low stepstool in a corner, his violin and bow laid out across his lap. They squeezed in, and Miles closed the door behind them.

"Are you okay?" Daisy asked.

He looked up. "I'm missing part of the coda, specifically the last three notes. I thought I'd have them by now, but I don't."

"It sounded finished to us," Miles said. "Right?" Logan and Daisy nodded in agreement. "I'm sure you don't have to worry. It's awesome."

Philip adjusted his tie. "I'm not worried. I just know it could be better." Truth be told, his competitive spirit had started to surface. He didn't think he'd cared about winning this in the slightest, but the realization that he would soon lose his title as winner of the candymaking contest had finally sunk in. Winning this competition wouldn't do much to soften that blow, but at least it wouldn't hurt.

"We can't help you find your coda, or whatever you called it," Daisy said, "but we brought you snacks."

"I'm not really hungry," he said, but he held his hands together anyway. Two brownies, two sugar cookies, one fudge-like piece of chocolate, and one carrot stick tumbled into his palms.

"The carrot stick makes it a healthy breakfast," Daisy declared.

He shook his head, and she plucked it from his hands.

"I'll take the chocolate piece if you don't want it," Logan said.

"Take them all," Philip said. "I really can't eat anything."

Miles took the rest and left the chocolate square for Logan, who popped it in his mouth. As he chewed, feeling the ingredients differentiate themselves, a wave of homesickness for the factory hit him. By now his dad and Max would be well into planning where the new **Mmm Mmm Good** candies would be made. He tried to take his mind off of it by focusing on the taste lingering in his mouth. Out loud he said, "Just the right blend of chocolate, peppermint, and cashew, with a hint of marshmallow."

Because Philip was only half paying attention, it took a few extra seconds before Logan's comment reached his ears. When it did, Philip grabbed his violin and bow and stood up. "I'm such an idiot!"

The others exchanged worried looks. "Um, what?" Miles said.

Philip just shook his head. "I always thought my mom had come up with that combination. But the recipe is probably printed on the side of a cashew container! Anyone could make them!"

"That doesn't make you an idiot," Daisy said.

"It doesn't make me a genius," he countered. "Let's just get this over with, okay? I'll see you guys out there." He slid past them and left the closet before any of them could think of how to make him feel better.

"Musicians sure are emotional," Miles said.

"C'mon," Daisy said. "Let's go get seats up front. He's going to need a big cheering section right now."

CHAPTER TWENTY-FOUR

The young woman with the ponytail and the clipboard and the earpiece told Philip he was up fifth, directly following the girl who could memorize the order of a shuffled deck of cards in ten seconds, and right before the boy who played piano with his toes. Philip was glad to be going sooner rather than later. He probably should have eaten something.

While he waited his turn in the wings, he felt bad for his outburst in the closet. It had been silly. He was feeling sorry for himself, and how could he do that? He had three friends who were here for him. That was worth much more than realizing he'd been wrong about his mom's chocolate squares all these years.

He peeked out the side of the curtain. He could see them sitting front row center. He'd sworn those seats had RESERVED signs taped to the back of them. But leave it to Daisy to get in there anyway. The judges' table was only a few feet in front of them. The panel consisted of three women and two men of varying ages. He watched them each take turns shuffling the deck of cards before the girl took it back. She flipped through it card by card while the crowd shouted down from ten to one. Then she placed the deck back on the judges' table and began reciting them in order. *Three of clubs, nine of diamonds, king of clubs, two of hearts.*

The judges ticked off each one as she got it correct. When she got to the last two, Philip could see her forehead break out in a sweat. He knew the lights were hot onstage, but that wasn't the reason. She knew which cards were left, but she didn't know the correct order. He did, though. He'd seen them before she set them down.

Ace of spades, jack of diamonds. Ace of spades, jack of diamonds. He repeated them under his breath, and a second later she blurted them out into the microphone. He had no idea if she'd heard him or not. He'd never, ever helped an opponent in anything. He must be getting soft. He couldn't tell Andrew.

Each judge gave a nod, acknowledging she'd gotten all fifty-two cards in the right order. She got more applause than any of the contestants before her. She hurried offstage without giving him a glance. And now it was his turn.

The master of ceremonies was a tall man in a suit that Philip could tell from across the stage needed a tailor's attention. Philip felt an unfamiliar flutter in his stomach as the man flipped to the next index card—the one that would have Philip's name on it.

He shook out his right hand a few times and hoped it wouldn't tense up before the end. None of the other musicians in the competition were performing their own compositions. It was risky, but hopefully it would pay off.

He took a series of deep breaths as the ponytailed woman gave him a gentle push onto the stage. He walked slowly, head high, with his bow hanging from one hand and his violin from the other in imitation of the videos he'd seen of professional violinists walking onto the stage.

"Ladies and gentlemen," the announcer began, "it is my pleasure to welcome Philip Ransford the Third to the stage." The crowd clapped politely and the tall man continued. "He will be performing an original violin composition titled 'Bioluminescence.'"

The audience murmured, clearly impressed. Philip took center stage, blinking in the bright spotlight. He tucked the violin between his chin and left shoulder, placed his fingers in starting position, and poised the bow above the strings. But he didn't lower it. He couldn't help notice the activity below him. Daisy was waving a poster over her head, but that didn't bother him. In fact, it was pretty cool. No one had ever made that kind of poster for him before.

What he found distracting was the fact that one of the judges— the oldest of the women—had excused herself from the judges' table. Her heels clacked on the floor as she walked up the aisle. The bright lights shining in his eyes didn't allow Philip to see if she had left the room. Was he supposed to wait for her to return to the table?

"You may begin," one of the other judges said. Well, he had his answer for what to do, at least. Maybe the lady just didn't like violin music. Or maybe she had to go to the bathroom. You'd think she could have waited until the intermission.

He shrugged it off, tried to pretend he was alone in his mom's old room at home, and began to play. Any shuffling or chatting abruptly stopped as the music filled the auditorium. When he neared the end, he hoped that somehow his arm would know how to hit the right strings for the last few notes.

It didn't.

He ended by striking the strings with a flourish of his bow, then lowered the violin dramatically to his side. As he suspected, the audience didn't notice anything was missing, or if they did, they didn't care. They clapped loudly, a few whistled (he was pretty sure the whistles came from the three kids giving him a standing ovation from front row center), and some even stomped their feet. He had played his best. Or at least his second or third best.

As he walked off stage he could see the one judge returning to her seat like it wasn't at all strange that she'd missed someone's whole performance. The other judges turned over their voting cards, and the announcer prepared to introduce the next contestant.

Ponytail Woman ushered him back to a large dressing room to wait with the few others who'd already performed. She handed him a cup of cold lemonade and a brownie. He'd rather have had one of those chocolate squares that Logan had eaten, but he took the brownie anyway. Now that all their stock of candy was gone, he had to admit he was looking forward to eating real food again when he got home. Hopefully Marietta's cooking skills had improved in his absence.

He felt a tap on his shoulder. "You were really good," the girl who'd gone before him said. She pointed to a screen on the wall. "We can watch on the monitor."

"Thanks," he said, stepping closer to the screen. The boy playing piano with his toes was oddly mesmerizing. The camera must have been shooting from the side of the stage, because he could see the judges' table and the first few rows of the audience.

"Guess she doesn't mind piano playing," Philip muttered.

"What?" the girl said.

"Nothing. Sorry."

But she didn't let it go. "Who doesn't mind piano playing?"

"The judge," he said. Figured he might as well talk, since they were stuck there until intermission.

The crowd clapped politely. The piano was wheeled away, and a girl began singing the national anthem. Her voice was full of richness and depth. It reminded him that the kids here were really the best of the best. This was no middle-school talent show.

The girl spoke again. "If you're talking about the judge who left during your performance, I thought that was weird, too."

"You saw?"

She nodded. "It's even weirder because of who she is. I mean, all the judges are at the top of their fields—some are world famous, even. But out of all of them, you'd think she'd be the best at judging a violinist!"

That got his full attention. "What do you mean?"

"You don't know who she is?"

Philip shook his head. Piano Foot Boy came in and got his snacks. They all nodded politely at each other.

"Anne Turner," the girl said. "She's first violinist in the National Symphony Orchestra."

Philip's jaw dropped. "Really?"

The girl nodded and sipped her drink. Philip moved closer to the monitor. He'd watched a lot of videos of professional violinists over the years while he was teaching himself. Now that he could see her better without the glare of the stage lights, she did look vaguely familiar. He'd mostly focused on the musicians' hands, though, so he wasn't surprised that he hadn't immediately recognized her.

"But why would she have left?" he wondered out loud.

The girl shrugged. "Maybe she wanted to stand in the back to hear better. You know, like how the sound would echo off the walls."

Philip considered that. It wasn't a bad theory.

"Okay, everyone," Ponytail Woman said, making a final check mark on her clipboard. "You have twenty minutes to go visit with your families. Dessert tables have been set up in the rear of the auditorium. It is mandatory to regroup back here for the second half. When the contest is complete, you will sit in the auditorium while the judges tally their scores and announce the winner."

Miles and Daisy were waiting for him in the area between the front row and the stage. "Great job," Miles said, pumping his hand up and down. Daisy gave him a hug. "Did you see the poster?"

He nodded. "Hard to miss." He glanced around the crowded room. Everywhere, parents and siblings were hugging relieved contestants. A janitor rushed out to mop up the stage where a raw juggled egg had met its untimely end. "Where's Logan?"

"He wanted to beat the rush to the dessert table," Daisy said. "Here he comes." They saw him weaving his way back to them, a plate piled high in each hand, mostly with those chocolate squares.

Daisy and Miles exchanged a worried look. They knew how hard it was for him to hold on to slippery things like plastic plates. They both grabbed a plate as soon as Logan got close enough.

"Ick," Daisy said as her fingers stuck to the bottom of it. Miles tried to move his fingers, too. They kept sticking to different parts of the plastic.

Logan grinned. "It's my new trick. If I put something sticky on whatever I need to carry, I don't drop it!"

Miles licked one sticky finger. "Mmm, honey."

"Good trick," Daisy said halfheartedly. Philip gave her a wet wipe that he kept in his pocket to wipe down his violin's chin rest. While she was wiping her fingers, he reached for one of the chocolate squares.

Logan began telling him how cool it was to watch him up there, and that he liked the title of the piece, and that Miles had recorded it on his vid com, but Philip only half heard him. The chocolate mint square tasted exactly as he remembered from when his mom made them. Mint and crushed cashews and marshmallow inside a pillow of soft milk chocolate. It was his strongest memory of her. If it was this easy to replicate the candy, it was a good thing Henry had talked him out of making it for the contest. The judges would have known right away, and he never could have won.

"Excuse me," Logan said, calling out to a silver-haired woman in a blue-and-white dress standing a few feet away by the stage. She turned around. Philip could see the laminated badge on a string around her neck that said JUDGE in bold black letters. This was the judge who'd left! Was Logan seriously about to confront her?

Philip shrank back a little. It took a lot to make him feel intimidated by anyone, but first violinist of the NSO? That would intimidate anyone.

But instead of asking why she'd left, Logan surprisingly held up a chocolate square. "These are really, really good. You made them, right?"

The woman's gaze shifted around their group. She gave a small nod.

Logan brushed his hair away from his eyes and said, "My family owns the **Life Is Sweet?** candy factory, and honestly, these are really special. Would you ever consider selling the recipe? Or maybe going into business together?"

Miles and Daisy raised their eyebrows high at each other. Logan Sweet had suddenly turned into a businessman! The Candymaker would be proud of how well he was representing the factory.

Philip wanted to crawl into a hole. Here was arguably one of the best violinists in the entire world, and Logan was asking her about chocolate!

She glanced around at all of them again and then shook her head. "I don't think so. It's an old family recipe. I've only shared it once . . . with my daughter." Her eyes flashed to Philip and, inexplicably, filled with tears.

For a split second Philip thought she must have heard him play after all. It wouldn't be the first time he'd seen people get emotional after hearing music.

And then *boom!* A rush of images hit him, and he fell back into the nearest seat.

Logan said, "Well, if you change your mind, please think of **Life Is Sweet?**."

The woman gave another small nod, but she didn't turn away from him. Logan shifted his weight from foot to foot. Was she waiting for a business card or something? It took longer than it probably should have for him and Daisy and Miles to pick up on Philip's distress. It was the raspy breathing and clammy white skin that finally did it.

"Philip?" Daisy asked, shaking his shoulder. "Are you okay? You look like you've seen a ghost."

Philip stared past her at the woman. She had more gray hair than when he'd last seen her, and it wasn't on one of the violin concert videos he'd watched. She hadn't excused herself from judging his performance because she needed a bathroom break, or to hear it better, or any other reason he'd considered. She did it because the rules of every single contest he'd ever been in were the same—a contestant cannot be related to a judge.

CHAPTER TWENTY-FIVE

Philip tried to get his mouth to form words, but all that came out was "Gr...ah...wha..." So he stopped trying. Even though the room was full of contestants and their families chatting and laughing, all he heard was his heart thumping in his ears.

"What's going on?" Miles asked, looking from one to the other. The judge stepped cautiously over to Philip and lowered herself into the seat beside him. She put her hand on his arm. Instinctively, he jerked it away and shifted to the far side of his seat.

"Philip!" Daisy scolded.

But the woman held up a hand. "It's okay. I deserve that."

Daisy shook her head. "Why? Because you left during his performance? It was really great, by the way. He's the best young violinist in the nation."

She nodded. "I agree. I wasn't half as good at his age. But if I had to guess, that's not why he's angry."

Philip sprang up from his seat. "Where have you been the last decade? How come I didn't even know you existed?"

Shocked, his friends backed away. "What's going on?" Logan asked in a shaky voice.

"Guys," Philip said, gesturing back and forth between them and the chair. "Meet my grandmother."

Their jaws fell open.

The woman stayed seated with her fingers laced tightly together. "Annette Turner Rickman," she said quietly. "You can call me Anne."

Philip didn't want to call her anything. He began to pace between the seats and the stage. "Did you even know Mom died? Why didn't I know about you? How did you know I'd be here?"

People had started to notice. The violin boy and the judge were fighting! Daisy snapped into action. She reached for both Philip and this judge, who was somehow his *grandmother*, and marched them both out the side door of the auditorium and into a classroom, where she closed the door. "I don't know what's going on," she said to Anne, "but my friend here deserves answers to his questions."

"I know he does," she said calmly. "I'm just waiting for him to finish asking them."

Philip glanced around at the room—a history classroom, judging by the many posters of past presidents. Logan and Miles stood pressed against a wall, scared, or freaked out, or just trying to be supportive and invisible at the same time.

Anne held out what looked like an ordinary black flash drive. "Your mother trusted me with this, and it's something I've treasured. Please, take it."

Philip crossed his arms.

Daisy stepped forward, took the device, and slid it in her pocket. Anne gave her a grateful look.

"I'd like those answers," Philip said. He had a hard time meeting her eyes, but he forced himself to. Up close she looked so much like his mother. It felt like someone was trying to pull out his heart with a rusty pair of pliers.

"You're almost grown up now," she said, "so I'm going to give it to you straight. Marshall—my late husband and your grandfather—owned a paper business. Cardboard boxes, mostly. He built it from nothing, working day and night to grow it into something big that employed dozens of people. Your father—barely out of college and eager to prove himself to his own father—offered to buy Marshall's company so he could sell off the pieces to our competitors. Marshall refused, but your father was relentless. One by one he destroyed every relationship your grandfather had built with his suppliers over decades. Marshall lost his business, and his employees lost their jobs." Anne paused to catch her breath.

"And then your father met Karen, our only daughter and your mother. Beyond all reasoning, they fell in love. And why not? Phil was dynamic, handsome, brilliant, and charming. Everyone could see that he truly loved her and perhaps even regretted what he had done to our family's business, but there was no undoing it at that point."

Daisy hung on every word. This was better than a soap opera! She glanced at Philip. He, too, seemed rapt. His face was dark and angry, but he didn't take his eyes from his grandmother's face.

Anne sat on the edge of the teacher's desk and rubbed at weary eyes. "I'm sure you can guess the rest. She married him and broke her father's heart. Karen always believed Marshall would come around, but he never did." She let out a long, shaky breath. "Don't get me wrong—I was deeply hurt by your mother's choice, too. How could I not be? But I couldn't close her out like Marshall did. Karen would send me updates on you and your brother, pictures and little video clips. She'd insisted on naming her firstborn after me, so that's why you got to be Philip Ransford the Third, instead of Andrew inheriting the name."

Philip had always wondered about that but never questioned it. Having his father's name had opened many doors over the years.

"And I got to meet you both a few times, too," his grandmother was saying. "Once Karen was even able to bring you to my house when Marshall was out for the day. Sneaking around was very stressful for both of us. But for Marshall, who wore that grudge and anger like a second skin—well, he had it even worse. For him it was like his daughter had died."

Philip made a guttural sound in his throat, and Anne stood up and walked toward him. When he stiffened, she stopped. "I got a job with a new symphony, and we moved across the country a few years before Karen got sick. She hid it from me until Reggie—bless him—found me and let me know. I only got to see her once after that—in the hospital. The nurses told me your father had been at her bedside from dawn to dusk. That he'd thrown half his fortune at medical procedures to save her. But...well..." She trailed off.

They all knew how that part of the story ended. She made another movement toward Philip, and when he didn't back away, she kept going. She put her hand on his arm. "The regret I feel about losing those last years with your mother haunts my every waking hour. I channel that pain into my music, as I suspect you do into yours. Yours has more joy in it, though, which I was very grateful to hear. Marshall passed away a few months ago, and I reached out to your brother first, to test the waters. I thought that by his age, he'd have a greater understanding of human nature and of how complicated relationships could be. I hoped he'd have compassion."

She lifted her hand off Philip's arm. Philip felt the absence of it and wished she'd put it back. This surprised him.

"But in the end it was you," she said, her kind voice finally soothing him. "I only came to your house perhaps three times after your parents moved in, and only when your father was away on business trips. One time I got the heads-up he was headed home early. In my haste to leave, I left some items there—a birthday scarf I'd been knitting for your mother, along with some books and a violin.

Your mother asked if she could keep them, since she had so little of me. How could I refuse her anything?" She gave a small smile. "It appears leaving the violin was perhaps my only good decision in all this mess."

Philip felt the last of his anger fade away, leaving sadness, and maybe a little hope. He glanced over to see what his friends thought of all this and was surprised to see they must have slipped out the door.

"I really could have used a grandmother all these years," he finally said.

"I know. I could have used a grandson. You have thirteen hand-knit sweaters waiting for you at my house. One for every birthday."

"So it was Andrew who told you I would be here," he said. "No wonder he was so eager for me to come."

She shook her head. "It wasn't Andrew."

Philip thought for a minute. "Reggie! I knew he was being unusually nice to me before I left. He called me *kiddo*. No one calls you kiddo unless they're trying to hide something and feel guilty about it."

She shook her head again. "It wasn't Reggie, although I am deeply indebted to him. He sent me every newspaper clipping about you and your brother's accomplishments. You certainly are an ambitious and successful duo."

She didn't comment about ambition running in the family, but she didn't have to. They'd definitely inherited their competitive streak from their father. He tried again. "Don't tell me you were already signed on to judge and saw my name?"

She shook her head. "Not exactly." She took another deep breath. "When your father found out about your violin playing, he called me. I was so surprised I literally dropped the phone. Still have a bruise on my left pinky toe. Make no mistake, your father was not a fan of ours, either. Your grandfather had been very vocal in letting others know about your father's ruthless tactics. But a lot of time had passed. Your father wanted some guidance on what to do with you and couldn't think of anyone else to ask. After the shock wore off enough for me to talk, I told him about this talent contest. Your father knew we would meet if you came here, but he signed you up anyway. Perhaps he's changed."

Philip wouldn't put too much faith in that.

"Pretty nice violin you played up there," she said.

"It's a Stradivarius," he replied.

"Yes, I know. I'm sure there's a good story to explain why you have it."

"There is."

Anne glanced up at the wall clock. "Looks like intermission ended a while ago. Pretty sure I'm fired now."

Philip nodded. "Probably. And I'm probably disqualified for not returning to the dressing room."

She smiled. "Probably."

He found her face looked less like his mother's now and more like her own. He smiled back. A real smile. "So now what?"

"Now I hope you'll let me be your grandmother."

He thought for only a few seconds. "This is some trip for me. New friends, a new cat, and a grandmother. And those are only the parts I can tell you about."

She grinned and linked her arm through his. "A cat? Tell me about that."

"Come meet her." They headed for the classroom door.

"You have her with you?"

"We have a lot of stuff with us!" he said as he pushed open the door. Daisy, Logan, and Miles tumbled to the floor.

"We weren't listening with Daisy's spy ear!" Miles insisted.

A spool of what looked like silver thread with a tiny suction cup at the end rolled itself up from under the door and back into Daisy's hand. She immediately ditched it in her pocket. Her attempt to look innocent failed miserably.

"It's okay," Philip said. "Saves me the trouble of having to fill you all in."

The hallway had emptied out, and they could hear the sound of tap shoes scuffing up the high school's stage. "Hmm, the tap-dancing cowgirl," Anne said. "That means we have about ten acts left."

"Can we go in and watch?" Miles asked when they got to the lobby. "We could sit in the back."

Before Anne could answer, AJ came bounding around the corner, Philip's violin case swinging from his hand. "There you are, Philip! I've been looking all over for you. I was getting really worried. You're supposed to be in Dressing Room B, but no one has seen you since intermission!"

Anne squinted at him. "This isn't your brother, Andrew, is it?"

Philip shook his head. "This is AJ. He's our chaperone. And Daisy's cousin. Sort of."

"Hey!" Miles said brightly. "Speaking of cousins, did I tell you guys I have a cousin now, too? Her name is Jade and she's three. Supersmart and funny. Can't wait for you to meet her."

"Huh?" Logan said. "Your friend Arthur's daughter?"

"Yes! Turns out—"

But AJ cut him off. "You'll have to finish what's no doubt a fascinating story that I myself will look forward to hearing, but right now we have to get Philip back to the dressing room or he'll be disqualified." He finally noticed Anne's judge's badge. "Unless that's already happened? I'm sorry if he caused any trouble. It's been a very eventful last few days. Maybe you can let him back into the contest?"

She pulled the badge over her head and tossed it in the lobby trashcan. "I'm not a judge anymore," she said. "Just a grandma."

"She's *my* grandma," Philip said proudly, pointing his thumb at his chest.

AJ looked stunned. "What?"

"She's also first violinist with the National Symphony Orchestra," Philip added.

Anne waved that off like it was no big deal. "Come, let's go see that cat you told me about." And off they went out the front doors, laughing like old friends as Philip told her about Aurora's barking.

Logan and Miles followed them, Miles excitedly filling Logan in on the DNA discovery.

AJ shook his head. "Man, I take a nap for a few hours and half the group get new relatives! What else would I have missed if I'd slept a little longer?"

Daisy grinned and linked her arm through his as they followed the others back to Harvey. "Things move pretty fast around here," she said. "Ya snooze, ya lose."

 **DAISY** reached over the stable door to stroke Magpie's nose once more before heading out of the barn. The Candymaker had invited all of Spring Haven to the factory's first picnic in seven years, and from what Daisy had seen so far, most of them had shown up!

A group of kids ran past her, different-colored streamers billowing out behind them from each hand. She sat down on a nearby bench and held up her copy of *Knitting for Dummies* that hid her vid com. Philip had given them each a copy as a joke, but she'd already made two mittens and a bookmark. It would be nearly impossible to find the boys with all the activities going on outside, so she'd have to look for them the high-tech way. As long as they had their vid coms, she could find them, and they nearly always had them.

When they'd returned from the trip, she'd replaced the boys' usual little red dots and names with their *Role with It* avatars. Seeing them pop up made her laugh each time. Cowboy Miles blinked onto the screen first. When she zoomed in to his location, it looked like he was standing in the pond behind the factory. Like, *in* the pond. Odd! He'd sure come a long way from the boy who was allergic to rowboats!

Logan's chess piece showed up in his bedroom, but Daisy figured he must have left his vid com behind when he went to the picnic. No way he would miss even a minute of it. The Philip-headed goat popped up in a car a few blocks away. She had only seen him twice since they got back, and only for a short time. He said he was busy with "official Harmonicandy business," but she wasn't so sure.

She was about to head down to the water to see what was up with Miles when her vid com buzzed. AJ's face filled the screen. All she could see behind him was white, as if he was standing in front of a blank wall. "I finished setting up the holojection," he said, sounding like a little kid who'd just built a LEGO castle all by himself. "It's awesome. I created three layers of it, so even if someone were to walk through one of them, they still wouldn't see Paradise."

"That's great, AJ," she said. "What does Frank think of it?"

"He's thrilled. He's jumping around and walking back and forth through it. Evy loves it, too," he said. "She was here to take down her mirrors. She turned a bunny into a deck of playing cards."

"Cool."

"Yeah, it was. Haven't found the bunny yet, though."

"Why are you standing in front of an empty wall? Are all Frank's maps gone already?"

He reached his hand over his head and pushed it into what she'd thought was the wall. "It's sand," he said. "I'm lying in the sand."

She peered closer. "Oh. Yeah, I see now. Cool. I'm glad you're relaxing now, but I really want to join the picnic. I bet no one will beat me at Toss the Icy Mint Blob into the Giant Hat. You know how good my aim is."

"Okay, one last thing. I shouldn't be telling you this, but I'm feeling generous. Something about being in this place . . . well, you know what it's like. It makes you hope the whole world is happy. Plus you gave me this guy." He held up the stuffed unicorn Daisy had bought him when they got home. "Hi, Corny," she said.

"So here it is." He lowered his voice and whispered, "*Cinnamon.*"

Daisy held the book closer to her face. "Sorry, it's kind of noisy here. It sounded like you said *cinnamon*?"

"I did."

She frowned. "Is that code for something I should know?" She'd memorized the list of code words for spies when she was six. Her memory rarely failed her, but she didn't remember any that had to do with spices.

"Gotta go," he said, slipping on his sunglasses. "I've already said too much."

"Wait, no, you didn't. You didn't say anything."

But he waved, and the screen went dark.

"Grrr."

More kids ran by, shouting about the duck race starting soon. She really wanted to go around to where all the action was, but AJ's call couldn't be ignored. It was the second time in a month someone had randomly brought up cinnamon—her mom had suggested cinnamon tea when they'd spoken on the road trip, and now AJ? She thought hard but couldn't put anything together. She knew one place that might help, though.

She jumped up from the bench and ran inside the factory. The picnic would have to wait a few more minutes. She kept running until the heat from the Tropical Room reached out into the hall. She glanced around to make sure no one could see her, then yanked the door open. Everyone made such a big deal about how heavy the door was and how you had to press the button to loosen the seal first, but she almost never got to use her full strength anymore, and she never passed up the opportunity. Use it or lose it, as they say.

As always in the Tropical Room, the heat wrapped itself around her like a cozy blanket. Paradise had been hot, but definitely not a wet, thick heat like this. That felt more like a tropical island. This was the jungle.

"Avery?" she called into the cavernous room. She figured if anyone knew information about cinnamon, it would be him. She wound her way through the vanilla vines, which had grown much taller since she'd last been there, and scanned the treetops but didn't see him or any of the other workers. Everyone must be out at the picnic.

She headed over to her favorite cinnamon tree, the one Logan always teased her about hugging, even though she knew he liked that she did it. After all, he was a tree hugger, too.

She could see the vertical knife marks where Avery had scraped the bark until it came off in small brown spirals. She moved some grass away with her foot, and sure enough, a few spirals sprang up. She slipped one into her pocket and leaned against the tree to think.

She got about a minute to relax there before her vid com buzzed with a video message from Philip. He'd recorded it from the back-seat of the limo. "Meet me in fifteen minutes in the storage room by Max's lab."

That was just like him. He didn't ask, he just told. She had something to give him anyway, and he probably wouldn't want others around to see it. Right as he was hanging up, she could hear Reggie calling to him from the front seat. It sounded like he was saying the Candymaker was on the phone.

Daisy tucked the vid com away and leaned against the tree again. As usually happened when she was near it, she felt a pull to hug it that didn't come from any conscious choice. She faced the tree and put her arms around the narrow trunk. Since she knew she was alone, she went one step further and laid her cheek against the smooth bark. She closed her eyes and breathed deeply, letting the sweet, spicy smell fill her up. Why had AJ said *cinnamon*? Why had her mother? A coincidence?

She knew Philip would start bugging her again if she was late, but she couldn't make herself move. She just let her mind go blank, focusing purely on the smell, trying to get some kind of clarity. She went through the steps that AJ had done when he got Logan to conjure up the memory of Frank's address. Without thinking, she pulled the small piece of bark out of her pocket and began chewing on it.

Suddenly her mind began to spiral. She felt as if her thoughts were going around the inside of a long tunnel, grasping for something—a memory—at the end. And then *bam!* She heard the sizzle of cinnamon bark on a skillet and heard the voice of a little boy giggling and her shushing him. She and this boy were hiding under a kitchen table while grown-ups talked at the stove. They were young, really young—like, she was maybe three, and he was two at the most. Out the window she could see a flat dirt yard and low, brownish-orange rock plateaus in the near distance. Where was she?

But as soon as she'd asked it, she knew the answer. She was on a Native American reservation. Why? And who was she with? She focused hard, and her sharp memory finally kicked in. She could recognize her mother's voice talking in hushed whispers. "He'll stay here for another month, then," she was saying. "Then his mother will be back for him."

She saw herself reach for the boy's hand. They remained like that until the grown-ups found them. They thought they were going to get scolded, but instead the women laughed. "Looks like we've got a couple of future spies on our hands," the other woman said.

"Was there ever any doubt?" Daisy's mother asked.

The memory faded. Daisy's arms flew away from the tree. That boy had been her brother! Or at least she'd called him that? But her mother had said his mother would be back for him. She called AJ.

"What?" he said instead of hello. "I'm busy."

"You're lying in a hammock with a stuffed unicorn, drinking ice tea with a tiny umbrella in the glass!" Which, in fact, he was. "Just tell me one thing. Did I have a brother who we left behind at a Native American reservation?"

"Cinnamon worked, then, eh? They cooked with it all the time. Whole house smelled like it."

"Do I need to repeat the question? Was that my brother?"

"Yes," AJ said. "And no. Not your real brother, by blood, but your parents raised him with you until his own parents could take him again."

She sucked in her breath. "Why?"

"Are you alone?"

"Just me and the trees."

"Okay. His parents were spies, too, for a different organization. They were deep undercover, very important government gig. His mother couldn't have a baby with her. Your mother and the boy's mother had gone to school together, and they made this arrangement between them. Even your grandmother doesn't know about it to this day."

"That's good to know," Daisy said. "One less person to be angry at for keeping this from me."

"You're old enough now to understand," AJ said. "You can't compromise his family's safety by looking for him. He and your mother have stayed close—he called her *Mom* for those two years. She might be gearing up to tell you on your next family mission. Or maybe she'll chicken out again. I don't know." He leaned back in the hammock again. "Now if you don't mind, I've got some suntanning to do. Go eat some chocolate pizza and have fun at the picnic. You now know the secret of the mystery brother."

The screen went blank before she could ask the boy's name. She—whose memory was nearly perfect—had forgotten someone that important in her life? Granted, she was only four, and so much in her life changed soon after that. She moved to the mansion, started spy training. And of course she had AJ to occupy—and annoy—her. He'd stepped into the brother role.

She walked in a daze toward the Harmonicandy Room. She wasn't surprised about the little boy's mom not being able to care for him for a while. After all, Daisy's grandmother had pretty much raised her—was *still* raising her. She knew the adult spies did very important work, and someday she would, too. Protecting identities was their number one priority. She wouldn't press her mom for more details. She was grateful for what she'd gotten. And at least she finally knew why she always wanted to hug that tree!

The factory was supposed to be off-limits to picnic-goers, but many of the workers had brought their families in for tours. Daisy got a lot of hellos and high fives, which helped her pull herself out of her own head and be present at this special occasion. As she passed the Taffy Room, Fran whipped a piece of purple taffy at her. Daisy caught it with one hand. "Thanks!" she said, popping it into her mouth.

"You know there's always a summer job waiting for you here," Fran replied.

Daisy nodded. "I may take you up on that one day!" She got as far as the lobby before her vid com went off again. She answered by saying, "Hold your horses, Philip. I'll be there in two minutes."

"No horses," Grammy replied. "Just a couple of pelicans."

Daisy grinned. "Sorry! Hi, Grammy. I see you're back in your waterfall."

"I took your advice and wet my hair. Better?"

"Much. What's up? I'm at the candy factory." It felt so good to be able to say that instead of hiding her visits from her grandmother.

Once Daisy had gotten back from the road trip, she'd told her grandmother everything—about the trip, and Paradise, too. She hadn't seen Grammy in over a month at that point, and she didn't want to spend the next five years, until she was eighteen, lying. Grammy hadn't been thrilled, but she hadn't been surprised, either. In the end all she'd said was "Sounds like a successful mission."

"I figured you were at the factory," Grammy said now. "Unless you've installed a chocolate fountain in your bedroom without telling me."

"Nope."

"I'll be brief, since clearly Philip is anxiously awaiting your arrival."

Daisy felt her cheeks reddening. Maybe telling Grammy about her friends had been a little hasty.

"Do you remember that before you left for your mission at Camp Tumbleweed I told you I was considering a big mission for you when you got back?"

Daisy nodded. She'd been thinking about that recently but had been afraid to ask. She was enjoying her time off. "Mom told me we have a family mission out west. Is that it?"

Grammy shook her head. "If you take this mission, you'll skip that one. Marissa or Clarissa will step in for you."

A stand-in daughter? "Why wouldn't I go?"

"Because you've been accepted here." Her grandmother pressed a button on her screen, and a typewritten letter appeared.

Daisy's eyes widened when she read the letterhead. "The Unit? The best spy school in the country? You sent in an application for me?"

"I did."

Daisy couldn't believe it. "You'd let me go to boarding school two thousand miles away?"

"It's not my first choice," her grandmother admitted, returning to the screen. "But I think it would be good for you to be with kids whose lives are similar to yours. And before you say anything, no, it's not to keep you away from the candy factory kids. You'd still be home on vacations and for summers, and you'd still get to do some gigs, although you'd get graded on those."

Her eyes opened wider. "Graded on missions?"

Grammy nodded. "The spies who did your Camp Tumbleweed dead drop got an A on the project."

"What?! That crazy scytale thing? And the fake bear poop? And the birdhouse?"

"Yup. Extra points for creativity."

"So if I went there, I'd meet them?"

"Yes."

Daisy had a thought. "How old do you have to be to go there?"

"It accepts boys and girls between ten and seventeen."

And maybe mystery brothers, she thought.

"You don't have to decide now," Grammy assured her.

"That's good," Daisy said, relieved.

"You have till tonight." Her grandmother winked, patted a pelican on its head, and hung up.

 **LOGAN** returned to his room after dropping off a gift on Avery's desk. He'd forgotten to get him a postcard from "someplace supercool," as Avery had requested (Paradise didn't have a gift shop!), so he'd painted him a picture of the River of Light with the red-and-green sky above it. On the bottom, he'd written the poem Miles

had given him on the trip, about returning home and seeing it—and life—with new eyes.

He hoped the heat in the Tropical Room wouldn't make the paint run before Avery got to see it. The painting had taken him three weeks to do, since the paintbrush kept slipping. He found it didn't help to put something sticky on his hand first, because he had to keep shifting the angle of the brush to paint. Still, he was proud of how it had turned out. It had a lot more detail than the map his grandfather had made, which now hung on his wall next to the painting Daisy had sent at the beginning of summer. His mom had suggested they research the artist—Ava Simon—but they hadn't been able to turn anything up on her. They decided he had a one-of-a-kind piece of art that was probably worth a lot of money. Not that he'd ever sell it.

His walkie-talkie crackled, and his father's voice came through. "They've reached a decision! They're going to call a meeting in a few minutes. Stay tuned."

"Roger that!" Logan said, fumbling for the button. Finally!

Old Sammy—the long-time president of the Confectionary Association—and the other judges and committee members of the New Candy Contest had been in heated debate over the future of the Harmonicandy. As soon as they'd returned from the road trip, Logan, Philip, and Miles had gathered all the people who'd attended the Harmonicandy's first tasting when it came off the conveyor belt. It wasn't easy, but they explained how they'd used the old batch of Magic Bar chocolate by mistake, and therefore using the factory's current chocolate supply would break the contest rules. They couldn't tell the part about Henry giving Philip the bowl of chocolate, or anything about Paradise, which made it really hard to convince them.

Openly upset, the Candymaker and Max had insisted that maybe they could find more of the old beans, but Randall was quick to put that argument to rest. He'd been around in the days of the Magic Bar, and something in his eyes told the boys he knew at least a little bit about what had happened back then.

Once the situation was brought to the Confectionary Association's attention, they'd agreed that Philip would, regrettably, have to step down as winner, but they had to debate whether or not **Life Is Sweet** would still have the right to produce the candy. Essentially, every candy company that had sent competitors to the contest would have to agree to it, and that would be very tough.

Even though no part of the apartment looked out on the great lawn in the back, Logan could hear the cheers and the music through the walls. He'd waited seven years for the picnic, and he couldn't believe it was finally happening. He grabbed one of his grandfather's old notepads and slid it in his back pocket. He liked keeping it close. Frank's original letter had proven true—seeing his grandfather's trials and errors really did make him feel better. It showed how every time you learn what doesn't work, you get closer to what does.

To keep his mind off the Harmonicandy situation, he'd been experimenting with the Bubbletastic ChocoRocket recently. The chocolate-to-gum part was really quite simple—the sugar and gum base (made from chicle harvested from his favorite sapodilla tree) went in the dehumidifier, which pulled out the moisture overnight and turned it into powder. He then added cocoa powder and corn syrup and pressed the mixture into the shape of a rocket. He'd already done those steps for the contest, although not as well. So he could turn the chocolate into gum, but every attempt to turn it back to chocolate had failed. He couldn't extract the chicle back out. It just wasn't within the laws of nature.

Finally he realized something that on some level he'd known all along—life moved in only one direction. Forward. He'd never been one to look back, ever. So why did he want his candy to do it? Besides, he had his sights set on another candy, one he'd have to figure out how to mass-produce—what equipment would be necessary, what kind of packaging to use, basically all the questions a real candymaker would have. He could tell that Philip's grandmother was caving a little each time he spoke to her. Which was every day. If he'd learned anything from Philip, it was to go after what he wanted, if it was important enough.

"It's time!" the walkie-talkie announced. "Gather your friends and meet us in the Harmonicandy Room. Over and out."

Logan didn't need to be told twice! Whatever the answer, at least it would finally be over. He ran out of the apartment and was halfway down the main hallway before he realized he didn't have his vid com with him. He'd have to find his friends the old-fashioned way—by actually looking for them!

Running through the factory wasn't as exciting when he knew Henry wasn't there to tell him to stop running. He'd been in touch with people from the factory who had marshmallow-related questions, but he still wouldn't tell anyone Henry's whereabouts. When they were feeling optimistic, they told themselves he'd found a doctor somewhere to fix his eyes, or maybe he'd gone to visit Frank. When feeling pessimistic, they feared he'd gone completely blind and couldn't come to work.

Out of habit, Logan glanced into the Marshmallow Room as he approached it, then stopped short. Marshmallow production had continued in Henry's absence, but none of the candymaking machines were running today because of the picnic. But the door was open, and only one man had the key during off-hours.

"Henry!"

Henry stood by the largest of the Bunsen burners, his back to the door. He turned at the sound of his name, and Logan's heart plummeted. Henry wasn't wearing glasses, but Logan knew it wasn't because he didn't need them. His eyes were completely glazed over and unfocused. An angry purple bruise burst across one cheek. Both knees had bandages on them. For a moment, neither of them spoke.

"Has anyone seen you yet?" Logan asked.

Henry shook his head. "Only the nice nurse who walked me in. She's waiting out back. Probably cheering on a duck."

"Don't move," Logan commanded. "Don't you move, Henry. I'll be right back."

He ran from the room, then stuck his head back in. "I mean, you can *move*, but just don't leave the room, okay?" He ran away again without waiting for a reply. Grabbing his walkie-talkie off his waist, he called his dad. "I still have to find everyone, so it's going to be a little while."

"Old Sammy's not getting any younger," his father said. "And I'd like to get back outside. Your mother's here, and it's almost our turn for the three-legged race!"

"Roger that," Logan said. "Over and out."

As soon as he got outside and saw that the great rubber duck race was beginning, he knew where to find Miles, at least. He and his new cousin, Jade, had been talking about the race for days. They'd each picked out a duck earlier and had been carrying them around and whispering to them all day. "Trying to build its confidence," Miles had told him, as if the ducks were real instead of made from bright yellow rubber.

Even more people had come to the picnic than had attended the Kickoff. That was more for candy insiders, while this event was intended for the Spring Haven community. Logan loved seeing the shopkeepers from town and all the workers' kids and families. It was very tempting to stop and join a potato-sack race, or to make a s'more at the Some More S'mores campfire, or to measure himself against the tallest sunflower, which had indeed grown higher than his head, but he was on a mission.

While dodging a game of chess played with giant chess pieces, he nearly tripped over a bench near the strawberry fields. He bent down to rub his leg and saw something sticking in the dirt. A discarded candy wrapper, no doubt. But knowing that his mom hated trash, he didn't want to give her any reason to cancel the picnic in future years.

"Huh?" he said as he picked it up. It wasn't trash at all, but a six-of-diamonds playing card. He turned it over. *The Great Shoudini!* The fancy letters, though faded and dirty from mud, were unmistakable. Evy had been here! She's who Henry was out meeting that night before the road trip. That's why she knew about his eyes. Logan sped up again.

"Go, ducky, go!" Jade's cheers blended in with the shouts of the huge crowd gathered on the banks of the pond. She jumped up and down, her bare feet squishing in the shallow water. **MILES** jumped right along with her, backpack bouncing, while both sets of parents looked on with delight. The ducks had left the starting line of the great duck race a while ago, and on such a clear, windless day, it was going to be a long time before any of them reached the other side. Miles popped a sample of a new candy, temporarily named You've Never Tasted Peanut Butter Like THIS, into his mouth. *Hmm*, delicious!

A lot had changed in the three weeks since AJ dropped Miles

off back home. He'd spent most of the first night staring up at the stars and remembering the view of the Milky Way and the billowing waves of the aurora. It comforted him to know that even though he couldn't see it from Spring Haven, the vast universe of stars and planets was still up there, even in the daytime, reminding him he was a part of something huge, something that maybe went on forever.

The maps that covered his walls also gave him a sense of the hugeness of the world. When Frank had told him he could pick out whichever ones he wanted, Miles had thought he must be kidding. But Frank just stepped aside and said, "Take them. Love them. Do whatever you like with them. So many maps wind up forgotten in basements of universities and libraries. If you take them, I know that won't happen." While Miles picked through the bounty, Frank gazed on, clearly pleased. "I envy you," he said. "You and the other mapmakers of the future. With new telescopes to see the biggest things, and new microscopes to see the smallest, you'll be at the forefront of amazing discoveries. You'll get to map time and space! The brain! The atom!" Miles had hugged him for a long, long time until Frank reminded him how late it was and ushered the kids out.

Every night since he'd left Paradise, he'd traced the lines of Smoranthia, which covered most of one wall in his room. He tacked up the small pencil drawing Henry had given him beside it. He realized he'd had an original Frank Griffin map all those months! He knew he'd donate them both to a museum someday, on the condition that they wouldn't end up in the basement.

On their last night in the RV, the others had helped him hatch a plan for the best way to break the news to his dad that he had a brother. He'd considered bringing his dad out onto the garage roof because they always had good talks out there. But what if his dad fell off in shock? Probably better not to risk it.

His next thought was to invite Arthur and his family over to the house, but that could be really awkward, since his dad would have nowhere to go if he was upset. Daisy suggested geocaching, but his dad hadn't been overly excited about it the last time he and Arthur took him, so that was out, too.

Logan was the one who suggested Miles find a neutral place, somewhere both men felt comfortable. And so it was that during the seventh-inning stretch of the Spring Haven Pirates versus the Willow Falls Hawks, the two men embraced as brothers for the first time. Since then there'd been a flurry of meetings, dinners, pictures, stories, and tears. And now, the **Life Is Sweet** annual picnic!

"There you are," Logan said, reaching them through the crowd lined up ten rows deep on the banks of the pond.

"Do they have a decision?" Miles asked hopefully.

"Yes!" Logan shouted over all the people cheering for their duck. "But that's not all. He's back! Henry's back!"

Miles grabbed Logan's arm. "He is? Finally! Let's go!" He told Jade that he had to attend to candy business but that if his duck won, she could keep his two dollars and they would buy Pepsicles with them. The girl was insane for Pepsicles. That turned her frown upside down very quickly.

Every one of Miles's senses lit up as they ran across the great lawn toward the factory. The smells of chocolate, spun sugar, corn dogs, and ripe fruit filled the air, along with the dance music coming from hidden speakers. Hundreds of balloons and colored lights hung from tree branches. Kids (and parents) laughed with glee when Paulo from the Bee Room fell into a dunk tank full of powdered sugar. Potato-sack races ran all day, along with contests to see who could make their High-Jumping Jelly Bean jump the highest and (for those eighteen and over) who could keep a Fireball Supernova in their mouth the longest.

When they reached the back door and the crowds had thinned, Logan stopped Miles. "Do you have your vid com? Can you tell

Philip and Daisy to meet us at the Marshmallow Room as soon as they can?"

Miles nodded and reached around to his backpack. Before fishing out the vid com, though, he pulled out a small brown notebook tied with a rubber band. He had planned on giving this to Logan at the end of the day, but no time like the present. The larger item hidden in his backpack was for Daisy. The afterlife map had been hers all along.

He pressed the small notebook into Logan's palm. "This was in Sam's box. The contract was stuck inside it."

Logan held the notebook, surprised. Then he flipped the pages. "It's all blank."

Miles shook his head. "Actually, if you look really close, you'll see he'd written in it. Filled up all the pages. I think it talks about finding Paradise." He'd tried to think of a better name for it but so far hadn't been able to top the name it already had. At least he had his own geocaching handle now—and if Mr. Sweet approved of the spot, MiddleEarthBoy would soon be hiding his first cache inside the jug on the front porch of the factory!

Logan's eyes lit up. "This is great. Maybe Daisy can do that thing she did with the contract and get the words back!"

"Maybe she can," he agreed. "She said if it was written in real lead pencil that had faded with time, she could turn it into black lead sulfide first, then use some kind of hydrogen gas to get it to darken."

"I don't know what that means," Logan said.

"Yeah, me neither," Miles admitted. "But I know one thing about the notebook—the words didn't fade over time. They were erased. Maybe Sam planned to reuse the notebook, or maybe he just wanted to leave no trace, but either way, he didn't want someone to read it. I think we should let him have his privacy. Doesn't everyone deserve that?"

Logan examined the notebook while Miles sent the message to Philip and Daisy to meet them in the Marshmallow Room.

"I agree," Logan said. "I can use it to write our story."

Miles tucked the vid com away. "Perfect. Now let's go give Henry his eyesight back!"

"I'm proud of you, **PHILIP**," Reggie said as he left him at the factory door. He placed the two large suitcases beside the old milk jug on the porch.

"Don't go getting all soft on me," Philip said. "It's not that big a deal." But even Philip couldn't say that with a straight face. They started laughing. "All right, it's a big deal."

His vid com buzzed in his pocket. "I'll see you later, okay?" he told Reggie. "Thanks for . . . well, all of it." When Philip had gotten back from the trip and told Reggie about his grandmother and what he'd learned, it was as if ten years disappeared from Reggie's face.

His father had only said, "So I take it you met your grandmother." Philip nodded. Then his father asked, "Did you win the competition?" Philip shook his head. "You'll do better next time," his dad replied. Stunned by this response, Philip's first thought was that perhaps his father had been taken by aliens and this man had been left in his place. But then he decided that maybe even Philip Ransford the Second could change for the better. Either way, that was the last they spoke of either matter. Philip actually didn't know whether he might have won if he hadn't left. But he decided then and there that his contest days were over. He didn't have to prove anything to anyone other than himself.

Reggie tipped his hat as he walked away. "Good luck in there."

"Thanks, Reggie," Philip said, then pulled out his vid com. The message from Miles to meet in the Marshmallow Room came up first, followed by Daisy asking where he was. He quickly grabbed the suitcases and pushed open the door. Even on wheels they were heavy. But he couldn't risk leaving them behind. He got a lot of "Moving in?" jokes as he hurried down the hallway.

"I thought you were standing me up," Daisy joked when Philip pushed the suitcases through the door and then closed it behind him. "But now I see it's because you were packing. Are you leaving town, too?"

He stopped straightening his tie in the mirror. "Too? Are you going on another gig already?"

She shook her head tentatively. "I think I'm going away to school for a while. Spy school. Like, with other kid spies."

"I figured that's what spy school would be," he said. "That's cool, though. It'll be good for you."

"Yeah, that's what my grandmother said. So, you gonna tell me what's in the biggest suitcases I've ever seen?"

"I'll show you." But he didn't move.

"Well, while you're apparently frozen, I've been meaning to give you this." She handed him a flash drive. It took a few seconds, but he recognized it as the one his grandmother had given him—or rather, *tried* to give him—after his performance.

"Did you open it?" he asked.

"What do you think?"

"Of course you did."

"Yup. I think you'll be surprised."

"Maybe later," he said. "Miles wants us in the Marshmallow Room, and it's the annual picnic, and I really need to show you—"

She plucked the flash drive from his hand and stuck it into the side of her vid com. A video booted up and began to play. Philip tried to turn away, but hearing his mother's voice made him whip his head around. She was sitting on a patch of grass, and behind her were a hundred rubber ducks floating on a pond. Philip's mouth formed into an *O* shape. "C'mon, sweetie, come to Mommy."

"I think he's going to do it!" his father's voice said, offscreen. Philip realized his dad must have been holding the camera.

A few seconds later, a baby in a pair of red shorts and a blue shirt pushed to his feet and began walking—Frankenstein-like—toward his mother. Philip pointed to the screen. "Is that . . . that's me?"

Daisy nodded. "I knew your essay wasn't a lie."

"I didn't," he said. The camera zoomed in on him and his mom as she lifted him up and whooped. Up close he could see how tired she looked, with dark circles around her eyes. Tired but joyous.

His eyes filled up. She was sick, even back then. He wondered if she knew it. She probably just thought she needed more sleep.

Daisy slowly pulled the vid com away and switched off the video. "You okay?" she asked.

He nodded slowly.

"Hey, why don't you just tell me what's in the suitcases? That'll take your mind off things."

"They're filled with cash."

"Come again?" she asked.

A loud knocking on the door made them both jump. "We know you're in there." A second later the door opened. Logan held up a key. "Got my own now."

"We have to go," Miles said. "Henry's back!"

Daisy jumped to her feet. "Let's go!"

Philip reached for the handles of one of the suitcases and gestured for Daisy to take the other. She just grabbed them both and took off as if they were stuffed with feathers.

"Moving in?" Miles joked.

"Not exactly," Philip said.

When they got to the Marshmallow Room, they found the door closed but unlocked. Henry sat on one of the stools, passing a marshmallow from one hand to the other.

"You're all here," he said. "How was your trip?"

Philip stopped short at the sight of him. Miles gasped, then put his hand over his mouth.

"Henry!" Daisy yelped, rushing over to him. She took his hand. "What happened?"

Henry gave a soft, sad chuckle. "You should see the other guy."

The four of them looked at each other. One by one, they nodded. Philip went over to the cabinet above the fridge. He pulled out a small glass container. It held only two of the beans he and Logan had harvested. AJ had the other two, along with the Magic Bar. He had access to a special lab and was working on learning more about them. Philip unscrewed the lid, and the scent quickly overpowered the vanilla marshmallow smell that hung in the air.

He handed the jar to Logan, who took the marshmallow off Henry's palm and placed two beans there instead. "Please," Logan said. "Eat."

Henry lifted his other hand out of Daisy's and felt the beans with his fingers. He shook his head.

"Please," Logan repeated more firmly. "Protecting the tree is not your job anymore."

Henry opened his mouth to speak again but then closed it. Philip stepped forward. "Come on, Henry. You've helped all of us. I have a feeling you've done a lot more around here than anyone knows. You gave your life to this place. Let us give you something back."

Henry shook his head. "*Only at the right time*," he said, reciting the words on the tree. "It is not meant for me."

"You don't know that at all," Logan insisted. "And how do we know this *isn't* the right time?"

Henry seemed to consider that thought for a minute, until he finally said, "Then you take one, too." The way he said it sounded almost like a dare.

Philip dared not breathe. He wanted Logan to agree so badly. The others looked like they were holding their breath, too. Logan's face darkened, a rare sight. "I already told you guys. I won't do it."

"Then neither will I." Henry crossed his arms. Logan did the same.

Miles cleared his throat. "Um, not to rush this or anything, but we were supposed to be in the Harmonicandy Room, like, half an hour ago."

Logan began to pace. "Henry, this isn't going to cure you. You probably won't be able to drive again. It's not going to let you see the stars. But it can give you back a little of your sight, enough to work and get around without beating yourself up with walls and tree branches."

Henry let out a long breath and then finally a nod. "If you consider doing it, too. Not now," he said, holding up a hand to quiet Logan's argument. "But in a few years if the doctors can't help you."

Logan hesitated but said, "I'll think about it."

Henry gave one quick nod. "Good enough." And he popped the beans into his mouth.

Philip pulled Logan away toward the cooling racks and whispered, "You're never going to do it, are you?"

Logan shook his head and whispered back, "I'm sorry. I know you really want me to. But my scars aren't a health concern, not really. It doesn't feel right. Who knows how many more of those beans will grow? Or what they're really meant for?"

Philip wanted to press him to reconsider, but he couldn't make himself do it. He had to accept his friend's decision, like it or not.

"How do you feel?" Miles asked Henry eagerly.

"Nothing yet," Henry said.

The walkie-talkie on Logan's belt buzzed, and his father's voice came through loud and clear. "Are the others with you?"

"Yes," Logan said, stepping back toward Henry. "I know we're late. We, um, got caught up."

"Pretty important meeting to be late for," his father said.

"I know," Logan said. "We're really sorry. We'll come as soon as we can."

"Don't bother," the Candymaker said, but he didn't sound too angry. "Old Sammy wanted to join the fun out on the lawn, so we're outside now. I'm about to take my turn in the dunk tank. Here's Sammy."

They heard fumbling and some music before Old Sammy's voice came over the line. "Greetings, young candymakers."

"Hi, Sammy!" the four of them called out. It felt too rude to call him *Old* Sammy, even though he used it himself! Philip felt his heart start to pound even faster than it was already beating. This was it. This was the moment they'd learn the Harmonicandy's fate.

"I'd like to start by saying that if a certain fellow who shared my first name had allowed me to purchase his beans fifty years ago, you'd have plenty to use now."

Their eyes widened. Old Sammy must have been the one who'd made the offer Frank told them about! Of course he didn't know that the issue ran much deeper than simply not having a big enough supply.

"The committee has made a decision," he continued. "𝐋𝐢𝐟𝐞 𝐈𝐬 𝐒𝐰𝐞𝐞𝐭 can make the Harmonicandy as long as every reference to its winning the contest is deleted from the wrapper, sales material, advertising, et cetera, and the thousand-dollar prize is returned."

They all whooped and cheered, even Henry, who was still chewing and had started rubbing at his eyes. Philip had already expected to have to return the prize. That'd be easy, since he'd never actually cashed the check.

But Old Sammy had more to say. "Additionally, a percentage of profits will go into a special fund that will allow the Confectionary Association to donate money to various charities. An anonymous donor has just pledged enough money to build mobile burn units for communities in need. And that's only the beginning, I'm sure! Isn't that wonderful? I have to go now, children. Time to throw a ball at the dunk tank. Over and out."

Logan, Miles, and Daisy slowly turned to look at Philip. Daisy put her hands on her hips. "Philip Ransford the Third! Did you bribe the Confectionary Association so they'd let the factory make the Harmonicandy?"

"*Bribe* is such an unpleasant word," Philip said. "I prefer to think of it as a win-win for everyone. We get to make our candy, communities in need get new burn units, and the Confectionary Association gets to look like heroes. Hey, if you have to have a ruthless businessman for a father, at least pick up a few pointers to help in times of need." He didn't add that Old Sammy had agreed to give him the leftover promotional posters. They'd make the perfect wallpaper for Andrew's room.

"You really pulled it off," Daisy said, shaking her head in wonder. "You saved the Harmonicandy and found a way to still do what you wanted with the profits. It's possible I may have underestimated you."

"Yeah, well, don't do it again," he joked.

"I won't," she said. He could tell she meant it.

"But I don't get it," Logan said. "*You're* the anonymous donor, right? How did you have the money to buy two mobile burn units?"

"I didn't," Philip admitted. "But the National Symphony Orchestra did."

"You sold your *violin*?" Miles practically shrieked.

"I have another one that's just as good," Philip assured him. Well, not really *as* good, but it had been good enough for him to use before he found the Strad, and he'd loved thinking it had belonged to his mother. Finding out the truth hadn't changed anything.

Logan turned pale. "Philip, I told you that violin wasn't a real Stradivarius. My grandfather made it. You can't sell the National Symphony a fake!"

Philip shook his head. "Samuel Sweet may have been a great candymaker and a good enough woodworker. But he did *not* make that violin. Antonio Stradivari constructed it in 1698. I only sold it with your father's blessing, since of course it really belonged to your family. My grandmother will use it, and then it will get passed to whoever becomes first violin in the symphony after her." He paused. "Wanna see it?"

"Do we want to see what?" Miles asked.

Philip walked over to the two suitcases. He unzipped them to reveal bundled stacks of hundred-dollar bills. Daisy, Logan, and Miles gasped and dropped to their knees to get a closer look.

"That's a whole lotta dough!" Henry exclaimed.

They all whirled around. "Henry!" Daisy shouted. "You can see?"

Henry had put his latest pair of glasses on, the ones with lenses half an inch thick. "I can see your faces again," he said. "That's more than enough for me."

Logan threw his arms around Henry first, followed by Miles, Daisy, and Philip, who was still getting used to these group hugs. It felt both nice and awkward in equal measure.

Henry untangled himself from the group and pointed at one of the suitcases. "Looks like there's a note for you, Philip."

He was right. Sticking up between the neat stacks of bills was a corner of a yellow envelope that he hadn't noticed before. Philip opened it up and slid out three pieces of paper. He laughed when he saw the top one and held it up for the others to see. "Looks like Aurora has made herself at home." The photo showed his grandmother in her living room, trying to play her violin with Aurora draped around her neck. The caption underneath said:

My new scarf. P.S. Did you know she's toilet trained??

The second paper had Logan's name at the top. "This one's for you," Philip said, passing it over.

"It's the recipe for the chocolate mint squares!" Logan shouted. "Henry, wait till you try them! There's marshmallow in them too!"

Philip smiled. It would be wonderful to smell them baking when he came to the factory. It took him a few seconds to realize what the last piece of paper meant. His grandmother had drawn three musical notes and the letters *G-A-B* followed by a smiley face. He played them in his head and knew exactly what they were for. The last three notes of his original composition.

The perfect ending.

$$\bullet \; \bullet \; \bullet \; \bullet \; \bullet \; \bullet \; \bullet \; \bullet \; \bullet \; \bullet \; \bullet \; \bullet \; \bullet$$

LATER THAT NIGHT

$$\bullet \; \bullet \; \bullet \; \bullet \; \bullet \; \bullet \; \bullet \; \bullet \; \bullet \; \bullet \; \bullet \; \bullet \; \bullet$$

After the last guest had left the picnic, and all the lights had been taken down from the trees, and all the left-over food had been packed up for donation, one person stood at the far end of the Tropical Room, out past the long rows of sugarcane. The soil had arrived an hour before, still wet and smelling like new beginnings. It took only the lightest poke to push the blue bean deep into the dirt. A swipe of the hand refilled the hole.

He knew, even if the others hadn't figured it out yet, that the tree was dying, or at least the microbe that made the blue beans so powerful was weakening. Frank's reaction when he heard each pod only contained one blue bean told him that it had once been very different.

He gave the ground one last pat before making his way back out of the room. If this seed took, the new tree wouldn't bear fruit for another three to five years. They wouldn't know until then how many blue ones survived. That seemed both like an eternity and like no time at all.

Tantum ad tempus. When the right time came to use them, they'd be ready.